An Instant *New York Times* Bestseller!

An Indie Next Pick for the Spring 2019 Kids' List!

A Most-Anticipated Book of the Year for *Seventeen,
Book Riot, BuzzFeed, Cultress, Epic Reads, Syfy,*
and *The Nerd Daily,* among others!

"If you like your young adult fantasy full of ice, blood, and angst,
Wicked Saints will sweep you up in its wintry embrace."

—NPR

"This dark fantasy starts off with a bang. . . . The upfront
presence of the gods adds an intriguing twist to a brutal story.
The ending is as powerful as the opening, and there are explosive elements waiting to detonate in the expected sequels."

—*Booklist*

"If you love dark fantasy, this book promises to be a brutal, enchanting gem, full of terrifying blood magic."   —*Book Riot*

"Rarely does a dark, magical epic have so effective a character-
grounded sense of humor."

—*The Bulletin of the Center for Children's Books*

"Emily A. Duncan's debut YA novel does not disappoint. It's
thrilling and brutal, reading like a heavy metal song. And
it's the first book in a trilogy! I cannot wait for books two and
three—and for whatever else this blistering new talent writes.
For fans of: authors of dark fantasy novels, like Leigh Bardugo."

—*Paste*

"Will leave readers hungry for a sequel." —*Publishers Weekly*

"I highly recommend *Wicked Saints* to fantasy readers. Emily Duncan's writing style reminds me of Leigh Bardugo's. If you enjoyed the setting of the Grisha trilogy and the characters of *Six of Crows,* I believe you will enjoy *Wicked Saints.* Duncan's debut novel is perfect for readers looking for intrigue, dark magic, and betrayal on every page." —*Teenreads*

"Prepare for a snow-frosted, blood-drenched fairy tale where the monsters steal your heart and love ends up being the nightmare. Utterly absorbing." —Roshani Chokshi, *New York Times* bestselling author of *The Gilded Wolves* and *The Star-Touched Queen*

"Full of blood and monsters and magic—this book destroyed me and I adored it. Emily is a wicked storyteller; she's not afraid to hurt her characters or her readers. If you've ever fallen in love with a villain, you will fall hard for this book." —Stephanie Garber, *New York Times* bestselling author of *Caraval*

"This is the novel of dark theology and eldritch blood magic that I've been waiting for all my life. It's got a world at once brutal and beautiful, filled with characters who are wounded, lovable, and ferocious enough to break your heart. A shattering, utterly satisfying read." —Rosamund Hodge, author of *Cruel Beauty* and *Bright Smoke, Cold Fire*

"*Wicked Saints* is a lush, brutal, compelling fantasy that is dark, deep, and bloody—absolutely riveting! With a boy who is both man and monster, mysterious saints with uncertain motives, and a girl filled with holy magic who is just beginning to understand the full reaches of her power, this Gothic jewel of a story will sink its visceral iron claws into you, never letting go until you've turned the last page. And truthfully, not even then—the explosive ending will haunt you for days!"

—Robin LaFevers, *New York Times* bestselling
author of the His Fair Assassin trilogy

"Dark, bloody, and monstrously romantic. This is the villain love interest that we've all been waiting for."

—Margaret Rogerson, *New York Times* bestselling
author of *An Enchantment of Ravens*

"Seductively dark and enchanting, *Wicked Saints* is a trance you won't want to wake from. Duncan has skillfully erected a world like no other, complete with provocative magic, sinister creatures, and a plot that keeps you guessing. This spellbinding YA fantasy will bewitch readers to the very last page."

—Adrienne Young, *New York Times* bestselling
author of *Sky in the Deep*

ALSO BY

EMILY A. DUNCAN

RUTHLESS GODS

wicked saints

EMILY A. DUNCAN

WEDNESDAY BOOKS
NEW YORK

Published in the United States by Wednesday Books, an imprint of St. Martin's Publishing Group

www.wednesdaybooks.com

Designed by Anna Gorovoy

Map by Rhys Davies

The Library of Congress has cataloged the hardcover edition as follows:

Names: Duncan, Emily A., author.
Title: Wicked saints : a novel / Emily A. Duncan.
Description: First edition. | New York : Wednesday Books, 2019.
Identifiers: LCCN 2018055527 | ISBN 9781250195661 (hardcover)
    ISBN 9781250195685 (ebook)
Subjects: | CYAC: Fairy tales. | War—Fiction. | Assassins—Fiction. | Princes—Fiction.
    Gods—Fiction.
Classification: LCC PZ8.D917 Wic 2019 | DDC [Fic]—dc23
LC record available at https://lccn.loc.gov/2018055527

ISBN 978-1-250-19567-8 (trade paperback)

First Paperback Edition: April 2020

10 9 8 7 6 5 4 3 2

For Mom & Dad—most ardent of supporters

1

NADEZHDA LAPTEVA

Death, magic, and winter. A bitter cycle that Marzenya spins with crimson threads around pale fingers. She is constant; she is unrelenting; she is eternal. She can grant any spell to those she has blessed, her reach is the fabric of magic itself.

—Codex of the Divine, 2:18

The calming echo of a holy chant filtered down from the sanctuary and into the cellars. It was late afternoon, just before Vespers, a time where psalms to the gods were given up in an effortless chorus.

Nadezhda Lapteva glared up at the mountain of potatoes threatening to avalanche down over the table. She twisted her knife hard against the one in her hand, narrowly missing skin as she curled the peel into a spiral.

"A cleric's duty is important, Nadezhda," she muttered, mimicking the dour tone of the monastery's abbot. "You

could change the tide of the war, Nadezhda. Now go wither in the cellars for the rest of your life, Nadezhda."

The table was covered in potato peel spirals. She hadn't anticipated losing her entire day to remedial labor, yet here she was.

"Did you hear that?" Konstantin acted like she hadn't spoken. His paring knife hung limp in his fingers as he listened.

There was nothing but the service upstairs. If he was trying to distract her, it wasn't going to work. "Is it our impending death by potato avalanche? I can't hear it, but I'm certain it's coming."

She received a withering look in response. She waved her knife at him. "What could it possibly be? The Tranavians at our doorstep? They have seven thousand stairs to climb first. Perhaps it's their High Prince and he's finally decided to convert."

She tried to be glib, but the idea of the High Prince anywhere near the monastery made her shiver. He was rumored to be an extremely powerful blood mage, one of the most terrifying in all of Tranavia, a land rife with heretics.

"Nadya," Konstantin whispered, "I'm serious."

Nadya stabbed her knife into yet another potato as she glanced at him. It was his fault they were down here. His pranks, conjured from a mixture of boredom and delirium after early morning prayers, had been innocent at first. Switching out the monastery's incense with lemongrass, or snipping the sanctuary's candlewicks. Minor offenses at best. Nothing to deserve death by potato.

Filling Father Alexei's washing bowl with a red dye that looked like blood, though, that was what had done them in.

Blood wasn't a thing to be made light of, not in these times. Father Alexei's rage didn't end in the cellars. After they scaled Potato Mountain—*if* they scaled Potato Mountain—they still had hours' worth of holy texts to copy in the scriptorium. Nadya's hands were already cramping just thinking about it.

"Nadya." Her knife slipped off course as Konstantin nudged her elbow.

"Damn it, Kostya."

My perfect streak of fifty-four intact spirals, ruined, she thought mournfully. She wiped her hands on her tunic and glared at him.

His dark eyes were focused on the closed door that led upstairs. There was nothing but the—

Oh.

The potato slipped from her fingers, falling to the dusty floor. She hadn't noticed when the service above had stopped. Kostya's fingers dug into her sleeve but his touch felt distant.

This can't be happening.

"Cannons," she whispered, somehow making it more real by saying the word aloud. She shifted the grip on her knife, flipping it backward as if it were one of her thin-bladed *voryens* and not a half-dull kitchen blade.

Cannons were a sound every child of Kalyazin knew intimately. It was what they grew up with, their lullabies mixed with firing in the distance. War was their constant companion, and Kalyazi children knew to flee when they heard those cannons and tasted the iron tinge of magic in the air.

Cannons only meant one thing: blood magic. And blood magic meant Tranavians. For a century a holy war had raged between Kalyazin and Tranavia. Tranavians didn't care that their blood magic profaned the gods. If they had their way, the gods' touch would be eradicated from Kalyazin like it had been from Tranavia. But the war had never reached farther than the

Kalyazin border. Until now. If Nadya could hear the cannons, that meant the war was slowly swallowing Kalyazin alive. Inch by bloody inch it was seeping into the heart of Nadya's country and bringing death and destruction with it.

And there was only one reason why the Tranavians would attack a secluded monastery in the mountains.

The cellars shook and dirt rained down. Nadya looked at Kostya, whose gaze was flint-eyed but fearful. They were just acolytes with kitchen knives. What could they do if the soldiers came?

Nadya tugged at the prayer necklace around her neck; the smooth wooden beads felt cool against the pads of her fingers. There were alarms that would go off if the Tranavians breached the seven thousand stairs leading up to the monastery, but she had never heard them. Had hoped she never would.

Kostya grabbed her hand and shook his head slowly, his dark eyes solemn.

"Don't do this, Nadya," he said.

"If we are attacked, I will not hide," she replied stubbornly.

"Even if it means a choice between saving this place and the entire kingdom?"

He grasped her arm again, and she let him drag her back into the cellars. His fear was justified. She had never been in real battle before, but she met his gaze defiantly. All she knew was this monastery, and if he thought she wasn't going to fight for it, then he was mad. She would protect the only family she had; that was what she was trained for. He ran a hand over his close-cropped hair. He couldn't stop her; they both knew it.

Nadya tugged out of Kostya's grip. "What use am I if I run? What would be the point?"

He opened his mouth to protest but the cellar shook so hard

Nadya wondered if they weren't about to be buried alive. Dirt from the ceiling dusted her white-blond hair. In an instant, she was across the cellar and nearing the door up to the kitchens. If the bells were silent, that meant the enemy was still in the mountains. There was time—

Her hand touched the doorknob just as the bells began to toll. The sound felt familiar, as if it was nothing but another call to the sanctuary for prayer. Then she was jarred by the urgent screeching tone they took on, a cacophony of high-pitched bells. No time left. She yanked the door open, running the last few stairs up to the kitchens, Kostya at her heels. They crossed the garden—empty and dead from the bitter winter months—into the main complex.

Nadya had been told the protocol countless times. Move to the back of the chapel. Pray, because that was what she did best. The others would go to the gates to fight. She was to be protected. But it was all formality, the Tranavians would never make it this far into the country, all these plans were simply if the impossible happened.

Well, here is the impossible.

She shoved open the heavy doors that led behind the sanctuary, only managing to move them enough for Kostya and herself to slip through. The tolling of the bells pounded against her temples, painful with each heartbeat. They were made to pull everyone out of sleep at three in the morning for services. They did the job.

Someone slammed into her as she passed an adjoining hallway. Nadya whirled, kitchen blade poised.

"Saints, Nadya!" Anna Vadimovna pressed a hand to her heart. There was a *venyiashk*—a short sword—at her hip, and another, long, thin blade clutched in her hand.

"Can I have that?" Nadya reached for Anna's dagger. Anna

wordlessly handed it to her. It felt solid, not flimsy like the paring knife.

"You shouldn't be here," Anna said.

Kostya shot Nadya a pointed look. In the monastery's hierarchy, Anna—as an ordained priestess—outranked Nadya. If Anna ordered her to go to the sanctuary, she would have no choice but to obey.

So I won't give Anna the chance.

Nadya took off down the hall. "Have they breached the stairs?"

"They were close," Anna called.

Close meant the very real likelihood that they would make it to the courtyard and find the Tranavians already there. Nadya pulled at her prayer necklace, her fingers catching across the ridged beads as she searched for the right one. Each wooden bead was carved with a symbol representing a god or goddess in the pantheon, twenty in all. She knew them by touch, knew exactly which bead to press to attune to a specific god.

Nadya once wished she could blend in with the other Kalyazi orphans at the monastery, but the truth was, for as long as she could remember, when she prayed the gods listened. Miracles happened, magic. It made her valuable. It made her dangerous.

She tugged her necklace until the bead she wanted was at the bottom. The sword symbol carved into it felt like a splinter against her thumb. She pressed it and sent up a prayer to Veceslav: the god of war and protection.

"Do you ever wonder what this would be like if you were fighting against people who also petitioned for my protection?" His voice was a warm summer breeze slipping up the back of her head.

Truly we are fortunate our enemies are heretics, she replied. Heretics who were winning the war.

Veceslav was always chatty, but right now Nadya needed help, not conversation.

I need some protection spells, please, she prayed.

Her thumb caught Marzenya's bead, pressing against the symbol of an openmouthed skull. *And if Marzenya is around, I need her, too.*

Magic flooded through her veins, a rush of power that came with chiming chords of holy speech—a language she only knew when the gods granted it. Nadya's heart raced, less from fear than the intoxicating thrill of their power.

The wide courtyard was blessedly silent when she finally pushed through the front doors of the chapel. To the left ran a path leading to the men's cells; to the right, another trailed off into the forests where an ancient graveyard that held the bodies of saints centuries gone was kept by the monastery. Snow from the night before piled on the ground and the air was frigid. It snowed most nights—and days—on the top of the Baikkle Mountains. Hopefully it would slow down the Tranavians.

Nadya scanned for Father Alexei, finding him at the top of the stairs. The priests and priestesses who trained for battle waited in the courtyard and her heart twisted at just how few of them there were. Her confidence faltered. Barely two dozen against a company of Tranavians. This was never supposed to happen. The monastery was in the middle of the holy mountains; it was difficult—almost impossible—to reach, especially for those unused to Kalyazin's forbidding terrain.

Marzenya brushed against her thoughts. *"What is it you require, my child?"* spoke the goddess of magic and sacrifice—of death. Marzenya was Nadya's patron in the pantheon, the one who had claimed her as an infant.

I want to give the heretics a welcoming taste of Kalyazi magic, she replied. *Let them fear what the faithful can do.*

She felt the press of Marzenya's amusement, then a different rush of power. Magic granted by Marzenya felt nothing like magic granted by Veceslav. Where he was heat, she was ice and winter and cosmic fury.

Having their magic at the same time itched under Nadya's skin, impatient and impulsive. She left Kostya and Anna, moving to Father Alexei's side.

"Keep our people away from the stairs," she said softly.

The abbot looked over at her, eyebrows drawn. Not because a seventeen-year-old girl was giving him orders—though if they survived he would scold her *thoroughly* for that—but because she wasn't supposed to be there at all. She was supposed to be *anywhere* but there.

Nadya raised her eyebrows expectantly, willing him to accept her place here. She had to stay. She had to fight. She couldn't hide in the cellars any longer, not while heretics tore apart her country, her home.

"Move back," he called after a pause. "I want you all at the doors!" The courtyard was a cramped enclosure, not made for fighting. "What are you planning, Nadezhda?"

"Just some divine judgment," she replied, bouncing on the balls of her feet. She was going to shake out of her own skin if she stopped moving and allowed herself to think on what was about to happen.

She heard his weary sigh as she moved to where the stairs met the courtyard. It was the only way for the enemy to make it to the monastery and even then sometimes the steps were so coated with ice they were impossible to climb. No such luck today.

How could the Tranavians know she was there? The only people who knew Nadya existed were in the monastery.

Well . . . there was the *tsar*. But he was far, far away in the capital. It was unlikely news of her had spread into Tranavia.

Her breath whispered out in a prayer of holy speech, symbols forming light at her lips and blowing out in a cloud of fog. She knelt, trailing her fingers over the top of the stairs. The slick stone froze, forming the stairs into a single block of ice.

Idly twirling the *voryen* in her hand, she stepped back. The spell was a ploy for time; if the Tranavians had a blood mage who could counteract her magic, it wouldn't last.

No going back now.

Nadya could fight an average blood mage. But the possibility of a Tranavian lieutenant or general—a mage promoted because of sheer magical power alone—made her feel like running back into the sanctuary where she belonged.

Marzenya scoffed at her doubt.

I belong here, Nadya told herself.

Kostya stepped up beside her. He had abandoned his kitchen knife for a *noven'ya*—a staff with a long blade on one end. He leaned against it, watching the slope where the stairs dropped out of sight.

"Go," he said. "It's not too late."

Nadya grinned at him. "It's too late."

As if agreeing with her, the bells cut off with a disconcertingly final ring. The air around the monastery was silent but for the steady sound of cannons, now pounding clearly at the base of the mountain.

If Rudnya fell, the monastery would be next. The city at the base of the mountains was well fortified, but they were in the heart of Kalyazin. No one had ever expected the war to push this far west. It was supposed to stay on the eastern border where Kalyazin and Tranavia met, just north of the border on Akola.

A crack trailed up the solid block of ice on the stairs like a spider web. It spread, forming a pattern of fractures before the whole thing shattered. Kostya pulled Nadya into the courtyard.

"We have the high ground," she murmured.

She was holding a single *voryen*. Just one dagger.

We have the high ground.

There was a tremor in the silence and a sharp touch jabbed into the back of her skull.

"Blood magic," Marzenya hissed.

Nadya's heart lodged in her throat, doubt sliding cold tendrils down her spine. She felt her magic shivering, and without thinking, shoved Kostya aside just as something exploded near where he had once stood. A hard chunk of ice slammed into her back, pain ramming down to her toes. She was thrown onto Kostya and they both went crashing to the ground.

He was back on his feet before Nadya had even registered what happened. The courtyard became thick with magic and steel as soldiers swarmed up the stairs. She scrambled to her feet, keeping to Kostya's side, his blade moving at a dizzying pace as he defended her against the Tranavian soldiers.

Children of a war-torn land were expected to know how to react when the enemy finally came calling. Kostya and Nadya had their strategy perfected. She was fast, he was strong, and they would do anything to protect each other. Unless she caused their downfall with her fraying nerves. Her limbs shook as more magic than she was used to swept through her body.

I have no idea what I'm doing.

Panicked prayers to the gods would only be met with more magic; Nadya had to decide for herself how it was used.

She ran her hand along the flat of her *voryen*. Pure, white light followed her touch and though she wasn't entirely sure what it would do, she found out quickly enough when she sliced a Tranavian soldier. She only caught his arm, but like a poison, the light blackened his flesh at the point of contact. It spread up his arm to his face, choking his eyes with darkness before he toppled over, dead. She staggered back into Kostya. The urge to drop her *voryen* needled at her hand.

I killed him. I've never killed anyone.

Kostya's hand dropped to brush against hers.

"Keep going," Marzenya urged.

But there was so much magic swirling through the air and it was so powerful and Nadya was just *one* cleric. Fear consumed her for another long heartbeat until Marzenya jabbed the back of her head with a sharp, pointed pain.

Keep going.

Frost tipped her fingers and she ducked under a Tranavian's blade, slamming her frostbitten hand against his chest. Like the last, blackened skin crept up his neck and onto his face before he fell, the light flickering out of his eyes.

Nadya's chest constricted. She felt like throwing up and Marzenya's bitter nudge of disgust at her weakness jolted her. There was no room here for misplaced sentiment. This was war. Death was inevitable. Necessary.

"Nadezhda!" Marzenya's warning came too late. Flames engulfed her, licking underneath her skin, her blood boiling. Pain blackened her vision. She stumbled, and Kostya caught her, slipping them out of the fray right before she crashed to her knees in the shadows of the chapel doorway. She gritted her teeth, catching the inside of her lip; blood coated her mouth, metallic and sharp. She struggled to breathe. It was like being burned alive from the inside out.

Just when she thought she could take no more, Veceslav's

presence swept in, enveloping Nadya like a heavy blanket. He soothed out the magic, pushing it away until she could breathe. She hadn't called on him; he had simply known.

She didn't have time to be shaken by the gods' omnipresence. She struggled to her feet, her limbs trembling. The world spun dangerously, but it didn't matter. Whatever that had been, it had come from a powerful mage. She scanned the courtyard and when she found him, her once-boiling blood froze.

Oh, she had made a horrible mistake.

I should have hidden.

Thirty paces away, at the entrance to the courtyard, stood a Tranavian with a bloodied piece of paper crumpled in his fist. A vicious scar slashed over his left eye. It started at his temple and ended just at his nose. He watched the violence with a slight sneer. Nadya didn't need to notice the red epaulets and gold braiding of his uniform to recognize him.

There were whispers of the Tranavian High Prince throughout the monastery. A boy made general a mere six months after venturing to the front when he was sixteen years old. One who had used the war to fuel his already terrible grasp of blood magic. A monster.

Every doubt Nadya had pressed away crashed back on top of her. This couldn't be real, not the High Prince; not *him*.

He was young, only a few years older than her, with the palest eyes she had ever seen. As if sensing her, those pale eyes met Nadya's and his lips twisted into a wry smile, his gaze straying to the magic swirling like light at her palms.

She let out a stream of curses.

I need . . . I need something powerful, she prayed frantically. *He's going to come for me. He's looking right at me.*

"You risk injuring the faithful," Marzenya replied.

The world tilted. Black tunneled Nadya's vision at the corners. The courtyard was a nightmare. Crimson splattered snow, the bodies of those Nadya had lived, worked, prayed with, fallen and broken across the stones. It was a slaughter and it was her fault. The Tranavians wouldn't be there if not for her. If she died, would that make this massacre worth it?

The prince started across the courtyard toward Nadya, and her panic blanked out everything else. If he took her, what would her blood give him? What could he do with the magic she had? There were so many Tranavians, they had so much magic, and everyone she knew was going to die.

Kostya shoved her back into the shadows. Her magic slipped away as her back slammed against the door.

"Nadya," Kostya whispered, looking frantically over his shoulder. The prince was out of sight but he had so little space to cross. There was no time left. It was over. Kostya tucked a lock of her hair behind her ear. "You have to go, Nadya, you have to run."

She stared at him, horrified. *Run?* After everyone she loved had been cut down she was supposed to flee to safety? What would that make her, if she ran to save herself? The monastery was the only home Nadya had ever known.

"You have to go," Kostya said. "If you fall to him the war will be lost. You have to live, Nadya."

"Kos—"

He kissed her forehead, lips warm, slipping something cold and metallic against her palm. "You have to live," he repeated with a rasp. Then he turned away to call out to Anna. Nadya dropped what he'd given her into her pocket without looking at it.

Anna fought a few paces away, bodies piling around her

feet. Her head whipped up when she heard her name. Kostya jerked his head in Nadya's direction and understanding cleared Anna's features.

Kostya turned back toward Nadya, an expression on his face she had never seen before. He opened his mouth to speak only to violently jerk forward, his knee buckling out from underneath him. A crossbow bolt stuck out the back of his leg.

A scream ripped out of Nadya's throat. "Kostya!"

"Time to go, Nadya." Anna grabbed her arm and dragged her toward the path leading to the graveyard.

I can't leave Kostya. Kostya who, when they'd first met, had considered her unusual gift with a serious expression before wisecracking that she could never do a single bad thing in her life, else the gods would know immediately. Kostya, who disregarded her status with the divine and cajoled her into all manner of pranks and mischief. Kostya, the boy who rolled apples to her during prayer. Kostya, her friend, her family.

He waved a hand at them to go, pain vivid in his face. Nadya struggled against Anna, but the priestess was stronger. *Not Kostya.* She was losing everything, she couldn't lose him, too.

I will not trade my safety for his life.

Her throat closed with tears. "I won't leave him!"

"Nadya, you have to."

She couldn't break free. She could only stumble as Anna pulled her to a mausoleum, kicking the door open. The last thing she saw before Anna pulled her into the dark was Kostya, his body shuddering as another bolt thudded into him.

2

NADEZHDA

LAPTEVA

*When the faithful turned to the god of protection against a
wandering horde from the north, they expected his blessing,
only to be slaughtered in the war that followed. Their folly
was in forgetting Veceslav was also the god of war, and iron
must be tested.*

—Codex of the Divine, 4:114

Anna pushed past Nadya, slamming the door closed and
barring it. Nadya struggled to stop her—Kostya was going
to die if she didn't do something—but Anna moved in
front of the door, blocking Nadya's way.

"*Nadya,*" she pleaded softly, everything she wasn't saying thick in her voice.

This had always been a possibility; Nadya knew her
friends were willing to die for her. The only thing she could
do now was make sure their deaths were not in vain.
Mourn the loss later, survive now.

She clenched her fists and turned away. Stairs descended into darkness before her. She nearly tripped on the first step and learned the hard way just how far down they went. Anna grabbed her arm to steady her and she realized the priestess was shaking.

"Can you get us some light?" Anna asked. There were tears in her voice, just barely restrained.

The darkness was choking, but Nadya found the silence even more disconcerting. There was nothing, even though the battle raged on just outside. They should be able to hear the clash of metal and screams of battle nearby, but all was quiet.

Light Nadya could do. She pulled at her necklace, finding Zvonimira's bead and the candle flame that marked the goddess of light. She sent up a weak prayer; nothing but a feeble petition for something that could not save them.

A thread of holy speech moved through her lips in a whisper as Zvonimira acknowledged the prayer. White light sparked at her hands. Pressing her fingertips together, she formed a ball of light that could be spun into the air, illuminating the space around them.

"*Golzhin dem,*" Anna cursed under her breath.

Helpless, Nadya could do nothing but follow as Anna started down the steps. Her best friend was probably dead. Everything she had ever known destroyed. Each time she blinked the High Prince's cold smile flashed before her. She would never be safe again.

I would take months of carving out a mountain of potato peels over this.

Nadya didn't know if any of the nearby military camps were still standing, or if the Tranavians had ravaged them as they moved deeper through the country. If she could make it to the capital city of Komyazalov and the Silver Court, there was some hope, but she doubted it possible with the High Prince only steps away.

Nadya was supposed to remain a secret for another year, training in the holy mountains with priests who—while they did not have magic themselves—understood the fundamentals of divinity. Like how a peasant girl could be the one thing that would save Kalyazin from the heretics' torches. But war didn't care for carefully laid plans.

Now the war had taken everything from Nadya, and she didn't know what she was supposed to do. Her heart ached, the vision of Kostya staggering with crossbow bolts slamming into his body the only thing she could see.

Anna led her down the stairs and into a long, dank tunnel. It didn't look like anyone had been down here in decades. After a few minutes of silent walking, Anna paused in front of an aged wooden door set into the wall. She shoved her shoulder into it until it opened with a pained groan. Dust rained down on their heads, spattering Anna's headscarf like snow.

Inside was a storeroom filled with traveling clothes, racks of weapons, and shelves of carefully preserved food.

"Father Alexei was hoping this place would never be necessary." Anna sighed wistfully.

Nadya caught the warm violet tunic and pair of dark brown trousers Anna lobbed at her. She pulled them over her thin garb. Anna tossed her a thick, woolen black coat and a fur-lined hat. Anna pulled on her own set of clothes before she moved to the weapons rack. She gave Nadya a twin set of ornate *voryens*. She paused, staring at the blades in Nadya's hand, then wordlessly handed her a third, considered further, then a fourth.

"You lose them all the time," she explained.

That was true enough. Nadya strapped two of the blades to her belt and slid the other two into her boots. At least she would be armed when the prince caught her. Anna pulled a *ven-yiornik* from the weapons rack—a long, single-edged sword—and strapped it to her hip.

"That should do," she murmured. She took two empty bags and started to carefully pack them with food. "Strap those bedrolls and that tent to the bags, would you?"

The entire room shook, a deafening crash coming from the direction of the doorway. Nadya yelped in surprise. She ducked her head into the hallway. Nothing but darkness. Anna carelessly dumped a shelf of preserved food into one of the packs.

Panic clutched at Nadya's chest. The tunnel wasn't very long. The Tranavians could be there in moments.

Anna shouldered one of the packs and moved out into the tunnel. The world shifted dangerously as words in a rapid-fire language Nadya only barely understood floated down from the direction they had just come.

She didn't need to understand the words or recognize the voice. It was the prince. It had to be. She could not last against him.

Then she was running, running, *running* after Anna. She had to trust that the priestess knew the twists and curves of the tunnel; she had to trust that wherever this led wouldn't just spill them out into a company of Tranavians.

The sound of magic striking the walls hissed behind them. Something brushed Nadya's ear, heat coming off it in waves. It slammed into the curve of the tunnel before her, bursting into a shower of sparks. He was close; he was too close.

"*Tek szalet wylkesz!*" The shout echoing through the tunnel didn't sound angry. If anything it sounded amused. A laugh rang out, clear and sardonic.

Nadya slowed just long enough to look back into the darkness. A pattering sound came from within the black. It started slow but rose in intensity, sounding not like one but many things. Many moving things. She squinted. A thousand small flapping wings.

Anna yanked her down just as a teeming mass of bats swarmed into the cramped space of the tunnel.

Nadya's light spell cut off, plunging them into a living, moving darkness. The bats caught their hair and tore at any unprotected skin. Nadya followed Anna blindly, the priestess's hand in hers the only thing she had that was not the living darkness. It was like being swallowed alive by the dark.

They were trapped within the shifting flurry of wings and claws until finally Anna slammed through a doorway and the girls and the bats went spilling out into the snow.

The bats disappeared into wisps of smoke the second they hit the fading light. Nadya jumped to her feet, helping Anna up. Her gaze was fixed on the opening, the yawning slash of black against the glaring white snow of the mountainside.

"We need to move," Nadya said, backing away from the cave entrance.

She glanced at Anna, concerned when she didn't get a response. Anna stared at the open doorway. No Tranavians appeared.

We'll die if we don't move. Nadya lifted a hand as the other scrambled for her necklace, catching on the right bead. She sent a simple prayer to Bozidarka, the goddess of vision. A vivid image took over her sight. The prince, leaning back against a stone wall, a nasty, sneering grin on his face, his arms crossed over his chest. At his side, glaring at the opening of the tunnel, a short girl with black hair cut severely at her chin, a spiked patch over one of her eyes.

Nadya snapped back to herself, vision clearing. Her head swam from the effort, eyes blurring until there was nothing but the white of the snow. Swaying unsteadily on her feet, she exhaled, centering herself. The Tranavians weren't following them. She didn't know why, but she wouldn't question it. They would come soon enough.

"We're safe for now," she said, exhausted. No more magic. Not until after she'd slept.

"That doesn't make any sense," Anna murmured.

Nadya shrugged, looking out over the severe mountainside. Snow was piled high, and where they were standing the trees were sparse. There was little to use for cover when the Tranavians finally ventured out from the tunnels.

Anna gasped and Nadya turned. She tried to steel herself, but when her gaze drew up toward the top of the mountains, it still felt like a punch in the stomach.

Black clouds of smoke billowed up from a point high in the summit. It filled the sky as though to swallow it completely. Nadya's knees gave out from underneath her and she dropped down into the snow.

Kostya was gone.

Everything was gone. It was as if there were a gaping wound where Nadya's heart should be, a void in her chest that had sucked everything away leaving her with absolutely nothing. She had *nothing*.

She dug a fingernail into her palm, letting the sharp pain clear her head just long enough to blink away her tears. Tears were useless. There wasn't time to mourn, even though she wanted to. They couldn't win this war; the Tranavians were going to take everything and burn Kalyazin to ash. Fighting felt useless.

Why didn't the gods stop this? She refused to believe this destruction was the will of the gods. They couldn't have wanted this.

Nadya startled as Anna slipped her hand into hers.

"Iron must be tested," Anna said, quoting the Codex. "We cannot know the gods' intentions."

Intentions were not always kind nor just.

As if conjured, Marzenya's warm presence slipped over Nadya like a cloak, but the goddess did not speak. Nadya was grateful for the silence. Any words would only ring hollow to her mere mortal ears.

Giving up now would mean everyone in the monastery had died for nothing and Nadya couldn't allow that. She rummaged in her pocket and pulled out a small pendant on a delicate, silver chain. Drawing it closer, she found numerous spirals all swirling into each other and disappearing in the center of the pendant. She had never seen it before, and she made a study of knowing every symbol of the gods.

What had Kostya given her?

"Do you know what this means?" She held out the chain to Anna, whose eyes narrowed as she took the pendant.

She shook her head slowly, handing it back. Nadya slipped it over her head, letting the cool metal settle against her skin underneath her clothes. It didn't really matter what it meant. It mattered because it was from Kostya. Because he had looked at her with an expression that could only be described as longing, he had kissed her forehead, and he had died so she could escape.

This wasn't fair. War wasn't fair.

Nadya turned away from her burning home. She would escape so Kostya wouldn't have died for nothing. That had to be enough, for now.

They would have to travel all night to put enough distance between them and the Tranavians.

"We need to head to Tvir," Anna said.

Nadya frowned, tugging her hat down over her ears. Tvir was to the east. East was Tranavia. East was the front. "Wouldn't Kazatov be wiser?"

Anna messed with the scarf over her hair, adjusting the headband and temple rings. "We need to get you to the closest camp and Kazatov is too far north. Your safety is my top priority. The king would have our heads if anything happened to you."

"Well, the Tranavians have the heads of everyone in the monastery already."

Anna winced, shooting her a wounded look. "General Golovhka can decide what we do from there," she said slowly.

Nadya didn't like it. She didn't want to be tugged around, endlessly shuttled to safety only so others could die in her stead. She should be fighting. But if Tvir was the closest camp, then to Tvir they would go.

Anna glanced at her, sympathy in her long, dark eyes. She looked over her shoulder, expression fracturing. Nadya couldn't look back. She had seen enough destruction and if she looked back again it would break her completely.

"Let's worry about finding shelter first, yes? There's an abandoned chapel nearby. We can reach it within a day or so. We'll figure out what to do from there."

Nadya nodded wearily. She was too tired to fight or panic about her seemingly inevitable capture by the single person who should never have access to her power, who never should have known she even existed.

All she could do was put one foot in front of the other, pretend it wasn't so cold she could feel frost icing her lashes, and pray. At least she was good at prayer.

3

SEREFIN

MELESKI

Svoyatovi Ilya Golubkin: *Born a farmer's son, Ilya was struck with a disease that prevented him from walking. Healed by a cleric of Zbyhneuska, he was imbued with superhuman strength and went on to become a warrior monk. Ilya single-handedly protected the city of Korovgrod against invaders from across the sea.*

—Vasiliev's Book of Saints

Serefin Meleski leaned against the tunnel entrance and squinted out into the snow. The sun had nearly set, but the reflection was blinding against his—admittedly terrible—vision.

"You're letting them get away," Ostyia whined at his side.

He ignored her, instead picking up his spell book from where it was strapped to his hip, flipping it open. He

riffled through the pages in silence before tearing one out. He dropped the book and held his arm out to Ostyia.

Her eye narrowed and she glanced down at the knife in her hand. She snatched his wrist and dragged the blade over his palm.

"Not his *hand*," Kacper protested from where he was leaning against the opposite wall of the tunnel.

Serefin ignored him as well, lifting his hand. He watched the blood quickly well up from the cut and drip in slow rivulets down his palm. It stung, but the surge of magic that would come canceled out any minor pain. He moved the spell book page into his bleeding hand, letting the blood soak into the paper. Magic ignited hot in his veins, and as the page slipped into dusky tendrils of smoke, his vision sharpened. A trail leading straight to the cleric showed vividly as red streaks against the snow.

He smiled. "She can run."

"Is it wise to tether yourself to her with that spell?" Ostyia asked.

"She won't be able to feel it. It's not a tether, just a trail."

It wouldn't matter how far she ran; he would be able to keep track of her as long as he fed blood into the spell at occasional intervals. Easily done.

"Confident," Kacper noted.

Serefin shot him a bland look. "Even if she feels it, she won't be able to break it."

"You don't know anything about the magic she was using. How do you know she won't feel it?"

Serefin frowned. Kacper was right, but he wasn't about to admit that.

"Have the men round up those still alive and contain them," he said to Ostyia.

She nodded and disappeared down the tunnel.

Kacper watched her go. "Why aren't you going after her?" The sleeve of his coat had nearly been shorn off during battle; it was holding on by a few threads, and his gold epaulet hung haphazardly off his arm. He tugged a brown hand through his dark curls and appeared surprised when he found them matted with blood. "We've been looking for evidence of a bloody cleric for ages and we finally found one."

"Do you want to be stumbling around in the dark in the middle of the Kalyazi mountains?" Serefin asked.

Their company had already experienced firsthand how deadly a Kalyazi winter could be to those unfamiliar with the terrain. Besides, Serefin could barely see on a good day and his night vision was worse. Understanding lit Kacper's dark eyes and he nodded.

Serefin had been on the front in Kalyazin for almost three years with only the occasional leave to return home. In all that time it was as though winter never ended. Even Kalyazin's melt season felt cold. It was only snow and frost and forests. For the last five months Serefin had charged his company to look for evidence of Kalyazi magic. His father had been adamant it existed, that it was vital Serefin find these clerics. They could tilt the course of the war in Kalyazin's favor and that would not do, especially now, after a decisive strike against Kalyazin had finally been won. Tranavia had claimed the Kalyazi city of Voldoga only weeks earlier, a vital outpost for the enemy. It was the first step in finally turning this endless war to their side.

"With any luck, she'll lead us to more of her kind," Serefin said. He started back into the tunnel, but paused.

Passing an absent hand over the scar that cut across his eye, he turned to Kacper.

"Light?" The word came out condescending, a brittle command instead of a request. Any other time he would have had slightly more consideration for Kacper's feelings, but exhaustion made him callow.

"Yes, sorry." Kacper fumbled for a torch that had fallen to the ground and relit it.

They passed the storeroom where the Kalyazi girls had been hiding and found Serefin's lieutenant general, Teodore Kijek, poking around.

"Send word to my father about today's events," Serefin told him. He didn't bother mentioning the cleric. Best if his father thought the cleric escaped; he didn't need to know Serefin had let her go.

"Of course, Your Highness."

"Do we have a count for how many Kalyazi survived?"

"I estimate about a dozen," Teodore replied.

Serefin made a soft sound of assent. He would have to decide what they were going to do with the prisoners and he could not say he relished the task.

"Do we know if the girl was the only cleric among them?" He couldn't imagine luck shining on him in such a way, but he could dream.

"If there are others, they have not yet revealed themselves to us," Teodore said.

"Perhaps they can be persuaded?" Kacper mused, his dark eyes sparkling with anticipation.

Serefin had a proven aptitude for being particularly convincing.

He nodded curtly. Persuaded indeed. "We will remain here for the night." He glanced into the storeroom; the Kalyazi girls had not looted it entirely. "Clear all this out as well," he continued, waving a hand. He would ferret out information while keeping tabs on the cleric as she ran. It seemed like a valuable way to spend his time before he heard back from his father.

"Of course, Your Highness," Teodore said.

Serefin motioned Teodore away and continued on with Kacper.

"Why on earth have you not sent him back to the front yet?" Kacper asked.

Serefin glanced over at Kacper, who stood to his left, on his blind side. Kacper fell back a step, moving to Serefin's other side.

"Can you imagine what my father would do if I got rid of his spy?"

Kacper winced. "Well, at least when we fetch the cleric we can go home. There won't be a reason for the king to keep us out here any longer."

Serefin raked a hand through his brown hair. It desperately needed a trim. He was tired—no, not tired, *bone-deep* weary. Finally discovering the cleric was a stroke of brilliant luck, but it didn't change that he had been in an enemy kingdom for years yet dreaded the thought of returning home. The war was all he knew at this point. They walked the rest of the tunnel in silence before finally reaching the graveyard.

The monastery was a larger complex than Serefin had expected, with far better guards. He found Ostyia observing the prisoners as they were rounded up in the courtyard. He sent Kacper to find a suitable place for him to spend the night, though he sensed there would be nothing in this dour prison that wasn't a stone slab and threadbare blanket. Why were monks so damned austere? There was nothing wrong with sleeping comfortably. But he would accept a concrete slab and threadbare blanket over yet another night spent out on the snow.

Ostyia fiddled with the patch over her eye before finally taking it off and stowing it in her pocket. A jagged, ugly scar crossed her face over the ravaged, empty socket of her left eye.

When Serefin and Ostyia were children, Kalyazi assassins had infiltrated the palace disguised as weapons masters meant to train the young prince and nobleman's daughter. The assassins had gone for their eyes first. Perhaps blinding the children of the enemy before murdering them was a religious thing.

Ostyia often liked to leave her scarred eye socket uncovered. She relished looking terrifying and claimed she was saving her eye patch days for the sea if the war ever ended. Her gaze cut to the spell book at Serefin's hip.

"That looks thin," she pointed out.

He sighed and nodded, picking up the book and riffling through it. He was running out of spells.

"Something tells me we won't find a book binder in the heart of Kalyazin who does spell books."

"No, probably not," Ostyia agreed. "Besides"—a teasing note entered her voice—"even if we did, she wouldn't be half as good as Madame Petra."

Serefin shuddered as he thought of the overbearing elderly woman who bound all of his spell books. He could never figure out if she treated him like a long dead son or lover. He was disturbed he couldn't tell the difference.

"Did you not bring any extras?"

"I've worked through all my extras." Which meant the possibility of being trapped in the middle of enemy country without a spell book.

"Well," Ostyia said, "I suppose you could take one of the lower ranking mages' books if you need to."

"And leave them defenseless?" Serefin raised an eyebrow. "Ostyia, I'm heartless, but I'm not cruel. I can manage fine enough with a blade in my hand."

"Yeah, and leave me to work my ass off, keeping you safe."

Serefin shot her a dirty look. She glanced up at him, smiling cheekily.

"Forgive my tone, Your Highness," she said, curtsying dramatically.

He rolled his eyes.

They were splitting up the prisoners into containable groups where they would be locked in the sparse, cell-like bedrooms. Serefin's eyes narrowed on a boy about his own age who was holding himself up on the shoulder of an older man.

"That one," he said, pointing out the man to Ostyia. "Pull him out. I want to question him."

Her face lit. "The boy?"

"Not like that. He already has a crossbow bolt sticking out of his leg, and no, the old man. I'll speak to the boy later."

Her face fell. "His Highness will forgive me if I say he is absolutely no fun."

"I will not."

She had the man brought over to them. Serefin guessed him to be the leader of the monastery. Did those have a title? Serefin wasn't sure.

"Do you train all your people for war now?" Serefin asked pleasantly, resting his hand on his too-thin spell book. Before the man could answer, he held up his other hand, stopping him. "Forgive me, I should introduce myself, my name is Serefin Meleski, High Prince of Tranavia."

"I am Father Alexei," the man said. "And yes, even those not conscripted into the army receive some training. It's necessary, wouldn't you say?"

Maybe the tactic was necessary for Kalyazin, but the war had never breached Tranavia's borders. Regardless, Serefin was surprised at the civility in the old man's tone.

"A holy war that has raged for near a century calls for extreme measures," Alexei continued.

"Yes, yes, *we're* nasty heretics that need to be eradicated from the earth and you're just doing what's right," Serefin said.

The priest merely shrugged. "Simple truth."

Ostyia was tense at Serefin's side. He shoved his hands into his pockets and smiled at the old man.

"But you have magic of your own, don't you? Tell me, how many of your mages—what do you call them, clerics?—are hiding in Kalyazin? We know about the one here, don't bother trying to protect her, she'll be in our custody within the day."

The old priest smiled. "They are called clerics, yes. I have no information that can aid you in this, young prince."

Serefin frowned. He wished the man was patronizing him so he could at least work up the necessary righteous anger, but there was nothing of the sort in his voice.

He wasn't going to press the point, not right now and not with the priest. The boy with the crossbow wound was the one who had shielded the cleric and helped her escape. He was the one to talk to.

Serefin directed a soldier to take the priest away.

"Do you want to question someone else?" Ostyia asked.

"No." Serefin caught Kacper's eye from where he was speaking with a mage nearby and waved him over. "Religious folk drink wine, correct?"

Ostyia shrugged.

"There are casks of wine in the cellar," Kacper offered.

Serefin gave a quick nod. "Perfect. I want to be blind drunk before the night is out."

4

NADEZHDA

LAPTEVA

*Horz stole the stars and the heavens out from underneath
Myesta's control, and for that she has never forgiven him.
For where can the moons rest if not the heavens?*
—Codex of the Divine, 5:26

"*It's certainly not my fault you chose a child who sleeps so
deeply. If she dies it will very much be your fault, not mine.*"

Startled by bickering gods was not Nadya's preferred
method of being woken up. She rolled to her feet in the
dark, moving automatically. It took her eyes a few seconds to catch up with the rest of her body.

Shut up!

It wasn't wise to tell the gods to shut up, but it was
too late now. A feeling of amused disdain flowed through
her, but neither of the gods spoke again. She realized it
was Horz, the god of the heavens and the stars, who had

woken her. He had a tendency to be obnoxious but generally left Nadya alone, as a rule.

Usually only a single god communed with their chosen cleric. There once had been a cleric named Kseniya Mirokhina who was gifted with unnatural marksmanship by Devonya, the goddess of the hunt. And Veceslav had chosen a cleric of his own, long ago, but their name was lost to history, and he refused to talk about them. The recorded histories never spoke of clerics who could hear more than one god. That Nadya communed with the entire pantheon was a rarity the priests who trained her could not explain.

There was a chance older, more primordial gods existed, ones that had long since given up watch of the world and left it in the care of the others. But no one knew for sure. Of the twenty known gods, however, carvings and paintings depicted their human forms, though no one knew what they actually looked like. No cleric throughout history had ever looked upon the faces of the gods. No saint, nor priest.

Each had their own power and magic they could bestow upon Nadya, and while some were forthcoming, others were not. She had never spoken to the goddess of the moons, Myesta. She wasn't even sure what manner of power the goddess would give, if she so chose.

And though she could commune with many gods, it was impossible to forget just who had chosen her for this fate: Marzenya, the goddess of death and magic, who expected complete dedication.

Indistinct voices murmured in the dark. She and Anna had found a secluded place within a copse of thick pine trees to set up their tent, but it no longer felt safe. Nadya slid a *voryen* from underneath her bedroll and nudged Anna awake.

She moved to the mouth of the tent, grasping at her beads,

a prayer already forming on her lips, smoky symbols trailing from her mouth. She could see the blurry impressions of figures in the darkness, far off in the distance. It was hard to judge the number, two? Five? Ten? Her heart sped at the possibility that a company of Tranavians were already on her trail.

Anna drew up beside her. Nadya's grip on her *voryen* tightened, but she kept still. If they hadn't seen their tent yet, she could keep them from noticing it entirely.

But Anna's hand clasped her forearm.

"Wait," she whispered, her breath frosting out before her in the cold. She pointed to a dark spot just off to the side of the group.

Nadya pressed her thumb against Bozidarka's bead and her eyesight sharpened until she could see as clearly as if it were day. It took effort to shove aside the immediate, paralyzing fear as her suspicions were confirmed and Tranavian uniforms became clear. It wasn't a full company. In fact, they looked rather ragged. Perhaps they had split off and lost their way.

More interesting, though, was the boy with a crossbow silently aiming into the heart of the group.

"We can get away before they notice," Anna said.

Nadya almost agreed, almost slipped her *voryen* back into its sheath, but just then, the boy fired and the trees erupted into chaos. Nadya wasn't willing to use an innocent's life as a distraction for her own cowardice. Not *again*.

Even as Anna protested, Nadya let a prayer form fully in her mind, hand clutching at Horz's bead on her necklace and its constellation of stars. Symbols fell from her lips like glowing glimmers of smoke and every star in the sky winked out.

Well, that was more extreme than I intended, Nadya thought with a wince. *I should've known better than to ask Horz for anything.*

She could hear cursing as the world plunged into darkness. Anna sighed in exasperation beside her.

"Just stay back," she hissed as she moved confidently through the dark.

"Nadya . . ." Anna's groan was soft.

It took more focus to send a third prayer to Bozetjeh. It was hard to catch Bozetjeh on a good day; the god of speed was notoriously slow to answer prayers. But she managed to snag his attention and received a spell allowing her to move as fast as the vicious Kalyazin wind.

Her initial count had been wrong; there were six Tranavians now scattering into the forest. The boy dropped his crossbow with a bewildered look up into the sky, startling when Nadya touched his shoulder.

There was no way he could see in this darkness, but she could. When he whirled, a curved sword in his hand, Nadya sidestepped. His swing went wide and she shoved him in the direction of a fleeing Tranavian, anticipating their collision.

"Find the rest," Marzenya hissed. *"Kill them all."*

Complete and total dedication.

She caught up to one of the figures, stabbing her *voryen* into his skull just underneath his ear.

Not so difficult this time, she thought. But the knowledge was a distant thing.

Blood sprayed, splattering a second Tranavian, who cried out in alarm. Before the second man could figure out what had happened to his companion, she lashed out her heel, catching him squarely on the jaw and knocking him off his feet. She slit his throat.

Three more. They couldn't have moved far. Nadya took up Bozidarka's bead again. The goddess of vision revealed where the last Tranavians were located. The boy with the sword had managed to kill two in the dark. Nadya couldn't actually see the last one, just felt him nearby, very much alive.

Something slammed into Nadya's back and suddenly the chilling bite of a blade was pressed against her throat. The boy appeared in front of her, his crossbow back in his hands, thankfully not pointed at Nadya. It was clear he could only barely see her. He wasn't Kalyazi, but Akolan.

A fair number of Akolans had taken advantage of the war between their neighbors, hiring out their swords for profit on both sides. They were known for favoring Tranavia simply because of the warmer climate. It was rare to find someone acclimated to Akola's deserts willingly stumbling through Kalyazin's snow.

He spoke a fluid string of words she didn't understand. His posture was languid, as if he hadn't nearly been torn to pieces by blood mages. The blade against Nadya's throat pressed harder. A colder voice responded to him, the foreign language scratched uncomfortably at her ears.

Nadya only knew the three primary languages of Kalyazin and passing Tranavian. If she wasn't going to be able to communicate with them . . .

The boy said something else and Nadya heard the girl sigh before she felt the blade slip away. "What's a little Kalyazi assassin doing out in the middle of the mountains?" he asked, switching to perfect Kalyazi.

Nadya was very aware of the boy's friend at her back. "I could ask the same of you."

She shifted Bozidarka's spell, sharpening her vision further. The boy had skin like molten bronze and long hair with gold chains threaded through his loose curls.

He grinned.

A thud sounded nearby, startling him, but it was the recognizable sound of someone slamming face-first into a tree. Anna's muffled swearing followed. Nadya rolled her eyes and sent up an apology to the heavens. The stars and moons relit in the sky, making the world seem three times brighter.

"We'll be hearing prophesies about the end of the world for the next twenty years now!" Anna cried. She had her *venyiashk* drawn, her gaze wary as she looked just past Nadya's shoulder.

Nadya crouched, stabbing her bloody *voryen* into the snow. She looked up at the Akolan boy, lifting her hands as she straightened. Caution was necessary, they were in the middle of a war zone, but she had just saved their lives. He eyed her before letting out the tension on the crossbow.

She glanced behind her to see a tall Akolan girl sheathing her curved dagger. Her thick, dark hair fell in waves around her shoulders and she wore old, weather-beaten Kalyazi clothes, but her gold nose ring glinted new in the moonlight.

When Nadya turned to shoot Anna a pointed look, the priestess sighed and dropped her blade as well.

"Who are you?" Nadya asked.

The boy ignored her. "Did you do that?" he asked, pointing at the sky.

"Don't be ridiculous," she snapped.

"Ridiculous, as you say. My name is Rashid Khajouti, and my lovely companion—"

"Can speak perfectly well for herself," the Akolan girl said, sounding amused. Her hand no longer lingered near the hilt of her dagger and she moved away from Nadya to show she meant no harm. "My name is Parijahan Siroosi. I suppose we should be thanking you, not threatening you." She glanced at Rashid. "There were more Tranavians than we initially thought."

They had made quick work of them, regardless. Nadya's gaze landed on a crossbow, dropped by a Tranavian soldier, near her feet. She picked it up. The image of Kostya flashed in her vision. It took everything she had to not smash the weapon to pieces.

"Why were two Akolans planning on taking down a group of Tranavians in the middle of the night?" she asked, running her fingers over the wood of the crossbow, trying to dispel the image of her dead friend.

"I could ask the same," Parijahan said.

"We have a clear and obvious reason to be killing Tranavians, in general," Nadya pointed out.

Rashid chuckled. Parijahan shot him a look and he fell silent.

Something felt off, but Nadya couldn't place what it was. The way the Akolans had relaxed after initially being so aggressive, the stillness of the night air around them: the pieces weren't lining up right.

Horz?

"Yes, love?"

That wasn't all of the Tranavians, was it?

"I thought you knew."

She cranked the crossbow to set the bolt and turned it on the Akolan boy. Anna moved at the same instant, her *venyiashk* drawn against Parijahan's neck. There was no possible way she could have known the reason for Nadya's sudden defense, but she trusted Nadya enough to move without question.

It was that kind of blind trust that made Nadya uncomfortable.

"You're our voice to the people, love," Horz said. *"You'd best get used to blind adoration."*

"There are more Tranavians nearby," Nadya said to Anna.

The Akolans just exchanged a knowing glance. There was something else going on here.

But before she could think of what to do, Rashid hefted his own crossbow and fired.

She ducked instinctively, in an attempt to knock the bolt into her shoulder or arm, somewhere less deadly than her heart.

But she heard the thud of the bolt hitting flesh and a strangled cry and it took her brain a handful of painful seconds to catch up. It hadn't been her. She hadn't been hit.

"You *missed*." A new voice spoke, this one rich with a thick Tranavian accent.

A chill dragged down Nadya's spine. Tranavian words bouncing off the walls of a dark cavern as her home burned above. Was the voice the same? It sounded the same. The same lilt—even though the words were Kalyazi this time—and a distinct presence of authority.

How had the prince caught up already? It was too late, it was over.

She turned.

There was a Tranavian soldier on his knees in the snow, a crossbow bolt sticking out of his shoulder. His face was expressionless, his eyes glassy. Behind him stood a tall, wiry boy with sharp, wild features and long black hair. The boy's hands were covered in blood, a crumpled spell book page in one, the other held outstretched toward the soldier in the snow.

"I go and find the one *you* let get away and you don't even have the decency to kill him," the boy said, and tutted at Rashid.

His fingers twitched, just slightly, and whatever spell he had caught the soldier up in changed and the man crumpled to the ground, dead. He dropped the page and used the snow to wipe the blood off his hands.

It wasn't the prince. Nadya wanted to be relieved—because

maybe this meant she was safe—but she had felt the wave of power as the boy cast his magic. It was strong. Far stronger than the power she had felt from even the Tranavian prince during the attack.

"We could have gotten information out of him," Parijahan pointed out, then simply moved away from Anna's blade.

Anna shot Nadya a desperate look, but she just shrugged, equally bewildered. The only Tranavian she could now feel nearby was the mage, but he clearly knew the Akolans.

They needed to leave. This commotion was happening dangerously close to the monastery, to the prince. Nadya saw her chance when Rashid began picking through the soldiers' belongings. But the Tranavian boy took a step closer and she froze, suddenly aware the situation had moved from benign to deadly in only a few short seconds.

The way he looked at her was too discerning, too focused. Even in the darkness, Nadya could see his eyes were such a pale shade of blue as to be nearly devoid of color. He was the second Tranavian with eyes like ice she had seen in as many days.

His gaze flicked to Anna, but then returned to her.

"Names?" he asked.

Parijahan shook her head.

"We very politely gave them *our* names, but I suppose Kalyazi don't appreciate manners," Rashid said.

A smile slid over the Tranavian's face, slightly feral. His canine teeth were oddly sharp; everything about him was sharp in the most unnerving way. There were three vertical lines tattooed down his forehead in black ink, ending at the bridge of his straight nose.

"Wise of them."

Nadya was beginning to see her mistake in not taking the opportunity to run. There were only three of them, and none of them could be much older than her, but there was something so off-putting about the Tranavian. She couldn't put a name to it, but she knew—intrinsically—he would not hesitate to kill her if she made any indication of hostility.

Would he hand her right back to the prince? Or would he kill her here and take whatever power her blood might harbor for his own?

She might have failed to protect the monastery, but she would die before she let herself fall into the hands of a Tranavian.

He stepped closer. She froze, all cavalier thoughts of heroism escaping her. She didn't know if she could actually fight off this boy if it came to it, and maybe waiting out the situation would get her to the other side alive. He took her string of prayer beads in one hand. A hiss of displeasure escaped her lips. No one touched her beads but *her*.

"You both came from the monastery, yes?" His Kalyazi was almost perfect but for the crackling Tranavian accent that hardened his words. Beating the consonants into submission.

The answer was too obvious to deny. She fought against the urge to step back because even the foot of space he was giving her was much too close. This boy was a heretic, he profaned the gods and cast blood magic. Around him the air snapped with wrongness.

"So which one of you is the one with magic?" His voice lowered.

"Kalyazi don't have magic," Anna said, a beat too quick.

The boy gave her a shrewd glance before returning to Nadya. "It was you."

"Don't be ridiculous," she said, but her traitorous voice shook. Each moment they stood out in the open was another chance for the prince to come upon them. Maybe that was exactly what he wanted. Maybe he was just stalling.

He smiled, the expression dangerous and chilling and far too appraising. He reached down and took Nadya's hand, pressing it to his lips as if he were a court nobleman and not a renegade blood mage out in the middle of enemy territory. "My name is Malachiasz Czechowicz," he said, and she couldn't shake the feeling that she had just been given something. Something she had not asked for and could not envision ever wanting.

She did not give him her name and he dropped her hand. *What was that?*

Nadya elected to ignore it, clenching her teeth and fighting the urge to step away.

"We need to get out of here," Anna said, moving closer to Nadya.

She nodded, and stooped down, carefully picking up her *voryen* and sheathing it, aware of the way Malachiasz tensed as she did so.

"The danger has passed, and we haven't yet finished our introductions," Rashid said pointedly.

Nadya couldn't see any reason to lie. "There's a prince on our trail and the longer we spend out here, the closer he gets. We thought the group you had your sights on was part of his company, but it looks like they were merely stragglers. We'll be on our way now before he has the chance to catch up."

Rashid's eyes narrowed. Malachiasz's head tilted to one side, his hand lifting to rest on the spell book at his hip.

"Prince? The Tranavians have as many princes as you Kalyazi. You'll have to be more specific," Rashid said lazily, but his expression creased with alarm.

"The High Prince," Anna snapped.

Parijahan glanced at Malachiasz. "The High Prince is this far into Kalyazin?"

They don't know, Nadya realized, an almost giddy sense of relief rushing through her. The Tranavian was a problem, but he wasn't a part of the prince's company.

"The monastery burned yesterday," Nadya said, tripping over the words. It was too raw.

Parijahan pushed Malachiasz out of the way. "So you need somewhere safe to wait him out?"

Nadya blinked. "What?"

"Parj . . ." Malachiasz said, his voice a warning.

She ignored him. "Come with us," she said earnestly. "We can keep you safe from the prince."

Nadya's gaze strayed to Malachiasz. Parijahan followed it.

"He won't harm you." It would have been more reassuring if she sounded confident.

"I make no promises," he murmured.

"I won't have anything to do with any Tranavian," Nadya said. "Except to kill them."

"Yes, I can see that," Malachiasz said. He nudged one of the dead soldiers with the toe of his boot. "An admirable skill set. She's not going to take you up on your offer, Parijahan. We should go."

"The *actual* High Prince is near?" Rashid asked.

"Blood and bone, I should have left you both in those gutters," Malachiasz snapped. He bent down and snatched a spell book off one of the dead soldiers, then stalked into the trees.

Rashid shrugged at Parijahan and took off after him. Parijahan watched the boys disappear.

"Technically," she said conspiratorially to Nadya, "he would have been killed by the Kalyazi soldiers he was antagonizing had we not come along. But Rashid did end up unconscious in a gutter."

Nadya felt like she was going to explode with nerves. The most she and Anna could do would be to hike a few more miles into the mountains and hope the High Prince didn't already have their trail.

"Can you truly keep us safe?" she asked as Parijahan turned back to her. Nadya didn't like the thought of being anywhere near that blood mage, but if there were straggling bands of Tranavian soldiers this deep into the mountains, they could happen upon another at any time and not be so lucky. Nadya didn't want to think about what this could mean for the war effort.

Parijahan nodded. "There's an abandoned church nearby. We found it a few weeks ago and have made it almost livable. It could fall around our ears at any second, but at least it's warm."

Anna let out a sharp breath. Nadya glanced at her, but Anna just shook her head.

"And you'll do this . . . why? You put a dagger to my neck."

"I did, but it *was* very dark. And you helped us. I have a bad habit of picking up those who've helped me." She smiled wryly, but her expression became deadly serious as she glanced up at the sky.

It was clear she knew Nadya had cast the magic. There had never been any true point in trying to hide it. Using her power was inevitable, and the minute she did, people would know Kalyazin had clerics again after a thirty-year absence.

One cleric, at least.

Parijahan rubbed the hilt of her dagger. "I think you can aid us in doing the impossible."

5

SEREFIN

MELESKI

**Svoyatovo Radmila, Nymphadora, and Agrippa Mar-
tyvsheva:** *Triplets blessed by the god Vaclav, the Martyv-
shevas lived in the center of the dark Chernayevsky Forest
in quiet communion with their patron until the heretic Ser-
giusz Konicki invaded. When he tried to force the Mar-
tyvshevas to renounce their patron, they resisted. Konicki
killed Nymphadora and Agrippa, burning them and half
the Chernayevsky Forest. Radmila fled to safety, spent seven
years in contemplation with Vaclav, then hunted Konicki
down and burned him alive like he had her sisters.*

—Vasiliev's Book of Saints

The next morning, Serefin woke with a raging hangover
and a prisoner to interrogate. It was early, before dawn,
and he lay on the stone-hard pallet, staring up at the ceiling and contemplating his fate.

If they found the cleric within the next few days—he

was certain they would—it meant a speedy return to Tranavia. It had been years since he had been in Tranavia for longer
than a few months. The war was all he had.

He wasn't sure he remembered how to be the High Prince
instead of the blood mage general at the helm of the army.

Serefin sat up and was rewarded by a headache pounding
a hammer against his temple. He groaned, running a hand
through his hair. He shrugged on his coat and tried to ignore
that his mouth tasted as if he had chewed on sawdust all night.

He opened the door to find his entire company in a panic.

"Your Highness, I was just coming to wake you," Ostyia
called.

He blinked at the pair of soldiers who were crashing through
the hall past her, shouting something about the end of the
world.

"I'm going back to bed," he said. He'd had enough of this
ridiculous country and their ridiculous religion and maybe the
end of the world would stop the absolutely blinding headache
he had acquired.

"Serefin!"

"Oh, yell a little more, Ostyia, please."

He turned back, regretting the motion immediately as the
room spun. He pressed a hand to his face, slouching against
the doorframe.

She was fighting a smile. He was going to kill her. "Do you
want me to get you something for that hangover?" she asked
sweetly.

"No—yes, water, just water." He waved a hand. This wasn't
fair. He was *certain* she'd had more to drink than him the night
before. "Then someone tell me what's going on." He rested his
forehead against the stones, cool against his skin.

Ostyia returned a few moments later, handing him a full

skin of water. It didn't help. He kept a hand pressed to his temple as he signaled her to brief him.

"Sometime around three o'clock in the morning everything in the sky went out."

He flinched as he raised an eyebrow. Why did *that* hurt? "What is that supposed to mean?"

"It means the whole world went dark for about fifteen minutes last night."

Serefin's eyes narrowed.

"Also a scout we sent in the direction of the Kalyazi girls never returned," Ostyia continued. "Are you allowed to kill people if you're the hand of the divine?"

He ignored that.

"Should I order the rest of the company to move out? We can have them sent ahead."

He considered her suggestion. "Hold that order." He wanted to send the rest of the company with Teodore while he sought out the cleric.

"You're giving her time to get away."

"I still have her trail. I need something more to ground the spell. We're going to get it now."

Serefin followed Ostyia through the sparse and cold hallways of the monastery and into the opulent sanctuary. He didn't understand why so much money was poured into creating something for the purpose of gods who would not care a bit for it, but he could still appreciate beauty for what it was.

Pews of rare blackwood lined the sanctuary, with the smallest of statues carved at each of the ends. The altar was huge, reaching up to the vaulted ceiling and made of gold and blackwood and silver. The tiers of the Kalyazi gods pictured on either side, the highest tier not depicting figures of the gods themselves, but columns with words in an ancient language Serefin could not make out. The first through third tiers showed the gods in more human forms: regal, beautiful, terrible.

Serefin paused in the doorway, eyeing the ceiling. Paintings of haloed saints and forests stretched over them. Icons were placed along the walls of the sanctuary, depictions of more saints. How could one country have so many raised to purported holiness?

Light filtered through the clear glass—Serefin was surprised it wasn't stained glass like the abandoned chapels of Tranavia. Ostyia was watching him and he turned to her, rolling his eyes derisively.

"We could make good coin out of all this gold," he noted.

"Only if you wanted to carry it back to Tranavia yourself," she said.

We'll have to find new ways to fund this war eventually, Serefin thought. The army had looted the Kalyazi churches near the border, but anything farther away was too difficult to transport. Serefin wondered if he could have a method looked into for moving the riches into Tranavia. At least then the gold would be put to some actual use instead of collecting dust in tribute to empty air.

Why waste all that money and time in service to gods who did not even know you existed? He would never understand the Kalyazi and their devotion to a thing of the past.

The future was magic, it was power, it was mankind stepping out of the shadows and finding out the world had been kept in the dark by these gods. Not even gods, but rules and rigors kept in place by men of the church. Of course, the war was about more than just religion—there was a stretch of land between Tranavia and Kalyazin that both claimed as their own. And there were other, minor issues that had compounded during the near century the war had stretched.

"The abbot gave you nothing?" Ostyia asked as they approached the door where the young monk was being held.

"An old man content to speak only in riddles. I have a mind to execute him." Removing their leader would ensure the prisoners remained placid. He had used the tactic before with the Kalyazi. It always worked. He had never used it with church folk, though; he was hesitant to do anything that might turn one of their own into a martyr. The Kalyazi loved their martyrs.

He paused before the chosen door, stopping Ostyia before she opened it. She shot him a look that was altogether too knowing.

"If you'd rather not, I would be more than happy to do this for you," she said.

Serefin shook his head. It didn't really matter that he was tired of torturing prisoners, tired of this tour.

"No, I'll do it." He shot her a half-hearted smile. "Besides, this could be fun, yeah?"

Ostyia kicked open the door. It led into a room nearly identical to the one Serefin had slept in. The Kalyazi boy sat on a hard wooden chair with his wrists tied behind his back, the position yanking his shoulders over the chair. Someone had patched up the crossbow wounds in his leg and side, Serefin noticed. That was good. He didn't want the boy bleeding out while he was trying to get answers from him.

"We could bypass all this unpleasantness, you know," the boy said in fairly smooth Tranavian. He had obviously been taught Graznki, a rougher daughter language to the mother tongue. "I'm sure you don't want to stain your nice coat."

Serefin raised an eyebrow. *"Zhe ven'ya?"* His coat *was* nice.

The boy appeared surprised to hear his own language out of the Tranavian High Prince's mouth. His dark hair was cut close to his head; three diagonal lines were shaved into the side. His robes seemed too thin to keep him properly warm, but Serefin supposed a Kalyazi monk would enjoy pain. .

"You are going to ask where our missing sisters went. I will tell you I have no idea. You will kill me, end of the story."

"That wasn't a particularly good story," Serefin said as he moved a chair across the room, placing it in front of the boy. He flipped it around and sat on it backwards, leaning his forearms against the back. "The rising action did nothing for the climax, it all fell short at the resolution."

"Tranavians don't like stories. They're too busy writing down blasphemes to use for sacrificial magic."

"Ah, that's not true." Serefin looked at Ostyia, who shook her head, looking rightly dismayed by the accusation. "What a malicious rumor." He fell silent. The boy stared back stoically, but a flicker passed over his expression. He was finally taking a good look at Serefin's scar and eye. "What is your name?"

The boy blinked. "Konstantin."

"Well, Konstantin, you are correct, I would like you to tell me where your little acolyte ran off to."

Konstantin leaned forward as far as his bound arms would allow. "And I would like to tell you to shove that spell book up your ass."

Ostyia took a step forward, but Serefin held out a hand to stop her. He smiled and reached down for the book at his hip. "This one?" He held it up.

"That's the one."

"Hm." Serefin opened the book and riffled through it. "Not really the proper use for it." His other hand shifted his coat sleeve down, his thumb pressing gently against the razor sewn into the cuff. Just a bit more pressure would send the razor through his flesh and draw up the blood needed. "You and

I both know I saw you protecting the cleric before she disappeared. Where did she go?"

"Who?"

"Feigned confusion is quaint, truly. What's the girl's name?"

Konstantin regarded him with stony silence. Serefin hadn't
expected him to answer. It would take encouragement. He
needed her name to clarify the spell. Serefin pressed his thumb
down on the razor in his sleeve. He barely even felt the blade
slice open his flesh. Konstantin's eyes went wide as Serefin took
his bleeding thumb and pressed it against one of the pages of
his spell book.

"No. Of course you wouldn't know such a thing."

His magic jolted, just once, as the blood ignited with what
was written on the pages. Konstantin went rigid, a vein puls-
ing in his neck betraying his fear. Sweat poured down his forehead and Serefin watched with thinly veiled interest as blood
dripped down from the corners of the boy's eyes. He was boiling him from the inside out. After a few seconds—which surely
felt like years to the Kalyazi—Serefin let the spell break. Konstantin slumped back in his chair, gasping for breath.

"Still nothing?" Serefin asked pleasantly.

Konstantin spat at his feet, the wad of bloody saliva landing on Serefin's boot. Serefin regarded it with distaste.

"I sensed this would happen, but I did so wish to avoid it."
He sighed, waving a hand to Ostyia, who quickly stepped out
of the room. The other boy stared at Serefin with some confusion, blood now dripping from his nose.

It didn't take long for Ostyia to return and Serefin kept his
gaze firmly on the Kalyazi boy as panic stripped his features
raw. Ostyia brought the second prisoner forward, kicking the
back of his legs to force him to kneel. Serefin finally glanced
over to see who Kacper had chosen. Kacper was a master of

secrets and information; ferreting out who would break their prisoners fastest was his specialty.

The boy appeared to be about fifteen years of age, with a subtle resemblance to Konstantin, his eyes huge and wide with fear. He kept them straight ahead, staring at the wall. Ostyia drew her blades and held them crossed over the boy's throat. Serefin turned his head lazily, his attention returning to Konstantin.

"Let's try this again, shall we? Tell me the girl's name and where she went."

Konstantin set his jaw even as his gaze went to the younger boy; his expression softened, but Serefin could see they didn't have him yet.

"It would appear I need to be more convincing," Serefin said. His thumb was still bleeding, so he carefully tore a second page from his spell book.

Fear etched onto Konstantin's face as Serefin leaned his chin on his forearm and inclined his head toward the second, younger boy. The spell caught and the boy spasmed in silent pain, tears running down his face. Serefin was impressed with his stoic grace in the face of agony.

"No!" Konstantin struggled against the bonds on his arms. "Don't hurt him! D-don't hurt him."

"Oh? Should I stop?" Serefin shifted the spell, causing the boy to whimper.

Resignation and a hint of anguish passed over Konstantin's face. "Nadezhda. Her name is Nadezhda."

"Full name, please?" Serefin reached over and slid one of Ostyia's daggers out of the sheath at her hip. He began to clean his fingernails with the point of the blade.

"Lapteva. Nadezhda Lapteva."

Serefin had to hide a smile. Now he had her. "And the other girl?"

"Anna Vadimovna. I . . . I do not know where they were going. There are multiple safe houses in the area. She could have chosen any one of them."

Serefin watched as the boy crumpled, the agony of betraying the information breaking him. Funny. For all he knew it was paltry information at best. Multiple safe houses were hardly surprising. He would have to comb the area thoroughly. There was also the matter of certain end-of-the-world incidents Serefin would like answers for.

"Is she powerful enough to take the stars out of the sky?"

The boy's head lifted and Serefin was faintly disgusted to see something that looked suspiciously like hope flicker across his face.

"No, but the gods are."

Serefin snorted softly. "Right, of course."

He stood up. "Thank you, Konstantin, for your time." He tore a third page out of his spell book and crumpled it in his hands.

Ostyia took a step back as the younger boy fell over, dead.

Serefin left just as the Kalyazi monk's shock was beginning to wear off—just as the screams of rage began.

Ostyia shut the door, muffling them. "I will have someone collect the body," she said.

"Thank you." Serefin glanced at Ostyia. "I'll have to ask that you convince me not to get drunk again."

"Anything for you, Serefin."

As they entered the sanctuary, Serefin paused in front of the ornate altar. He skimmed his hand over a carving of a forest that covered the top.

Pain suddenly lanced through his skull as if spikes were being driven through his eyes. He clutched his head with one hand, fingers fumbling for his spell book and razor. He fell to the ground.

"Serefin!" Ostyia cried, dropping to her knees.

He held out a hand. The pain was already dissipating, ebbing away like a trickling stream. He leaned back, expelling a long breath of air.

"What was that?"

He internally accounted for all the threads of magic he had active. The spell he had cast to track the cleric had been severed. He scrambled for it, his index finger sliding over the razor in his sleeve, but even with fresh blood he couldn't reconnect it. He had her name but it wouldn't help if he lost the trail.

She'd found his spell, broken it, and kept him from bringing it back. And last night she had taken the stars from the sky. She was more powerful than he'd thought.

He had to find her. He had to take her power for his own.

"Have Teodore placed in charge of the company," Serefin said slowly. "You, Kacper, and I are going after the girl. Now."

6

N A D E Z H D A

L A P T E V A

Though Bozetjeh is the god of the wind, he is considered to
be the essence of speed and of time itself. He is everywhere
and nowhere all at once.

—Codex of the Divine, 10:114

Sweat beaded at Nadya's temples but relief flooded her
as the prince's spell snapped away. She let out a hiss of a
breath, the odd sense of something *wrong* leaving her.

Up ahead the Tranavian boy paused. He looked back
at her, a frown creasing the tattoos at his forehead.

He shouldn't have been able to sense that, Nadya thought.

"No . . . he shouldn't have," Marzenya agreed. She sounded curious. *"You will dispose of him soon, yes?"*

He's Tranavian, Nadya replied. The answer was obvious.

Nadya was disconcerted Marzenya had to tell her the
prince was tracking her every move, that she hadn't felt

the taint of his blood magic. There were still too many things Nadya didn't know how to do on her own.

After Parijahan had offered them a place to hide, they had swiftly caught up with the two boys. Rashid grinned at Nadya, whereas Malachiasz eyed her silently before turning away.

They arrived at a large, ramshackle church that sprawled down across a valley. It looked like whoever built it had planned for it to rival the Church of Adrian, the Martyr in Khavirsk, but got distracted. It was made entirely of wood—even the round onion domes—and there was unfinished red paint peeling from the bottom of the walls. Carvings over the doorway revealed a dedication to the goddess of the sun, Alena.

This is yours? Nadya asked, thumbing the appropriate bead on her necklace.

She felt amusement in return. *"It was never truly dedicated."*

Nadya eyed the church. She could fix that. She wondered how these refugees would take to having their space suddenly inhabited by a goddess. If they *were* refugees. She wasn't sure what other word to use to describe them, all three foreigners and one of them the enemy, no less.

Rashid shoved open the door. It was dark in the foyer, the stumps of half-used torches unlit in their sconces, only one of them left burning. The inside of the building looked nothing like a church. There were three long hallways that were utterly black, two on either side of the entrance, and one down the middle. Nadya had to assume the middle one led to the sanctuary—the church would have been built around an intended sanctuary space—but the rest of the building had clearly been repurposed somewhere along the line.

"It was like this when we found it," Parijahan said.

The dark hall opened up into a large, airy nave that had been gutted. There were piles of weapons against the far wall, clearly picked off Tranavian companies. The room was cut by a chill draft from a hole in the ceiling, but there was a fire smoldering in a makeshift fireplace at the far end of the sanctuary that likely worked to combat it. At the opposite end of the room was a pile of worn pillows and blankets that Rashid immediately sprawled on top of. He pulled the crossbow onto his lap and began meticulously going over it. Beside him was a long table with benches that appeared as though they had been dragged in from the church's kitchens. A few ragged maps rested atop them.

The wall between the nave and the sanctuary had been torn down and the only thing that remained of the original space was the icon of Alena that hung over the fireplace—where the altar would have been. It was a lovely piece. It would have been worth thousands of *kopecks*. Anna shot Nadya a wide-eyed look.

The icon was by Kalyazin's most beloved iconographer, Probka Vilenova. She was a saint now, martyred by Tranavians. Her fingers had been cut off and her eyes gouged out before they finally tied rocks to her ankles and drowned her in one of their hundreds of lakes. These three probably had no idea just how much the icon was worth.

"Are you sure this will be safe?" Anna asked. "It feels . . . conspicuous."

"Did it look like there was anyone in here from the outside?" Rashid said.

It had not. In fact, it looked like the church had been long forgotten by the world.

"We're not staying for long," Nadya said. "Just a day or so." She had cut the prince's spell when they were still far from the church so she had to hope they were safe, but they had to keep moving. They had to get to Tvir.

"No?" Rashid asked, sounding vaguely disappointed. "Didn't Parijahan explain the situation?"

"Situation?" Anna asked.

"Until they trust us, nothing I say will matter," Parijahan said. She hopped up onto the table. "But, I suppose knowing our intentions would be a start. We want to stop the war."

"Oh, something as simple as that?" Nadya asked, breathing out a startled laugh. "It's been nearly a century, and you think *you* can stop it? You're right. There's no trust here."

"She has a point," Malachiasz said. He leaned back against the table next to Parijahan. "But we are the ones with the nasty heretic in our midst. I think, first, we should find out just who is the one with magic." His eyes lingered on Nadya, a smile flickering at the corners of his lips, before cutting to Anna.

He wore the uniform of a Tranavian military blood mage, though his black jacket was ragged, fraying at the sleeves and hem. There was a patch sewn onto the elbow and the silver epaulets at his shoulders looked like they had seen better days.

Rashid looked expectantly at Anna and Nadya.

Neither of them spoke. Nadya chewed her lower lip. If the layout of this church was anything traditional, there would be multiple exits. It would only be a matter of finding the right door and the right hallway and getting out. But Nadya couldn't let her driving reaction to every situation be acting upon the desire to flee. There was a reason two Akolans and a Tranavian were camped out in the Kalyazi mountains. There was a reason they were speaking cryptically, why the Tranavian seemed unsettled. There was a reason for all of this and Nadya had to believe the gods had thrown her path against these foreigners for a reason, whatever it might be.

"I could always test them," Malachiasz said.

"No!" Anna's outburst made Nadya jump.

Malachiasz lifted an eyebrow. His pale eyes slid back to Nadya. A chill ran through her.

He knows it's me.

It was a deeply uncomfortable thought.

Malachiasz pushed off the table, drawing a wicked looking curved knife from a sheath at the small of his back. He flipped it between his fingers as he walked over to where the girls stood.

Bloodletting to test for magic was a heretical act in itself, made worse by the fact a heretic blood mage would be doing the deed.

Malachiasz's pale gaze locked on Nadya.

Fine. If he tries to kill me for my power, I'll just have to kill him first.

He took her hand, fingers curling around her wrist. The heat of his touch made Nadya's skin crawl. She saw the flash of silver as the blade lifted, felt the shift of fire to ice as the metal touched the top of her index finger.

"No," she whispered. She tensed, pulling back, but his grip was firm, locked around her like a shackle.

Without breaking eye contact, she drew her *voryen,* using his hand around her wrist as leverage to yank him closer, snapping the dagger to his throat. He tensed, head forced back to keep her blade from cutting flesh. A slow smile tugged at his mouth.

"You already know it's me," she said, voice low. "Don't think I'll be complicit in your heresy."

"Suspicion and confirmation are two different things. And heresy is such an ugly word."

Nadya glanced at Anna. It looked as though the other girl had stopped breathing. Anna shook her head, alarmed.

"Well, I want proof," Rashid said.

Malachiasz's hand was still clenched over Nadya's wrist and there was a thin trickle of blood trailing down his pale neck, damage from her less than steady nerves. He moved his other hand up, his movement cautious, and wiped the blood from his skin with his thumb.

"Complicit in heresy, indeed," he murmured.

Nadya pulled her dagger back.

"The *moons* going out wasn't enough for you?" Malachiasz asked Rashid, dropping Nadya's wrist and sheathing his knife. She darted back to Anna's side. "I am a bit curious about the long-term ramifications of a spell like that. What havoc will be wrought on the tides from canceling out the moons for that long?"

"We're thousands of miles away from any oceans, Malachiasz," Parijahan said wearily.

"It's something to think about."

"He's Tranavian. They always have water on the brain," Rashid said. "Their country is practically under water as it is."

"A few lakes—" Malachiasz said.

"And swamps."

"So many ponds!" Parijahan said.

"Bordered by an ocean on the north *and* the east," Rashid continued. "Why do you really think your war has never moved into Tranavia? No one in Kalyazin can swim. Can you swim?" he asked Nadya.

She shook her head.

"When you put it that way, buried alive under snow does seem like an altogether more satisfying way to die," Malachiasz mused.

"I can think of a hundred better ways for you to die," Anna muttered.

He smiled, pressing a hand to his heart. "Surely all one hundred are deserved."

Parijahan said, quite solemnly, "Tides are controlled by gravity. My people figured that out centuries ago."

Malachiasz made an indignant sound and looked at Rashid, who nodded seriously.

Nadya wondered if their idle chatter meant her magic had been forgotten, but she found she wasn't so lucky as Rashid pointed to her. "Magic."

"What will you do with the proof?"

"Marvel at how a country who lost their mages and have been hanging on to a war *against* mages by the skin of their teeth may finally have a chance again."

She glanced at Malachiasz, wondering what his reaction might be, but his face was impassive. "What will *he* do?"

"Oh, he'll probably want to kill you for your power. Isn't that how all your clerics died out in the first place?"

Malachiasz grinned.

Nadya shuddered. That had definitely had a hand in it.

"But," Rashid continued, "he will not do that. Because he is not in the Kalyazi mage killing business."

"I could be," Malachiasz mused.

Parijahan rolled her eyes but a shock of terror ran through Nadya at his quiet contemplation of her death. The Akolans weren't taking him seriously and she couldn't understand it.

Nadya ran her hand down her necklace, fingers catching against the beads as she considered what spell she could use, until she reached Krsnik's bead. Perhaps simple was the way to handle this. She had already done flashy.

Little help?

Krsnik, an old and grouchy god, grumbled something that was apparently an assent because Nadya was given the spell a heartbeat later. She blew smoky, glimmering symbols onto her palm and her hand lit into flames.

Parijahan exchanged a delighted glance with Rashid. Nadya moved over to the table and trailed a burning fingertip over what was clearly a discarded spell book page. She picked up the paper and it burst into flames. When only ashes were left in her hand, she tilted them into the blood mage's palm. She brought her gaze up to meet his and was unsure of what she saw in his eyes.

Tension, curiosity, but underneath it all was something darker. Something that made a shiver jolt down her spine. It made her wonder why a heretic had been placed before her path. To kill him? What other reason could there possibly be?

A smile flashed on his lips, as if he could read her thoughts the way the gods did.

"So, what is the difference between you and our blood mage friend here?" Rashid asked. "Forgive a handsome young foreigner his ignorant questions."

The blood mage in question flopped down on the pillows beside Rashid, opening his spell book in his lap. Nadya never saw him cut himself, but the back of his hand was bleeding. He used a quill to scratch the blood onto the pages of his book.

"I think your mage is making the differences fairly blatant," she said. "Blood. Spell books. Heresy. That's Tranavian magic."

Malachiasz smiled without looking up from his work.

He smiles too much, she thought.

"My *power* is divine. I am not. There's no blood. No spell books."

"Just the requirement of constant approval from the gods," Malachiasz said. "No pressure. One misstep and it's all over."

"Is it so hard to live by the will of the gods? They ask for so little. You give them no credit."

He shook his head. "So little?" he asked incredulously. "They ask for far too much. Why do you think Tranavia broke with the gods? Who yearns for life yoked to another being's whim? We wished to choose our own destiny."

Nadya rolled her eyes. "And is your destiny worth the torture and mutilation of a century of innocents to reach the means for your magic? Hundreds upon *thousands* of people."

His expression flickered but he recovered so quickly Nadya questioned if it happened at all.

"Sacrifices were made willingly. No one is forced into tests."

"Except prisoners of war," Nadya shot back.

He leaned forward. "Even prisoners of war are made to understand the greater good they're serving in the end."

"Greater good?" Nadya cried, finally losing her temper. "How *dare* you speak of a greater good, like your kind has any right to pretend you are anything but heretics and abominations revolting against the gods."

Malachiasz was grinning now, sharp-toothed and dangerous. He lolled his head to one side, lazily closing his spell book. He took a bandage out of his pocket and slowly wrapped his hand. "All right, you win. She'll be useful," he said to Rashid.

Nadya didn't like the sound of that. "Useful? Are you going to experiment on me as well?"

Malachiasz stood and crossed the room until he was standing over Nadya. He was very tall. He took her chin in his ink-and blood-stained hand and tilted her face up toward his.

"You would not be so lucky," he said, his voice soft, his breath a whisper against her cheek.

"Malachiasz . . ." Parijahan said.

He released Nadya, taking a step back. "We can keep you safe," he said. "The High Prince could be right outside the door and never realize the church is even here. I've made certain."

"The High Prince, maybe, but what of Tranavia's other horrors?" Anna shot back.

Now it was Malachiasz's turn to go still.

"What?"

"The monsters you Tranavians let foul once-holy churches. What about them?"

"The Vultures do not venture onto the battlefield," he said, but his voice was strained. One of his hands absently rubbed his forearm. "They haven't left Tranavia in . . ."

"About thirty years," Nadya said. "Funny, that."

His eyes narrowed, but he shook his head, backing down.

Woven into the darkest of Kalyazi nightmares were the Vultures of Tranavia. Blood mages so twisted by their heretical magic they were no longer human, nothing more than violent monsters. It was true, they hadn't been seen in Kalyazin in a long time. It was also true they had been one of the final nails in the last of the clerics' coffins.

If they came for Nadya, she wasn't sure she could escape so easily this time.

"Why would you help us?" Nadya asked after a beat of uncomfortable silence.

"We're no friends to Tranavia," Parijahan said.

Nadya shot a pointed look at Malachiasz. He smiled at her.

"We're here because Tranavians burned down the last, what, three refugee camps we found?" Malachiasz said, moving back to the tables and hopping up next to Parijahan.

"Three camps, two outposts, one military encampment, and one village," Rashid said.

"The military camp was before my time," Malachiasz said, answering the question Nadya was about to ask: how could they ever get *him* into a military encampment?

"Again, we want this war to end," Parijahan said simply.

"Don't we all?" Anna muttered.

"Yes, well, keeping a Kalyazi cleric alive would do that, wouldn't it? Even with the differences in ideology."

"It's a start," Nadya allowed.

"What if we go further?" Parijahan asked. "The boys kept telling me to wait until an opportunity arose, and now here you are. So, tell me, how do you feel about assassinating the Tranavian king?"

7

SEREFIN

MELESKI

Svoyatova Alisha Varushkina: *A cleric of Bozidarka and a seer, Alisha's visions protected Kalyazin from an uprising in the western provinces. This protection did not extend to her. Years later, a low prince from the west, Dmitri Zyuganov, would burn out her eyes with a flaming poker for interfering with his plans.*

—Vasiliev's Book of Saints

"Your Highness?"

Serefin clenched a fist, reflex causing his index finger to brush against the razor in his sleeve. He forced himself to relax. Being on edge wasn't going to help anything. "Yes?"

He was relieved to find Kacper trailing along behind Teodore, less relieved to notice Kacper had something in his hand that looked suspiciously like a royal missive. Dread coiled in his stomach.

"Did you speak with my father?" he asked Teodore.

"I did, Your Highness. He expressed—" he paused and Serefin sighed, knowing what was coming "—displeasure at the outcome of yesterday's attack."

"Well, he wasn't here," Serefin muttered.

Teodore said nothing, and Kacper handed Serefin the missive. He took it gingerly between two fingers. The seal was his father's. The king generally sent messages via courier instead of with magic in an effort to mask the disappointing reality that he was a less than impressive blood mage. Contact *could* be made with blood magic—like Teodore had done the night before—but it was discouraged.

"Did this arrive this morning?" he asked.

Kacper nodded.

There was no telling how long it had taken to reach Serefin's hands. He broke the seal, scanned the letter, became confident that his eyesight was finally failing him completely, scanned it again, and looked up at Kacper with a frown before reading it closely once more.

"Did my father mention this?"

"He did not," Teodore said.

"Nothing? Nothing at all? Not even the littlest hint that he had been planning this for months without giving me so much as a warning?"

"It would help, Ser—Your Highness," Kacper said, shooting Teodore an irritated look, "if we knew what the message was?"

"He wants me to return to Tranavia," Serefin said, handing Kacper the missive and ignoring Teodore's scandalized expression. "Immediately, apparently, as there's a matter of an upcoming *Rawalyk*."

"What?" Kacper looked startled.

"The ceremony to choose a royal consort—" Teodore started.

"I know what a *Rawalyk* is—" Kacper said, just as Serefin snapped at Teodore, "He's aware of the tradition."

Teodore gave Kacper a dark look.

"I need to go after the cleric, I don't have time for this," Serefin said. "We are *so close* to a turning point with the war, and he wants me to drop everything for a pointless charade."

"He did mention that the Vultures requested to be sent after the cleric," Teodore said.

Serefin raked a hand through his hair. Kacper's eyebrows lifted.

"So he's stripping me of my command and ordering me home," Serefin said softly.

Teodore didn't respond.

It made sense, of course, for the Vultures to want to get their hands on the first Kalyazi cleric in more than thirty years. There was a new generation in the cult, ones who had never seen Kalyazi magic before. It stood to reason.

But Serefin hated the idea of his victory going to someone else. His father was the one who had sent Serefin to the front when he was only sixteen; he wanted a war hero for a son so that was what he got, and all the mess that came with it. It wasn't fair to ask him to fill a role he had grown unused to for the sake of tradition when they were so near the end.

There would be no arguing. It was not a choice. If he left that day, he could reach Grazyk in a few weeks, potentially longer depending on what they found when they reached the border. If he took only Ostyia and Kacper with him, he could make the journey in even less time. But they were behind enemy lines. Anything could go wrong.

"I will," he started slowly, each word a sharp arrow piercing through him, "leave you in charge of the company. You are to take the prisoners to Kyętri, am I right?"

A nod from Teodore.

"Right. Lieutenant Neiborski will be coming with me," he said.

Kacper looked relieved, as if he briefly thought Serefin was going to leave him behind. Ridiculous.

"General Rabalska, as well, obviously. I expect you to have the prisoners outfitted and removed from here by tomorrow morning at latest."

Teodore was aware he was being dismissed. He bowed and Serefin waved him away. If he was lucky, he wouldn't have to see the man again for months.

He moved through the cold, unadorned hallways until he reached the vast wooden doors that opened out into the courtyard. While they were plain on the back, the fronts of the doors were covered with ornate carvings and icons of saints. Six of them, three to each door. Serefin gazed at them after the doors closed before turning and jumping down the stairs leading to the courtyard where Ostyia was waiting. She was perched on the wall that led to the seven thousand steps down the mountain.

Serefin dropped his pack on the ground and hopped up onto the wall beside her. Kacper sat on his other side.

"I have to go home and get married."

Ostyia had the decency to wince. "What about the cleric?"

"The Vultures have gone to fetch her."

"She'll be dead within a day."

Kacper shuddered. "I wouldn't wish that fate even on a Kalyazi. Can you imagine?" He flashed a hand over his face. "Those masks are terrifying."

The Vultures were a complicated part of Tranavian society

and politics. They were the blood mage elite, a cultic sect of individuals, closed off from the rest of their kingdom, living in the hollowed-out carcass of an ancient cathedral in Grazyk under the leadership of a king of their own, the Black Vulture, who sat on the Carrion Throne.

When Tranavia broke from the gods, the Vultures filled in the gaps left behind by the church. They acted on their own, citing magic as a higher voice of command than any mortal king could ever be. The Vultures could have gone after the cleric without permission from the king, but Tranavia had in place a careful balance of power. The Vultures would act as advisors to the throne, but their authority only extended to the realm of magic—which in Tranavia was a vast reach. They skulked through the palace with their iron claws and torn robes, more monster than human, yet revered nonetheless.

For decades, the image of Tranavian politics was that the king kept the Vultures on a careful leash. They were to train the royal children to harness their magic as well as maintain a certain level of security in Grazyk, but they were not to leave Grazyk or Kyętri, the two cities that housed the cult's leaders.

They were kept away from the front owing to an unfortunate measure of unpredictability to their actions that made them more liability than asset on the battlefield. That said, Serefin had been through many a battle that would have been turned if they'd had even one Vulture in their midst. But he would never request one. They unsettled him.

Serefin scratched the back of his head as he squinted up at the monastery's onion domes. The glare from the whitened stone irritated his bad eye. "My father wants the prisoners to be taken to the Kyętri mines."

"That's a lot of activity from the Vultures suddenly," Ostyia said.

"It's odd, isn't it?"

A hush fell over them. Contemplating the Salt Mines where the Vultures held their experiments was hardly pleasant.

"I don't like this," Serefin said finally.

Ostyia glanced at him.

"The timing, the Vultures, that my father had this"—he waved the missive still in his hand—"sent instead of just having a mage contact me, which gives me less than no time to return home. I don't understand what he's doing."

It was no secret that Serefin's relationship with his father was strained. He didn't know if it was fear, distaste, or the simple reality that sending Serefin away to war at such a young age had put a rift in their relationship. Whatever it was, erratic behavior from the king was becoming increasingly normal, so Serefin didn't know why all these strange things converging at once surprised him.

Ostyia shot him a disbelieving look. "He's been stepping on you for ages now."

"Has he?"

Serefin hadn't had a moment's respite in years. With the country at war it stood to reason, but anytime he returned to Grazyk to remind the country that they *did* have a prince, he was turned around and sent right back to the front. He was tired, beginning to fray at the edges, as if the barest touch would shatter him. He didn't want to play political games as soon as he returned to Tranavia, but that was his fate.

Ostyia was right, the rift was growing deeper. His father had been trying his hardest to gloss over the truth. His son was a talented blood mage, and he was not. If he pushed Serefin out of sight, the *slavhki* of the court would never recall the son was more powerful than the father.

Serefin jumped down off the wall, sliding on the icy stone

of the courtyard before turning around and facing his friends. "Well? We might as well put on a good show."

"Is that what it will be? A show?" Ostyia asked.

"If it's a *Rawalyk,* then yes," Kacper said.

"Meaningless dramatics for the sake of the nobility," Serefin said, then shrugged. "There's something else here. I might as well see what it is. I'm sure it won't be good."

Ostyia's eye narrowed. "I know that look. What are you planning?"

Serefin wasn't sure he was planning anything *yet.* He had a feeling, a creeping dread that wouldn't allow him to run home and play the part of the prince without some misgivings first. Maybe it was a product of being battered alive by this war, of seeing death and destruction every day for years. Maybe he was just growing irrational. Either way, it was there.

"What if my father is using the *Rawalyk* to install a puppet as his heir? Someone who can be manipulated." Serefin was too opinionated, too powerful, too much of a threat to Izak Meleski's sovereignty. "If he ties someone to the throne through me and then I meet an unfortunate accident . . ." he trailed off.

"Oy," Ostyia murmured.

"Just how paranoid do I sound?"

"Very."

He nodded. "I've been leading armies for three years," he said, voice soft. "And you don't go onto a battlefield without a strategy. But sometimes, reconnaissance is necessary. So I'm going to go home. I'm going to see what this nonsense is about, and then I'm going to deal with it as necessary. That may mean playing the prince and participating in needless dramatics. It could mean something entirely different. We may as well go and find out what this battle is going to look like." With that, Serefin started down the seven thousand steps.

NADEZHDA

LAPTEVA

The goddess of vision, Bozidarka, is a goddess of prophecy. Be warned: for her gifts can break a mortal's mind and her blessings are not so easily interpreted.
—Codex of the Divine, 7:12

No more was said about plans to kill kings. After Nadya had stuttered through her disbelief that it was even possible, Parijahan had suggested they speak more in the morning.

Killing the Tranavian king could end the war, but better still—at least for her—it would be some small justice for Kostya's death. She would take the risk for that. She didn't know if it would be possible—doubted it immensely—but the conversation made her warm to the Akolans. Even if she was still waiting for the right moment to put one of her *voryens* in the Tranavian's heart.

Nadya passed a restless night in a chilly room with

hard beds and thin blankets stolen from Tranavian soldiers. She was up before dawn breached the horizon, slipping out of the room and down the hall. She was used to waking before the sun to pray and wanted to be somewhere suitable to do so.

Anna was still asleep when she stepped out into the hallway. She found Parijahan in the gutted sanctuary, sitting at the table with ragged maps spread out in front of her.

"You were serious, weren't you?" Nadya asked. She sat down across from the Akolan girl.

"Why would I joke about something like this?" Parijahan replied, without looking up. She wore her dark hair in a loose braid that curled over her shoulder. "There were more of us, once. A boy who lost everything when the Tranavians burned down the forest he and his family used as their livelihood, a girl who grew up in a refugee camp, Kalyazi siblings from Novirkrya who were conscripted into the army when they were children but then defected."

Novirkrya was a village just on the southern border, near Lidnado, a small country that hated both its neighbors in equal measure and had remained miraculously apart from the war for the near century it had been raging, likely out of spite alone.

There are so very few faithful left in that country, Marzenya noted.

"What happened to them?" Nadya asked.

"This country, this war. The siblings had to flee north to avoid the army catching them, but it was like that for most."

But the two Akolans and the *Tranavian* remained?

The others trickled into the room. Anna sat down next to Nadya, leaning her head against Nadya's shoulder.

"Well," Anna said, "we're still here."

"No High Prince," Parijahan said.

Rashid brought food into the room; bowls of *kasha*—a thin gruel Nadya knew well—and loaves of hard, black bread which he set on the table before he curled up on the pile of pillows in the corner. He was dressed in layered, golden brown Akolan robes with long, slit sleeves.

"Nobody warned me that Kalyazi assassins rise before dawn." He yawned.

Malachiasz entered the room clutching half a loaf of black bread and looking like he hadn't slept at all. His long hair was tangled and there were dark smudges of shadow underneath his pale eyes. He flopped onto the pillows beside Rashid and put an arm over his face.

"They don't, but acolytes who have to answer the call to prayer at three in the morning do," Nadya said.

"And they call *us* barbarians," Malachiasz mused.

"We call you heretics. It's different. *And* accurate," Nadya snapped.

He sat up and rolled his eyes, then stuck most of the bread in his mouth. He opened his spell book and dropped a quill in the crease between the pages.

"Don't you dare start bleeding all over that while we're eating," Parijahan said.

Malachiasz looked up, a knife already in his hand, the blade poised on his forearm, bread still half in his mouth. Parijahan stared him down. After a long silence he meekly lowered the blade.

Nadya looked down at the map, Parijahan passing her a bowl of *kasha*. "I need to get to the military camp in Tvir," she said. She couldn't *truly* entertain their wild plans about assassinating kings. There were things expected of her, she couldn't just abandon those duties at the first obstacle. She was the vessel that would flood the world with the gods' touch once more.

"Tvir? Are you planning to waltz straight into the hands of Tranavia, *towy dżimyka*?" Malachiasz asked.

She wracked her basic understanding of Tranavian for what he'd called her. *Little bird?* Confused by both his meaning and the vaguely condescending way he'd said it, she elected to ignore him completely.

"Clearly, you had a protocol to follow, yes?" he continued. "An important mage like you?"

Nadya found it difficult to ignore his continued condescension.

"But if you go to Tvir, you're going to die. It fell to Tranavia two months ago."

Anna paled. Nadya tried to ignore the despair that hit her in the chest. It settled right between her ribs, hammering at her with each beat of her heart. This was hopeless; she was going to die before she had a chance to do anything for her country.

"Everything was destroyed," Parijahan said softly, cutting through some of the tension between Nadya and Malachiasz. "The military camp, the nearby village. We were close by when it happened. We got lucky and escaped. Others were not so lucky."

Anna rubbed her forehead. When Nadya looked to her for some kind of direction, or *something,* she just shrugged. "That was all I ever was told to do," she said. "The next outpost is . . ."

"Not close," Rashid said.

A door slammed shut before Nadya. "So I should listen to the plans of two foreigners who have welcomed my enemy with open arms?"

Malachiasz smiled.

Parijahan pursed her lips. "When I was thirteen, my older sister was to be married to a Tranavian *slavhka*. There was no love, it was a political marriage, but Taraneh was hopeful. They had met once before the marriage and he seemed . . ." she trailed off, shaking her head. Her gaze was firmly locked on a corner of the room. "Normal. A blood mage, but what Tranavian isn't? Regardless, the wedding went fine—"

"The wedding was *not* fine," Rashid interrupted.

Parijahan's face twisted. "We thought nothing of it, it stood to reason there might be some tension."

Foreboding weighed heavy in the Akolan's words and Nadya shifted uncomfortably. She glanced at Malachiasz, but he was watching Parijahan with a careful expression on his face, not hostile or mocking, just gently attentive.

"My family is well off—"

"Be honest, Parj," Rashid said softly.

She sighed. "My family is one of the three high Travasha of Akola. My sister was murdered a month after her wedding, in a foreign land, for her dowry."

"And Akola didn't go to war over that?" Anna asked.

"There was never any proof the Tranavian did it. It looked like an accident, my sister drowned in one of Tranavia's hundreds of lakes." Parijahan laughed bitterly. "Of course, because Akola is a land of deserts, why would a *prasīt* know how to swim? But Taraneh was a fine swimmer; her favorite place in the world was the oasis near our family home."

"So what are you doing here?" Nadya asked. *And what are you doing with a Tranavian blood mage?*

"There were some rash decisions made," Rashid said.

"I took revenge," Parijahan said matter-of-factly. "And now there is one less *slavhka* in the Tranavian court."

"Why not return to Akola after? Why stay here?"

"I don't want anything to do with a family that will not avenge the death of their daughter. Tranavia cannot win this war," she said fiercely. "Let them live with their blood magic and their corrupt politicians in their own country, but they cannot be allowed to spread beyond their borders."

Nadya thumbed at her necklace, searching for the god of truth—Vaclav's—bead. She was bewildered when Vaclav confirmed that all three were being truthful with her. Even the Tranavian.

"None of this explains him," Nadya said, pointing to Malachiasz.

"I'm an enigma," Malachiasz replied archly. "There were rumors about you, *towy dżimyka*, on both sides of the war. The Kalyazi cleric come to save the country from the Tranavian scourge."

A chill cut through Nadya. She couldn't tell if he was goading her or not.

"What are you saying?"

"Tranavia knows you exist, clearly, why else would the High Prince himself—prodigy tactician of the war—attack a monastery in a location that provides no strategic advantage? And if Tranavia knows, then all of Kalyazin knows as well."

There was something else he was saying and it took Nadya longer than she would have liked to catch up.

"You three are here . . . because of me?"

"Doesn't that make you feel important?"

He was mocking her again. She sighed.

"We followed the rumors to this area, yes," Parijahan said. "I didn't think anything would come of them, but here you are."

Nadya knew divine intervention when she saw it, but something still felt wrong. There was a path she was supposed to walk and this wasn't it. Working with a *heretic* wasn't it. It couldn't be.

She ran her spoon around the now empty bowl. "I need time to consider this, to . . . pray. Do you have a plan for getting into Tranavia?"

"You can't be serious," Anna said.

"What choice is there?" Nadya retorted.

"They don't have a plan," Malachiasz answered, cutting off Rashid before he had a chance to reply. He closed his spell book with a loud snap. "Go pray," he said to Nadya, putting the full weight of his loathing on the word *pray*. "Ask your gods to accomplish the impossible."

A pathway led through the trees to the remains of a small stone altar. All that was left was a bench and a carving of a purpose-fully ambiguous figure meant to portray Alena. It was calm outside, early morning light flickering through the empty tree branches, striking the carving so that it drew the sunlight into itself. Nadya settled herself down cross-legged on the bench.

She tugged her necklace over her head, rubbing her fingers over the beads. She needed to refocus, to work through the trauma of losing her home and her friends. She only felt blank when she thought about the monastery, about Kostya. Where would she be when the agony of losing everything finally caught up with her; would she be in a place where she could handle it?

She had spent too many sleepless nights wishing she had some small part of her parents to hold on to. All she had was the knowledge her mother had always possessed that her daughter was touched by the gods. Her mother had shown up nine months pregnant on the monastery steps, staying only long enough to give Nadya her name before she was gone, so Father Alexei always told her.

Lapteva wasn't even an uncommon surname. It was every-where. It wasn't until Nadya was fourteen when she realized no family was returning for her, that her fate lay within the monastery walls and nowhere else. The abbot was the closest thing to a father she would ever have.

Thinking about Father Alexei made her heart ache. He was dead now, along with everyone else she had known and loved. Kind Marina with her warm laugh, who would smuggle Nadya *probov*—flat, but tasty, flour cakes—when no one was looking. Dour but talented storyteller Lev, who could spin fables and legends that always made Nadya fear to go to bed at night.

One evening, he told her a story about a Tranavian mon-ster known as *Kashyvhes* who drank blood and controlled vic-tims with its mind. While she was walking through the dark halls of the monastery to her chambers that night, Kostya had jumped out of a closet. She punched him so hard he had to go to Ionna, the healer, for a split lip.

Now they were gone, and the monastery was empty. Its golden relics gutted and icons defaced. The altar probably lay shattered, the statues of saints had likely lost their heads and their hands. All that beauty—holiness—desecrated for the sake of magic and blood.

But she couldn't force the feelings and so she sat with an empty heart and a blank mind and waited to see if her gods would talk to her. This time she was alone.

Ask the gods to do the impossible. The arrogance, Nadya thought. She wasn't convinced they could do it, but if Malachiasz was right, there was nowhere for her to go. Maybe she should take that as a sign and accept that circumstance was forcing her into this situation that could very well end in disaster.

She was walking back to the church when she spied Mala-chiasz slipping through the trees. Curious, she followed, pulling at her prayer beads. She had only taken a few steps when he stopped. Her hand immediately dropped to her *voryen*.

"Are you going to put one of your pretty blades into my heart, *towy dżimyka*?"

"I'd like to," she said. "Why do you call me that?"

He turned to face her, one hand lifting to rest against the spell book strapped to his hip. "What am I supposed to call you?"

She still hadn't told them her name. She didn't know why it felt important to keep it to herself; why she felt like giving this boy her name would be giving him more than he deserved. Maybe she was just being irrational.

"Nadezhda Lapteva," she said, then added, "Nadya."

Malachiasz looked almost relieved, but Nadya was probably just imagining things. He nodded.

"Well then, Nadya, please, you are welcome to join me."

Her eyes narrowed. "So you can take me back into the woods and murder me?"

"You were following me," he pointed out.

Heat rushed to her face.

He smiled, then turned to go. "We're not enemies, Nadya."

"Not right now, you mean."

He paused, glanced back at her, then nodded. "You have nothing to fear from me."

Yet. Nadya heard it in his tone, even if he didn't mean it— even if he never meant it. He was a Tranavian mage and they were enemies by default.

She followed him.

The trees were thick in this stretch of the mountains and even with their leafless, snow-covered boughs it was hard to see through them. All was quiet except for the crackle of ice underneath their feet. Nadya was trying to figure out just where they were going when Malachiasz held out a hand, stopping her. He pressed a finger to his lips.

They had stopped at a high point on an overhang where the mountainside cut off precariously. Malachiasz shifted to the edge, dropping down into the snow. Nadya hesitated, then moved beside him.

It took her a second to parse out what she was seeing below, and when she did she nearly shot back to her feet and fled.

Malachiasz clamped his hand down on her shoulder, pressing her down into the snow. She froze like a startled rabbit; the only defense mechanism she had left. His fingers tensed against her, a pressure that maybe was supposed to be reassuring. He pulled his hand away.

He had led her straight to the High Prince.

Malachiasz leaned close to Nadya and she tensed as he tipped his face down to hers, lips at her ear.

"My magic will be felt the moment I use it." His voice was a low murmur. "They won't feel yours."

She cast him a sidelong glare and then yanked her glove off and thumbed at her necklace until she found Zlatek's bead.

The god of silence loathed granting Nadya power; he'd once voiced they should revoke her magic completely. It was a shame his power was so damn useful because he was so crotchety that Nadya avoided dealing with him whenever possible.

She sent a tentative plea and, assuming she'd been denied, was shocked when suddenly a string of holy speech swept through her head. She felt the barest surge of irritation.

Thank you, Zlatek.

There was no response. She passed her thumb over Marzenya's bead. If she needed to kill the Tranavian here, she would be ready. He wasn't going to catch her unaware.

Her senses grew fuzzy as she whispered Zlatek's spell, but

when she shifted the ice underneath made no sound. She glanced at Malachiasz.

"Fascinating." His lips moved but there was no sound. His eyebrows shot up in surprise.

Zlatek had spread the spell to Malachiasz as well.

Cheeky. She held a finger to her lips, grinning. Even her breathing was made silent by Zlatek's spell. The drawback was her senses were dulled as well.

Just below the overhang were the prince and his lieutenants. The girl with one eye was still on her horse while both boys had dismounted. She looked bored, her chin on her hand, elbow resting on the pommel of her saddle.

"If we continue east, we'll be fine," she said.

The prince shook his head and rummaged in his saddlebags, pulling out a map. "Unroll that," he said as he handed it to the boy with dark brown skin. "We'll ride straight into the front, and I, personally, would rather not deal with the entire Kalyazi army."

"A detour will take us days, Serefin. We'd end up skirting the lake country."

Serefin ignored her, moving over to where the other boy had the map laid out against a tree. He faced the ridge where Nadya and Malachiasz were hiding. Nadya would be fine if he glanced up, her hair was practically the same color as the snow. Malachiasz, though . . .

She tugged her white scarf off her neck, shoving it at him. If he wasn't going to toss her over the side for the prince to capture, then she didn't want them caught because his hair looked like ink against paper. He stared at her blankly. She rolled her eyes, setting the scarf over his head. Realization sparked and he tied the scarf over his hair before settling back down in the snow.

Their timing couldn't have been better as the prince chose then to glance up at the top of the cliff. Her palms were sweating even as they pressed against the snow. She lifted her head again after a few tense seconds passed.

"We have to go farther north," the prince was saying, his voice a low, musing hum. Nadya, only passably fluent, had to concentrate to keep up with his Tranavian. "I would love to tack on as many weeks to this journey as possible, but I suppose there's no point."

"It's only marriage, Serefin," the other boy teased.

The prince just sighed. "Tranavia hasn't had a *Rawalyk* in generations. The illusion of choice is worse than just being told to marry some random *slavhka* I've only met once in my life."

Nadya slid her fingers over the hilt of her *voryen*. Malachiasz's hand landed over hers. He shook his head at her scowl and she yanked her hand away. Her skin crawled from his touch.

Nadya missed the prince's next words as Malachiasz moved backwards so he could stand without being seen. She rolled out of sight and to her feet.

Once they were a safe distance away from the prince, he cut a finger over his throat. She broke off the spell and he let out a breath as the magic lifted. Nadya shivered as her senses realigned. Malachiasz untied the scarf from around his head and handed it to her.

"Blood and bone," he murmured. "Are there other clerics who can do what you can?"

Nadya shrugged. "I'm the only one I know of. That doesn't mean I'm the only one. And the spell nearly didn't work; Zlatek isn't known to be cooperative."

He crooked his head to one side.

"God of silence? We don't have many churches dedicated to him. I think there's one in Tobalsk."

Malachiasz shook his head.

"Right. You're Tranavian."

He smiled slightly. It was the first genuine smile she had seen from him, and he looked younger, less intimidating. He couldn't be much older than her. He started to walk back to the church.

"That was a perfectly good assassination opportunity you foiled," she said as she crunched through the snow after him.

"Assassinating the High Prince while he's on Kalyazi soil will achieve nothing but renewed vigor from Tranavia," Malachiasz replied.

"Him being dead would be an achievement of its own," she muttered. "I failed to catch the significance of him going home . . ." Nadya trailed off as Malachiasz hesitantly pushed open the doors to the church, a frown forming on his face.

The churchyard was utterly silent.

"We weren't out there for very long," Nadya said.

"It's not that . . ." he murmured. Then he swore under his breath.

Suddenly he was pressing two bloody fingers against the doorframe, his dark eyebrows furrowed in concentration. He reached for the book at his side, tearing out a page and pressing it against the door. Blood seeped into the paper. The lines of blood formed a three-pronged symbol that spread out over the entire door.

"Stay back," he said.

"Why?"

"Something's been cast on the church," he said slowly. "Someone from Tranavia wants to know who's here."

Nadya took a wide step back. "The prince?"

"No. Wrong direction. I don't suppose you have a god for curse breaking?"

Nadya let out a breathless laugh. She couldn't ignore the significance of his asking, even if he meant it as a joke. "No, sorry."

"Shame. I'll have to do it myself."

He used his wicked-looking dagger to cut a line down his forearm. Nadya winced. His arms were riddled with scars and half-healed cuts, layers of them arranged in a ridged, messy, cross-hatching pattern.

"Hold this, please?" He handed her his spell book.

She took it, bewildered.

When he stepped away from the page on the door it remained stuck to the wood, the symbol glowing faintly around the edges. He swiped two fingers through the bleeding cut on his arm and moved to the wall next to the door. He scrawled a series of symbols onto the wood with his blood. Suddenly he stopped and something akin to horror crossed his face.

"Oh," he said. "This is very bad."

He turned to her, flipping open his spell book while it was still in her hands. She held it up, only moderately disgusted he was using her as a book stand.

"It's a good thing I have practice at this from my acolyte days," she muttered.

"I was going to say," he said absently as he flipped through the pages. "You're very good."

"I have many talents."

His lips quirked into a bare smile.

"Are you going to tell me what's bad, or . . . ?"

He looked up at her, all color draining from his face.

"You're Kalyazi."

"Yes. I am."

"Nadya," he breathed out, and there was something in the way he used her name that made her feel too warm and too cold all at once. She blinked up at him, sudden terror gripping her. He looked shaken, and she didn't really want to contemplate just what could frighten this blood mage.

"It's the Vultures."

A chill swept through her. She felt a stirring in the back of her head. The gods were distressed. Her joints locked up and ice wormed its way into her bones. How was this happening? First the High Prince, now the Vultures?

She couldn't run from the Vultures. She couldn't run from the darkest nightmares of Tranavia.

Malachiasz tore out multiple pages of his spell book and frantically scrawled blood over the wood and torn pages. "If they come here, you and I won't be long for this world."

"Why would *you* be in danger?" she asked. If she focused on the little things, maybe terror wouldn't swallow her alive. "Because you defected from the army?"

He stopped writing, closing his eyes and whispering something fast under his breath in Tranavian that Nadya couldn't catch. He let out a bitter laugh and turned to look at her, his pale eyes full of fear. "Because I defected from *them*."

9

SEREFIN
MELESKI

Svoyatovi Roman Luski: *Appointed as a bishop in secret by half of the Council of 1213, Luski fought to maintain Kalyazi control of the eastern provinces. It was a losing battle, as Dobromir Tsekhanovetsky gained the votes of the other half and betrayed his country's trust by handing the provinces to the Tranavian king.*

—Vasiliev's Book of Saints

Three mages against two dozen soldiers, and Serefin only had a bare handful of spells left. The Kalyazi camp was just down the hill, the predawn dim revealing only a few soldiers awake.

Ostyia flipped twin *szitelki* in her hands, impatient while Serefin carefully shifted through his last five spells. If they ran into any more Kalyazi on their journey home, he would be in trouble.

"What do you have left?" Kacper asked, his voice low.

He leaned on his staff. Razor-sharp metal was tied to the tip of it.

Serefin showed Kacper his painfully thin spell book. Kacper selected one of the remaining spells. The chosen spell would burn for a while, creating a sufficient distraction while Ostyia and Kacper finished off any soldiers not already boiling from the inside out from Serefin's magic.

Serefin eventually made his way down the hill once the sounds of struggle had ceased. He found Ostyia cheerfully riffling through rucksacks with provisions. "I don't think we'll have to stop by the border now," she said.

"Should we do something about the bodies?" Kacper asked.

Serefin shook his head, squinting up at the morning sky. "No, let the buzzards have them."

Ostyia tossed Kacper a rucksack as he went to fetch the horses.

"Hey now, what's this?" Serefin heard Ostyia murmur as she lifted a tent flap and peered inside.

He followed after her and watched as she picked up a book discarded on the tent floor. There was a small pile of them inside. She flipped through it before handing it to him and picking up another.

"These are Tranavian spell books," she said, frowning.

Serefin knew the Kalyazi burned the spell books they picked off Tranavian bodies. If they could help it, they avoided even touching them.

"There's Kalyazi written in some of them," Ostyia noted.

Serefin found a page in the book he was holding where blocky Kalyazi script was scrawled in the margins. He frowned. It was a cross between a Kalyazi diary and musings on the functions of the spells written in the book.

Well, it seems not every Kalyazi is so rigidly devout, he thought.

He recognized the structure of Kalyazi prayers amidst the spells. Were they trying to merge the two?

"Are they all like this?" he asked.

She opened a few more, flipped through them, then nodded.

"Collect a few," Serefin said. "I want a closer look."

"What do you think it means?"

"Desperation." Serefin stepped over a dead officer's body. "The Kalyazi are losing the war. One might even say they're becoming heretical."

The border came and passed without trouble. Serefin tried not to worry. They were so far north they skirted the front entirely, but they had found the border unmanned and unguarded.

It was as if the war had grown routine. This stretch of border used to be carefully watched, but they were losing resources. He would have to remember to post a company to keep the border, even in the north. It would be too easy for Kalyazi troops to slip into Tranavia using this same route through the mountains into the marshlands.

"I can't decide if you complained more when we were in Kalyazin or now that we're back in Tranavia," Ostyia said.

While the change in temperature had not been immediate, it was obvious they were no longer in Kalyazin. There was barely any snow on the ground or trees. It was still cold—the long winter that had struck Kalyazin had graced Tranavia as well—but it was nothing like the frigid bite of Kalyazi air.

Also, it was raining. Serefin might have mentioned his dismay at traveling through the rain.

"It's simply my nature," he replied.

"I can't argue with that," she muttered.

"I've mentioned I hate the marshlands, right?" Kacper said. "While we're all getting our complaints out."

"No, Serefin's complaining is *inherent* to his system. Everything he says must be a complaint," Ostyia said.

"I'm going to demote both of you when we get back to Grazyk," Serefin replied. "Have fun guarding the Salt Mines."

Serefin didn't particularly wish to travel through the marshlands either, but the main roadways would be clogged with Tranavian nobles traveling to Grazyk. He wanted to avoid dealing with the nobility for as long as possible; they were the one thing that could make him miss the front.

The Tranavian marshes had wooden boardwalks, built centuries ago, else they would be impossible to cross. Serefin had always been certain the reason the front stayed on Kalyazi soil had nothing to do with the strength of Tranavian forces and everything to do with Tranavia being too soggy. Staging any battle in the marsh or lake lands would be difficult and miserable for both sides.

Unfortunately, the marshlands were perpetually dark. Light struggled to get past the thick foliage. There were legends of demons that lived in the dark corners where the light never touched and the boardwalks never reached. Dziwożona, the marsh hag, or the flesh eating *rusalka*. Creatures who waited in the damp for the unsuspecting to venture to watery graves. In Tranavia, there was always another monster around the corner waiting to devour you.

They reached an inn early in the evening, managing to go undetected by the few travelers they passed. Few ventured this way, Tranavian superstition holding most of the country in check. After all, it was *always* better to simply not risk being dragged underneath the water by a *wolke* to serve as his slave.

Serefin sent Kacper inside as he unpinned his badge of office and handed it to Ostyia. Normally he would enjoy using his status in a backwater inn like this one, but Serefin was tired and didn't want to attract unnecessary attention. The scar on his face was telling enough. He couldn't go anywhere in Tranavia without being recognized. Hopefully he was dirty enough he would go unnoticed.

The inn was thankfully quiet, holding only a handful of peasants and a pair who looked like soldiers. Bundles of dried herbs were nailed to the walls, giving the inn a vaguely pleasant aroma. Serefin found Kacper at a table in the corner.

"Do you want to clean up?" Ostyia asked.

"Later."

She gave him a questioning look.

"No one has groveled at my feet as yet. I'd like to keep it that way." He leaned across the table, pitching his voice lower. "I'd also like to get drunk."

Ostyia rolled her eyes, grinning.

"Well, you smell terrible," Kacper said. "Two weeks of traveling doesn't look good on you, my prince."

"Salt Mines," Serefin said, distracted, as he flagged down the older man behind the counter. "And what did I *just* say? Why do you both use my name at the most inappropriate times and my title when I don't want you to?"

"To irritate you," Ostyia said.

"Definitely, also, you need a new threat."

"It's a perfectly apt threat," Serefin replied.

"It's a reasonable threat," Ostyia said to Kacper. "I sure don't want to hang out with the ancient Vultures and their experiments."

"But you *do* want to hang out with the younger Vultures and their experiments?"

Ostyia's face flared red. Serefin watched with amusement as Kacper pressed further.

"What was her name? Reya? Rose?"

"Rozá," she muttered.

"I'm surprised she has a name," Serefin mused.

"They're supposed to only go by their order title," Ostyia said. "The court Vultures stopped following that rule years ago, but the current Black Vulture has been working to have them reinstate it to hide their names from the court."

The barkeep set three tankards of *dzalustek* on their table without a word, lumbering back behind his counter.

Serefin took a sip of ale. It wasn't good but it wasn't watered down, either, so it would do. "Did you ever meet the Black Vulture?" he asked Ostyia.

She nodded. "He's not your type."

Serefin exchanged a dry glance with Kacper. Ostyia grinned at him before getting up to order them dinner.

It wasn't until Serefin was on his fourth—maybe fifth? It was hard to keep track—tankard of *dzalustek* that the uncomfortable meeting he had been so ardently avoiding finally came into being.

"Your Highness?"

Ostyia was looking over his shoulder, her face pained. *Slavhka*, she mouthed.

Serefin knew he was not supposed to groan aloud at a subject, but that knowledge felt very unimportant after two tankards of ale, let alone four . . . or five. He turned in his seat.

At least he recognized this particular noble. It would have been awkward if it had been some backwater princeling Serefin had never seen before.

Lieutenant Krywicki was a bear of a man who had gone to

fat after his tour ended. He was one of the tallest men Serefin had ever met and his width near made up his height. He had a thick head of black hair and eyes the color of coal.

He was also, Serefin recalled, insufferable. But most people were insufferable, Serefin reasoned, so Krywicki wasn't anything special.

Serefin stood, only wavering a little on his feet.

"Lieutenant Krywicki," he said, vaguely aware he was going to be slurring every word he spoke. "What brings you to this backwater swamp?"

Is Krywicki from this backwater swamp? Serefin wondered. He rejected the idea. He was from somewhere else. The north? Probably the north.

"My daughter, Your Highness," Krywicki said, with a laugh that was probably a normal volume but sounded uproarious to Serefin.

He tried not to wince. He didn't know if he succeeded or not.

"Daughter?" *Did I know Krywicki had a daughter?* He glanced over his shoulder at Ostyia. She nodded encouragingly. *Apparently, yes.*

"Felicíja!" Krywicki said. "Here, Highness, let me buy you another drink. Did you just return from the front?"

Serefin was suddenly back in his seat with another tankard in front of him. Kacper and Ostyia exchanged a glance that Serefin barely noticed as he concentrated on the sweating glass in front of him.

He should definitely not drink this.

Well, sacrifices must be made, he thought as he picked up the tankard. Was this five or six? He had absolutely no idea.

"The front, yes, we've only just returned," Serefin said.

"How goes the war?" Krywicki asked.

"Same as it bloody ever has." Serefin took a drink. "Barely anything has changed in the last, what, fifty years? I don't expect anything ever will. It feels too optimistic to hope our victory at Voldoga will turn the tide."

Krywicki looked bewildered. Ostyia shot Serefin a wide-eyed look. Oh, he wasn't supposed to express his disdain about the war out loud, right. Certainly not as the poster child for the war effort.

"But we'll beat the superstitious Kalyazi down," he continued, now utterly self-conscious that he was backpedaling. "They'll break soon." He leaned across the table toward Krywicki, who unconsciously leaned toward him in return. "I can feel it. The war will end during my reign, if not sooner." The signs were there: Voldoga, the appearance of the cleric implying desperation, that they were able to make it all the way to the Baikkle Mountains, and yet Serefin did not usually give in to hope.

Krywicki raised his eyebrows. A Tranavian prince did not treat his upcoming reign as if it were a given. No Tranavian treated their future as though it were a given. Serefin had spent far too much time in Kalyazin.

"So soon?" Krywicki asked.

Serefin nodded emphatically. He frowned. Wasn't Krywicki just talking about his daughter? Where was she? He realized he was inquiring after her before his brain had a chance to catch up to his mouth.

He definitely should not have had that last drink.

Krywicki looked all too delighted to introduce his daughter to the High Prince. He left the table, returning with a girl who looked like she was barely old enough to be free of her nurse-maid.

Serefin shot a desperate glance Kacper's way. Kacper just shrugged.

Felicíja looked nothing like her father. She had waves of blond hair and pale violet eyes. She looked gentle, pretty. Serefin would have to keep an eye on her.

She bowed to Serefin. Court niceties would have her curtsy to him, but they weren't at court.

Blood and bone, she's young, he thought. In reality she was likely only a year or two younger than Serefin. She just *looked* young. Dimly it occurred to him that by calling all of the potentially eligible *slavhki* into Grazyk, his father was weeding out the weak and settling the strong blood in the heart of Tranavia.

"It's a pleasure to finally meet you, Your Highness," she said as he took her hand and pressed it lightly against his lips.

He hoped it was lightly. He'd lost any real feeling in his hands two tankards ago. His vision was also far more blurry than usual, which only happened when he was really drunk.

"The pleasure is mine," he replied. "Is it safe to assume you are traveling to Grazyk?"

Ostyia's single eye widened in alarm. Serefin had no idea why until Krywicki answered for his daughter.

"Of course we are," he said. "There hasn't been a *Rawalyk* in generations, it's not to be missed. In fact, Your Highness, you are more than welcome to join us for the rest of the journey."

Oh, that's why Ostyia is making that face. Serefin watched as Ostyia dropped her head onto the table. He didn't particularly relish the idea of traveling with the lieutenant and his daughter, either. It would be rude of him to refuse the invitation, but he didn't particularly care for being polite. Besides, this was an obvious ploy to get Felicíja on his good side before the *Rawalyk*.

Serefin squirmed his way out of it. "I must beg your forgiveness, I have been riding all day and it's late. It truly was a pleasure to meet you."

Serefin escaped to the second floor of the inn. He let out a groan as soon as they were in the hallway.

"It is so disconcerting to watch you play the nobleman," Kacper said.

"I'm the *prince*," Serefin replied. "I'm not supposed to be playing at anything."

But Kacper shot him a dry look, to which he waved a dismissive hand. He leaned back against the wall.

"How old do you suppose Felicíja is?"

"Seventeen or so," Ostyia suggested.

"There's no chance she'll last very long, not amongst anyone actually raised at court."

"No."

Serefin winced. He wanted to say more, but Ostyia gently pushed him toward the door to his room.

"Go to bed, Serefin. We have to wake up early enough to leave before Krywicki notices, and you're going to have a hangover tomorrow."

"I'm really not ready to begin dealing with the nobility again," Serefin mused, frowning, as she pushed him down the hall.

"Well, welcome home, Your Highness, you don't have a damn choice."

10

NADEZHDA

LAPTEVA

Krsnik, the god of fire, is quiet, calm, but ruthless, and when his followers call upon him—when he chooses to listen—his attention is destruction.

—Codex of the Divine, 17:24

Nadya stared at Malachiasz, horror trickling down her spine. He moved down the wall of the church, scrawling his blood onto the boards. She took a step back, then another, and another, until there was enough space between them, until she felt like she could flee. Her breath jolted in panicked gasps because this couldn't be happening, he had to be lying.

"What does that mean?" she asked, her voice hushed.

"It doesn't matter now."

Nadya clutched her prayer beads in a fist. Maybe she had been wrong to wait for an opportunity to put down this heretic. Her other hand twitched toward her knife.

Prodding agreement came from Marzenya. A needling feeling to rid the world of this terrible boy before he spilled any more blood.

His eyebrows were drawn in concentration and he had spent so much of his own blood that Nadya wasn't sure how he was still standing. Horror flashed against his features and he stepped back from the wall, wavering on his feet.

"*Kien tomuszek,*" he murmured. He ran a trembling hand down his face, streaking blood down his cheek.

"What are the Vultures truly like? Could we fight them?" she asked. Surely the stories were exaggerated.

Malachiasz coughed out a panicked-sounding laugh. His gaze was glassy. "Amplify an already talented blood mage's power tenfold. Grind their bones into iron and salt their skin in darkness until nothing can break it but their will alone. Until their blood burns so hot in their veins that when it spills it creates magic of its own. Burn out every memory, every thought, until they can become nothing at all, until they *are* nothing at all. When there's nothing left but magic and bloodlust and rage, then they are finished. When they are empty, they are ready." His eyes closed, eyebrows furrowing. "No, *towy dżimyka,* we cannot fight them."

Nadya took a step back, heart thudding so hard in her chest that she shook. She shouldn't have asked; she already knew the truth. Was that what he was? Or had he fled before any of that was done to him?

He cut another line down his forearm, hissing through his teeth. "Do you trust me?" he asked.

"*No,*" she said.

He laughed, taking another spell book page and soaking it with blood. He slapped it against the door as he went into the church. She darted after him, feeling the threshold push against her. She shuddered at the close contact with his magic.

It was like she could feel them just over her shoulder, lurking, waiting. She didn't know if they were close, or how much time they had before the monsters struck.

She almost ran into Malachiasz's back when he stopped dead in the sanctuary.

Parijahan jumped to her feet. "What is it?"

He held out a hand, keeping Nadya from fully entering the room. His eyes were strangely cloudy, murky and dark. "I thought we had time," he said, some thread of something *else* crackling in his voice.

Cold panic pressed against Nadya, driving in between her ribs. The temperature seemed to plunge so quickly that Nadya wasn't surprised to find her breath clouding out before her face.

"Abominations," Marzenya hissed.

An earth-shattering crash resounded through the church, shaking it to its foundation. Nadya stumbled into Malachiasz and it was like slamming into a stone wall. She shoved away from him though it seemed like he didn't even notice.

He glanced up at the ceiling, head tilting. Nadya watched with horror as his eyes grew unfocused and a trickle of blood began to drip out of the corner of his eye. A small part of her had been convinced Malachiasz had fled the Vultures before he had been turned into a monster. Apparently that wasn't the case.

"You said we couldn't fight them," Nadya whispered.

"We don't have a choice," he replied. "There are two of them inside: Ewa and Rafał." His voice sounded different, dropping lower, grit scratching through. His lips twitched into a sneer. "And one in this room."

Nadya was almost knocked to her knees at the refrain of holy speech that slammed through the back of her head. Her hands were nowhere near her necklace.

What is this?

"What you need."

It was raw, unformed magic. *This could kill me.*

"Yes, it could."

She was grateful for the odd collection of weapons scattered around the sanctuary because it meant the others moved fast and without questions. Anna shot Nadya a terrified look.

Nadya could barely fathom that this was happening, that her elbow was an inch away from the arm of a boy who was everything she hated, everything she had been trained to destroy. A boy whose trembling had ceased to a stillness so complete it was like he'd turned to stone next to her.

Malachiasz scanned the ceiling. His sneer turned into something closer to a smile. "Rozá." The way he said the name sounded like a song, a tease, a challenge.

Something materialized on the ceiling and began to drip down to the floor like blood. It *was* blood, Nadya realized. It dripped faster, becoming a torrent.

Malachiasz finally noticed the blood leaking out of the corner of his eye. He shuddered and wiped at it with his thumb.

Parijahan's face was white as chalk. "Malachiasz . . ."

What is going on?

The blood moved as if it had a life of its own until it formed into the shape of a girl, materializing in the center of the room. Iron spikes wove through an auburn braid. A thick black book hung from straps on her hip. Her face was covered by a crimson mask crafted in strips. It left only her eyes visible, black as onyx. Blood dripped from her bony shoulders.

"Perfect. Saves me a double trip to this wasteland," the girl said. Her voice sounded wrong. Everything about her was off-putting and otherworldly, as though Nadya's brain couldn't comprehend she was even real.

Blood was leaking from the corners of Malachiasz's eyes again. He looked down at his hands with something too close to resignation, shaking as iron claws grew and lengthened from his nail beds. Blood fell from his lips, landing on the back of his hand—crimson on pale skin.

Nadya was still too close to him and now there was nowhere for her to go. The Vulture girl stepped closer, her movements odd, too fast and jerky, like Nadya's eyes lost seconds as they tried to track her.

"Look at you," the girl said. Nadya shuddered at the sound of her voice. It was like death and madness clashed in dissonant chords when she spoke. "Debased, unmasked, diminished." Her hands looked perverse: the fingers too long and the joints thin and spindly. Her nails were also iron claws.

A vein pulsed in Malachiasz's neck. His gaze was flinty as he eyed her. There was blood dripping from his nose now, catching on his upper lip. Rozá stepped closer. Malachiasz was trembling. Not from fear, though, it wasn't that. It took her longer to put a name to it: restraint.

"How much further do I have to rile you before I can make you face me as you truly are?" Rozá asked.

She was much shorter than him, probably Nadya's height. Even so, she leveled to him, reaching up with an iron claw and trailing it down the side of his face. It opened a thread-line cut, welling blood.

"Not much further," he replied.

He had said there were two other Vultures. Three of them was too many, Nadya knew, but at least the Vultures were outnumbered. She drew her *voryens*.

Rozá's head shifted, birdlike, her onyx gaze honing in on Nadya. There was no warning before she struck. She was there and then she was gone. Nadya didn't have the opportunity to defend herself, she barely had enough time to realize the Vulture had moved.

Then the world shifted. Two more Vultures materialized into the room, then a third. Nadya's heart plummeted in horror as she realized there were more than just the three that Malachiasz named.

The others jolted into motion. Rashid sidestepped a flash of dark magic and whipped two Akolan blades from the weapons rack. He spun one in a lazy arc, a smile on his face. Anna's terror had chilled to something deadly.

A split-second, a blink, and Rozá was impaled on Malachiasz's long iron claws. He gritted his teeth and Nadya felt her chest tighten as metal glinted in his mouth; his teeth rows of iron nails, too-sharp canines now deadly fangs. Pale eyes darkening as his pupils dilated, expanding to swallow the ice of his irises, then more, further, until the whites of his eyes were gone.

"It won't count if I don't kill you as you truly are," Rozá said. There was no hint of pain in her voice, nothing to suggest she was even injured as she pulled herself almost elegantly off Malachiasz's claws.

He sneered.

The air stirred behind Nadya and she whirled, drawing her *voryens* up in time to catch a second Vulture's claws. Tall, probably male, likely Rafał. His mask was studded with jagged spikes and he retracted his claws and lashed out at her again so quickly that when she jumped away she jolted into Malachiasz's back. Her magic swept out around her with her movement and it brushed against him. She shuddered involuntarily. The power roiling underneath his skin ached like a poison, a blackness that spread in his veins and coursed out into his aura. She didn't want to be this close to him but if she was going to get out of this alive she was going to need a monster who knew how to fight monsters.

Nadya gathered her divine magic around herself like a shield, throwing it back over Malachiasz as Rozá and Rafał struck at the same time. The magic only barely held against them.

Malachiasz tilted his head back. Nadya felt him shift his footing and then suddenly he was leaning against her. She stumbled as a spray of blood precluded her spell shattering in front of her.

Malachiasz had looked dizzy when they were outside the church. Blood mages could only press so far before their resources needed to be replenished. But then he straightened and moved away from her and Nadya frantically murmured words in holy speech as Rafał's claws came perilously close to tearing open her chest. A sphere of light formed at the tip of her *voryen* and she flicked her wrist down, shooting it off into the Vulture in front of her, slamming him back into the wall.

Rozá vaulted past Malachiasz to get to Nadya. For a tense heartbeat, Nadya thought he had let her, but he was moving toward the Vulture that had a defenseless Anna backed into a corner, her sword just out of reach.

Nadya tugged her second *voryen* from her belt, fusing Krsnik's heated magic into the metal. She spat out symbols of smoke and pulled threads from Marzenya's death magic into her other blade.

"This is what the Kalyazi have rested their hope upon?" Rozá said when she was steps away. "This is pathetic."

"You talk too much," Nadya snapped. She pulled the essence of Bozetjeh's power and cut the distance between her and the Vulture, slamming her flame-tinged *voryen* into her shoulder.

The blade passed through as if the girl was made of blood and nothing more. Rozá's clawed hands snapped toward Nadya's torso, but she slipped out of her grasp, fluid with Bozetjeh's power. She slammed the other blade—coated in the essence of the goddess of death and magic—into the Vulture's stomach.

Rozá choked, pain fluttering over her visible features. Her eyes closed and she pulled herself off Nadya's blade. She took a step back, pressing her hand to her abdomen. There was blood pouring from the bottom of her mask.

There was movement at Nadya's side and she turned, but Malachiasz was already there. A spray of blood arced between his hands, shifting into blades, slamming into Rafał. He grabbed the Vulture by the front of his shirt, driving the nails of his other hand into the opening of his facial mask.

The magic in her head was growing more insistent, aching to destroy. She was already pulling on so many threads. It was far more than she had ever used before and she didn't know how much her body could take, how much divine abuse she could channel before it ruined her.

But the Vultures were shaking off her attacks as if she was nothing but a mild irritant. Rashid grasped at Rozá's moment of distraction and attacked; she slammed him into the wall where he crumpled like a discarded doll.

Nadya heard Anna's sword clatter to the ground, the sound too loud yet distant, as if it came from miles away.

They're here for me. Rozá's claws sunk into Malachiasz's chest. *They're here for him, too.* One of the smaller Vultures slashed open Parijahan's side.

Malachiasz freed himself from Rozá's grasp and staggered back. His inhuman, onyx eyes locked with Nadya's and she experienced a moment of clarity. A passage of a singular thought between her and this nightmare of a boy she did not know and did not trust.

She ran. He followed.

The monsters gave chase.

Just before they passed the threshold of the sanctuary, Nadya turned, calling on Marzenya and Veceslav both. One to ensure destruction, the other for protection for those she did not wish harmed.

Then she brought half of the sanctuary down on the Vultures.

Malachiasz tripped over his own feet, just barely missing being caught by falling debris. His features shifted between something *human* and something *not*. They settled on something less than. Nadya shuddered.

"It won't be enough," he said, voice tangled. "We need to get farther away."

"And abandon the others?" Nadya's spells wouldn't hold forever.

"The Vultures will try to come after us; they'll leave the others, they're inconsequential," he said.

Nadya nodded, then turned to run. Malachiasz grabbed her arm. She froze, staring in horror at the iron claws that were inches away from brushing against her skin.

"*Let me go.*"

He did. Immediately. "That won't be enough."

There was no *time*. The rubble was already starting to shift. It took her a second to realize what he meant. They wouldn't outrun the Vultures on foot. They needed magic.

None of the gods could give her magic like that and he looked like he was about to faint. He was swaying on his feet, skin ashen.

A hand pushed through the rubble. Malachiasz swore. Then

there was more blood, dripping down his face, from the corners of his eyes and from his nose. The skin at his wrist split, an iron spike pushing through as if his bones were made of metal. The spike shot off his arm and slammed into the hand in the rubble.

Nadya was going to be sick.

"I could get us away, but . . ." he trailed off.

He seemed too drained to use any magic. And if they stayed, the Vultures stayed, and Anna and the Akolans would end up dead.

Malachiasz shuddered. He raked a hand through his hair, smearing blood on his forehead. Watching this boy whom she had just witnessed become something horrific, this boy who had appeared so untouchable, be shaken to his core and worn to his limits made her contemplate doing something unthinkable. Nadya had her beliefs that she would never forfeit, but she also understood the necessity for self-preservation. She had to stay alive to be any good for her country.

This is walking a dangerous line.

Nadya was no longer in the monastery; she had to make her own choices.

"Do blood mages have to use their own blood for magic?" she asked, her voice barely above a whisper.

"It's messy to use anyone else's so we try to avoid it," he remarked, voice absent. Then he blinked. *"What?"*

She swallowed hard and met his gaze. Her stomach roiled. His black eyes were too disconcerting and she had to look away.

"I know what you believe about my magic. It's easy to spread the rumor that blood mages use human sacrifices," he said slowly; his voice almost sounded normal. "It doesn't mean it's true."

"But can you?"

He nodded. She swallowed hard, hesitated, feeling her own hands shaking as she fought with the weight of her decision. He would get them out; it would save the others.

Would she make a dangerous exception of her own principles for the safety of her friend, the only one left, and two potential allies? For the possibility that this ragtag group could turn the war?

Swallowing hard, she rolled her sleeve back and held her forearm out to him.

He didn't give her a chance to change her mind. His iron claw was a shard of ice dragging down her skin, parting her flesh. Her breath swept out of her and she prayed she would not live to regret this. She watched with her heart in her throat as the cut welled crimson.

Blood was not to be spilled for the sake of power. Magic was a divine appointment from the gods. But here her gods-given magic was useless. Doing this one unspeakable thing would keep her alive, keep those she needed to protect alive. She couldn't destroy these monsters if she died.

Malachiasz's eyes narrowed, his fingers tensed around her wrist. "Our secret?" he said.

She snapped his grip off, flipping it so her hand was clenched around his forearm. "I don't know what you are," she said slowly. "But I swear by the gods, if you use this against me it will be the last thing you ever do."

The silence that followed was so fraught Nadya could feel him trembling underneath her hand. She had the sense it was the sheer effort of keeping himself in a form that resembled human.

Who was this boy? Or, rather, *what* was he? And what had she just done?

"I understand," he said.

She nodded.

He pulled her to his chest and the surge of power she felt around them nearly knocked her out. She felt herself slipping, felt him materialize into a spray of blood and magic. Then Malachiasz was gone and he took Nadya with him.

When Nadya woke, it was on top of crimson snow. She shivered violently, sitting up. After a quick check, she realized the blood wasn't hers. She was in the forest, in a snow bank, and still alive. She felt terrible.

There was a dark form lying a few feet away. She hesitated before stumbling over to Malachiasz, unsure what she would find.

But whatever had taken over his features was gone now. He was just a boy, pale and unconscious in the cold. He was covered in blood, they both were, but somehow unwounded. Nadya leaned back on her heels and eyed him. He had a soft mouth and his nose was stately. His face was lovely, all the feral, unsettling qualities absent when he wasn't awake. She wasn't pleased with herself for noticing, *especially* not now. As heat rose on her face, it occurred to her she wasn't sure he was breathing. She had ducked her head down to listen to his chest when his eyes opened, black as pitch.

"Kill him."

Then she was on her back, the weight of Malachiasz's body pressed onto her. His mouth opened in a snarl and iron teeth glinted against the light; she could feel the ice of his claws press against her neck.

"Malachiasz!"

His eyes cleared, the black leaking away until there was almost no color left at all but the palest blue. He stared down at her, slowly moved his hands away from her neck. And then like a startled animal he shot off, staggering backwards until he tripped and landed a few feet away. His expression was troubled. He scanned their surroundings, his face becoming more concerned.

"Nadya," he said softly. As if he hadn't expected for them to escape, to be alive, for him to be *himself*.

"Where are we?" she asked, sitting up. She moved to pick up a *voryen* lying in the snow nearby. She didn't sheathe it.

He looked up at the trees. "I don't know." His voice sounded broken and unnatural.

She felt her heart stutter. "Are the Vultures still around?"

His eyes closed and he grew still. "Well, there's one," he said weakly, cracking half a smile as he opened his eyes.

She glared. His smile faded and he leaned back on his hands, seemingly oblivious to the cold. Nadya was shivering.

"If this didn't work . . . If we just abandoned our friends . . ." Nadya trailed off, panic snapping at her chest. If she had just left Anna behind at the behest of this *monster* she was going to kill him. She might just kill him anyway. She didn't know what was holding her back.

"Nadya—"

"No," she snapped, cutting him off. She stood up, clutching her *voryen*. She pointed it at him. "Give me a reason not to kill you."

"You would be dead if not for me?" he offered, looking up at her, squinting at the glare from the sun off the snow.

"Not good enough. You would be dead if not for *me*."

He nodded, allowing that. She pressed the tip of her knife underneath his chin, tilting his head back farther.

"What I just did was heresy," she said softly.

"Was it worth it?" he asked, sounding curious.

Of course it wasn't worth it. Every breath more he spent alive Nadya was disobeying her goddess. They had saved each other but it didn't mean she should let him live. It was her *duty* to rid the world of monsters like him. She moved to press the blade against his neck, cut his artery and be done with him. His hand landed over hers, fingers digging into the spaces between hers. His pale blue eyes met her dark brown. He didn't struggle, instead he bared his throat farther to her blade.

"You could do a lot with blood like mine," he murmured. "That's always the first step, you know. Spilling the blood is the hard part. Using it is easy. Using your blood was enlightening; that's quite a power you have. It could be greater, if you had mine as well."

Revulsion charged through her body and she pulled back. "What *are* you?"

Malachiasz shrugged. She watched as he stood, unnerved by how much taller he was than her. Her head only just came to his shoulder. She'd liked it better when he was at her feet.

He took a step closer; she forced herself to hold her ground. Then his hand—anxious tremors gone—was underneath her chin, directing her gaze up to his. She couldn't help feeling the chill of iron nails graze her flesh, even as his hand was steady and warm against her cold skin. He studied her face and all feelings of distaste quieted as she studied him in return, trying to piece together what it was that kept staying her hand. His dark tangle of thick hair that he had pushed away from his face was caked with blood and snow and made him look all the more feral. A curiosity she couldn't quite name took root within her. Here was the very thing she had been taught her entire life was an abomination—and he was very much the worst kind of abomination—but he was also just . . . a boy.

A boy whose hand was *still on her face*. She fought between wanting to wrench away and resting her face against his palm because it was warm and she was so very cold.

"Nadezhda Lapteva," he said contemplatively. When he shared his own name, she couldn't help feeling as if he were pulling her under into some dark depth from which she would never escape. It was a similar feeling now.

But it was only a feeling.

"What?" she said irritably, upset with herself for whatever this was, and with him for acting strange after she had just watched him turn into a monster.

"You could be exactly what these countries need to stop their fighting," he said. He dropped his hand and she was colder for its absence. "Or you could rip them apart at the seams."

11

SEREFIN

MELESKI

Svoyatovi Valentin Rostov: *A cleric of Myesta, Rostov infiltrated Tranavia at the beginning of the holy war, utilizing his goddess's powers of deception. For years, Rostov fed information back to Kalyazin, until a Tranavian prince who suspected him of using magic other than heretical blood magic poisoned him.*

—Vasiliev's Book of Saints

Serefin hated when he had to admit Ostyia was right, but he woke the next morning with a hangover to compete with all others. To her credit, she wordlessly handed him a waterskin as they left and her smile was only slightly sly.

"How much of a fool did I make of myself last night?" he asked once the inn was out of sight.

"You promised Felicíja Krywicka the entire western reaches as a wedding gift," Kacper said.

Serefin's eyes narrowed. The prior evening was hazy but he was *fairly* certain that was a lie.

"It was fine," Ostyia said. "You were a little too *Serefin* at times, but overall, no harm done."

"Blood and bone, not my true face," Serefin said, mock horrified.

"While you were talking to Felicíja, Krywicki mentioned he was in Grazyk a month ago and was alarmed by how many Vultures were skulking through the palace," Kacper said.

Serefin straightened in his saddle. "Did he say anything else?"

Kacper nodded. "The Vultures are recruiting at a fast pace, as if they're preparing for something."

"We know that Vultures are taken to the Salt Mines when they're instated," Ostyia mused. "And we've been sending a lot of Kalyazi prisoners there the past few months."

Serefin felt a shiver creep up his spine. They were still missing something.

Sunlight glittered off the deep blue of the lake, nearly blinding Serefin if he looked at it directly. Grazyk was a port city by Lake Hańcza, open to many channels and wide rivers that eventually flowed into the sea.

Boats floated lazily near the docks. Serefin wondered if anything was ever done about the pirates preying on Tranavian ships as they met the open waters. It had become enough of a problem to garner his father's attention, but that was before Serefin left. A port city in the middle of the kingdom. Sometimes it felt like Tranavia was more water than land.

There would be a string of small villages to pass through before they finally reached the city. Those always smelled foul and looked worse, what with the beaten shacks only barely holding together and racks upon racks of fish drying out in the sun.

Serefin watched a young woman cross the street, two buckets attached to a rod over her shoulders. They were full of water and moving, live fish. Her clothes were tattered, her skirts ragged and dirty at the hem. A small boy ran up to her from where he had been sitting in the doorway of a house with shutters that hung on single hinges. He pulled on one of the buckets, knocking her off balance. She was laughing as she set them down and reached inside, pulling a fish out and showing it to the boy.

The war was running Tranavia into the ground. Kalyazi villages were in a similar state, but he didn't care about starving Kalyazi villagers; he cared about starving Tranavians.

When they were nearly at the city, Ostyia spurred her horse to a gallop to reach the gates first so the guards would be prepared for the High Prince's arrival.

"Well," Serefin said softly, "so it begins."

"Cheer up, Serefin," Kacper said. "It won't be too bad. You just have to do some groveling and lying and then you can stab your old man in the back and be done with it."

Serefin tamped down his paranoia. He shoved it out of his head, pushed his empty spell book into his pack where it wouldn't be noticed—an empty spell book on a prince was considered disgraceful—and prepared to face his fate.

Grazyk was the most opulent city in Tranavia, built long before the war, when Tranavia was at its peak in wealth, and the fashion was color and light and gold. Serefin didn't think gold ever went out of fashion, but it was certainly too expensive now to line doorways and molding with golden bricks and gold inlaid wood. A few of those buildings still stood, a testament to when Tranavia was not so poor. Most had been destroyed long ago for the paltry wealth that could be sucked from their foundations.

There was a cloud of smog that hung over the city. It was an oppression everyone had simply learned to ignore. The fog came from magic experiments gone wrong, filtered up from the ground where there had been mines nearby—not unlike the Salt Mines. While the experiments had been moved to Kyętri, the smog never cleared. It just hung black in the air, a reminder of what happened when mages reached for too much.

Not that any mage in Tranavia would heed the reminder. Mostly it made the whole city smell like ash. Nobles attempted to counter it by wearing pouches of expensive herbs and spices or dousing themselves in fragrant oils imported from Akola. Neither worked, but nothing would keep *slavhki* from their outrageous solutions for things that weren't problems.

Ostyia had a runner sent to the palace, marking the start of needless formality. Serefin tried to work up the feelings of homesickness he had experienced while out on the front, but now he realized it had been wistful delusion.

If the city was lavish, the palace was magnificent. It glittered in the distance, a promise of beauty watching over the city and its shameful fog. Spires twisted up into the sky, their hundreds of windows reflecting such a glare that Serefin had to lower his gaze.

The guards swung open the large wooden gates when they approached. Even those were hammered with gold. A servant waited in the courtyard to take their horses.

The courtyard was paved with smooth granite that turned to lush grass just past the front of the palace. It buzzed with a low hum of activity. He could hear the sound of clashing blades from the northern side of the grounds. He braced himself for the inevitable summons from his father. It arrived immediately by way of a servant wearing a plain brown mask that left only his eyes visible. One of his father's personal servants. The servant bowed to Serefin, who spoke before he could even deliver his message.

"Yes, yes, my father wishes to see me."

The servant nodded. Not being able to see his face was disconcerting. Serefin wasn't fond of the masks that had been the fashion at court the past few years.

The style took after the ones worn by the Vultures. The only people who did not wear masks at court were usually the royal family. Serefin loathed wearing anything that might make his vision even worse. His mother was never in Grazyk long enough for it to matter, and the king transcended court trends completely.

Serefin raked a hand through his hair, then waved to the servant again. "Well? Take me to him. We can't keep His Majesty waiting."

12

NADEZHDA LAPTEVA

Very little is known about the goddess of the sun. Quiet and eternal, she has never granted her power to any mortal; none know what would happen if she ever did.
—Codex of the Divine, 3:15

Nadya and Malachiasz were lost. Apparently direction was not one of his many blood mage talents.

Nadya wrapped her arms around herself, shivering violently. He glanced back at her before shrugging out of his bloody military jacket. She hesitated, frowning at the symbol of everything she had spent her life fighting against. But her coat had been torn to useless shreds and he didn't appear to notice the cold so she accepted his offer. The jacket was still warm from his body heat. She tugged the sleeves down to cover her hands.

He eyed her before starting back into the woods.

"You should have cut his throat. I'm disturbed you chose to

spare him again," Marzenya said. The thought slid into the back of Nadya's mind like a suggestion.

Nadya had noticed a distinct increase in Marzenya's presence, in her interjections and nearness. She found she liked it, comforted by the knowledge her goddess was nearby and watching her. But a small part of her was unnerved by the pressure that came with it. Thoughts like that wouldn't do for someone chosen by the gods. One of the most important lessons Father Alexei had taught her was to keep her mind schooled, to keep doubts away. While it was perfectly human to doubt, it was not something she could indulge.

As much as Marzenya might wish for it, more death was not what Nadya needed. There was a chance that when—or at this rate, *if*—she and Malachiasz returned to the church there would be nothing left. Neither of them was willing to admit that.

It would be her breaking point. If it was delusional to hope their flight had saved the others, then so be it, but Nadya couldn't entertain the notion that her last friend in the world was gone and she had been left with a Tranavian abomination as a companion. Anna *had* to be alive.

But Nadya couldn't shake the feeling that she'd abandoned Anna the same way she'd abandoned Kostya. Running to save herself for some greater purpose was a bitter survival when it meant losing everything and everyone with each step she took.

"We won't survive a night out here," Nadya noted when they'd stopped in a clearing for a brief respite.

Malachiasz was gazing into the trees with a puzzled expression on his face. "What would kill us first, do you think, the cold or whatever lurks in these mountains?"

"That's not a question I want answered."

He smiled softly, turning to where she was sitting on a downed tree.

"And it will be your kind, won't it? It's only a matter of time before they find us out here."

"Does Kalyazin have no monsters?" he asked.

She narrowed her eyes, puzzling over his question, but clearly he meant it as rhetorical because he continued speaking.

"Rozá is arrogant," he said. "She left Aleks, the Vultures' best tracker, in Tranavia. She has no way to find us now."

Nadya ran her hand down her prayer beads. The spell book tied to Malachiasz's hip was thick. She found it hard to believe the other Vultures couldn't just cut their arms and find their way there.

He followed her gaze and seemed to know what she was thinking. "Most Tranavians buy their spell books with the spells already written by arcanists, Vultures included. I write my own."

"But you can't know for certain Rozá didn't have someone write her a handful of tracking spells before she came."

"Of course not. It's just incredibly unlikely."

"Which doesn't make anything *better*. They could still be at the church. Anna, Parijahan, and Rashid could be dead, and now we're lost in the middle of the mountains slowly freezing to death." Distantly, she knew she was panicking. Everything was falling through her fingers and she was powerless to stop it. This wasn't how things were supposed to happen.

Malachiasz sat down beside her, careful to keep space between them, but she could feel heat radiating off him and it was almost enough for her to lean into him. Almost.

She dropped her head into her hands. There had to be a way out of this. She would risk returning to the church for Anna, she had to. After that, she had nothing. She could continue running, it was apparently all she was good at.

Or she could end this. She glanced at Malachiasz, who returned the look, eyebrows lifting.

"Would killing the Tranavian king destroy the Vultures as well?"

He shook his head. "They have their own king, the Black Vulture." He caught the disappointment on her face because he was quick to continue. "You can rattle the order, Nadya. You already have."

"The Vultures destroyed my country's clerics," Nadya whispered. And he was *one of them*.

But he was also sitting quietly beside her as she worked to reassemble the pieces of her shattered life. She didn't have to trust him, or even like him, but he had ignored the multiple chances he had already been given to kill her, just as she kept sparing his life. That had to count for something. She could stand this begrudging uneasy truce, even if she was reminded of onyx eyes and iron teeth every time she looked at him. Except now his fingernails were just those of a boy with too much anxiety, jagged and red from being chewed at.

"Do you want revenge for that?" he asked.

"I don't know what I want," she whispered.

"There's nothing wrong with that."

Except the hope of a nation was pinned on her. She had spent her whole life studying the Divine Codex and preparing for something vast and great that would shake the world. She just hadn't known what it would look like. She didn't know if it was in front of her now, or if she needed to take a different path.

Could that path mean she would have to work with this

Tranavian? That was what she didn't understand. Because it was clear Marzenya wanted him dead.

"Why are you here?" she asked softly. "Why would you entertain Parijahan and Rashid's plans for killing your king?"

"He's not my king."

Nadya's brow furrowed. If he had been a Vulture, then his king would have been the Black Vulture. Is that what he meant?

"Tranavia is crumbling," Malachiasz said, voice low. "The throne is corrupt. But if you break off the Meleskis' grip on the throne, replace the king with someone who has Tranavia's well-being at heart, maybe the kingdom can be saved. Despite how you judge me, I hate this war. I would like to see it end, too."

As if he realized he had said too much, his eyes tightened and he looked away. She tugged her necklace off, running it through her fingers until she landed on a bead that felt right. Nadya had touched Alena's power only once in her life and it had been humbling. She was always nervous when she prayed to the older gods, the ones who rarely granted their magic to mortals at all. The Codex said Alena never had, but Nadya knew that wasn't exactly the truth.

Will you take me back to your church? Nadya prayed.

The goddess's warm touch filled Nadya. She stopped shivering. Then something pulled at Nadya's chest, right over her heart. A thread she could follow straight back to the church. Back to danger, back to this strange world of monsters and dark magic she had found herself in. If this was where she was supposed to be, then so be it, even if it took her to Tranavia, right into the monsters' nest.

She stood, prayer beads held loosely in her hand.

"What were you doing?" Malachiasz asked.

"Praying. I know how to get back to the church. We can make it before nightfall if we hurry."

She couldn't read the expression that flickered over his face. It was a mixture of discomfort and awe rolled into one jumbled pile. She found it oddly heartening that her magic disconcerted him just as much as his did her.

They weren't as far away as Nadya initially thought. When they reached the church they found the front door hanging off its hinges. The walls were covered with blood. Nadya stumbled as she imagined the worst and Malachiasz put out a hand to steady her. He didn't immediately remove his hand from her arm and she didn't pull away from its steadying warmth.

"The Vultures aren't here," he said, voice soft.

She swallowed hard. Her hands were shaking when she pushed open the door.

"Hello?" she called into the dark, stagnant air within the church.

There was only silence. She felt her heart drop. She glanced over her shoulder at Malachiasz, who stepped past her, farther into the church.

He was immediately knocked aside as Anna tore into the foyer. She threw her arms around Nadya's neck and Nadya finally relaxed. Anna was safe; she hadn't lost everything, not yet.

"I thought you were dead," Anna whispered fiercely.

She pulled back, reluctantly, but then a steely look appeared in her dark eyes and she whirled. Malachiasz's eyes widened and he took a step back, lifting his hands. There was a sharp crack as Anna punched him in the jaw.

"How *dare* you," she snapped.

"Anna, leave him alone," Nadya said, grabbing Anna's arm as she prepared to strike again. "We didn't have a choice."

"We?"

Malachiasz slowly worked his jaw. Nadya heard it clicking from where she was standing. He was definitely going to have a bruise.

"The Vultures left after we did?" Nadya asked hopefully.

Anna was still glaring daggers at Malachiasz. He back stepped once, then fled to the sanctuary. She ground her teeth, but nodded.

"They wanted me . . . and him."

"Because he's one of *them*."

Nadya nodded.

"We have to leave."

Nadya shook her head. "I'm going to Tranavia. I'm going to end this war."

Anna turned, but her movements were slow, horrified. "Nadya . . ."

"If this war were at a different place, if we weren't losing, then I would go to Komyazalov from here. I would go to the Silver Court and let the king decide what to do with me. But I don't have the luxury, Anna. You have to understand that."

"So you'll throw your lot in with that *monster*?"

"He saved my life," Nadya said.

"Only so he can ruin it later!"

Nadya didn't respond.

"Is this what the gods want?" she asked.

"It's what I want."

Anna tensed. "That doesn't make a difference. You know that."

"It's still my life and I get a say in how I use it."

Anna reared back, making the sign against evil over her heart. Nadya rolled her eyes.

"I have had the gods chattering in my head my whole life.

I've had this . . . this destiny hovering over me and I think the least I can ask for is the choice in how I see it into being. If it means going with these foreigners and that monster, then so be it."

"Do you *hear yourself*?"

Nadya didn't understand why Anna was reacting so strongly. It was like Nadya was shattering the image of the innocent, holy cleric Anna had, but Anna knew her better than that. She was chosen by the goddess of death. She never had a chance at innocence.

Anna took Nadya's face between her hands, forcing her to meet her gaze.

"I don't want your name added into the book of saints," she said quietly. "I thought—" Her voice cracked and she swallowed. "When half the sanctuary collapsed and we couldn't find you, I thought . . ."

Nadya hugged her. Anna smelled of incense and a lingering reminder of home. The roads before her went in opposite directions but they would lead to the same end. The child in her yearned to see the famed Silver Court once more—the last time she had been there she was far too young to really remember. She wanted to see the *dolzena* with their *kokoshniks* and the *voivodes* before all that gold and splendor melted away for good. But to them she would be a soldier, nothing more, a holy relic, a symbol, perhaps. Nothing human.

Nadya loved her country—more than life—but she wanted to do something that mattered. She could bring the gods back to Tranavia if she did this. They would need to fine-tune the details of the plan on the road, but she felt a confidence she had never really known before. There was an element of divine providence—strange as the circumstances appeared—and Nadya wasn't going to ignore it for the safer option.

She pulled away, heading off to find the others. She nearly ran into Malachiasz in the hallway. He looked frantic, making fear immediately spike through Nadya. He took her by the shoulders. "Can your magic heal?"

Nadya's eyes widened and she nodded.

"Parijahan was fine," Anna said.

"She's decidedly not fine now," he said, voice tight. The skin on his jaw was starting to purple as blood settled underneath the spot where Anna had punched him.

"Calm down," Nadya said, touching his arm.

He blinked, his gaze dropping to where her fingers lightly pressed against his scarred forearm, and seemed to realize he still had her by the shoulders. He let go and stepped back.

He's genuinely worried about her, Nadya thought, shocked. *He cares.*

"Is there any incense left in this place? I'm going to need it. A censer would be wonderful as well, if you saw any when you moved in. What kind of injury is it?"

"Her side is torn up. And yes, I can find some." He took off at a run down the hall.

He returned swiftly with a dented censer, a pouch full of incense, and a few sticks that seemed to puzzle him. He handed them to Nadya with such an earnest expression on his face that her heart tripped over itself. She handed the censer to Anna, following Malachiasz into one of the side rooms.

Whoever had initially wrapped the wound on Parijahan's side had done a good job but there was a darkness Nadya could sense in the jagged gash that was making it fester. Anna lit the censer. The scent of spice and holiness flooded the room almost instantly. Nadya relaxed and let her eyes shut. The smell was familiar, it was *home.* She tucked a slow-burning stick of incense behind her ear, hearing Anna's breath of a laugh. It was a bad habit of hers and she had singed her hair on multiple occasions, but she liked having it burn nearby. Rashid was pacing and Malachiasz was putting out such a frantic energy that before Nadya could even do anything she sighed.

"All right, boys, get out of here. Parijahan will be fine. Her wound got worse, she has a fever, but she's going to be fine." She shooed them out.

She wrapped her necklace around her hand, finding Zbyhneuska's bead and pressing her fingers against it. Opening her eyes, she scanned Parijahan's unconscious form. The girl's breath was shallow and sweat beaded her forehead, her brown skin ashen and pale.

The healing goddess was a mute one, working in feelings and visions. Of the pantheon, she was the gentlest, though soldiers had a tendency to send all their prayers to Veceslav instead of her; something about how a god of war was more likely to shield and heal them during battle than a goddess. A ridiculous superstition. Most would live through battles longer if they burned a candle to Zbyhneuska.

Thanks to Zbyhneuska's silence, Nadya always felt like she could work through her problems with her.

Marzenya is upset I haven't killed the Tranavian yet, Nadya said. *I know we're at war and Tranavians are heretics, but murder feels needless to me.* She felt Zbyhneuska's chime of scolding, but also understanding. Zbyhneuska thought death was needless too.

But Zbyhneuska, goddess of health, was not Nadya's patron. Marzenya, goddess of death and magic and winter, *was.* It wasn't something that usually bothered Nadya. But the way Malachiasz had dug his fingers into hers, the resignation with which he had readied his neck for her blade, had left her off balance.

She didn't understand it. She didn't want to kill him until the time came when she did. When she no longer had a choice.

Nadya pulled the spell Zbyhneuska gave her apart in her head, trying to decide how to channel it properly. There was a darkness to Parijahan's wound that unnerved Nadya. She tugged at her magic, feeling a chorus of holy speech swirling in the back of her head. It felt clean; hopefully, it would be enough to heal the damage done by monsters.

Could this be more than just blood magic? Are the Vultures something else? It was thought not meant as a prayer, but Zbyhneuska reacted all the same. Her confusion startled Nadya.

But the gods were not infallible. The Tranavians had found ways to shield themselves from the gods; that was one of the reasons the war had begun in the first place. It meant that if they had found some darker method of harnessing magic, then the gods would not know. It was terrifying.

Nadya returned her focus to the task at hand, murmuring prayers under her breath. She wasn't entirely sure she had succeeded when she finally lifted her hands away and opened her eyes. What she *was* sure of was her spinning head and the sudden glaring awareness that she couldn't remember the last time she had eaten. She felt like she was going to pass out.

Parijahan's breathing steadied, and the wound had closed, so Nadya left to let her sleep and picked her way through the rubble into what remained of the sanctuary.

"She'll be fine," she said, collapsing beside Malachiasz on a pile of pillows now covered with dirt and bits of debris. "Now let me fix that while I have Zbyhneuska's attention."

"Your goddess won't allow her magic to heal someone like—"

"Shut up, Malachiasz," Nadya said wearily.

He tensed, going utterly still as she brushed his long hair

back, gently pressing her fingers over the blackening bruise. His eyes closed and she thought she heard his breath hitch. Healing the bruise was a simple task, but it wiped out the last of her reserves. So *then* she fainted.

13

SEREFIN

MELESKI

Svoyatova Evgenia Zotova: *Zotova hid herself in the guise of a man and lived for most of her life prophesying from a cave at the base of the Baikkle Mountains.*

—Vasiliev's Book of Saints

The palace's throne room was one of the most over-the-top places in all of Tranavia. It was a huge space, lined with columns of glass. Carved floral etchings ran up them in delicate spirals. The floor was made of black marble, so polished it was practically reflective. A lush carpet of deep violet ran along the length of the hall, leading up to Serefin's father's throne. The throne was the physical manifestation of power, blood, glory, and magic. Iron flowers with sharp thorns curled around the back and intricately twisted metal made up the arms and legs. It commanded attention.

Serefin had never been able to picture himself on it. He was a weapon, never a prince.

Izak Meleski sat upon the throne now, tall and straight-backed with his ivory military coat emblazoned with medallions and black epaulets. He had a severe face—one Serefin loathed to admit his own resembled—a neatly trimmed beard and finely kept dark brown hair. His crown was a simple piece of iron that was somehow just as commanding as the throne if not nearly as dramatic.

It's the bearing, not the symbols, Serefin mused.

Serefin narrowed his eyes at the sight of the king's close advisor, Przemysław, hovering near the throne. The slippery old man had been Serefin's adversary at court for as long as he could remember. Anytime he returned home, Przemysław was there to turn him around and send him back to the front.

"You took your sweet time returning, I see," Izak noted as Serefin approached the throne, bowing low before his father.

"Why, thank you, Father, yes it *has* been a long time. What's that? Oh, it's only been eight months since last I was in Tranavia. Yes, that *is* a long time to be at the front, but, as you see I am here now mostly unscathed." He tapped his temple. "Some scars aren't so visible."

His father appeared anything but amused, and while Izak had never been truly appreciative of Serefin's wit, he could usually at least dredge up a half smile from him. Serefin sobered. This was not a good start.

"I returned in exactly the amount of time the journey called for," he said. "I was in the heart of Kalyazin when your missive arrived."

"Yes, Lieutenant Kijek informed me of that debacle."

"I had it perfectly under control and would have finished the job if not for this summons. And I admit—" Serefin paused, swallowing down the anxiety threatening to choke him. He was suddenly unspeakably nervous. "I'm curious about the necessity of this *Rawalyk*. It feels rather sudden."

"It is tradition, Serefin. Are you arguing against that?" Izak's voice rose in a way that immediately struck fear deep in Serefin's bones.

"I'm arguing against being called away from the war effort seemingly on a whim," Serefin replied, voice even. He was toeing dangerous territory with his father and he knew it. But if he was just being paranoid, his father would ignore his snark as he usually did and this would end with perfect civility. "We have no need for alliances. Voldoga was a turning point, the Kalyazi won't be able to hang on much longer, we have no need to go crawling to our neighbors. This is a tradition that hasn't been acknowledged in *years*."

"And now we're acknowledging it," Izak said, his tone chilling.

Serefin met his father's cold gaze and shrugged. "It's a needless waste of resources."

"Your concern is noted, yet you're here."

It wasn't like he was given a choice. He did as he was told, no matter what he was told. It was . . . exhausting. He rejected the idea of bringing up the Kalyazi spell books he had found on his way home. If the king didn't ask, why should Serefin tell him? Before he would have brought it up to his father right away, desperate for approval. Now it was painfully clear his father didn't care. He still wasn't sure his suspicion was justified, but this was . . . not the father he knew. He was stern, he was serious, yes, but he was never cold.

There was movement in the shadows behind the king's throne.

A loose-limbed figure lounging on the steps around the dais. Serefin's stomach dropped. It was a Vulture, masked and listening in the king's throne room.

It was wrong. That was not how things worked in Tranavia. Serefin clenched a fist behind his back.

"Have the Vultures captured the cleric?" Serefin asked, pulling his gaze away from the one in the corner.

Izak frowned. A muscle in his jaw tightened almost imperceptibly. Serefin raised an eyebrow. Was it because he mentioned the Vultures or something else altogether?

"Have they not?" Serefin asked innocently.

"Apparently, there were complications in her retrieval," Izak said, standing. He was a tall man; Serefin was only the barest inch taller. He folded his hands behind his back and stepped down from the dais. "The Vultures reported she was with a rogue group who were especially cunning."

The Vultures had *failed*? That was rich. Serefin had to stifle the smile threatening to slip through his mask of composure.

"A rogue Kalyazi group who can stand against the Vultures?"

"They apparently had a defected Vulture in their midst."

Serefin let out an incredulous laugh. "A traitor? Do we know who it was?"

Izak shook his head. Serefin glanced at Przemysław.

"The Vultures have been as they always are," Przemysław said. "Recalcitrant about their dealings. We were informed one of their number had fled. He was a boy who had a difficult transition into their order. His indoctrination was messy. His family are members of the court so extra precautions had to be taken to ensure there were no residual attachments nor capabilities of recognition. From what I understand, they used new methods when indoctrinating him. Painful methods."

"So, we have nothing!" Serefin said cheerfully.

"Serefin!" Izak snapped, casting him such a dark look that he felt like turning and bolting out of the room.

This is worse than I feared.

"The Vultures sent were young," Przemysław said slowly. "They were bewildered to see one of their own amongst enemy rabble, though that brings up questions of their training—"

"Their training is fine," a new voice cut in. The Vulture slunk forward. His mask was a visceral affair; jagged edges cut into the leather made it look like it was dripping blood.

"Then why isn't the cleric here now?" Serefin asked.

The Vulture stepped closer to Serefin. "We do not answer to you," he said, voice low.

"No," Serefin replied, "of course not. You just can't offer any explanation as to why one of your own was found with a Kalyazi cleric."

"When our king realized the extraction had gone badly, he had them return to better decide how to deal with the girl," the Vulture said. He turned away from Serefin to address the king. "I assure you, everything will be handled as it should."

"See that it is," Izak said. "I cannot spare another visit to your Salt Mines so soon."

Serefin stiffened. *Why would he go to the Salt Mines at all?*

"I should have gone after her," Serefin muttered.

The Vulture turned but the king spoke over him.

"You should do as you're *told*." Again, a lace of venom. An erratic swing from ice to hot anger.

"Father?" Something slipped in Serefin and his voice was no longer composed. Less the blood mage general and more the boy who wasn't sure what was happening and still—after all these years—didn't understand why he had been shoved aside to fight a war he barely believed in. It was a moment of weakness he immediately regretted.

He didn't know what he expected from his father. A second of silent understanding? Something to assuage his fears?

He received only his father's cold, dismissive glance. His father continued as if nothing had happened.

"We are allowing three weeks before the *Rawalyk* begins for the proper delegates to arrive. Until then, your time is your own."

Serefin nodded. "Thank you." *What am I supposed to do for three weeks? Especially under the watch of the entire palace.* Serefin knew a dismissal when he heard one, so he turned to go.

"Serefin," his father called after him. He turned back, some part of him lifting with hope that perhaps this was when his fear would be dispelled, that his father would smile and welcome him home like a son, not an interloper. But all he said was, "Your mother is in Grazyk. You should speak with her."

And something in his tone chilled Serefin utterly. Panic flared in Serefin's chest. "Of course, Father, right away."

There was his reconnaissance. Now it was time for strategy.

When he stepped out of the throne room, Kacper was waiting by the door. He was leaning against the wall, picking at his fingernails and ignoring the guards, who were studiously ignoring him in turn.

"How bad was it?"

Serefin glanced at the guards and inclined his head down the hallway. Kacper trailed along behind him. Where could they go to speak freely?

Nowhere in this damn palace is safe, Serefin thought.

"I have concerns," Serefin finally replied, pausing in the hallway and looking out the window.

Kacper paled.

Serefin considered his mother's return to Grazyk. She would

not have come just for the *Rawalyk*, he knew that much. He wished he could speak with her about his father, but Izak Meleski would know. She would not tell him, but he would know. Serefin ran an absent thumb down the scar on his face. If his mother was back she would have brought her witch back with her. The witch's tower might be safe from his father's informants, but that would mean speaking to Pelageya Borisovna.

His father gave Pelageya a wide berth. The Kalyazi woman had left her own country after rejecting her gods. While she did not have magic, per se, she was *something*. A seer. A madwoman.

"Do you know if Pelageya is in her tower?" Serefin asked mildly.

Kacper's eyes widened. "What do you want with her?"

"Someplace my father won't think to look." He reached for his spell book, forgetting he had cleaned it out. He sighed. "We have three weeks until the *Rawalyk*."

Kacper nodded. Hopefully it would be enough time to piece together what was going on. If this *Rawalyk* was just as it appeared, or if it was . . . something darker.

Serefin turned to Kacper, opened his mouth, and closed it again. He glanced down the hall. "Come with me," he said.

He wove through the labyrinthine halls of the palace, passing servants wearing dull, gray masks, aware of their lingering glances. They reached one of the three spires. Serefin opened the door, ducking into the entranceway.

A voice formed of ancient promises and death called down: "His Highness has decided to grace me with his presence? We *are* in dire times."

Serefin smiled at Kacper, who looked distressed.

There was no way to see the top of the tower, but Serefin

knew Pelageya was up there, leaning her head down over the railway, looking like a sixteen-year-old *dolzena* when in truth she was nearly ninety years old. He wondered how she would look when they reached her, if they would get the young woman or the old. Frankly, the young one terrified him.

"Serefin . . ." Kacper groaned as Serefin started up the spiral stairs, taking them two at a time. "This is madness. You hate her."

"She terrifies me. As she terrifies everyone." Serefin paused, pulling on the railing as he leaned back. "Like she terrifies my *father*."

Kacper frowned. "She's Kalyazi. Your father probably has a hundred spells on this tower to know what she gets up to."

If Serefin had his spell book, he would have cast a perception spell. Even still, he sliced a finger on the razor inside his sleeve and pressed it against the window.

"Get your bloody hands off my glass!" Pelageya called.

The spell wasn't as strong as it would have been if Serefin had his spell book, but it was sufficient. The witch's tower was void of his father's magic, but choked with something ancient and dreadful.

"There's nothing of my father's here."

"Blood and bone, of course not. Your mother made sure of that, princeling."

Serefin reached the landing only slightly winded—being back at the palace was already getting to him; he had climbed all those ridiculous stairs in Kalyazin and had been *fine*. He found the young Pelageya at the top. She stood in the doorway to her chambers with her hands propped on her hips. Her black hair was wild and tangled against her pale skin, her sharp eyes dark. Whatever magic she had, whatever it was that allowed her to shift from young to old and back at a whim, it showed in her eyes.

"My mother?" he asked. Of course his mother. Izak and Klarysa only outwardly tolerated each other. Bringing the witch back to Grazyk was just another way for Klarysa to get under Izak's skin.

"Aye. Come in, princeling, I can see you want somewhere to speak without your father's snooping rats hearing you." She turned, stepping into her rooms.

Kacper shot a desperate look at Serefin. "Come on, there are better places for this," he murmured. "Places that don't involve being around a crazy Kalyazi witch."

"Don't try so hard to compliment me, Zyweci," she called.

Serefin entered Pelageya's rooms. Black rugs overlapped on the floor and deer skulls hung from the walls, tied up by their antlers. The witch sat in a plush ivory chair, her legs crossed underneath her, twisting a lock of black hair in between her fingers, eyeing Serefin with her head cocked to one side.

"You've realized your father isn't so good a father to you, eh?" she asked.

"What is he planning?"

"No one but he knows. Klarysa has her suspicions, but of course she could do little from her seclusion in the lake country. She can do a bit more in Grazyk, now, but . . ." She waved a hand to the ragged chair across from her. Serefin sat cautiously.

"Your people put little stock in prophecy and foretelling," she said, gazing off into the middle distance. "So odd, for a people so entrenched in blood magic, that the Kalyazi are a more superstitious lot. You have your monsters; they have their demons." She fell silent.

"But?" Serefin prompted.

"Your father has become quite interested in prophecies made by a Tranavian mage named Piotr. Apparently he killed himself right after the foretelling. Threw himself into a lake with a brick tied around his neck. That's a death you read about in the Kalyazi book of martyrs."

"What kind of foretelling?"

"Damned if I know." She grinned.

Kacper shot him a pointed look. Serefin leaned back in his chair.

"But, topically," Pelageya continued. "Piotr *himself* was quite fascinated with an apocryphal Kalyazi story about a woman named Alyona Vyacheslavovna. She was just another Kalyazi martyr and yet the story goes that she ascended to godhood. Wouldn't *that* be a fate?"

Serefin raised an eyebrow. Apocryphal Kalyazi stories weren't going to do him any good right now.

He still felt too unsafe to say the words aloud. To say he suspected his father was going to kill him in the midst of the *Rawalyk*. He didn't have any proof, just a foreboding shadowing his every thought. "I think my father wants to put the winner of the *Rawalyk* on the throne," he said.

"Of course he does. It's all a test to find our next royal consort, is it not?" Pelageya said, but her black eyes returned to Serefin's face. She knew what he was suggesting.

"I think he wants me out of the picture."

Kacper shook his head. "The people would riot. The low princes would—"

"The low princes would see it as an unfortunate death, but be thankful the *Rawalyk* had decided a new line now that the High Prince is gone," Serefin said, interrupting him.

Kacper blinked. "It still doesn't make sense. You're his only heir."

Serefin lifted his eyebrows. He was the only heir, yes, but he was also the stronger mage, the one shifting the war to

Tranavia's favor, the one history would remember. Kacper's expression darkened.

Pelageya nodded. "Blood and blood and bone. Magic and monsters and tragic power."

Serefin heard Kacper's irritated huff of breath and shot him a warning look.

"This whole world is going mad," Pelageya said. "The war is eating at us all. Can it continue? Will it continue forever? Will someone finally break the cycle or will we be plunged into a new century of death? The Kalyazi have their hope; what do the Tranavians have, eh? Their king. Their prince. The knowledge that their king and their prince are undeniably mortal. Their Vultures? That terrible cult."

Serefin's eyes narrowed. Kacper stiffened.

"What if the prince were a harder one to kill? Blood and blood and bone. What if those gods the Kalyazi worship aren't gods at all? Demons of superstition, monsters and magic."

"This is getting us nowhere," Kacper grumbled. He put a hand on Serefin's shoulder, trying to get him to leave.

Pelageya stared past Serefin's shoulder. "You drive a spike into their neck. You wait until the wailing stops, you give them a draught of blood. Drink it! Drink it all, never mind whose it is for you will be dead in—ah, three, two, one. Again. Another. That one failed. That did not work. Mortals are so fragile, so easy to break, but blood . . . Blood and blood and bone. The Salt Mines work so hard, the Vultures so meticulous in their specific brand of torture. The answer is here. The answer has always been here. Gut the Kalyazi churches, melt their gold, grind their bones. Divinity and blood and blood and bone."

Kacper's hand tightened. Serefin could feel his speeding pulse through his fingertips.

Pelageya twitched. Her hand reached out, long fingers

stretched into the air. "The girl. The girl and the monster and the prince . . . and . . ." She twitched again, waving her hand by her ear against some imaginary irritant. "And the . . . queen? Not a queen but a queen. The queen of the wraith or the dark. But no. Power and blood and this pageantry is just a facade and there is more, there is more. The signs will come as they do and they will be ignored or heeded but they are signs, only signs."

"Serefin!" Kacper tugged on Serefin's arm. He pulled away.

"You have time! Time is slipping but it's there, it's there, it remains to be captured. You take it, you hold it. The girl and the monster and the prince and the last one is wrong, the last one hides in the darkness, in the shadows. And maybe the boy made of gold and the boy made of darkness are mirrors. And maybe all will be swallowed by the things you hide from; maybe, *maybe* you will be consumed." Pelageya abruptly stopped.

A heavy silence fell over the room, the only sound coming from the crackling fire. Serefin glanced at Kacper, who was staring at Pelageya with barely concealed horror on his face.

"Thank you, Pelageya," Serefin murmured, his voice strained as he stood up.

"You are always welcome to return here, princeling," she said sweetly. "But be warned, your father will notice, and you don't want that."

Serefin brushed a moth off his shoulder. The gray insect fluttered away and landed on the arm of Pelageya's chair. She stared at it with interest as they left the room.

14

NADEZHDA

LAPTEVA

*Zbyhneuska has healed dying men on battlefields, cured
slow, killing illnesses, given vision to the blind. When Svoyatova Stefania Belomestnova's head was cut off in battle,
Zbyhneuska's blessing healed her completely. But the goddess has never spoken; her voice has never been heard.
If she ever speaks, all the good she has ever done will be
unraveled.*

—Codex of the Divine, 12:114

Zbyhneuska's magic was enough to return Parijahan
to her usual self. Rashid wanted to leave immediately,
Malachiasz didn't want to leave at all. Nadya decided
they would give Parijahan a day to rest and then set off.
Parijahan—being Parijahan—refused to sleep while they
made plans, so she sat imperiously on what was left of
the pile of pillows.

"How do we know the Vultures won't try again?" Anna asked. "We're in the same place they left us."

"They won't," Malachiasz said.

"How do you *know*?"

"Because the Vultures cannot act against their leader. I fled from them, but I'm still one of them. I know exactly what they've been told to do."

Oh. Nadya didn't like how that sounded.

"How can we trust that you won't turn us over to the Tranavians? What if you're *ordered*?" Anna persisted.

Malachiasz merely looked tired. "Because wouldn't I have done that already? I wouldn't be here. Threads fray, even ones of magic created to command."

Nadya pressed at Vaclav's bead. Malachiasz was telling the truth.

"But you don't care about that," he continued. "You don't care what would happen to me if I went back to Tranavia. You're just a girl who's done nothing but live in a monastery her whole life yet can't see indoctrination when it's right in her face, probably because it's all she's ever known."

"Excuse me?" Nadya said. He couldn't talk to Anna like that.

His pale eyes flashed. "They'll just clear me out again."

The room chilled.

"I was ten years old when the Vultures took me," he said, his voice hard. "That's all I know, because I don't have anything left but my name. They always think it so *benevolent* of them. Take away everything that makes children human but let them keep their names as a reminder of everything they've lost."

Horror trickled through her veins, replacing the anger. She

thought of his whispers to himself, hushed words that sounded like his own name. Was it a reminder? Was he so close to losing that, too?

He sighed, raking a hand through his hair. "If I go with you I cannot promise I will not destroy everything you are trying to accomplish. The magic that has frayed and allows me to act against them can very easily be reforged if they catch me."

Except she couldn't do this without him. No one else was going to be able to teach Nadya what she needed to know to fool the court. He sat down at the table, movements heavy. Clearly he realized that as well.

Malachiasz steepled his fingers together and pressed them against his lips. Nadya sat down across from him.

"How is your Tranavian?" he asked her, switching to his native tongue.

A beat. A second too long as Nadya translated his words in her head. He shook his head before she even had a chance to speak.

"You won't get past the border if it takes you that long."

"*Nuicz zepysz kowek dzis,*" she muttered under her breath.

He cracked a smile. "Well, your accent isn't the worst I've heard."

It took her a second to translate. She grinned.

"You can't pause for so long, though," he said. "We'll practice in Tranavian until you get there."

"How are you going to get around the fact that everyone I'm supposed to be avoiding knows exactly what I look like?" Nadya asked in halting Tranavian.

The way he slowly ran his eyes over her face forced her to look down at the table. She felt heat burning at her cheeks and frowned, thrown by her reaction.

"Your hair is distinctive; we'll have to dye it."

"I can manage that," Parijahan said. Anna nodded in agreement.

"Everything else will be easy," Malachiasz said. "A simple spell, nothing more."

"A simple spell that the High Prince won't see straight through?" Nadya asked. Her stomach roiled at the thought of wearing his magic on her skin for the next few weeks.

"Not if I'm the one writing it," he replied.

"That reeks of overconfidence," she muttered.

He smiled slightly. "That's not the right word for that context, but you're close."

Nadya winced. This was never going to work.

"We can get into the palace by forging paperwork."

Before Nadya had a chance to ask how they were possibly going to accomplish that, Rashid perked up.

"Leave that to me. I worked as the Travasha's scribe in my youth. There is very little I cannot forge."

Nadya glanced at Parijahan for confirmation. She just grinned.

"If she says she's from a border town her accent will be less noticeable. Reasonable explanation will hide just about anything from unsuspecting eyes," Malachiasz said.

"But that will put her close enough to Kalyazin to instantly be suspicious," Rashid argued.

"If I'm traveling with two Akolans anyway, would it not stand to reason that I be from somewhere close to both borders?" Nadya interjected.

Malachiasz nodded thoughtfully then abruptly stood and left the room.

"Where's he going?" Nadya asked, forgetting she was supposed to be speaking in Tranavian.

"Tekyalzaw jelesznak!" She heard Malachiasz call from the other room. *Wrong language.*

She rolled her eyes.

He came back and unrolled a map on the table, using his spell book to hold it down on one end and Rashid's elbow on the other. After frowning at the Tranavian side, he tapped at a point near where the Tranavian border met Akola.

"Łaszczów," he said. "It's just far enough from Kalyazin that you won't be instantly suspect, but near enough that a hold-over of a Kalyazi accent might be possible."

"Are there any low royalty in the area?" Parijahan asked.

Malachiasz shook his head. "Low nobility only. Inconsequential. The nearest low prince is in Tanów, which is farther north."

"So, it would be easily explained if Nadya didn't know all the finer points of court life," Rashid said.

"If Józefina didn't know, exactly," Malachiasz confirmed.

"Is that my name?" Nadya asked. "Did you come up with it yourself?"

He narrowed his eyes. "Józefina Zelenska. Your father, Lucjan, has tragically departed this world, but he died fighting for his country. Your mother, Estera, is an invalid, and," he paused, thinking, "you have a younger sister named Anka."

Nadya blinked. "Did you *just* come up with all of that?"

Malachiasz raised his eyebrows. "Yes, why?"

How many false realities has he constructed for himself? she wondered. If all he had was his name and his magic, how many nights had he lain awake and wondered where the people he might have called family were? Who they were? This was easy for him. Just another false family that would never be real. She had to stop herself from crossing the suddenly paltry distance to where his hand rested on the table, black lines of ink tattooed

on his pale fingers. The urge to give some small scrap of comfort to her enemy startled her enough that she dropped her
hand down to her lap to better pretend like it never happened.
His quick glance at the spot where her hand had once been
only made her feel more like she was doing something she
shouldn't.

Rashid shifted away from the map and Malachiasz gently
shoved him back down so it wouldn't roll up.

"Can you cast magic without using those beads?" Malachiasz asked.

She fingered her necklace. "Not really."

"We'll have to figure out how to work around that. What
about," he waved a hand over his mouth, "the symbols? Those
make it too obvious you're using magic."

"Oh, like how you cut your arm open and bleed over everything? Very subtle."

Parijahan snorted. Malachiasz's expression wearied.

"You know what I mean."

"I'll speak to Marzenya. Perhaps she and I can come to an
agreement," Nadya said.

"Also, if Rashid and Parijahan are posing as part of my en-
tourage—"

"I'm *much* too pretty to be a servant," Rashid said with a
sigh.

Malachiasz shot him an amused look. "You could pose as
nobility—"

"No, Malachiasz," Parijahan said quickly. "Too much paperwork. We're already risking it with Nadya. I don't want a keen
slavhka who visited Akola's courts recognizing me, and I definitely don't want my Travasha hearing word that I've reappeared,
so let's change the context. I pose as Nadya's maidservant, I

hide in plain sight. I can swallow my pride for a short time."
She smiled wryly. "And so can Rashid."

"What about Anna?" Nadya asked.

"I'm not coming with you," Anna said softly.

Nadya turned to her, speechless. Anna had to come with
her. She couldn't do this without her.

Anna's smile was tinged with acute melancholy. She had
clearly been thinking about this for some time. She looked at
Malachiasz. "Tranavia will be focused on the *Rawalyk*, won't it?"

"They've just pulled their prodigy tactician out of the war,"
he said. "All of the country will have its eyes on Grazyk. There's
a good chance Tranavia is so confident victory is in sight that
they will loosen their hold for the time it takes to see this ceremony through."

"I'm going to Komyazalov," she said. "Or, at the very least,
the biggest military base I can reach on the way while you all
deal with this." She pressed her index finger down on the map
over Tranavia. "I'll make sure Kalyazin is ready for what happens next. Besides, the prince knew we fled the monastery together. It's better for me not to even be present to arouse any
kind of suspicion."

Nadya leaned her head on Anna's shoulder and willed herself to keep her tears at bay. She had thought at the very least
she would have Anna beside her, but what Anna wanted to do
was important—vital, even—so she wouldn't argue against it.

"Don't go alone," Nadya said in Kalyazi. Malachiasz didn't
chastise her for switching languages. "Come with us for at least
a little while. There's still a military presence to the east, right?"

Rashid nodded.

"Don't travel through the mountains alone."

Anna cast her a long look. She didn't want to make this

harder, and it was already going to tear at them both to part. Anna was all Nadya had left of home, and now she was losing her, too. Finally, Anna nodded. Nadya relaxed, hooking her arm through the other girl's.

"What are you planning to do?" Nadya asked Malachiasz.

He chewed on his thumbnail. It looked raw, the edges jagged and red. "I'll get you into Grazyk, into the palace, whatever. We'll figure it out from there."

That wouldn't work. Every part of this needed to be spotless or they would be caught. She stared at him. Nadya knew she shouldn't care about this Tranavian abomination sitting across from her. He was doomed in his fate just like the rest of the Tranavians—even more so, as he was a Vulture, one of the worst. But she stared anyway, at this boy—this strange boy with his tangled black hair and tattooed forehead—and half of her wanted to help him.

The other half wanted to destroy him, but that half was strangely quiet.

Nadya sat outside in the cold gray mist of early morning, Malachiasz's jacket around her shoulders. Though the Vulture attack had been only yesterday, it felt like years had passed. They would leave later in the morning. Anna had dyed Nadya's hair a dark red, and she could feel the strands freezing against her neck. She tugged her necklace over her head and wrapped it around her hand.

She had an idea—probably a very bad one—definitely one that would take a lot of effort on her part to keep Malachiasz safe in Tranavia.

"You are asking me to shield a heretic," Veceslav said. *"Not only that, but one who has forfeited his soul for evil."*

Now, that seems a touch melodramatic.

"Nadezhda." Veceslav's tone was a warning. He thought Nadya was being utterly mortal, utterly petulant, utterly unlike how someone chosen by the gods should act.

Nadya tugged Malachiasz's jacket tighter around her shoulders. She hadn't meant to keep it, but when she left to go outside she couldn't find anything else.

Yes. I am asking you to shield a Tranavian. If this is going to work—if you want the High King dead—then I need him to be protected.

"You cannot presume to know our will," Veceslav replied.

Then what am I to do? If my methods are not right by you, I understand, but I cannot work miracles. I can only work magic. I am human. I am mortal. I am doing the best I can. I'm scared, Veceslav. All the time. I don't know what's going on or what I'm supposed to do. I'm just doing my best with the circumstance I have been given, with the power I've been given.

He was silent. Nadya was discomfited by how cold he was being with her. He was one of the gods she could usually count on to be kind.

"What are you proposing?" Veceslav's voice was a welcome nudge at the back of her head.

She let out a breath, watching it hiss out in the cold air before her.

I need him to be able to return to Tranavia and hide amongst his kind in plain sight. If I am to wear his magic on my skin, then he must be forced to wear mine on his. She paused, considering further. *The heretics cannot win this war and I fear they are close. If we protect this single Tranavian for the time being—abomination that he is—then we can cleanse Kalyazin of the heretics entirely.*

"Then you will be given the spells and magic to shield him from his enemies and yours."

Nadya noted his phrasing. It would do.

Thank you, Veceslav.

"You tread dangerous ground, child. Our touch on Tranavia is weak. If you journey there, you take yourself away from our protection. You must do your duty when you arrive."

Nadya shivered. *Break Tranavia so the gods can return.* Destroy it entirely, if that was what it took. And tell no one what she intended. The conversation was dropped when she heard footsteps crunching in the snow.

"Can't you do this inside where it's warm?" Malachiasz settled himself down on the bench beside her. He looked sidelong at her. "I was wondering where that went."

She felt her face flame. "I don't exactly have anything else at this point."

He laughed. Her face flushed even hotter. She ducked her head, confused by the odd feeling in her chest. It was the first time she had heard him truly laugh, and it struck her that she liked the way it sounded.

"It doesn't bother you to be wearing a heretic's coat?"

She rolled her eyes, but his words struck home and sent something churning within her. It *should* be bothering her to be wearing the enemy's uniform, even if it was just a piece.

"Why do you have a soldier's coat?" she asked.

"When I fled, it seemed rational to flee as a Tranavian soldier, not a Vulture. We're a bit more conspicuous."

They grew quiet until only their breaths broke up the silence. She glanced at him. He was gazing at the statue of Alena with a contemplative expression on his face. His black hair was tied back, but a strand had worked its way free. She watched as he mindlessly lifted a hand to tuck the lock behind his ear only to have it fall back against his cheek.

"I know how to help you cross the border," she said. The

words came out in a rush at the thought he might catch her staring. She unwrapped her necklace from her hand, stretching it out over her lap. She selected the right bead and held it up.

"That is entirely meaningless to me," he pointed out.

"Veceslav is the god of protection and war."

"Odd combination."

She waved that away. "Protection can mean a lot of things. Protection can mean shielding *all* of you from Tranavia."

He looked skeptical. She searched for the right words. "You're going to put a spell on me so everyone who sees me will see . . . someone else."

"More or less, yes."

"But if I were a blood mage, they would still be able to sense my magic, right?"

He nodded.

"Veceslav will disguise you as a weaker mage, or someone who has no magic at all. You could . . ." She searched for a scenario. "You could slip among the Vultures and they wouldn't know."

He grimaced, reaching over to brush a fingertip against the bead in her hand. "If they catch me," he said, his voice low against her ear, "they will pull the knowledge I have of you from my mind and set me after you to kill you."

Nadya swallowed hard, fear flooding through her. She resisted the urge to tuck his jacket closer around her. "I—I thought you were one of the strongest?" He never said it, but his demeanor implied it. He'd have to be to survive this long after defecting.

"But I'm not the oldest, Nadya." His pale eyes were faraway and one of his hands idly rubbed at his wrist where iron spikes had jutted from his skin. "I am so very young by comparison, and there are evils in this world far greater than I."

Her fingers closed over her necklace. "Don't make me regret helping you," she whispered. "Please."

He tilted his head back and she found her gaze drawn to the line of his throat, then he gave a lopsided smile. "I can't guarantee that, *towy dżimyka*." He stood. "We're leaving soon. You and I can wait till we're closer to the border to cast on each other."

"I'll be right in. Maybe go see if there's another coat in there for me," Nadya said. She wasn't sure what the pins on the left breast of his jacket meant, but she was fairly certain she didn't want them this close to her body.

He tugged a frozen lock of her hair through his fingers. "I'm not sure I will," he murmured. He turned and started down the path to the church. "Red was a good choice," he called back over his shoulder.

Nadya was left sitting in front of the altar, her face the same fiery shade as her hair.

"You didn't see that," she said, aloud, to whichever god was listening. "As soon as this is over, knife to the heart, just like that."

She didn't manage to convince herself. But none of that mattered, not yet.

15

SEREFIN

MELESKI

Svoyatova Viktoria Kholodova: *When Svoyatova Viktoria Kholodova was killed, a pomegranate tree burst forth from where her body fell.*

—Vasiliev's Book of Saints

Kacper let the door slam behind them. "That was one of your worst ideas, Serefin. Ever."

Serefin couldn't stop laughing. Kacper was looking at him in shock, unable to see the humor in earning a prophecy from a mad Kalyazi witch. Serefin wheezed, leaning back against the wall and sliding to the floor. A servant passed in front of them, pointedly not looking at the High Prince having a fit of hysterics on the ground.

"What did it mean?" Kacper continued.

"Did it have to mean anything?" Serefin asked after catching his breath. He wiped tears from his eyes.

Kacper shuddered.

Serefin brushed a moth off his knee, frowning. Where were they coming from? The insect left the barest sprinkling of dust on Serefin's black trousers as it flew away.

After heaving an exasperated sigh, Kacper slid down the wall until he was sitting on the floor next to Serefin.

"Now what?" he asked.

Serefin leaned his head back. He needed a way to dig deeper into the underbelly of the court without anyone suspecting him of stirring up trouble. He had a reputation for getting underfoot and antagonizing *slavhki,* most of whom weren't fond of him. While Pelageya was an oddity, it was comforting to know not everyone in the castle was under his father's spell.

"How quickly can a person travel to Kyętri and back?" he mused.

Kacper glanced sidelong at him. "You're leaving Grazyk?"

"I can't. But I need someone to go to the Salt Mines."

"Who would that be?"

"Well . . ."

"Definitely not."

"I trust you and Ostyia and no one else," Serefin said.

"That's touching, Serefin."

"Are you defying a direct order from your prince?" Serefin asked, pressing a hand over his heart.

"It wasn't a direct order, and I won't leave you with only Ostyia for protection while you're convincing yourself there are going to be assassins waiting for you around every corner. I'll find someone trustworthy to send to Kyętri."

"What am I supposed to do in the meantime?"

"Drink a lot of wine and prepare for your inevitable fate?" Kacper suggested.

Serefin considered that with a thoughtful nod.

"Maybe get a new spell book?"

That got Serefin to his feet. "There's an idea. With every piece I'm given about this business with the Vultures I grow more concerned, so first, let's go to the source."

"You're going to try to pull the Vultures away from your father?" Kacper asked.

"He shouldn't have them to begin with, so I'm certainly going to try."

Serefin's status earned him an interview with the Crimson Vulture, the second in command. Unexpectedly, she came to his rooms instead of requiring he go to the cathedral on the palace grounds to meet her.

The Vulture was a tall woman who wore an iron mask that covered all but her stormy blue eyes. Piles of black hair fell down her back in waves. Her head shifted to one side in an oddly avian way when she was brought before Serefin.

"Your Highness," she said, her voice graveled, "welcome back to Grazyk."

He motioned for her to sit and was grateful when she did; her height was intimidating.

"I hope His Excellency is well," Serefin said. He wasn't surprised that he had been denied an audience with the Black Vulture. The leader of the Vultures was notoriously elusive.

"I'll be sure to pass on your felicitations," she replied.

"Strange that he's not in Grazyk with the *Rawalyk* so near."

"Matters of state hold little interest to him. As it is now there will always be a war and there will always be state kings to fuel it, so he must see to the things of magic your king forgets or simply has no time for."

Or simply isn't powerful enough to comprehend. What must it be like, to be the king of a land that lauds its blood mages, surrounded by mages all more powerful than you? Serefin supposed he could sympathize with his father's position, if not exactly empathize.

"What kind of matters would those be?" Serefin asked.

"Curious about our ways, Your Highness? I would've thought they were too occult for someone with your sensibilities."

"I've just been given a lot of free time. It's not something one has a great deal of when they're continually at war. I may as well spend it putting together the pieces of just what has happened while I've been away."

She tensed. It was subtle, but Serefin caught it.

"Tell me, my lady, about the Vulture that was found in Kalyazin."

Her eyes widened a fraction of an inch. "I suppose we cannot keep every secret close."

"Did that sound like blackmail?" Serefin asked innocently. It would be a scandal if the common folk learned of someone defecting from the Vultures. They were the elite, a higher authority, the chosen blessed.

Her head tilt dropped a raven lock over the forehead of her silver mask. "Tell *me*, Your Highness, what do you want?"

"I was called from the front rather suddenly. The necessity for a consort seems like thin reasoning. I have no true proof of any dealings that should not be happening taking place, yet . . ."

"Yet you have suspicions."

He shrugged. "As I said, nothing founded."

"What makes you think my order would know the machinations of your political games?"

"There was a Vulture in my father's throne room," Serefin said idly. "The Vultures were also very eager to go after the cleric I found, only to fail . . . The latter is an unfortunate oversight on your order's part; the *former*, well, that looks like mixing magic and politics where they should not meet. I have no intention of blackmailing you, my lady—not yet, at least. Your order has traditionally played the role of advisor and nothing more, is that still the case?"

She swallowed. "Not quite."

He hummed an acknowledgment and waited for her to continue.

"Some amount of paranoia on your part may be well founded."

"What kind of paranoia?" he asked, letting his eyes close. He angled his head back. He would have expected more fear, more panic, anxiety that clutched at him and refused to let him think; instead he just felt calm. Here was a problem for him to decipher. Here was something to *do,* even if that something was surviving.

"It is rumored that your standing at court is tenuous, but they're whispers, nothing more."

Serefin couldn't help but smile. So his father had become so anxious about Serefin's power that he thought it best he was out of the picture entirely? How utterly Tranavian.

"And telling me this isn't betraying Tranavia?"

A flicker of amusement sparked in the Vulture's eyes. "It would hardly be the first time Tranavian politics were upheaved while the Vultures remained untouched. It's not like I told you anything you did not already know."

Regardless, it was confirmation he wasn't going mad, that he wasn't seeing knives where they were not, shadows where none stood. It was something, and it would have to be enough.

Serefin had nothing but time to figure out how to move forward. He might as well enjoy his last days.

The northern end of the palace grounds held a huge arena

built long before Tranavia discovered blood magic. Back when power was tested by might and strength alone. The traditions remained even as power became something far greater in concept. The arena was still used for mage duels, to settle grievances amidst the court, and—most importantly—for trials and executions.

It was a large building, made for seating a fair portion of the city if necessary. Iron spikes jutted around the circumference, and carvings of war lined the outside. The entrance was decorated with symbols for magic, and Serefin brushed his hand against one as he passed.

The inner arena was a circle of packed dirt that had been dug twenty feet down from ground level. It could be manipulated by mages during trials, but usually it remained as a training ground. There were a few individuals within when Serefin entered, Ostyia trailing at his heels. None of them took any notice of the prince. He moved to the railing and jumped up onto it, sitting down and swinging his legs over the far drop. Ostyia leaned against the railing beside him.

"Recognize anyone?" he asked. Faces were a blur.

She nodded.

"We have House Láta, House Bržoska, House Orzechowska, and House Pacholska," Ostyia said. "Ah, and dear lady Żaneta." She pointed to a young woman who was resting against the far wall of the arena, watching the other four girls as they sparred.

"They're all being so civil," Serefin noted.

Ostyia rolled her eyes. "When they become anything else, I want you to remember they're doing it for the crown, not you. Don't let it go to your head, dear prince."

"No, it's all for me," Serefin said with a wry smile.

Żaneta noticed them sitting in the stands and waved, bowing smartly after. That got the attention of the other girls, who bowed as well. Serefin waved a hand.

"Don't mind me," he called down.

He knew House Láta and Orzechowska were prominent blood mage families, but he was less sure about the other two.

Żaneta pushed herself off the wall and climbed the steps. Serefin felt his gaze follow her as if magnetized. Before his father's announcement, Serefin had been quite confident Żaneta would be Tranavia's next queen. Now, she would have to fight her way to the throne.

Her mass of dark auburn curls was tied back, throwing her tawny skin and refined features into sharp focus. There was a streak of blood smeared on the coat she wore over her dress.

Her mother was a noble from Akola, and Żaneta had her dark coloring. Her nose had a graceful hook to it that on anyone else might seem hawkish, but which looked regal on her. Her lips twisted into a smile as she neared Serefin.

"Your Highness," she said. Her voice had the barest hint of smoke to it, breathy and dark.

"Lady Ruminska," he replied, swinging around on the railing so he could stand. He took her outstretched hand and pressed it to his lips.

"Ugh, house name and everything," she said. "You leave for a few years and all my hard work goes to waste."

"Żaneta," he amended with a smile.

"Better." She stepped back, turning to the arena seats and a pile of the girls' discarded things. She picked up her belt and strapped it around her hips, attaching her spell book. "Did you get back this morning?"

"Yes, and I've already been thoroughly scolded by my father *and* discussed sensitive matters with a Vulture."

She lifted an eyebrow. "So busy so soon and without a drink

in your hand; war *has* changed you, Serefin." She picked up a heavily jeweled mask and let it hang from her fingers as she leaned over the railing. "Good luck to you, my dears," she called down. "Blood and bones will they need luck," she continued under her breath, turning back.

"The competition not up to your standards?" Serefin asked as he fell into step beside her. He tried to overtake her pace so it didn't seem as though he was trailing along behind her. He wasn't certain he succeeded.

"Is it ever?" She flipped the mask between her fingers before attaching it to her belt. "It's good to see you, and under such ideal circumstances."

Serefin found he couldn't agree with her on the circumstances, but at the very least he was away from the front. The likelihood of his death was about the same as it ever was, after all.

"Tell me something good, Żaneta," Serefin said as they walked through the gardens. "I have had nothing but bad news for years now."

"I'm going to catch you up on all of the best court gossip," she said. "You've missed so much! Did you know that Nikodem Stachowicz was caught in the palace archives with the youngest Osadik boy?"

"Don't those families—"

"Hate each other? And have been locked in a feud for three generations? Yes!"

Serefin laughed, and for the first time in what felt like years, he let himself relax.

16

NADEZHDA

LAPTEVA

*There are no ancient records of the goddess of light, Zvoni-
mira. There are whispers, rumors, threads of truth or fiction
that say that she is the youngest in the pantheon, but
who truly knows how the gods come to be? Like Alena,
Zvonimira has never bestowed her powers upon a chosen
cleric.*

—Codex of the Divine, 36:117

"Blood magic has become universally ingrained into daily
Tranavian life. Without it, the whole country would collapse."

Nadya had spent the morning letting Malachiasz's words
filter slowly through one ear and out the other. It wasn't
that she wasn't paying attention—she was all too aware
how vital it was she not misstep while deeply entrenched
at court—but it was *so much* information all at once.

His words made her pause. "How is that possible?"

He shrugged, burying his tattooed hands in his pockets. "It builds over time, magic does. Especially blood magic. It's so accessible. You don't have to have a true affinity for it to use it in small spells; you just need to know how to channel your own blood through the written conduits. After enough years pass, it becomes routine—fishermen cast spells to keep lines from breaking, bakers cast to keep their bread rising, the like—removing it would fundamentally destroy what has built the country up."

Nadya frowned. Her frown deepened when he handed her a slim razor. "Sew that into the sleeve of your coat. Cutting the palm of your hand and fingers hurts more than cutting the back. The razor is treated so the cuts won't scar."

She thought of the scarred plain of his forearms. If the scars weren't from his magic, then what?

Scattered along the mountain paths and wider roads were wayside shrines that Nadya would quietly attend to whenever they passed. It only ever took her a short while to brush dirt off the statues or pillars and remove the dead flowers before catching up to the others. After the third one they passed, Malachiasz stopped to wait for Nadya while the others walked on ahead.

She could feel his gaze on her as she worked. This shrine was dedicated to Vaclav so Nadya was taking extra time to ensure it was spotless when she left it. Vaclav was a darker god, chaotic and strong-willed, and Nadya was careful to stay on his good side.

"I don't understand," she heard him say quietly, an odd, agonized note in his voice. Like he was trying so hard to comprehend her strange, pagan ways but simply couldn't.

She leaned back on her heels and looked over her shoulder at him, raising an eyebrow.

"It's a carving on the side of the road. Your cleaning it doesn't make a difference," he said.

"The gods like when their altars are tended."

He shot her a look. "It's just junk."

"It's a place of holiness and you should treat it with a modicum of respect," Nadya replied, returning to her work.

She heard Malachiasz scoff. "So, your power and *this* are both holy?"

"What does my power have to do with anything?"

"If it's all holy." He waved a hand vaguely.

"I don't think you're in any position to say what's holy or not," she said, voice hot. "Besides, it's not like you can deny my power exists."

"Having power granted to you, and acknowledging that beings of power exist, isn't the same as acknowledging that those beings are benevolent or even sentient."

"But you're acknowledging they *exist*."

"Not in the capacity you do. You're saying your every choice is dictated by these beings. Everything you do is on their behalf and at their whim, so you have no free choice at all."

"I absolutely have a choice."

"Do you?"

"You're still alive."

He immediately fell silent. She half-expected him to leave—they were near where they were planning to camp so Nadya was in no hurry—but instead he moved so he was standing beside the altar, facing her, a puzzled frown still on his face.

"They talk to me, you know," she said as she used her sleeve to scrub a patch of lichen off the statue. "They all have their own quirks and desires. Some of them talk to me regularly:

Marzenya—my patron—Veceslav, Zvonimira. Others only give me magic when I ask. Some regularly deny my requests. They're not mere concepts."

He didn't look convinced; she didn't understand what was so hard to comprehend.

"How do you explain my power, then?" she said. "Since you clearly know everything."

He ignored her barb completely, which was infuriating in its own right. "It's the concept of gods that I don't accept," he said. He idly gathered his long hair back, tying it with the strip of leather he kept around his wrist. "You believe they care about your well-being. I don't think that's true. I don't . . ." he trailed off, quiet as he searched for words. "It's what we tie to the word 'god,' I think, that bothers me. This idea that these beings are so much more than we could ever be so they deserve our worship. Kalyazi"—he gave her an almost apologetic look—"pin everything on the gods. Creation, morality, day-to-day interactions, their own *thoughts*. But who's to say that the gods care at all what individual people think or feel or do? How do you know that you're interacting with . . . well, *gods* and not just beings who have attained a higher standing than mortals?"

"Because there's no proof that mortals have ever reached higher than what they are?"

Malachiasz pointed to himself.

"So you're like a god?" she said dryly.

He grimaced. "Obviously not. You see the problem?"

"I think your entire argument is based on semantics."

"Isn't that what everything is, though? Concepts that we give unnecessary weight. For all you know, you're merely communicating with incredibly powerful beings, but they are *only* that. Not beings that had any hand in this world's creation, or beings that determine the course of your life. Our kingdoms are falling apart, have been at war for a century, and it's because of these things."

Nadya straightened, shooting him an incredulous look.

He noted her reaction with a shrug. "There's no other blame to place for a holy war that's gone on this long. For just a moment, let yourself consider without your current religious hang-ups," he said. "What if the gods were unseated from their thrones?"

"Impos—"

He held up a hand, lifting an eyebrow.

She ground her teeth. "Who would remove the *beings of power,* then?"

"Another being of equal or more power, clearly."

"And what will that fix? Remove a foundation for how thousands of people structure their lives—for what?—the chance for blood mages to stop having their feelings hurt when we call them what they are?"

"Kalyazin is dying," Malachiasz said, and Nadya shivered as their hypothetical conversation stepped too close to reality. "Tranavia is, too. And you expect me to believe that removing the forces that have toyed with us for thousands of years wouldn't save us all from the ashes of what our kingdoms will soon become?"

She swallowed. "It's moot," she said, her voice too soft because she didn't want to even consider what he was implying.

He smiled cheerfully. "Impossible, of course. Musings, nothing more. Regardless, your power is only that. It's not like your people have been limited to only this so-called divine magic in the past," he continued.

He was referring to witches—apostate magic users outside the gods' approval—but there had been no witches in Kalyazin for decades. Their route of magic was considered just as heretical as blood magic and they had all but been eradicated by the old clerics during the time of the Witch Hunts. How did he even know about that? The chill of discomfort was gone and now she was righteously heated again. He was talking circles around her and she couldn't keep him *still* for long enough to show him how he was wrong.

"You're using heretics as an example," she said. Witches and blood mages, it was all the same. "It's not particularly compelling."

"It's proof that your holier-than-thou attitude about magic isn't all there is!"

"I don't have an attitude about magic."

"You keep calling me a heretic."

"You *are* a heretic. You just laid out sheer heresy in front of me. And my power is divine; calling me 'holier than thou' is just trite."

He sat down beside her and she stiffened, suddenly acutely aware of . . . *him*. The way he folded up his lanky frame to sit, one knee glancing against her leg because he was so close. She swallowed. He took her wrist, his touch unbearably gentle, and pushed her sleeve back, exposing the still visible cut his claw had dragged down her forearm. There was a beat of silence, the road suddenly eerily quiet as they both stared down at the culmination of Nadya's own heresy.

"Well," he breathed out softly, a flicker of something feral at his lips, "perhaps you're right. Maybe not so holy, after all."

This should not be happening. She should not be leaning close to this boy, his touch warm against her skin. Her gaze caught against the shape of his mouth; her brain slowly coming to register what he said.

She yanked her arm away and continued scrubbing at the

altar, trying not to seethe and failing. Trying not to think about the way it felt when his fingers curled around her wrist, the way his leg was still pressed against hers, and failing at that, too.

Malachiasz was quiet for a long time before he spoke again. "You never feel trapped?"

"Trapped by what?"

"The path you have to follow for your magic. That it could be denied at another being's whim. You have so little say in the direction of your own life. Isn't that stifling?"

"When you frame it that way, yes. Except my life isn't like that. My magic isn't like that either." But . . . for a flickering instant, she let herself consider just how carefully she had to tread with the gods, how a decision to survive had already cost her hours of guilt. She shoved the thoughts away.

"But you have all these rules and guidelines. What happens if you break them?"

"I don't."

He frowned. "What keeps you from testing them?"

She leaned back on her hands and her fingers brushed against his, heat burning up her arm. She shifted away. "What are you trying to say, Malachiasz?" she asked, too mortified to look at him directly.

He drew one knee up against his chest and rested his chin on it. "I'm trying to understand."

"Why?"

He appeared genuinely puzzled by the question. "Am I not supposed to be interested?"

"You're not supposed to care."

He opened his mouth, and closed it again, looking thoughtful. "I do care," he finally said, voice quiet.

Nadya swallowed hard. "Why?" she asked. He was Tranavian,

a heretic, a *Vulture,* every part of him was in opposition to what Nadya believed, and yet . . .

There was something else. She didn't know what it was. She was unnerved to discover she wanted to find out.

"Because I have known nothing but the Vultures my whole life," he said reluctantly. "And we have both spent our lives preparing to kill, well, each other, but here we are instead." He didn't need to indicate the decided lack of space between them.

"The Vultures destroyed Kalyazin's clerics," Nadya said.

He met her gaze before he nodded. There was no shame in his eyes, nothing like remorse.

"I will not harm the last," he said.

Nadya's heart felt erratic in her chest and she didn't know how to make the feeling go away. "We have no idea if I'm the last," she said finally, primly, hoping it would break the spell that was keeping her trapped here with him, even though she knew magic had nothing to do with it.

"Don't you wonder what it would be like? To be someone else, with no expectations upon you or the fear of retribution keeping you on the same path."

No. Yes. It's more complicated than he could ever know.

"You grew up in a monastery." He fidgeted, fingers picking at a hang nail. "And that's just a different string of rigid rules, isn't it? How to live, who to love, what you can and can't think."

"I don't mind rules, or having grown up in a monastery, but I can grant you that the magic, the destiny, knowing most clerics are killed young . . ." she trailed off. "It's hard living your life knowing you're probably going to die horribly. But this is who I am. It's a blessing, not a curse."

She hoped it didn't sound like she was rationalizing to herself, too. What was happening to her?

He seemed to be considering that.

"You disagree," she said.

He nodded.

"This is why our countries have been at war for nearly a century," Nadya said. "And I do feel a little like killing you right now, so I can see why."

"Just a little?"

"Don't press your luck." She returned to the statue.

In a flash, his hand was underneath her chin, thumb brushing against her jaw. He turned her face back to his. "I plan on doing exactly that," he murmured.

If Nadya hadn't been sitting down she suspected her knees would have given out on her.

Then, just like that, he let her go. He stood up and nodded to the altar. "Are you finished?"

She had been done for some time. She nodded, clearing her throat. He held out a hand. She hesitated before letting him pull her to her feet. He let go as soon as she was standing, digging his hands into the pockets of his coat as he started down the road to where the others had decided to camp. She watched him go. Something had shifted between them.

Spending days speaking only in Tranavian did wonders for Nadya's understanding of the language but little to mask her accent. It was frustrating Malachiasz more with each passing day, but she wasn't sure what she was doing wrong.

"It's soft. Your words are too soft. Like," he waved his hand in front of his mouth, "your words are mush. Tranavian is hard."

Nadya let her horse wander instead of tying it up, sending a short prayer up to Vaclav to keep an eye on the animal so it didn't stray too far.

"You're not making any sense."

"We could lose this whole game at the border because it's desperately obvious your native tongue is Kalyazi."

She waved a hand. It was out of her control. The only way to get any better was to continue doing exactly what they were doing. They still had plenty of time until they reached the border, anyway. "Then I'll keep my mouth shut. All they'll see is a Tranavian soldier split from his company, two Akolans seeking refuge, and a mute peasant the Tranavian picked up for pleasure. Because they're like that."

That earned her a dirty look. Anna snorted.

They reached the point where Anna would part with them and Nadya wished she could pretend it wasn't happening. She understood why Anna was staying behind—if they were successful, Kalyazin needed to be ready—but she hated it nonetheless.

Anna's final words to Nadya nestled down within her bones. *"Don't be a martyr. We have no use for yet another saint."*

Afterward she walked into the military camp where Nadya could not follow. Nadya watched as she spoke with a soldier at the perimeter, the soldier's eyes scanning the woods behind her. She watched as the soldier waved Anna inside, and watched as she disappeared. It wasn't fair that Nadya had to lose everything for this, but she should know better. She had read the Codex enough times; her goddess demanded sacrifice.

Parijahan hooked her arm through Nadya's. "You'll see each other again," she said softly.

Nadya didn't believe that, but it was a small comfort.

The mountains gave way to fields bitten by the frost of the long winter gracing Kalyazin. As each day brought them closer to the border, soon there was nothing but the burnt and blackened remains of what were once Kalyazi villages. Ravaged fields and decimated buildings where homes had once been. How

much death had to sweep through these countries before someone finally said *enough*?

Nadya distanced herself from Malachiasz during those days
of travel. She would rather lose the time learning about Tranavia than look him in the eyes and pretend she didn't want to
murder him.

Rashid was a gift from the gods during the bleak stretch
where they were surrounded by the constant taste of death in
the air. Nadya would spend her evenings next to him as he
spun tales with a skill Nadya wouldn't have expected from the
flashy Akolan. Kalyazi legends of princes and saints and old
magic, Tranavian stories of monsters and shadows, Akolan
tales of sand and intrigue. Every time Nadya learned something new about Rashid she found she was surprised; she
wouldn't have ever thought him a scribe or a storyteller.

Parijahan would listen with her head leaning against Malachiasz's shoulder or her hands idly braiding his hair, and Nadya
would forget they were probably doomed as soon as they
reached the border.

It was early evening, the setting sun creeping through the gaps
in the trees and flooding the clearing with warm, amber light.
Malachiasz and Nadya agreed that the moment where they
cast magic on each other should be kept between them, so they
had separated from Parijahan and Rashid.

Malachiasz leaned back against a tree, gazing up at a small
murder of crows that landed in the branches shortly after they
arrived.

"The *tolst* is an omen," Nadya whispered.

"Good or bad?"

She shook her head. "It could be either. It could be both."

His lips twitched into a smile. "You Kalyazi are certainly superstitious."

"Try my patience, Vulture boy, and I'll tell Vaclav to send a *leshy* after you. No one will know you're gone."

"No one would mourn my absence, either," he said.

Nadya blinked, faltering at his frank words. Her hands were trembling as she called on Veceslav and felt the holy tongue of the spell ease its way into her mind.

"Stand still," she ordered, lifting up on her toes. She rested a hand on his shoulder for balance. He stooped down a little so she could reach more comfortably.

She took her other hand and pressed two fingers to his forehead just at his hairline, where the trio of black lines were etched into his skin. She slowly ran her fingers down his face. Something sparked underneath her touch, something that wasn't magic at all. His lips parted when her fingers brushed against them, and the barest of sighs slipped through. She almost drew her hand back and away, frightened at the electricity jolting its way up her arm.

He tilted his head back and she let her fingers brush down his throat. His pulse sped under her fingertips. Lifting her hand again, trying to ignore its shaking, she touched his ear, dragging her fingers horizontally across his face to the other side. She felt her magic sweep over him, pause, hesitate, then cover him, shield him.

He looked the same to her. She recalled Veceslav's word: enemies. It would shield him from his enemies. Not his friends.

I guess that means we're not enemies after all, she thought grimly.

They were maybe something close to friends, skirting past that line into something else Nadya was afraid to consider.

She wasn't supposed to like him. He wasn't supposed to be

alive. She was helpless, all the control she had cultivated during her life crumbling because of this strange, wild heretic boy she should have killed. If she had done what she was supposed to none of this would be happening, her feelings wouldn't be a tangled jumble of wanting him far far away and being perpetually drawn to his side.

She wouldn't be so tempted by the idea of freedom he seemed to be holding before her. Letting him any closer was a mistake she couldn't afford to make.

His eyes had closed and he opened them, locking on hers. "That feels strange," he said, his voice thick. She pulled her hand away, shaking it as if that would help.

She reminded herself of the burned villages, of the desecration the Tranavians had caused to Kalyazin. That he was part of the cycle, had a hand in the horrors done to her people. She reminded herself Tranavians had destroyed her home, killed Kostya, and that she deserved revenge.

She reminded herself to blink.

"You'll have a false name, too?" she asked, trying to distract herself.

"Jakob."

"Well, that's certainly easier on the tongue than Malachiasz," she said.

He laughed softly. His laugh was so unexpected and came so rarely that it jolted her again. She felt her ears burning as a blush rose on her cheeks. She ducked her head to avoid looking at him.

She heard him flipping through his spell book and tearing out the page with the proper spell. His hand was warm underneath her chin as he brought her face up. He pressed the spell into her palm, using his bleeding thumb to smear blood against her forehead, down her nose, and against her lower lip and chin.

She kept her eyes on his face, watching as a frown pulled his eyebrows down. He tilted her head back farther, drawing a line of blood down her throat.

At first, it was as though nothing happened. Then the blackened, poisonous touch of his magic washed over her. She let out a sharp breath, one hand reaching to grasp his forearm.

"It's all right," he murmured, steadying her as her knees buckled.

"No, this is *wrong*." It hurt to speak. Hot waves of fire roiled over her with each breath. She felt tears burning at her eyes and wrenched them shut.

Then it stopped. The absence of pain was just as uncomfortable. She opened her eyes, realized slowly that her head rested against Malachiasz's chest, and forced herself to pull away without making it obvious she was panicking.

He bent down, dampening a rag in the snow, then straightened, holding it in his fist to warm it. He reached for her. She took a quick step back.

A thread of tension stretched taut between them. They wore masks created by the other on their skin—magic binding them together.

He didn't speak, but the expression on his face was a question. He reached his hand toward her again and this time she let him wash the blood off her face, his touch gentle.

"I should have warned you. You were probably rejecting my magic inherently because of what you are."

"It's over now, don't worry about it," she said. "Did it work? You don't look any different to me, how do I look?"

He had stepped back to wipe the blood off his hands and his gaze flicked up at her. "You look lovely," he murmured, and she wished she could put an adequate name to what she heard in his voice.

"Oh?"

He nodded, his expression perfectly blank. "Not quite so lovely as a Kalyazi peasant girl who spent her whole life locked in a monastery, though."

Nadya blinked at him, taking a step back. She turned and abruptly fled the clearing.

17

SEREFIN

MELESKI

Svoyatova Violetta Zhestakova: *When she was thirteen, Svoyatova Violetta Zhestakova led a Kalyazi army in the Battle of Relics in 1510. A cleric of Marzenya, Violetta was a ruthless killer who ultimately fell in battle, killed by the blood mage Apolonia Sroka.*

—Vasiliev's Book of Saints

The gardens were dark—no guards, no one at all. Just three Tranavian teenagers with jars of *krój* and time to waste. They were still waiting to hear back from the boy Kacper had sent to poke around the Salt Mines. Serefin had gotten to all the necessary tasks that came with returning home: collecting a selection of new spell books, speaking with the *slavhki* who requested an audience, and other duller affairs.

He still hadn't visited his mother. He wasn't putting it *off* per se, he just hadn't found the right time for it. The

second he went to visit her, everything would come spilling out of him. He wasn't so sure she could keep things from his father.

So, instead of investigating the plots swirling thickly through the air of Grazyk just as heavy as its magic smog, Serefin did the one thing he knew best: consumed a fantastic amount of alcohol.

It was fitting assassins chose to strike that same evening.

Ostyia was the one to catch them, shooting to her feet and drawing the thin *szitelki* at her waist in one rapid motion.

The world spun dangerously as Serefin stood, but he shook it away, forcing himself sober. Well, as sober as possible.

"How on earth did they make it past the walls?" Kacper asked in disbelief.

Ostyia and Kacper both moved instinctively closer to Serefin, shielding him. A spinning dagger cut through the air toward him.

He saw the blade coming and ducked out of the way, his fingers already paging through his spell book without his mind following. He cut open his forearm on the razor in his sleeve and it bled profusely.

"Kalyazi?" he muttered under his breath to Ostyia. A second assassin appeared down the garden path. The third shot out from the bushes, knocking Kacper down.

"Can't tell." She seemed torn about which assassin to go after, not wanting to leave Serefin on his own while Kacper grappled with the third.

Serefin knocked her toward the one down the path as he crumpled a spell book page. His magic ignited and he let the assassin in front of him draw close before he lifted a hand and blew on his bloody fist. The paper crumbled into dust in his palm and shot in an acrid spray into the masked face of the assassin. When the dust hit, it burst into flames.

Serefin lashed out with a booted foot that connected with the assassin's middle. The man went down in a heap. He turned to find Kacper had cut the throat of one assassin. Ostyia—shorter than her attacker by almost half—had cast a spell that made the last assassin falter. As he tried to regain his footing she threw herself at him, catching her legs around his waist and driving both blades into his neck. She gracefully leapt off as the man fell.

Well, that was short work. Serefin wasn't sure who would send such incompetent assassins after him, but apparently someone had too much faith in their purchase.

Ostyia turned. Her single eye widened.

"Serefin!"

Something hit the back of his head. Pain exploded through him and he stumbled forward. He felt the stone path scrape his knees open. He managed to roll into a crouch. His vision swam and he could barely make out another set of three figures in the darkness.

Of course there would be more. He tried to stand but his struggling vision and spinning head made it impossible.

Kacper moved toward the new group, but one of them was already at Serefin's side, a flash of steel at their hands. Suddenly they were gone and a figure Serefin couldn't identify was standing in front of him.

The new figure's face ducked before his.

"Get him up, I don't think he can see." He knew the voice instantly.

"Lady Ruminska, I don't think—" Ostyia called, but Żaneta was already turning to face the remaining pair of assassins.

Blood ran down her arms as she tore two pages from her spell book. She wiped blood over them both while dodging out of the way of the assassins' blades. One by one she let the pages flutter to the ground.

Iron spikes shot out from where the papers landed, skewering the assassins simultaneously and pinning them together. Both went down in bloody heaps. The pain in Serefin's head amplified and he pitched forward, barely catching himself before face-planting into the stones. He lasted there for a few tense seconds—he could vaguely hear someone's voice but he couldn't tell if it was Żaneta or Ostyia—before everything shuttered black around him.

This was worse than any hangover Serefin had ever experienced. And he always kept track of his hangovers and how badly they hurt. He had a list.

His head pounded. His mouth tasted like blood and was dry as a desert. When he opened his eyes, a vivid panic shot through him. He thought he had gone completely blind. Until he realized it was still dark outside.

Something rustled in the room and a candle lit. Żaneta set the candle by the bedside table before sitting down on the side of his bed.

"This is scandalous, Żaneta," he mumbled, resting his head back against the pillows.

"Definitely more scandalous than the prince being attacked in his own palace gardens," she agreed.

He lifted his hands and pressed his fingers against his throbbing temples. "Are you sure they didn't kill me?" he asked.

"Mostly."

Her auburn curls hung loose around her shoulders. He found himself tracking the freckles that dusted her warm brown skin.

"Did any of them survive?" he asked.

She nodded. "The one with the burned face. Your handiwork?"

He tried to nod but it hurt too badly. "Yes."

"A good spell," she said. "We have him in the dungeons."

"Does my father know what happened?" Serefin didn't want to know the answer, but he had to ask.

"He does."

Serefin groaned.

"I'm glad I wasn't there when he was told," she said.

Serefin needed to think, but the pounding in his head was making it difficult. There was no point in going back to sleep. He wasn't sure he would be able to, anyway. He needed answers. He wanted to demand an explanation from his father; surely this was his doing. Yet his rational side knew this couldn't be his father's doing. Because it had failed. Gloriously.

"My father is going to blame the Kalyazi," he mused.

"Was it not them?" Żaneta asked, standing up.

"I . . . don't know." The Kalyazi did not train incompetent assassins; his eye was a tribute to that. This could have been the work of the Crimson Vulture. Perhaps his father *was* behind the attack and she had shifted the pieces so incompetent assassins were sent instead to give him a better chance. He hated living with a black cloud of doom hovering over his steps, certain that his future was bleak but not having any clear answers.

"Would you fetch Kacper, please?" he asked.

Żaneta frowned. She hesitated, as if she wanted to argue, but then left. Serefin wondered what she was holding back.

Serefin let those thoughts fade when Kacper entered, a puzzled look on his face.

"Żaneta seemed upset," Kacper said.

"I said nothing to upset her."

Kacper let it drop. "A Vulture was sent to interrogate the
remaining assassin. I assume we'll be hearing of that by noon.
In the meantime . . ."

Serefin worked himself to a sitting position. He stared blankly
into the darkness at the opposite end of the room.

What information did he have? An attack on his life, a plan
to find a queen for Tranavia, and questions with no answers.
Why was his father sending thousands upon thousands of prisoners to the Salt Mines? Why was his father working so closely
with the Vultures? To what end? Why now?

What is happening?

"Have you seen the current list of families participating in
the *Rawalyk*?" Kacper asked.

"No, why?"

"It seems to be fluctuating," he said. "Names of girls keep
appearing then disappearing suddenly."

"What do you mean?"

Kacper shook his head. "I'm not sure. I want to look into it,
see if the girls are just getting nervous or if it's something else."

Serefin let out a breathless laugh. "We are so paranoid."
There was a beat of silence. "I need to talk to my mother," he
murmured.

He wasn't sure she could help him, not with anything. But
it was all he could do at this point. He was trapped in a cage
of gold and iron with no door to escape from and had been
given a dagger when he needed a saw to cut a hole in his prison.

"I can have a servant sent to her quarters," Kacper said. "Is
that all?"

Serefin nodded absently, before frowning and squinting up at Kacper. "Are you all right?"

Kacper blinked in surprise. "Me? Of course, why? They weren't trying to kill *me*."

Serefin eyed the other boy, taking in his dark hair and skin, the scar that cut across one of his eyebrows, and his sharp, brown eyes. He hadn't grown up fighting off assassination attempts like Serefin and Ostyia. By all rights, Kacper should have been just another soldier in the king's army; he was of low birth. His exceptional talent with blood magic and his sharp skills for espionage meant he had been shuffled around in the army until he was assigned to Serefin's company. Their friendship had been struck a month into Serefin's first tour of the front when he was sixteen. Kacper had gotten into a spitting fight with Ostyia. She broke his arm, he fractured three of her ribs, and it had taken Serefin knocking them both unconscious to get them apart.

Serefin still didn't know what the fight was about. Neither would tell him. It had taken another week for Serefin to promote Kacper to his personal service after Kacper had nearly lost his other arm on Serefin's behalf.

"I don't need formality, Kacper. Not from you. I was just making sure you weren't shaken up or anything. Assassins are new for you."

Kacper grinned, flopping down next to him on the bed. "To be honest, I was worried it was going to be boring here. The assassins keep it interesting."

"You thought Grazyk would be *boring*?" Serefin asked incredulously.

"I thought we were just coming here to have your father pick out a pretty girl for you to marry and then it would be back to the front."

Serefin groaned. "Don't talk about marriage."

"You sound like Ostyia."

"Ostyia would be in a far better position if she were in my shoes. She dumped the last suitor her father sent her way in a fountain. I think before this is over she'll have romanced at least half the girls here."

"At least?"

Serefin considered that. "Yes, you're right, perhaps more than half." Ostyia was very charming. When she wanted to be.

When Serefin finally rose to meet with his mother, his head had incrementally slowed its pounding. Every step he took was a mild agony, but he pressed through it. He needed to show Grazyk their High Prince would not be slowed by anything, not the prospect of marriage nor assassins in the night.

Ostyia knocked on the door to Klarysa's quarters before Serefin. The door was opened by his mother's handmaiden, Lena. She nodded crisply at Serefin and gestured for him to enter. Ostyia elected to wait outside.

"I have been in this blasted city for weeks now and my only son has just finally deigned to grace me with his presence." The graceful lilt of his mother's voice came floating down the hall. Lena shot Serefin a sympathetic look. Serefin had always found his mother to be a bit baffling. Both of his parents were larger than life, greater than reality. He had seen so little of them growing up.

His childhood had been spent with tutors and servants. His parents were figureheads who would move in and out of his life with little permanence. They sometimes appeared in the evening at mealtimes only to disappear once again at the start of a new day. Serefin had Ostyia—whose family had always lived in the palace—as well as a cousin on his mother's side, but that was all. The cousin had left when they were still very young, off to the country for his health. His aunt and uncle were still seen around the palace, Serefin knew that much, but he had never seen his cousin again, and had eventually stopped inquiring.

"I've been otherwise occupied," he said, pitching his voice to reach his mother and following along after it.

The sitting room was lavish, as would befit a queen. His mother sat on a velvet-embroidered chaise, a cloth mask covering her nose and mouth. Her brown curls were swept up elaborately, and her spell book rested on a nearby end table.

She stood, setting her book facedown on the arm of the chaise. "Serefin," she said, tugging her mask down.

She drew him into her arms, and he had to stoop so she could kiss his cheek.

"Mother, I'm glad to see you well," he said as she sat back down. She motioned to the chair opposite the chaise and he sat.

"Well enough for your father to drag me back to this dirty city." She paused, then conceded: "For a good cause."

"Is it a good cause?"

She raised an eyebrow. "Straight to the point?"

"I don't really have time for much else." He crossed his legs, resting an ankle on the opposite knee. "I've spoken to Pelageya *and* the Crimson Vulture, and I have to admit I felt safer at the front."

"And here I was going to ask if you were all right. I heard you were attacked last night?"

"I'm here, so I assume that means I'm fine."

Klarysa smiled wryly. "I do find it interesting that you went to Pelageya before me," she said, lifting an eyebrow. He knew that tone. She wasn't disappointed in him, rather she was telling him he had made a foolish decision but she wasn't about to say it aloud.

"Circumstances called for it," he replied.

"Yes," she said. "I'm sure they did."

I don't have time for this, he thought. But he did. That was the thing. He was trapped here—doing nothing, knowing nothing. He could feel the jaws of the invisible beast closing over him but he was powerless to stop it.

"Do you think I can turn the court to my side?" he asked.

She blinked, straightening in her chair. "Serefin?"

"Oh, I'm sure he knows anyway," Serefin said, waving a hand. "I just need to know how many steps ahead of me he is."

"Your father—" She put emphasis on the word *father* as if it meant something to Serefin. Maybe once it had. Years ago when he thought he might win his father's love. Not anymore.

"I found a *cleric* in Kalyazin. No one else seems to find that important. Doesn't it strike you as a bit strange? They sent the Vultures after her, but she escaped."

"The Vultures?"

"She escaped the Vultures. Why am I the only one troubled by this? What is Father planning that has made this a nonissue?"

Klarysa's eyes narrowed and Serefin realized he had hit upon something she had not been expecting. "What . . . did you speak to Pelageya about?" she asked.

He scoffed. "She told me a lot of nonsense that sounded like prophecy."

"Listen to her, Serefin. I know you don't want to. I know you think her mad. But listen to her. She could be the only thing that saves you."

"Saves me? Yes, I'm clearly trying not to die here, but I don't think the witch is going to help."

"Not from your father, from the Vultures. From the gods. From everything."

"Mother?"

"Pelageya knows what she speaks of." His mother was speaking quickly, her voice low. She knew whatever they said would return to the king. She cast a suspicious glance toward where the wall met the ceiling, the likeliest of locations for eavesdropping spells. "I can't help you, Serefin, you know that."

Serefin felt cold. "What has he done?"

Klarysa shook her head. There was fear in her eyes.

She can't tell me, he realized. *If she tells me, he'll kill her, too.* What did she know that he had yet to figure out?

"Give me something," he pleaded.

"Your father has always been a monster," she said. "But at least he had his own mind, his decisions were his own." She shook her head. "I fear he too has been taken by the Vultures."

She fell silent, but Serefin didn't need any more to put the pieces together. The Vultures had gone from their own agendas to whispering in the king's ear. The whispering had gone from suggestions to puppet strings.

It was altogether likely there was discord amongst the Vultures as well. That the Crimson Vulture was working apart from her own king, the Black Vulture. But who was holding the strings?

Serefin still had no answers.

18

NADEZHDA

LAPTEVA

Vaclav is rarely seen, rarely heard, and rarely worshiped. Dark forests and darker monsters heed his calls. His lands are vast and ancient and deadly and he is not kind. Truth is never kind.

—Codex of the Divine, 23:86

Nadya was the most surprised of everyone when her plan to get them across the border worked.

"Where's your company, son?" The Tranavian who confronted them looked older than Malachiasz, and thought by that principle he outranked him.

Malachiasz drew himself straight, his posture betraying the air of someone who was used to having authority. He flicked his hair away from where it was covering the pins on his jacket. Now Nadya was doubly certain she didn't want to know what they meant.

"Lost most of them to mercenaries hiding in the mountains," he said. "Lost the rest somewhere in between."

The soldier frowned at Malachiasz, but when he spoke again the condescension was gone. "Who are they, then?"

Malachiasz glanced back at the group. "The Akolans are fleeing Kalyazin, a wise decision. The girl is . . ." He faltered, convincingly. "Well, you understand." He winked at the soldier.

It took everything Nadya had to keep her expression schooled.

"I'll need you to come with me," the soldier said, giving Malachiasz a hard once-over. He pulled a second soldier over and ordered her to make sure the rest of them didn't go anywhere.

Nadya felt her heart speed up as Malachiasz followed the Tranavian into a shoddily constructed cabin. She glanced at Parijahan, whose expression was drawn and wary. The minutes Malachiasz was gone stretched on seemingly endlessly, but the soldier guarding them just looked bored.

Eventually Malachiasz stepped out of the cabin, his face pale. The other soldier followed behind him and waved a hand to the girl guarding them.

"Let them through," he said.

She looked like she was going to question him, but Malachiasz shot her a thin smile and tapped one of the pins on his jacket. He outranked her—he probably outranked everyone here—and she fell silent.

Malachiasz grabbed Nadya's wrist and pulled her away from the camp. She let him, fully aware it was all part of the show but also that he was clearly enjoying it.

Neither of them had addressed what had passed between them in the clearing. She didn't think they ever would. She just tried to ignore the stutter in her heart that was intrinsically tied to his hand around her wrist.

That initial danger behind them, now they had to make it to Grazyk before the real test began.

Tranavia was not what Nadya expected. There were lakes and rivers everywhere. They had to ferry across some, the boats run by haggard, elderly men and women, too old to fight at the front. But Tranavia was beautiful. The water clear and bright, studding the land like gemstones, untainted by the scourge of war that burned across the Kalyazi countryside.

On one of the many Tranavian boats they became acquainted with during the trip, Nadya leaned against the railing, gazing down into the water. Rashid was perched precariously at her side when Malachiasz came up next to her.

"It's lovely, isn't it?" he said.

"It is."

He was quiet, staring out across the water. There was a fondness in his gaze she had never seen before.

"It hasn't been particularly kind to me," he said. "But Tranavia is home. It's wild and vibrant and tenacious. Its people are bullheaded and innovative." He glanced at her. "I'll save it from destruction."

It was something they had in common—though she felt a pang of guilt because her actions would lead to Tranavia's fall. Her gods wanted it punished for its heresy and she would see that done. Even if it put her at odds with this strange, beautiful boy. But she could see he cared, deeply, the same way she cared for Kalyazin, and she could respect that.

He wordlessly unhooked the spell book from his hip and handed it to her.

She hesitantly took the thick, leather-bound book from him. She would have held it between two fingers, but it was too heavy for that. "What are you doing?"

"I can't be seen with that, and you need to appear like a competent blood mage."

She wanted to drop it in the water. She rested it against the railing, away from her body. He rolled his eyes, unhooked the belts that kept the book at his hip, and handed her those as well.

"I'll have to tear through it without using the spells," she said. While ruining a blood mage's spell book had always been a private goal for her, she would have preferred it not be *his*.

He tapped his temple. "They're my spells. I can rewrite them anytime."

"Are you going to come into the palace with us?" Nadya asked.

Here was what they had not addressed: just what Malachiasz's role would be once they reached the capital. He had dodged the question before in a way that made Nadya suspect he would simply disappear on their arrival.

"I will remain nearby," he said. He frowned and it furrowed the tattoos at his forehead. "It would not be uncommon for a *slavhka* to travel with a blood mage acting as their guard. It won't necessarily give me optimal reach of the palace, but I can certainly make do."

Nadya pursed her lips. That was a sound part for him to play and she found she had no arguments. "You won't get yourself caught by the Vultures?" She was still worried about what he had said about them not being able to act against their king's orders, even if the magic on him had eased.

"Worrying about him is a rather pointless endeavor, I've found," Rashid noted, nudging her with his elbow.

"You think I'm worried about him?" Nadya said flippantly.

Rashid shot her a disbelieving look. When she glanced at Malachiasz out of the corner of her eye, he was casually watching the water.

"I'm going to go see if Parijahan needs anything," Rashid said. "We should be on the other side of this lake within the hour."

Nadya wanted to pull him back, tell him not to leave her alone with Malachiasz, but Rashid was already gone.

"I've never had someone worry about me before," Malachiasz mused.

Nadya contemplated pitching herself into the water.

"Well, don't look to me to be the first," she replied.

He smiled. The breeze caught his hair, sending it out like tendrils of black smoke through the air.

"Our plan is as sound as it can be under the circumstances," he said. "*Rawalyki* are underhanded affairs. They draw the brightest and best into the heart of the city and after a mess of dramatics and sometimes blood a new consort is chosen. It's one of the only times the palace is accessible to nobility who are not in the upper reaches of the social spheres."

He was right, there was nothing further they could do at this point. Malachiasz had drilled her on court niceties until she felt like her brain was melting. Parijahan had taught her all she knew from growing up in a Travasha.

"Nobles are nobles," she had said, waving a hand. "Regardless of where they come from. The pettiness of court transcends all cultural boundaries."

Nadya was, for all intents and purposes, *ready*. She wished she felt it.

"You have to trust me," Malachiasz said. "Once we get inside, the moment where we can get close enough to strike *will* present itself. We've come this far, getting into Tranavia was half the battle."

She didn't want to trust him. Especially not after seeing him for what he was.

"Is . . . *that* something you can control?" she asked, knowing he would know what she was talking about. "It's not sparked by a certain time or incident?"

"I'm not a *wolivnak,* Nadya."

Wolf changers whose transformations were sparked by the cycles of the moon. She rolled her eyes. "Our word for those is *zhir'oten.*"

"Well, I'm not one of those," he said primly.

"Oddly, I get the distinct impression you're worse."

He laughed. "You're probably right."

"There's more to that form than what I saw, isn't there?" She wasn't sure how willing he would be to talk about this. His relaxed smiles did not mean he would answer her questions.

He nodded. "Not for every Vulture, but for me, yes."

"It felt horribly wrong," she said, feeling a shudder ripple through her.

He shrugged. "It really depends on what you mean by wrong."

"Monstrous."

"I *am* a monster," he said gently.

Her brow furrowed and she leaned her elbows on the railing, putting her chin in her hands.

Malachiasz angled his head back against the wind. "Tranavians value power and status above everything. It doesn't matter how that power is reached or what measures are taken to gain it. Monsters are seen as an ideal, because monsters are powerful, *more* than human." He held his hand out and his nails lengthened to iron claws. "Your people strive for divinity?"

She nodded, though it was an oversimplification.

"That is not a great deal different. It's striving for something that would be more than human."

"But not at the expense of killing people."

"Kalyazi kill Tranavians every day and do not see it as a

problem. Kalyazi were killing Tranavians long before this war began, and it was not an issue then either."

She whirled on him, anger flashing hot. His people were heretics and murderers and he would not twist her words on her. "It's not the same as *torturing* prisoners of war," she snapped.

He took her chin in his hand, his nails cold and sharp against her skin. He could press a little harder and rip open the flesh of her jaw. Her heart sped up, but she couldn't tell if it was from fear or something else.

"Perhaps not," he whispered, leaning down closer. She felt his warm breath feather her face. "Perhaps we should have this conversation again when you have tasted real power."

His hair brushed against her cheek, his mouth hovering so near to hers that she could feel her lips trembling. Her knees felt weak. His gaze lingered on her lips. The corner of his mouth twitched up and he leaned back.

He nodded over her shoulder, turning her head so she could see the city glittering behind them. "Welcome to Grazyk, *Józefina*," he said. "Now the real trial begins."

Nadya couldn't stop her hands from shaking.

Her prayer beads were safely in her pocket, so she clutched at the necklace Kostya had given her. What would Kostya say if he saw her now? Caught up in a plan forged by a group of potentially mad teenagers, a mask on her face made of leather painted white and stamped with impressions of thorns.

He would tease her, scold her, tell her she was getting in over her head. She missed him.

Marzenya had warned her the gods' presence while in Tranavia would be limited, but Nadya felt their absence like a physical wound in her side. As though the gods were ripped from her as soon as she stepped over the border. When she stretched she could brush against Marzenya's touch, but it took effort. It would be difficult to cast magic. She felt utterly and completely alone.

The entire city was shrouded in a stifling fog. Nadya could *feel* the blood magic that had caused such an oppressive taint in the air. It was difficult to breathe. This was why she was here, though, to rip apart that veil, to draw the gods back into this heathen country.

Once they entered the city, Nadya was overwhelmed by the sounds and crowds. She stuck close to Parijahan, grabbing her arm at times to keep from being separated. Unlike the villages they had passed through where the people looked worn and half-starved, everyone in the city dressed in rich, colorful clothes. Most wore masks over their faces—fanciful adornments that hid their identities. They were all nothing more than faceless enemies.

The closer they got to the palace grounds, the more agitated Malachiasz became. Nadya could feel her own nervousness feeding off his. She grabbed his wrist when they were near the palace gates, pressing down hard at the base.

She lifted her eyebrows when he shot her a questioning look. The magic they had cast on each other was all that would keep them safe; they had to trust in it. Nadya had anchored her safety to him and he would have to do the same for her. It was clear he didn't want to return to a place so near the Vultures, but he had to trust her spell would not falter. Finally he let out a long breath, the tension bleeding out of him. She let go of his wrist.

The guards at the palace gates went over Nadya's paperwork so meticulously that she convinced herself they were going to be arrested on the spot. A bead of sweat dripped down her spine. Rashid didn't appear concerned, but Nadya had learned the boy had a knack for calm in a similar way Parijahan did. She wondered what it was that allowed the Akolans to stare headlong into potential disaster without flinching.

After ten agonizing minutes, the guards waved her through the gates. Nadya wanted to collapse against Parijahan in relief, but she merely took the papers back from the guard and stepped past them.

Nadya felt Malachiasz tense when a massive black cathedral at the side of the grounds came into view. Its spires could be seen in the distance even past the overbearing palace with its glittering towers. She nudged the back of his hand, forcing his gaze away. He shot her a strained smile.

An attendant bustled out from the main palace doors, taking the steps with a grace that Nadya envied. Suddenly she was being swept through the doors and any chance she had to back out was gone.

"Your timing is impeccable, though we weren't expecting anyone from your part of Tranavia to participate." The attendant hadn't stopped talking since they stepped into the palace.

Nadya kept up with the chattering man, only shooting the occasional panicked glance Parijahan's way. A masked servant had taken Rashid to the servants' wing, and Malachiasz had disappeared when Nadya wasn't looking—he had warned her that he would probably be shunted off to the guard's barracks so she wasn't worried yet.

"Łaszczów is admittedly a bit out of touch with the rest of Tranavia," Nadya agreed. "But this opportunity was not to be missed."

The attendant smiled. "Quite right." The man wore a mask that looked like birds' wings on either side of his face.

Nadya had only been wearing her mask for a day and already she was fantasizing about ripping it off. It was hot and uncomfortable and she didn't want it on anymore.

The exterior of the palace was striking, with golden columns lining the entrance. Aged oak doors opened into the massive foyer. Marble floors were checkered in pale violets and blacks. Paintings of women in flowing gowns and soldiers in crisp military uniforms stretched across the vaulted ceilings.

As they wound their way through the palace, the paintings became darker in tone. The hallways closed in as the colors grew increasingly oppressive. Vultures—the birds and their human counterparts—their claws, and blood magic symbols scrawled by an artist whose frenzy could be felt.

Altogether opulent and terrifying, it was like a nightmare had bled its way into a nobleman's dreams.

"Feeling left out happens when someone goes *drinking* without you, Ostyia, not when someone visits a mad—oh." The droll voice that echoed down the hallway stopped.

A spike of adrenaline raced through Nadya. This was the defining moment, where this plan could succeed or burn to the ground and leave them all at the end of a noose.

The High Prince cut a completely different figure than he had that day at the monastery. His brown hair was shorter now, swept carefully back from his forehead. In this light, his pale eyes were less eerie, though the scar that cut across his face was still intimidating. But in the gilded halls of his palace he looked more like a prince than a monster.

He was trailed by the short one-eyed girl. She had been in the middle of pulling on his sleeve and cajoling him when he'd stopped abruptly.

"Who is this?" he asked the attendant. His lips quirked into a crooked smile.

Her heart was pounding so hard it felt like her entire body was shaking, but she forced herself to move past the attendant anyway.

"Józefina Zelenska, Your Highness," she said, executing a flourished bow that not even Malachiasz could complain about.

"Zelenska," the prince mused. "Do I know the name?" he asked the short girl.

She shook her head slowly, appearing puzzled.

"I'm not surprised. Łaszczów is a bit out of the way for royalty," Nadya said.

Something flickered over his expression and he took a step closer. His eyes narrowed on her face and she felt her pulse speed.

"Remove the mask," he said, then, as an afterthought, "please."

He's going to see straight through Malachiasz's spell, she thought, horrified, as she undid the catch and slowly pulled the mask away from her face.

With each beat of her heart she felt closer to death. He reached out and took her chin in his hand, lifting her face up to his.

"I've been to Łaszczów," he said softly. "I feel like I would remember such a face."

She resisted the urge to swallow. "I spend the better part of the year traveling," she said. "I was in Akola for the past few years, perhaps your visit overlapped?"

He glanced at Parijahan. She must have been confirmation enough that Nadya was telling the truth, because he dropped his hand, smiling in a way that was almost apologetic.

"Perhaps. A shame our paths did not cross. Good luck to you, Józefina."

She hastily put the mask back on. "Thank you, Your Highness."

It wasn't until Nadya had been led to her chambers that she felt like she could breathe again.

She tore the mask off her face and tossed it onto a chair. Taking in the room, she was met with the same level of splendor and intimidation she witnessed while walking through the palace halls. There was a lush chaise and a set of chairs in the sitting room, along with an end table and mahogany desk to one side. There were bookshelves that looked like they had never been touched except when cleaned. Oil paintings hung on the walls—portraits of Tranavian *slavhki*, probably.

Nadya looked up at the ceiling, and the sight chilled her bones. A massive mural of birds stretched over the entire surface—Vultures shown most prominently—surrounded by dripping, acidic flowers. She felt a stab of disdain that she knew came from the gods. Distant but still present.

Parijahan scanned the room, quickly pulling open the desk drawer, removing a pad of paper and pencil and scrawling a quick message.

This place is probably crawling with spells, she wrote.

Nadya nodded, reaching up for her prayer beads before remembering they were in her pocket. She had spent the better part of the journey carving the gods' symbols into thin circles of wood, which she attached to the cover of Malachiasz's spell book. It would work, in a roundabout way, and appear as though she was casting like a blood mage.

Can you clear the spells from these rooms, please? She sent the prayer to Veceslav, but it was Marzenya who answered.

"Can you feel it?"

Nadya paused. She leaned back against a chair and closed

her eyes, letting herself feel the invisible wall separating gods from men. She felt it the moment they had stepped into Trana-via, the weight of the veil pressing down against her, choking off her only access to the divine.

She was strong enough to fight through it, but this was man-made magic created to fight against the gods. This was greater than anything Nadya expected and would make her task all the more impossible.

I feel it.

"You came here to kill a king; I wonder if you won't uncover something even more terrible."

Nadya shivered. *Can't you give some warning as to what that might be?*

"I can barely see through the fog this country has cast, child. You have plunged yourself into the dark where the monsters dwell; now you must fight them off before you're consumed."

Holy speech whispered through her head and she moved to disassemble the spells woven through the walls. She couldn't take them apart completely—someone would notice, precautions in place—she was just making them fuzzy, bleeding them out. She dulled them so any information imparted back to the mages who set them would appear mundane.

Nadya liked taking spells apart, casting magic that wasn't flashy or dangerous. She had been trained for destructive magic—for spells that would turn the tide of battle—but she liked doing smaller things most.

She looked up at the ceiling. "I didn't realize how much they idolized the Vultures." *I didn't realize just what Malachiasz had run from.*

Parijahan sat down on the chaise, letting her calm spread into the room and wear down Nadya's frazzled nerves. The

Akolan girl had a knack for commanding attention then slipping away without notice. She was so closed and careful, from the way she bound her hair back into a tight braid to how she kept her sleeves always down to her wrists, her skirt hems brushing the ground. Nadya wondered if she had always been this way, or if this was a product of losing her sister and turning her back on her home.

Nadya placed Malachiasz's spell book on the table and sat down next to Parijahan.

"What happens now?"

Parijahan tugged off the leather strip tying her braid and ran her hands through her hair. "We've snuck in right as the gates were closing. Tomorrow the entire affair begins."

"I don't like that we've split from the boys."

Parijahan nudged her shoulder. "I think we can handle ourselves."

"Clearly." She grew quiet, still eyeing the painting on the ceiling. "Do you regret leaving your home? The time you spent in Kalyazin couldn't have been comfortable."

"Not regret, no. Having Rashid with me helped. I've known him my whole life. And we crashed into Malachiasz about six months ago after getting into trouble with some off-duty Kalyazi soldiers. Rashid ended up unconscious in a ditch; Malachiasz nearly had his hair shorn off and spent the entire next day after we got to safety panicking over the close call."

Nadya giggled. Parijahan gently turned her so she could undo her braid as well from where it was spiraled around the back of her head like a crown. Nadya was quiet as Parijahan combed her hair out with her fingers.

"Do you think we can actually do this?"

Parijahan's hands stilled. Nadya felt her fingers curl over her shoulders.

"We have to."

Her tone made Nadya's spine straighten. *She has some other stake in this I haven't heard yet,* Nadya thought. Something other than revenge.

"Then we will."

19

NADEZHDA

LAPTEVA

Myesta, the goddess of the moon, is deceit and deception and an ever-changing illusion of light in an eternal darkness.

—Codex of the Divine, 15:29

Nadya clutched Malachiasz's spell book against her chest and regretted every single decision she had ever made that had led her to this point.

"Relax," Parijahan said. "They're only dresses."

Nadya let out a strained whimper in response. Any *one* of the dresses in front of her was worth more than what would feed the monastery for five years. Rich fabrics in vibrant colors, pearls and gemstone beadwork spilled over the bodices and onto the skirts. Vague impressions of flowers were prominent amidst the glittering finery. The headdresses made Nadya's neck ache just looking at them. Some were tall, some looked like floral wreaths—though they

were made from fabric and lace and beads—some vaguely resembled the *kokoshniks* Nadya knew nobles wore in Kalyazin.

"Where did these come from?" Nadya asked.

"Officially? You have a wealthy Akolan patron."

Nadya glanced at Parijahan, who grinned at her.

"I guess unofficially that is also the case."

They eventually landed on a dress the color of midnight, close to black but flashing deep blue in the light. It was like slipping darkness over Nadya's skin, with just enough light to keep her from being consumed. Next she chose an ornate headdress that spilled strings of black pearls. Nadya fastened on a slim mask that only covered a strip of her face.

Parijahan stepped back with a nod.

Nadya reached for a delicate belt for her spell book before changing her mind and taking Malachiasz's instead. Instead of looking out of place, the worn leather seemed to fit over the rich dress.

She looked like a blood mage. She swallowed hard, hands fumbling for Kostya's necklace. She tucked it down in the bodice of the dress, out of sight but still close, still comforting. The last piece she had of home.

"Try to remain relatively inconspicuous," Parijahan said. "You don't need attention drawn to yourself yet, it'll just make all the other contestants try to take you out faster. We need to figure out how the king keeps himself guarded."

"Once we have that?"

"I've already heard more than one *slavhka* comment on the king's weakness with blood magic."

"An easy mark," Nadya said softly.

"It's the prince you have to worry about," she continued. "He surrounds himself with those lieutenants of his—both blood mages—and from what I've gathered, the prince is the opposite of his father in nearly every way."

Nadya couldn't worry about the prince yet. The king was the one she had come to topple.

"However," Parijahan said thoughtfully, "if you get close to the prince, that will get you a seat near the king. Then you'll have your opening."

"So, don't draw attention to myself, but also get the prince's attention?"

"Basically. You can do this, Nadya," Parijahan said softly.

She could. She had to. Kalyazin would win the war; the gods would reclaim their hold on the world. This was what she had spent her life preparing for.

It took Nadya exactly thirteen minutes to make a mistake big enough to land her in a terrifically uncomfortable situation. She was shuffled into a salon with the other participants and—in most cases—their chaperones. She knew what this was; a game of subtleties, Malachiasz had said. The first test.

This was where alliances would be forged and rivalry lines drawn. It was also where a number of the contestants would get their first true look at the High Prince. If Nadya messed up here she could lose the entire game before it even began.

The only thing Nadya initially noticed about the *slavhka* who flitted past her was that her large violet eyes were strangely off-putting. It took Nadya's brain a handful of seconds to translate the comment the girl made to her companion while still in earshot. It took her another second to realize it was a slight about Nadya's appearance. Her nose was crooked and her hair limp.

She can't even see my hair, Nadya thought, irritated and

bewildered. And she'd seen herself in a mirror, Malachiasz had done a perfectly fine job with her nose.

"*Porodiec ze błowisz?*" she called pleasantly. "I thought those with money could pay to learn how to properly associate with other people."

The girl froze. Chatter in half of the room ceased immediately. The girl turned slowly on her heels to face Nadya.

I should've let the slight pass.

She lifted her eyebrows as the girl stalked over to her and smiled. If she was going to get through this in one piece, she needed to act like this was something that happened to her all the time. Snide comments were a normal thing for her and so she would retaliate in kind.

"Excuse me?"

"I think you heard what I said," Nadya replied.

"How dare you speak to me like that. Do you know who I am?"

"Am I supposed to?"

The girl snatched her spell book open, tearing out a blank page and crumpling it in her fist. She tossed it down, grinding it underneath the heel of her shoe.

"Can you back that up with power?" she asked.

Nadya had literally no idea what was happening. No one had ever explained to her what this meant. Her confusion must have shown on her face because a tall girl with luminous skin like onyx threaded with gold glided over to stand near Nadya.

"She's challenging you to a duel, dear," she said gently.

Nadya looked over at the second girl, who smiled encouragingly. She fought the urge to glance back at where Parijahan was leaning against the wall.

Mimicking the other girl, Nadya flipped through Malachiasz's spells until she found a blank page. She crumpled it and stepped on it like the younger girl had. The girl gave her a vicious smile before stalking away.

"Well, that was unexpected, and we've barely begun!"

Nadya—still dazed—turned to look at the tall girl. She wasn't wearing a headdress and her spiral curls fanned out around her head like a halo.

"My name is Żaneta," she said. "And you just had the misfortune of being the target of an incredibly ambitious competitor."

"What just happened?"

Żaneta laughed. "Sit tight, my dear. There will be attendants now scrambling to prepare the arena for a duel. Congratulations—if you survive, this will significantly improve your chances."

The doors opened then and the High Prince entered. Żaneta smiled once more at Nadya before crossing the room to meet the boy who had destroyed everything Nadya held dear.

SEREFIN

MELESKI

"Serefin!" Żaneta greeted him by name as he stepped into the parlor, thus cementing her place as the one girl among the *Rawalyk* candidates comfortable enough with the High Prince to bypass formality.

He was already tired and the ceremony had barely started. He wasn't ready to speak to any of the nobles yet so he moved to an empty side of the room. Kacper stepped away as an attendant drew his attention.

"You will never believe what has happened," Żaneta started when Kacper returned.

"The arena is being prepared for a duel," Kacper said before she could continue, sounding puzzled.

Żaneta pouted. "I was going to tell him."

"I'm sorry," Serefin said. "I thought you just said a duel has been called."

Kacper nodded.

"The *Rawalyk* started this morning," Serefin said flatly.

Kacper nodded more emphatically.

"Is this your work?" he asked Żaneta.

She lifted her eyebrows. "I cannot begin to tell you how disappointed I am that I had nothing to do with this."

Serefin collapsed back onto the chaise. "Well, that's certainly a dramatic start."

Ostyia perched on the arm of a nearby chair, earning a venomous look from a middle-aged chaperone. She winked at the chaperone's charge, which only made the woman's glare more intense. "You'll never guess who it's between."

"Point them out to me."

Kacper handed Serefin a glass of wine before he flopped onto the chaise beside him. Neither of them should be acting this casual in present company, but Serefin couldn't dredge up the effort to care. Kacper pointed to the Krywicka girl.

"*No.*" Serefin didn't even have to pretend to be scandalized.

Żaneta laughed out loud. "The other is a latecomer," she said. "Over there."

Her name came to him immediately. *Józefina.* She had removed her mask, twirling it between idle fingers as she watched the parlor. There was a sharpness in her gaze Serefin found fascinating. Her other hand rested against the spell book at her hip. She glanced over just in time to catch Serefin watching her.

Her eyes widened but she didn't avert her gaze like he expected.

He smiled and stood, ignoring Żaneta as she hissed a protest. He was supposed to be observing, not interacting, but he was already bored and he wanted to know about this duel from the source.

"Lady Zelenska," he said once he was before her.

She was slow to stand, careful in her movements. She bowed her head as she dipped into a curtsy. "Your Highness."

"Shouldn't you be preparing for your duel?" he asked. "Lady Krywicka is nowhere to be found."

Józefina's fingers tightened over the spell book. It was a hefty thing, the sign of a skilled mage. But her knuckles were white, tension revealed in her iron grip.

"I'm prepared," she replied.

She sounded like she was trying to convince herself more than she was trying to convince him.

"Tell me," he said, "what did you do to stir up such a fuss?" He slouched against the wall, forcing her to move as well. Now her back was to the room, the eyes watching them less immediately noticeable.

"You assume I am at fault?" Her tone was too flippant. She wasn't used to functioning at court at all. Every interaction was a facet of the *Rawalyk* and she was completely inexperienced.

He grinned. And he was surprised when she smiled back.

She waved a hand. "It was nothing that would interest you, Your Highness, petty comments taken too far."

Serefin leaned closer. "I don't think you understand how petty I can be."

She shifted back. His favor would put a mark on her. She seemed to realize that.

"Would you explain something to me?" she asked.

Serefin lifted an eyebrow. "What do you wish to know?"

"This is probably ridiculous, but you must understand, my father died at the front and my mother is an invalid. I never had anyone to properly explain how this all works."

And she's brave enough to betray her ignorance to the High Prince? Serefin thought. He couldn't decide whether she was incredibly smart or terrifically stupid. The fact of the matter was that the *Rawalyk* favored the nobles who lived near Grazyk; it stood to reason those from the outer reaches of Tranavia would struggle. The entire game was in subtleties.

What this girl likely didn't realize was this duel would be to the death, and if she survived, it would give her an edge in his father's eyes. And an edge was all a person needed to be chosen.

Will this be the one who gets the throne after I'm done away with? he thought absently.

"It's a game," he said. "A game played in what you say, who you speak to, and how you act."

She paled.

"Think of it this way," he said. He ran his thumb over the rim of his wine glass, the crystalline tone sounding too loud amidst the hushed chatter of the parlor. "My consort—" He cringed. He had tried so hard to distance himself from this whole mess. "—will need to be someone who can prove she will hold her own against whatever Tranavia throws their way. Sometimes that will be underhanded slights in a ballroom. Mostly, with the state of the world as it is, it will be someone who can aid me in winning this war."

A frown flashed across her face, and he realized that she didn't seem nervous anymore. "You don't seem particularly invested in this, Your Highness, if you forgive my candor."

He couldn't fathom how she possibly could have seen that. He was doing his absolute best to hide how trying this all was, how much he just wanted to curl up and sleep until it was over.

He shot her a crooked smile. "I'm less than pleased about the circumstances surrounding it, but that is certainly none of the participants' fault."

"It would be difficult, though, to have no choice," she said, voice soft. Her hand went up to her neck, then fell. "You don't, do you? The choice will be the king's?"

Inexperienced maybe, but clever. *She's definitely clever.* "I'm used to it."

"Yes," she said. "Me too." Her thumb ran over the spine of her spell book.

He wanted to ask what she meant. He was fascinated by this backwater *slavhka* with her strangely soft words, but a stately Akolan girl stepped up to her side, whispering in her ear.

Józefina lifted her head, her smile like a knife's edge. "Apparently I have a duel to see to."

"Good luck, then," he said. "I'll be watching."

She was ushered away and Serefin returned to his friends. Żaneta straightened when he sat down next to her.

"So?"

"You have competition, darling."

Żaneta wrinkled her nose. "Really? She seems so . . . soft."

"You know better than to hold being from Łaszczów against her," Serefin scolded.

She rolled her eyes. "Well, if she dies in an hour, then it won't matter at all, will it?"

NADEZHDA

LAPTEVA

Malachiasz had found Parijahan and Nadya in the courtyard just outside the arena. He looked tired. She could relate.

"This certainly wasn't part of the plan," he noted sarcastically.

"I don't want to hear it," Nadya muttered. She had heard enough from Parijahan already. *Slip through under the guise of perfect mediocrity, indeed.*

She let the noise from the crowd in the arena filter out as she fixed the belts on her hips strapping down Malachiasz's spell book. It was so strange. All this time and energy spent on such a trivial affair when there was a war happening and people were starving, dying. It was just a game to them.

She was wearing the white leather mask again, and though it stifled, she took comfort in the anonymity. She was nothing but a name; a lesser noble from a forgotten city in Tranavia.

She heard her false name read to the crowd: Józefina Zelenska from Łaszczów, a blood mage of no military rank. Inconsequential. Insignificant by all standards. *My name is Nadezhda Lapteva,* she thought. *I am from the monastery in the Baikkle Mountains. I am a cleric of the divine. I am here to kill the king and end this war.*

She would bring this country to its knees.

Nadya let her fingers brush against the razor sewn into the sleeve of her shirt. She was wearing tight black trousers, high boots reaching up to her knees, and a loose-fitting white blouse with sleeves that constricted her forearms.

The gods were distant and Nadya would have the added difficulty of being forced to pretend to cast magic like a blood mage. The seed of fear she had been ignoring up until this point finally grew into something that threatened to topple her. She could barely feel the gods. How had she expected to do this— *be* anything—with the gods so far out of reach? What was she without them? Just a peasant girl who grew up in a monastery. A girl who would die for believing she was anything more than that.

20

NADEZHDA

LAPTEVA

The goddess of the hunt, Devonya, is known for her kind-ness to mortals, for her interest in their odd ways. She loves to grant them unusual talents in her name.
—Codex of the Divine, 17:24

My magic doesn't feel right. That was the first thought to cross Nadya's mind as the girl across the arena cut her arm and power whipped through the air like crossbow bolts. In comparison her magic felt weak, as if she was reaching through mud to grasp at mere threads. Her prayers were answered by magic only, no words, no touch of the gods. Just raw spells, cold power, and nothing more.

She slid the back of her hand over the razor in her sleeve, wincing as it cut, forgetting she wasn't supposed to react. Blood mages didn't react.

The girl—Felicíja—tossed a glass bottle onto the arena floor and poison sprayed out in an arc in front of her.

It got on Nadya's clothes and the fabric sizzled as it burned. She fought the urge to brush the droplets off.

She let ice form at her fingertips, grasping for Marzenya's power because she could form it to look the most like blood magic. The goddess was distant, her touch far away. Nadya's prayers felt like nothing more than pleas to empty air.

Then power. Claws of ice on her fingers shot off her hands. She didn't have time to see if they landed as she tore pages out of the spell book and crumpled them in a bloody fist.

She slammed the pages onto the ground and drew a circle of flames up from the dirt. The flames sparked underneath her boots and surrounded Felicíja. The girl staggered back as flames caught up her split skirt. She snarled, her fingers yanking out pages of her spell book.

Nadya was struck by a bolt of magic that sent her staggering back to the edge of the arena.

This isn't working. Using the spell book and pulling at threads of power at the same time was slowing her down. She had to end this fast or everything would unravel.

She raked bloody claws of ice over a spell book page, realizing seconds later it hadn't been blank. Panic slammed into her chest.

The flow of power she channeled shifted and became something dark.

This power was not hers to use. It wasn't hers *at all*.

She had no word for it but *wrong*. It was the only word running through her head. *Wrong wrong wrong wrong wrong.*

Seething and black and powerful—so powerful—and in a different way than *her* magic was powerful because where hers was clarity this was madness.

There was something else, too. A needling that Nadya realized was a spell Felicíja was attempting to cast on her, but it felt so weak by comparison that she barely noticed. Felicíja tried again, and again, tearing out page after page, but her spells were only glimmers, bare brushes of magic against Nadya and this power that tore through her, threatening to rip her apart.

Blood dripped down her nose. She had to get rid of the magic. The taste of copper bloomed in her mouth. She spat, pressing a hand against her chest because her heartbeat felt erratic.

She exhaled and let go of the magic. It shot out from her fingertips like bolts of lightning. One struck Felicíja, the crack of thunder reverberating through the arena. The girl went down.

For a tense second, Nadya was sure she'd killed her. Instantaneously. But the girl got back up, a *szitelka* in her hand and fury warping her face. Blood dripped from a wound in her side and was smeared across her face.

Gods, please stay down. Nadya grimaced. Echoes of the darkness rattled in her head. She drew her own blades.

She blocked Felicíja's strike, catching her blade on the hilt of the other girl's *szitelka* and using the leverage to pull her closer. She lashed out with her second blade but Felicíja twisted out of the way.

Recovering, Nadya twisted the hilt of her blade and yanked down. The *szitelka* was pulled from Felicíja's grasp and she staggered forward. Nadya caught the girl underneath her chin with her foot, snapping her head back and knocking her off her feet.

As the girl moved to rise, Nadya slammed the *szitelka* onto her hand, pinning her to the dirt.

Everything was too quiet. Too aware of the audience, Nadya hesitated, her other *szitelka* loose in her grip.

I don't want to kill her.

The only reason this fight had worked in Nadya's favor was

because of magic that had not been hers. It could have so easily been Nadya on the ground, Felicíja contemplating the killing blow.

Felicíja lifted herself up on her arm, glaring at Nadya. She didn't deserve to die here, with an audience, like an *animal*. And Nadya wasn't going to be the reason for her death. She wasn't going to perpetuate this Tranavian bloodlust.

It would be so easy, though, and it would further Nadya's mission. All it would take would be another icy claw into the girl's heart, or a stronger jolt of lightning. But the darkness lingered and Nadya feared what would happen if she pulled on it.

"I'm not going to kill you," Nadya said.

She was expecting relief, but what she received was a wad of spit that landed on her mask.

"Pathetic," the girl said, pain slurring her speech.

Nadya straightened. Felicíja's guard and a figure in a chilling mask that could only be a Vulture began to move toward them. It must have been clear she was backing off.

A hand brushed her arm. The dark echo reacted to the touch—*Malachiasz*—and Nadya's knees grew weak. She was shoved forward; knocked to her knees before the girl.

The girl who had blood dripping from her mouth, who stared at Nadya with eyes that were already dimming. A spike of iron was driven into her chest. As Nadya stared at it, the spike formed into the shape of a *szitelka,* then the girl pitched forward, dead.

Her stomach roiled as her vision tunneled. *No.* Mercy, she was going to give the girl mercy.

It took everything in her not to turn to Malachiasz. The girl's guard reached them along with the Vulture. Neither of them said anything. The flurry of activity would have masked what had happened. What Malachiasz had done instead of Nadya.

She finally glared at him. He raised an eyebrow at her. There was blood on his fingertips.

Blood dripped from Nadya's nose.

One day in this cursed city and she was already tired of the sight of blood.

Heat coursed through her veins. What point had killing the girl served? She dropped her eyes before someone noticed but not before shaking her head at him.

Idiot.

"You expected more from a Tranavian abomination?" Marzenya's voice was faint, as though coming through a fog. It sounded unbelievably sly, but there was another thread to her voice Nadya had never heard before: rage. *"You should have killed the bitch yourself. On your own."*

A warning. Attempting to spare another Tranavian and Nadya glancing against Malachiasz's power—unintentional as it had been—had sparked Marzenya's ire. Before the servants came to collect the body, Nadya stalked out of the arena.

SEREFIN

MELESKI

"What was *that*?" Ostyia asked, her eye wide.

Serefin shook his head. It had been ruthless, exactly what the Tranavian court was expecting. But more interesting, some elegance to her movements, innovation in her magic . . .

Ostyia perched on the arm of his chair. "No one uses elemental magic like that."

How had this girl not been drafted into the army? Why had

she not joined of her own volition? She was talented, quick, relentless, with an arsenal of spells Serefin had never seen before. He knew elemental spells were possible with blood magic, but no one ever used them because they were too difficult. It was manipulating magic in a way that was changing the power at its basest element. Blood magic drew from a person's innate ability and manifested in whatever way it was needed, but changing it to the elements—another base, another fundamental item in creation—was incredibly difficult.

Where had this girl been hiding?

"Żaneta is not going to be happy," Ostyia commented.

"She'll relish having real competition."

There was a flurry of activity in the arena and Serefin leaned over the railing. Two masked Vultures were carting off Felicíja's body.

Horror rippled through him and he exchanged a glance with Ostyia. What were *they* doing?

He dimly felt Ostyia's touch on his arm. He shouldn't be staring; it shouldn't be a sight he found uncomfortable. But it was another piece of the puzzle, another step closer. He hoped it wasn't coming too late.

21

NADEZHDA

LAPTEVA

*Silence and fear; those who worship the god Zlatek know
that above all else, those two things are paramount.*
—Codex of the Divine, 55:19

A healer ran after Nadya, fussing after her wounds—her entire body felt like it was on fire and her nose hadn't stopped bleeding—but she waved her away. She could handle it herself and she had to get out of this arena.

She couldn't stomach the stench of death any longer.

Malachiasz trailed behind her, silent. If he spoke, she was going to kill him, and he seemed to sense that.

They reached the hallway that led to her chambers. It was empty, devoid of servants or other participants who were boarding in this wing of the palace. She couldn't wait any longer.

She moved without warning, slamming him into the

wall, her forearm against his throat, *szitelka* drawn and pressed against his side.

He raised both hands in a sign of surrender, lifting one farther to unhook the mask from his face. It was made of iron and covered his mouth, stopping just where his tattoos started on the bridge of his nose.

"There was no need for you to interfere," she said, her voice a snarl.

He swallowed, his pale stare icing over. "Were you going to kill her yourself?"

She pressed up harder on his windpipe. "I can handle myself," she replied through clenched teeth. "Understand?"

"Perfectly," he wheezed.

She released the pressure on his throat but didn't pull away or sheathe her *szitelka*. "If anyone saw you—"

He cut her off, voice low. "Let's go somewhere a little more private for this discussion, shall we?"

His expression was carefully blank. Had she angered him with her outburst? Good. He deserved it. He couldn't place the whole plan's success on her and then not trust her to see through what was necessary.

Nadya kicked the door to her chambers closed after they entered. She begrudgingly sheathed her *szitelka*.

"You murdered her."

He was insufferably calm. "You hesitated. That was a duel to the death, there was no room for anything else."

"You're right, silly me, I forgot that Tranavians are all bloodthirsty with no capability of understanding concepts of mercy, thank you for reminding me."

Malachiasz blinked. Hurt flickered across his face and he turned away. Nadya thought seeing one of her jabs land would feel good, but it just made her more frustrated. How dare he play the victim here?

She grabbed his arm, yanking him back around to face her. "I did not need you to take matters into your hands. If anyone saw you—"

"Yet no one did. Yet here we are. Yet here you stand with a seat next to the High Prince at dinner this evening."

"You can't talk your way out of this. Her blood is on your hands, not mine." She leaned closer to him.

"I can live with that. You're trying to paint it as something it's not."

"It was *murder*."

"She was a *slavhka,* raised from birth to slaughter Kalyazi, and as necessary, other Tranavians."

"That doesn't make her a monster!"

"We're all monsters, Nadya," Malachiasz said, his voice gaining a few tangled chords of chaos. "Some of us just hide it better than others."

Now she was aware of just how close they were, her hand still clutching his arm. His gaze strayed to her lips. She managed to keep from blushing as she let go and stepped away—she didn't want to give him the satisfaction of knowing he could still fluster her while she was angry.

She closed her eyes. Heard him step away. When she opened her eyes again he was sitting on the chaise, elbow resting against the armrest, chin in his hand.

"The king will be there, a seat or two away from you," he said.

She had to take a breath to tamp down the immediate, crushing fear that swept over her. "Are you saying this is my chance?"

He shook his head slowly. "No, but this means you're getting closer. The time will come sooner than any of us expect. You need to be ready."

Nadya gritted her teeth.

The door opened. Nadya whirled, but relaxed when it was only Rashid. He grinned.

"Well, that was fun." His face fell as he picked up on the energy in the room. "Maybe not fun?"

Nadya sighed, finally collapsing into a chair. Malachiasz watched her carefully, like one watched a dog that had just bitten them. Had he assumed her harmless? That she would simply comply with any decision he made? They were still—at their core—enemies in this war. She hadn't forgotten, not even while she found herself worrying about his safety and wanting him by her side.

He wordlessly passed her a handkerchief. Blood was still all over her face and she felt herself weaken. He was a nightmare— the echoes she still felt of his power were troubling—but he was gentle. Anxious and strange, a boy caught up in a world that had broken him, all while trying to do something good for once. She wondered if her anger that was so quick to spark was just her fighting against the pull she felt. Was her fascination merely because she had been sheltered her whole life and never known someone so drastically different from herself? Or was it more? Was it because he was dangerous and exciting, all while being completely infuriating yet thoughtful?

She worked at washing off the blood, hesitantly reaching out to the gods. She would be in deep trouble for all of this, but she was met only with the strange fog. She would be more concerned if Marzenya hadn't spoken to her in the arena. They were there, watching, but at a distance.

"What's next?" she asked softly.

"Dinner," Rashid said. He was dressed in meek servants' garb that didn't look right on him. She missed the flamboyant gold chains that used to thread through his black curls.

"I've already failed the first etiquette test," Nadya said. "That bodes well for the next one."

Malachiasz stretched out towards her before thinking better of it and setting his hand on the arm of her chair instead. She found her eyes drawn to the tattoos on his long, elegant fingers. They were simple, straight lines: two on either side of each finger and one down the back that started at the bed of each fingernail and ended at his wrist in a single black bar.

"Everything is a game," he said. "It's all a play for power. We didn't want it, but you've caught the attention of the elite, so you may as well keep it."

She swallowed hard. "I can handle myself."

"I know, Nadya."

She continued furiously scrubbing at her face as Malachiasz asked Rashid if he'd found anything useful.

"Servant gossip keeps a palace running," he said cheerfully. "The king has barely been seen in months; the queen is in Grazyk, which apparently never happens due to her health. The tension between the king and the prince has reached astronomical levels but none of the servants seem certain as to why. It was quite clear the prince didn't want this *Rawalyk* to even take place. Also, the prince was seen in the witch's tower—"

Malachiasz perked up. "Pelageya?"

Nadya froze. *A witch in Tranavia?* "What?" she asked at the same time.

"No," Rashid said. "Calm down, both of you, and don't get any ideas. That's how we all get killed and accomplish nothing."

Nadya and Malachiasz exchanged a glance, their fight momentarily forgotten.

"Mages," Rashid said, sounding properly anguished. "Parj and I should have done this without you."

Malachiasz was smiling the faint, slightly feral smile she recognized from the first day she met him.

"Regardless," Rashid continued, "the witch is known to be the queen's personal advisor."

"But she's Kalyazi?" Nadya asked.

"Most consider it an obvious jab at king and country," Malachiasz said. "The royal family doesn't get along."

"Clearly."

"The prince had an interview with the Crimson Vulture," Rashid said. "The king has been paying visits to the Salt Mines, and the prince had someone sent to the Salt Mines who recently returned."

Malachiasz stiffened. A shutter snapped closed around him and he absently rubbed the scars on his forearm.

"That's not good," he murmured.

"Wait, which one is Crimson?" Nadya asked. The rankings didn't make any sense.

"Żywia is the second in command."

Nadya didn't like that he knew and used their names when no one else did. She didn't need to be constantly reminded of what he was.

"Why wouldn't the prince meet with their king?" Nadya asked.

"Perhaps the king's visits to the Salt Mines means he's working with the Black Vulture and the prince is attempting to undermine that?" Rashid said.

"I'd always thought a schism among the Vultures would be impossible," Malachiasz said. "But I think we've stepped into something bigger than just a silly pageant for a queen. If the Salt Mines are involved, definitely so."

"If we accomplish this, what will happen with the Vultures?"

"Theoretically, nothing. They would step back if Tranavia fell into chaos. Still . . ."

"Still," Rashid said, "the king seems to have forsaken his usual retainer of guards in favor of the Vultures."

"They're not *guards*," Malachiasz said.

"What are they, then, Malachiasz?" Nadya asked. He was becoming increasingly agitated. Nadya wasn't going to ignore the tremors of doubt she had when he appeared to falter.

He waved a hand. "It would be like your Kalyazi *tsar* having clerics act as guards. It's not their purpose, they're not supposed to be so deeply connected to the secular throne."

Nadya sighed. "Except religion is interwoven into our government. It's not a thing to be shoved aside." She didn't like comparing *monsters* with her religion, but it was an apt enough example. "But back to the point, we have to get past the Vultures to get to the king?"

Rashid glanced at Malachiasz, but nodded. Malachiasz leaned back on the chaise, pulling at his lower lip.

"That complicates things," Nadya said. "We can't just wait for the opportune moment. I need to know what I'm doing if this is going to work."

Malachiasz nodded. "You're going to go to the dinner. Watch the king. Charm the prince. He'll be your way to get to the king. Tell me *exactly* what the masks on the Vultures near the king look like."

He was going to deal with the Vultures. Fine. Good, even, because Nadya didn't know what to do when they were involved. They were a variable she feared and did not understand.

Rashid stood. "I'll go find Parijahan; you don't have much time before dinner."

That left just Nadya and Malachiasz.

"You should go as well," she said softly.

She could feel his gaze burning against her face, but she refused to look at him. She saw him stand and move toward the door out of the corner of her eye, but he changed his mind. Instead, he dropped down into a crouch in front of Nadya's chair so he was looking up at her.

"I acted without trusting your judgment, and for that I apologize," he said.

It's not an apology for murdering that girl, she noted. But it was a start. It was something from this boy who obviously had no morals and no regard for anything that didn't serve his own interests. She just wished she could understand what those interests were.

"Nadya," he started, then stopped. He let out a frustrated breath.

Inexplicably, she felt herself soften. She reached out and threaded her fingers into his soft black hair, letting her hand settle against the side of his head.

Why—after being so furious with him—did she find herself desperately yearning to kiss him? The heat of anger that *he* sparked was still fresh in her veins and yet she couldn't help but gaze at the bow of his lips.

She was feeling too many things in too little time. She wanted it all to stop. She wanted whatever this was she felt for him to stop.

If he was startled by her actions, he didn't show it. He let another moment pass between them—fraught with a tension still too new to her—before he spoke. "You have to trust *me,* Nadya," he said, his voice low. "I know I am everything you have been taught to hate and more. I have done terrible things in my life. If I disgust you, I understand. But—"

"We have to work together," Nadya whispered. "All four of us, or else this whole mess of a plan will go up in smoke and we'll all be hanged for it."

He leaned his head into her hand and she felt herself warm. To have another person react to her touch was a peculiar feeling, a connection she had never really had with anyone. The monastery didn't encourage relationships; one's devotion to the gods was more important.

This was a disaster. Anyone, *anyone* but him. Anyone but the enemy boy who had tormented her people, who was faithless, godless, monstrous. If she tore out her own heart would this stop? If that was the thing betraying her, then she would be rid of it. Anything to stop from being pulled to this terrible boy.

"It could be worse than hanging," he mused.

She couldn't help her strained laugh. "You would know."

"And you and I need to come to an understanding," he continued. "We can be enemies when all this is over."

It was fairly clear now that enemies wasn't quite what they were before, and an *understanding* probably wasn't going to be what either of them wanted.

Maybe she had knocked her head during the duel, but she found herself sliding her other hand up his neck to cradle his cheek. He grew very still, as if he truly thought her a little bird and sudden movement might startle her away.

"What if I don't want to be enemies when all this is over?" she asked softly, her voice betraying her by trembling. Her heart was pounding in her throat.

His expression didn't falter. "Then we can come to a different understanding."

"I think that would be best."

To steady himself, he put his hands on either side of her, one brushing against her thigh. She tensed and he started to pull back, so before the moment slipped away she pulled him closer and kissed him.

Something unspooled within her chest, something she had kept close her whole life. This act—the pressure of his lips against hers, and the heat that flooded her veins—this was heresy.

And she wanted more of it. She twisted her fingers into his hair and felt his hand slip up to her waist. His lips were soft and he kissed her back tentatively.

Sighing, he pulled away again. A flush tinted his pale skin and his hand on her waist tightened a fraction. He pressed his forehead to hers.

"The understanding I had in mind was one that kept you safer than this, *towy dżimyka*," he said, voice rueful.

"Oh so boring. I grew up in a monastery, I've been safe all my life," Nadya replied.

An achingly mournful half smile caught at his lips and it took all of Nadya's willpower not to kiss him again. He was struggling with the same pull. He lifted a hand and tucked a lock of her hair behind her ear, his touch burning down her cheek. His gaze tracked over her face, searching for something, but she wasn't sure what.

Anyone but him, she thought again desperately, but she was still drowning from the touch of his lips.

She thought of the echoes of power she had drawn on during the duel. Her expression must have changed because Malachiasz's eyes narrowed.

"Nadya?"

His spell book was still at her side and her hand moved to

shift it onto her lap. She trailed her fingers over the cover. How did she put to words that she had tasted the darkness he harnessed and she was terrified? How best to let him know there was still a part of him that she found *viscerally* unsettling? She flipped it open, landing on a spell scrawled page.

"Did you feel it?" she asked.

He paled and leaned back on his heels, swallowing hard. He nodded.

"You knew this could happen."

"I . . . did not. I thought nothing at all would happen if there was . . . no . . ."

"Blood," she finished for him. "Except this is all a grand performance, no? So, of course there was."

He seemed troubled for exactly seven seconds before the feral gleam returned to his eyes. "And? What was it like?"

"Horrible."

He hesitated, then lifted his hand and gently pressed his fingers over hers. She wanted to move away, she wanted to pull him closer.

They stared at each other. He smiled slightly. "It helped, right? You never would have gotten out of that duel alive if not for my magic."

The tension broke. She whacked his shoulder. He laughed.

"I have to go," he said, straightening up. There was so much of him to straighten; he was so *tall*. "We'll talk about this later? I'll be honest, I have no idea what it means."

"If we have a later," Nadya muttered.

He softly ran a hand through her hair. "Even so. Dazzle the monsters, Nadya. You've already charmed the worst of the lot; the rest should be easy."

She looked up at him, startled. He winked at her.

"I'm still mad at you," she said, but the words felt flat.

"I know." He grinned as he slipped his mask back over his face. He was gone before she could say anything more.

She pressed a hand to her lips, wrenching her eyes shut. There would be hell to pay for this.

22

SEREFIN

MELESKI

Svoyatovi Leonid Barentsev: A cleric of Horz, he lived in Komyazalov as an academic who taught the Codex of the Divine. It is believed Tranavian assassins poisoned him, but his body was never recovered nor found.

—Vasiliev's Book of Saints

Serefin's stomach dropped when he opened his door and Kacper staggered in. He looked haggard, like he hadn't slept in days. Serefin steadied him, pulling him into his rooms and shutting the door.

It wasn't safe for them to speak here and he had to be at dinner in an hour.

"Are you all right?" he asked.

Kacper leaned back against the door and slowly slid to the floor. "I was stopped in the hall by one of the Vultures that's been shadowing your father."

Serefin felt dizzy all of a sudden. He hadn't even had

anything to drink in hours. He glanced cautiously at the seam where the wall met the ceiling.

"And?"

Kacper shook his head. "Nothing. A warning? I don't know." He sighed. "I'm supposed to attend to you this evening," he said, his eyes flickering shut.

"Ostyia will be fine on her own."

Kacper raised an eyebrow, eyes opening. "Historically speaking, multiple people will die tonight."

"Historically speaking, it probably won't be me. Besides, you look terrible." He pulled on his coat, black with red epaulets and gold buttons down the front. He checked to make sure his razors were still sewn into the sleeves. "All right, tell me what you've found."

"You know how I mentioned I was going to look into the list of participating nobles?"

Serefin nodded.

"A number of them haven't backed out due to nerves, but are missing entirely." Kacper reached into his pocket and handed Serefin a stack of crumpled papers. "Also, my agent returned from the Salt Mines. It's not good, Serefin."

"When is anything?" Serefin asked as he unfolded the paper. His hands were shaking, he noted absently, an afterthought.

He read through the report, his heart sinking.

"Is this real?" His voice came out weak.

Kacper nodded.

The Vultures and the king *were* working together—though Serefin knew that wasn't quite true. Puppet strings. They had nearly succeeded in their goal with a new experiment, so said the papers. But their last was too strong-willed and difficult to control. They were moving to a new step in their gruesome process and placing his father at the center of it.

It felt like a sick joke. As if everything had been in front of his face the whole time but he had been too focused on the wrong things to see it. The Tranavians' flight from the gods hadn't been so simple and easy as magic and atheism.

"My father is a weak mage," Serefin rasped, his voice strained.

Kacper nodded.

If he was reading this correctly—and he wasn't sure he was—the Vultures had found a way to more power than any mortal should ever be able to reach, and they were going to give it to Izak Meleski. For a price. A sacrifice. That little anecdote from Pelageya about a mortal becoming divine now felt sickeningly ironic. It would only cost Izak his son, a paltry trade in the grand scheme of things. What was Serefin's life in comparison to unlimited power?

This was his father's chance to finally prove to his kingdom and his people that he wasn't just a weak king and weak blood mage. He would be more; he would be greater. He would become a god.

"He's . . . gone mad," Serefin said. It was the only explanation. The Vultures, his mother's skittishness, Pelageya's warnings. His father had lost his mind.

And Serefin would pay the price.

Kacper glanced at the ceiling. Serefin growled, pulled his dagger from its sheath and sliced open his hand. He slammed it down onto the table nearby and the smell of smoke filled the room as he snapped all the spells placed by his father. Damn the consequences.

"Do you know who this *former success* is?" Serefin pointed at a line in the report.

"The Black Vulture is likely, but, no, I have no idea."

Serefin rubbed his forehead. The Black Vulture wasn't important right now.

When had his father's mind snapped? He tried to think back further—he had been so out of touch with what happened in Tranavia while he was at the front; were there signs all along? He thought of the Tranavian villages he'd ridden through, destitute and close to fading away entirely. His father seemed indifferent about the plight of the country as a whole, the plight this war was spurring forward. It hadn't always been like that. He remembered when his father cared, even if it was years ago.

He might never know when things had changed.

Serefin leaned back against the table, suddenly weary. "How much blood would be needed to set this into motion?"

Kacper didn't respond.

The pieces were beginning to align, and the picture they were forming was too horrifying to comprehend.

"Perhaps the blood of the finest mages in Tranavia, brought into one place under the guise of the *Rawalyk*," Serefin whispered. "Common blood would do no good, it has to be blood with power. The girls disappearing, have any of them been from families that don't use magic?"

Kacper shook his head. "All blood mages. What if—" Kacper paused, unsure of what he was saying. "If this has never been done before, we don't know what will truly happen to your father."

"I'll be dead, so I don't really care what will happen to my father," Serefin countered. "But, what if . . . what if it *has* been done before?" he muttered, mind racing. "The answer is here."

Kacper lifted his head. "What?"

"The witch. The witch's words, blood and *bone*. 'Gut the Kalyazi churches, melt their gold, grind their bones.' What else did she say?"

"'What if those gods the Kalyazi worship aren't gods at all?'" Kacper asked, horror lacing his voice.

Serefin nodded slowly. He didn't care about the Kalyazi gods, but if they were something else entirely, what would that mean for Tranavia?

"So, what do we do?"

Serefin tried to think but came up blank. What *could* they do? What could they do when his mad father was steps away from godlike powers?

What could they do when the very girl who communed with these creatures had slipped from their grasp and was out in the world to wreak havoc?

"Do we truly have no way to find the cleric?"

Kacper's dark gaze met Serefin's pale eyes knowingly. "Is going back to the witch wise? Your father will suspect you're up to something."

Serefin waved to the blood smeared on the table behind him. His father already suspected. "I *am* up to something."

There was a sharp knock at the door and Serefin and Kacper both jumped. Serefin hastily wrapped his still-bleeding hand with cloth while Kacper got the door. Ostyia blinked her single eye at the sight of both of them.

"Are you boys all right?"

"Not at all, but I suppose that doesn't matter right now," Serefin replied as Kacper moved to a chair.

She held out a hand and Serefin gave her the report. Her face grew withdrawn as she scanned the pages.

"I see," was all she said. "Dinner is soon."

Serefin nodded.

"I'm going to burn this," Ostyia said, holding up the report. "This is bad, Serefin."

"I'm well aware."

"It's not just you who is in danger either, it's every blood mage here. Every noble, the entire Tranavian ruling class."

"I'm just in the most danger," he said, smiling thinly.

She nicked a finger against a hidden razor in her sleeve and the report went up in flames. Her solemn frown deepened at the effort of casting an elemental spell, but it faded as she brushed the ash from her hands.

"You have somewhere you need to be. We can figure out what to do about this later," she said.

Kacper stood. Serefin wanted to tell him to stay behind, but he knew Ostyia—as a *slavhka*—would be required to attend the dinner as nobility and not as Serefin's sometime body guard.

"You really look dreadful," Serefin told him, stepping closer and attempting to rake Kacper's hair back into the semblance of neatness. He tugged on his crumpled jacket, but nothing he did would straighten the wrinkles.

Kacper shot him a lopsided smile. "It's not every day I get to deliver news that the king is trying to turn himself into a god, eh?"

Serefin grimaced. *A god.* Hearing it aloud made it feel all the more real and all the more terrifying. There was a *reason* Tranavia had broken from the hold of the gods. There was a reason they had rejected the rules and the customs, the constant oppression of having a being greater than you rule over you by their own idea of morality. What his father was doing wasn't going to change anything; it was just going against the entire essence of being Tranavian.

If Serefin had to cut him down to restore the throne to what it *should be,* so be it. His father had lost his right to the throne by reaching for this kind of ideal. Reaching for more power was one thing—that was admirable—but this? This was too far. It would crumble Tranavia's already delicate government.

But there was no time for panicking. Serefin had to pretend

he was just a petulant prince home from the war and nothing more than that. He used to be so good at pretending.

The banquet hall was lit by crystal chandeliers that flickered golden light over the long table. Serefin found his place was beside Józefina, with Żaneta across from him. It was unusual, he was used to sitting at the high table, but apparently protocol had been shifted.

Żaneta smiled warmly at him as he sat down. He felt Ostyia perk up next to him.

"Surely they should be announcing your arrival?" Żaneta asked.

He glanced to where his father's seat remained empty at the other end of the table. No, the announcement would be for *that* arrival. Not for him, never him.

"Doubtful," he said cheerfully, waving a servant over. "But I much prefer it this way." He grinned at Józefina as he gestured for the servant to fill the glass in front of him. "What is this?" he questioned. "Please tell me it will help numb the drudgery of this evening."

"*Krój*, Your Highness," the servant replied.

Mead was good enough, he supposed. "I apologize, I'm certain present company will be sufficiently charming."

Żaneta rolled her eyes fondly. Józefina looked unsure but smiled.

It was going to be very hard to fake his way through this. He exchanged a look with Ostyia and she immediately began flirting with Żaneta, leaving him to focus on Józefina.

She was unhooking her white leather mask. The relief on her face was clear when she finally got it off.

"The mask not to your taste?" he asked.

"I'm not used to them," she admitted. "They're far more un-comfortable than I expected."

Without her mask on he could actually see her soft features. Her skin was lightly dusted with freckles, her eyes long-lashed and dark.

"You can elect to not wear them, but other girls, well—"

"The other girls will rip you apart," Żaneta chimed in, momentarily distracted from her discussion with Ostyia. She smiled. "Your duel was excellent. Though, next time, I would recommend setting a barrier down when the fight begins so you aren't caught off guard by a spell that works your blood."

Józefina looked puzzled for a split second, but the expression was gone so fast Serefin questioned if he'd even seen it. Had she not noticed Felicíja's spell? Unlikely.

"That didn't even occur to me."

"No, it wouldn't in the heat of the moment," Żaneta said, pulling a dinner roll apart with her fingers. "Many mages use internal spells because they're quick and dirty ways to take out an opponent."

"They were written specifically for torture," Serefin mused.

"Serefin, you are, as ever, the most charming of dinner companions," Żaneta said.

The doors at the back of the hall opened and silence fell like a smothering blanket. Serefin felt cold. Everything he and Kacper had learned came spinning back to him as his father entered the room. His father's gaze met his, a flicker of rage in his eyes, and fear flooded through Serefin.

He knows. He knows. He knows. A Vulture trailed behind the king. Serefin didn't recognize the mask. They were too late. It was all moving too fast out of his control—not that he had ever been in control—and now his father knew Serefin suspected and would not be complacent.

He was going to die.

He ripped his gaze away, noticed Józefina's hands were clenched so hard in her lap that her knuckles were bone white. She was glaring at the king with open hatred in her eyes.

She caught him looking at her and her entire face flushed. She ducked her head, murmuring a soft apology.

His eyes narrowed. She didn't need to apologize. Why did a girl from an out of the way city in Tranavia look at the king like that? Perhaps it didn't matter.

Or perhaps he had just found another ally.

23

NADEZHDA

LAPTEVA

Svoyatovi Yakov Luzhkov: *The founder of the Selortevn-sky monastery in Ghelovkhin, a place where clerics were trained in secret to fight in the holy war. When the monastery was destroyed in 1520, Yakov burned with it.*
—Vasiliev's Book of Saints

The High Prince of Tranavia was a charming boy who enjoyed self-deprecation and complaining. Nadya found herself laughing at his jokes and responding in kind as the evening went on. Żaneta was equally engaging, with biting wit and a keen intelligence that Nadya had not expected from one of the most impressive blood mages of the court.

Well, this is fast becoming a nightmare, she thought as she swirled her spoon through a bowl of borscht. There was soft music playing in the background, airy and light, and the atmosphere of the room didn't feel nearly as oppressive as when the king had entered.

"A nightmare that you are making for yourself." Nadya almost dropped her spoon when Marzenya's voice rang through the back of her head.

Not now, she pleaded. She couldn't keep this up and have a goddess pulling her apart for what she had done at the same time. *Admonish me all you like later but not here.*

"You are treading dangerous ground, child."

Dangerous ground that she was only making worse. Marzenya required full devotion. Nadya never could have dreamed that would be an issue. Yet here she was, a few days into Tranavia and already full of conflict.

There was a disturbance at the head of the table where the king sat. A crystal goblet went flying, crashing into the wall and shattering into thousands of glittering pieces, wine splattering across the stone like blood. Nadya couldn't parse the Tranavian the king shouted after the servant fleeing the hall.

She was chilled to her bones as one of the Vultures slunk off after the servant.

Serefin's face reddened and he tore his gaze away.

"He's getting worse," Nadya heard Ostyia whisper to Serefin.

He swallowed hard, nodded quickly. He reached for his glass only to find it empty and raked a hand through his hair, clearly agitated. After an uncomfortable silence, Serefin grinned brightly, his strain clear.

Nadya eyed the king. There was no clear sign as to why he'd thrown the glass. "Józefina?"

Nadya started. "Forgive me, Your Highness, I was distracted."

The prince leaned closer to her. "Please, just call me Serefin, the *Your Highness* thing gets very old."

She raised an eyebrow. This was all a game. "Of course."

"Trade places with me," the one-eyed girl demanded of Serefin.

"You can't flirt with every girl here, Ostyia," Serefin said.

"I can and I will," she replied primly.

He rolled his eyes and—casting another anxious look toward where his father sat—stood up and traded places with the girl.

Ostyia had a glittering eye patch covering her right eye in place of a mask. Her smile was electric, and she shined it Nadya's way.

"Your fight was the most interesting thing I've seen in *years*," she said, tucking a lock of black hair behind her ear. She wore it cropped at her chin, unlike any of the fashions Nadya had seen in Grazyk. "I mean," she leaned in conspiratorially, "I've seen Żaneta fight before."

Żaneta waved her hand. "Flatter the new girl, I don't mind."

"Your Highness." The boy who sat beside Żaneta caught Serefin's attention. "If it isn't too much to ask, are the rumors coming from the front true? Are we finally beating back the Kalyazi?"

Nadya didn't hear Serefin's response as Ostyia had leaned closer.

"Your spell book doesn't look like any I've seen bound here, who did it?" she asked.

Nadya's mind went blank. She saw Żaneta turn her gaze from the prince to her. One of her hands dropped to the spell book at her hip, feeling the ridges in the design on the cover, the icons of the gods she had set in the front.

"I have a friend who binds spell books, actually," she said, smiling. "He does beautiful work." She unclipped the book from her hip. "He's a bit obsessed with the Vultures, though, and it shows." Her smile turned sheepish. She desperately hoped a Tranavian noble wouldn't recognize symbols for the Kalyazi gods.

She offered the book for Ostyia to look at, heart pounding in her throat. The girl took it, running her hand over the cover.

Żaneta's eyes narrowed. Nadya caught the expression before the *slavhka* smoothed her features.

The gamble relied on something Malachiasz had mentioned offhand to Nadya: that no blood mage would dare open the spell book of another. If Ostyia ventured past the cover of the book, Nadya would be in trouble.

Each second felt like ages, but finally Ostyia handed Nadya the book back. Nadya clipped it to her belts with shaking fingers.

The food she ate was delicious, but Nadya barely tasted any of it. She was too focused on not making any more mistakes.

Somehow, she managed it. Well, she thought she did. The prince had caught her watching the king. It was sloppy of her, but she was trying to convince herself that both the king *and* the prince needed to die. Seeing the king in person, it was easy for her to remember the horrors Tranavians had done to Kalyazi over the years. The prince, though . . . he made it easier to forget. She shouldn't be so swayed.

Kostya. You're doing this for Kostya, she reminded herself. *Kostya would still be alive if not for Serefin.*

Just before dinner ended, the king rose, approaching Serefin. The prince tensed—Nadya saw his hand go for his spell book before he clearly forced it away. He didn't stand, though it didn't seem like the king was expecting him to. The king leaned down to whisper something in Serefin's ear. Their resemblance was clear, but Nadya noticed the king was careful to remain as physically far away from Serefin as possible. Serefin's face drained of color, his eyes flickering closed as his father spoke before a mask settled over his features, pale eyes dim when they reopened.

"Of course," he muttered, not turning to look at the king.

The king left in a flurry of servants, emblazoned guards, and masked Vultures.

Serefin offered to see Nadya back to her rooms. Whatever had passed between him and his father was forgotten or shoved aside.

"It'll put a target on your back and Serefin was told not to be seen favoring anyone in particular," Żaneta said to Nadya before turning to Serefin. "Don't get her in trouble while you engage in petty squabbles with your father."

Nadya froze. Serefin shot Żaneta an exasperated look. "There's no reason to scare her," he scolded.

"There's every reason to scare her," she replied sweetly. She stood and inclined her head to Serefin. "I bid you a good evening, Serefin. And Józefina?"

"Yes?" Nadya said a beat too quickly.

"Good luck, and I do mean that."

"Thank you," Nadya replied. "You as well."

Żaneta laughed, throwing her head back. "I don't need luck, but thank you."

Serefin held his arm out to Nadya, casting a sly look down the table at those who were openly staring at them. She hesitated before taking it. She met Parijahan's eyes as she passed where the servants were waiting. An echo of a smile touched her lips as she got up to trail behind them.

"So," Serefin said, his voice hushed, "what did my father do to Łaszczów to get you to look at him with that level of hatred?"

Nadya stumbled. She was fairly certain her heart stopped

for a beat. Did he know? There was no way. He *couldn't* know. She tried to smile but knew it came off false.

He chuckled. "Ah, that was cruel of me. Forgive me, but you are so charmingly provincial."

Nadya grimaced.

"Sorry," Serefin said with a slight frown. He ran a hand through his hair. "That was meant to be a compliment. It wasn't a good one."

"No."

He laughed sheepishly. "I've been at the front for years and lost all skill I formerly had at interacting with people, I'm afraid. Not that I was ever particularly good at it."

"I think you're doing fine," Nadya said. "However, I am probably the worst judge."

"It's refreshing," he said. "You are candid, and you hate my father; these are both things I appreciate."

The way he spoke of his father—the tightness around his eyes and tension that built in his shoulders—and the way he had reacted to his father merely speaking to him made Nadya suspect Malachiasz was right; they really had walked into something bigger than petty court games.

She wished she had more time to gauge if Serefin would make a better king. What she saw of him that evening made her hopeful, but it was not enough to stop the war. She had to press on.

"These are my rooms," she said, stopping. Parijahan walked around her to open the door.

She pulled away from Serefin but he caught her hand. He lifted it to his mouth, kissing it gently.

Nadya blushed instantly.

"Good luck, Józefina. I would not wish for you to lose your life for such a ridiculous reason as this *Rawalyk*."

"Thank you, Serefin."

His smile was crooked as he dropped her hand. "Good night."

"Good night."

He inclined his head to her before he loped down the hall. Nadya darted into her rooms, slamming the door shut. She leaned back against the door and slowly slid to the ground, her pale green skirts pooling around her.

Parijahan was grinning. "I think you charmed the prince."

"I think I did."

"Was it difficult?"

"I felt like throwing up the entire time."

Parijahan laughed. Nadya dropped her head into her hands. "He isn't what I expected." She had been expecting someone more like how she'd first seen Malachiasz—intimidating and powerful—and wasn't sure what to do with this charmingly awkward boy. That he was one of the most powerful blood mages in Tranavia—as well as a heretic—unfortunately caused her fingers to itch for the *szitelka* hidden in her sleeve. She had wavered too much already; she couldn't allow herself to feel any more.

Nadya had spent a fair portion of the evening tracking the king's movements, trying to decipher just how many guards he had around him at all times, just how difficult it would be to separate him and kill him.

Their odds weren't good. "Do you think I'll have to win this—whatever this *Rawalyk* is—to get us close enough?"

Parijahan considered, her gray eyes cast up at the painting on the ceiling. "I don't know if we have that much time. Be careful around any Vultures you see lurking around the palace."

Nadya pulled Kostya's necklace out from under the neckline

of her dress and flipped it between her fingers. She didn't need to be warned about the Vultures.

"What's your homeland like? Akola?" she asked. She didn't want to talk about the Vultures with that painting hovering over them.

Parijahan smiled, her eyes closing dreamily. "Warm. Even in the winter, it's not nearly so cold as it is in Kalyazin. The sands catch the sun and everything is golden."

"How long have you been away?"

"A long time. Much too long but still not long enough."

"Do you think you'll go back?"

Parijahan laughed. "I don't know." She stood. "Mistakes were made. People died. Rashid and I both learned that sometimes the only thing left is to disappear." She held out her hands to Nadya, offering to help her to her feet.

Nadya accepted. Parijahan was taller than her, and she rested her brown hands on Nadya's shoulders.

"We're asking too much of you, Nadya, I know that. We're asking you to trust us, foreigners that we are, and Malachiasz, monster that he is, and put your entire being on the line for the sake of something that may be impossible." She rested her forehead against Nadya's. "Please do not think just because you fell into our lives at an opportune moment that the three of us do not care about *you*. I do, and Rashid and Malachiasz do as well."

"I'm used to being used for my power," Nadya said. "You three are my friends. I'm just tired of secrets."

Parijahan nodded. "I understand."

Nadya didn't usually see this side of Parijahan. It relieved her to see there was a warm softness to Parijahan's flinty gaze.

"Well, I survived the court of monsters this far," Nadya said cheerfully. "Now it's just a matter of finding a weakness in their system and exploiting it."

Nadya tucked her prayer beads in her dress pocket. It was late, but not so late that it would be odd for her to be found wandering the palace halls. Besides, she was too nervous to sleep— and she hated feeling like she was alone in Tranavia. She needed the gods back. There had to be a way past the veil that was blocking Nadya's access to them.

"Where are you going?" Parijahan poked her head out of her room.

"To find some answers, ideally. You stay here in case one of the boys shows up. I wouldn't want them to worry their pretty heads about us."

Parijahan frowned.

"I'll be fine, Parj," Nadya said, clipping Malachiasz's spell book to her belt. "I have the prince's attention. Malachiasz will take care of the Vultures surrounding the king, and I'll use the prince to get close enough to strike."

Parijahan reluctantly let her go.

The palace was eerily quiet as Nadya wandered through the halls. As if everyone was waiting—a bated breath before a plunge. The flickering candlelight cast ominous shadows on the paintings that stretched over the ceilings.

The royal wing was on the opposite side of the palace and she found it watched by a handful of king's guards. No Vultures in sight.

One of them called her over to ask her business and believed her when she told him she got turned around looking for the library. A bored *slavhka* up too late wanting something as harmless as books. He pointed her in the right direction and then promptly ignored her.

She wasn't expecting to find anything on *her* magic in the library, but surely someone had documented the blood magic causing the heavens to be blocked off from the earth. Tranavians were so terribly proud of it after all.

There were a few people in the stacks when Nadya entered, but evening was growing into night and they paid her no mind. Nadya didn't have a firm sense of what she was searching for, but if growing up in a monastery had taught her anything, it was how to find exactly what she needed from a library.

She tucked her hand in her pocket as she wandered through the stacks—the library was large, and stairs spiraled up to multiple floors all filled with books. Her fingers rubbed over her prayer beads. The gods still felt too distant—but there was a faint nudge at the back of her head, pressing her to the back of the library.

Nadya had always thought she read Tranavian far better than she spoke it. Her fingers brushed over the spines of old, crumbling books, worn down with time and negligence. She wasn't entirely sure what she was looking at—the titles she glanced at didn't mean anything to her.

Am I supposed to be seeing something here?

No answer. She sighed, fingers twisting her prayer beads. This was probably a pointless endeavor. She wasn't going to find anything that could help in a *Tranavian* library.

A sharper nudge came just as her hand froze over a thin volume wedged between two books, pushed so far back it wasn't even visible. She carefully extricated it. The cover was blank, no title, no indication to suggest what the book was about. The cloth cover was ragged at the edges, and when Nadya cracked it the pages were yellowed—the hand that had written the text spidery and thin.

Nadya moved to a table. She was gentle when she opened the book fully. It felt as if it could crumble at the slightest touch.

The symbol on the first page was familiar. *Uncomfortably familiar.* She let go of her prayer beads, shoving them deep into her pocket, and reached for the necklace hanging around her neck.

The same spiral was etched into the round pendant.

She only had time to flip to the first page. Enough time to see the word *god* scrawled in that spiderweb hand. Enough time to realize she had stopped hearing the quiet sounds of other people in the room and to gather that someone was watching her.

24

SEREFIN

MELESKI

Svoyatova Małgorzata Dana: *A Tranavian who fled her family of heretics for a life in a monastery in Tobalsk. Her courage, and death at the hands of her brother, canonized her as a saint.*

—Vasiliev's Book of Saints

All of Serefin's senses felt disconnected. He heard the smack of flesh against flesh, felt his head whip so hard to one side he thought his neck might snap, but it took a few seconds for pain to flare against the side of his face.

Izak's ring sliced open Serefin's cheek and he felt blood slowly drip down his face.

As distant as his father had become with him—as strained as their relationship was—he had never struck him before.

"Now, what did I do to deserve that?" Serefin asked, dabbing at the blood on his face with his thumb. He had

known when his father had personally ordered him to his study after dinner it wasn't going to be pretty, but instigating his father was part of his plan and he would survive the bruises that would come of it. Besides, if this went wrong he would be dead in a few days anyway, so what were a few bruises?

"I ask for so little, Serefin, so little," Izak said. "A modicum of respect for the traditions of your country. It's so little."

That wasn't what this was about, but Serefin would play along if it kept them both from addressing the true issue. "I've expressed how I feel about these traditions. At this point in time, they're needless. We're at *war*, Father."

"Don't dare presume to remind me, Serefin."

He was struck a second time, and again, it took a bit for all of Serefin's senses to realign.

He worked his jaw, feeling it click. "Are you finished? Would you like to go a third time? By all means, I'm more than willing to be your human punching bag."

"Serefin . . ." His father's tone was a warning.

Izak finally crossed the room, sitting down behind his large oak desk. The room was spare; few items suggested it was ever even used.

Apparently that was the extent of the abuse Serefin would be suffering today.

Serefin eyed his father while he shuffled through the very few papers that were spread across his desk. What was stopping him from putting his dagger through his father's eye, right now? From throwing his spell book open and burning him from the inside out?

Politics. The fallout would mean Serefin's execution. His coup had to be more delicate.

"The answer has always been here." But the answer to what?

Why this war was still raging? Why his father, who vehemently denied the *existence* of gods, wished to become one? Though easily answered with his father's ego, that wasn't the reason. Serefin never denied the existence of the Kalyazi gods, he had just never seen their purpose.

He wondered if his father had already started the process. The way his crown was slightly askew and his hands shook were significant indicators where his father was concerned. But it was when his sleeve fell back and Serefin glimpsed dozens of fresh cuts scattered across his father's forearm that he *knew*. His stomach soured, finally having confirmation that this was all truly happening.

"I just think we're wasting resources on trivialities under the guise of tradition when there is a war going on and half the kingdom is starving," Serefin said sullenly, forcing himself to continue pretending this was just a normal conversation.

"When you rule you can forgo tradition and deal with the riots," Izak replied without looking up. Serefin's blood froze.

Nothing in his father's voice sounded remotely sincere. He shoved down the swell of panic rising in his chest. He had to change the subject. He thought back to a conversation he had with Józefina during dinner, about how her retinue was so small because she had run into Kalyazi inside Tranavia.

"One of the girls who lives by the border told me the Kalyazi had broken through."

That got his father to look up. "What?"

Serefin shrugged. "I can't confirm, but from what I saw of the Kalyazi while at the front, it doesn't sound unreasonable. We're winning, but that doesn't mean we've *won*."

One of his father's hands clenched to a fist, crumpling the paper in his hand. Serefin felt as though he had just won a small and completely insignificant victory.

An icy chill seemed to settle over his father's shoulders. "The Kalyazi have moved forces into Rosni-Ovorisk," he said.

Serefin frowned, unsure why his father was telling him this. Kalyazi forces moving that close to the border was strange, yes, but when Serefin was in Grazyk he was a prince, not a general, and his father usually made that point abundantly clear.

"It's almost as if they know something we do not," his father continued. "Like they're preparing for something . . . extensive." Abruptly his father smiled and fear clawed its way down Serefin's spine. "They won't survive whatever it is they're planning, of course. Tranavia is about to show them the true meaning of power."

"Are we?" Serefin asked, voice strained. His mind spun. If the Kalyazi were preparing an attack on the border, Tranavia might not be able to properly defend it. What did Kalyazin know that Serefin did not?

Izak didn't respond. He just waved him out.

"You walk on thin ice, Serefin. Stay away from your mother's brainwashing witch."

Is that what this was supposed to be about? Serefin almost relaxed. He was considering paying Pelageya a visit in the morning. Now, he most certainly would.

"Oh, I'm well aware of that, Father. Thankfully, I can swim, and I've been in Kalyazin, I know what cold is truly like. Because certainly, the ice is about to break."

His father looked at him sharply. Bowing, Serefin smiled, before turning to leave as quickly as he could.

In the hall outside his father's chambers, he pressed himself against the wall, his hands shaking. Kacper approached, putting a steadying hand on his shoulder. Serefin gravitated toward Kacper. He had to move fast. If Kalyazin was making preparations—and his father was planning to annihilate the

Kalyazi forces with the power of a god—Serefin was out of time.

"You all right?" Kacper asked.

Serefin dropped his head onto Kacper's shoulder. "No," he mumbled.

There was a beat of hesitation. Kacper shifted, nudging Serefin's head so his forehead pressed against his temple. "We'll get you out of this, Serefin," he said. "You know there's a pretty spectacular handprint on your face?"

Serefin laughed weakly and straightened. It was late and he was tired. There was nothing more he could do tonight.

They were walking back to Serefin's chambers when a tremendous crash resounded through the hallway coming from the direction of the library.

"Well that doesn't sound good," Kacper muttered as Serefin took off down the hall.

NADEZHDA

LAPTEVA

Nadya shifted so the *szitelka* under her sleeve dropped into her palm.

Let it be another contestant upset the prince was showing me favor, she prayed.

Her hand tightened over the hilt and she knocked the chair back as she stood, whirling around.

She found herself face to face with a blank metal mask.

Yelping, she jumped back, knocking into the table. The Vulture didn't move, just tilted its head from one side to the other.

Blonde, curly hair tumbled down its back. The candlelight glinted off the Vulture's iron claws.

Panic constricted Nadya's chest, a painful grip that made it hard to breathe. She couldn't fight off a Vulture. Not by herself. Not here.

She wasn't given the chance to reach for the gods and hope. The Vulture struck, moving so fast Nadya only barely had time to register the movement. Sparks flew up as the Vulture's iron claws clashed against Nadya's *szitelka*.

Do they know who I am?

What if they had found Malachiasz and twisted him back into a monster? Was that how they'd found her?

Nadya shoved the Vulture away, jumping onto the table. The Vulture's claws ground down over the wood as it narrowly missed Nadya.

She had no magic. She had nothing.

She had no hope without her gods.

25

NADEZHDA

LAPTEVA

Svoyatovi Vlastimil Zykin: A cleric of the god Zlatek. Vlastimil's mind was weak, unable to handle the rigors of silence his god required from him. Instead of striking him from memory, his failure is remembered as a lesson to those chosen by the gods that they are mortal and the gods are not to be trifled with.

—Vasiliev's Book of Saints

Nadya ran.

The Vulture followed, moving so fast that it was nothing more than a blur in the dim light.

Nadya didn't even make it out of the library. A brush of blood magic; the taste of copper filling her mouth. Something slammed into her, sending her crashing into a bookshelf, knocking it over with a deafening crash. Her breath left her in a rush and she gasped for air from the floor, too aware of the Vulture moving—slowly now—closer.

"Frightened little thing, aren't you?" the Vulture said, trailing an iron claw over a row of books, the spines fraying open underneath.

Desperation sent Nadya scrambling for a thread of anything that would stop the monster in its tracks. With each step the Vulture took toward her, Nadya shuffled back until she hit the wall and there was nowhere left to go. This was where it would end. In the dark. Alone. In the home of her enemies.

The Vulture was inches away from Nadya, crouching down in front of her. Its mask was completely blank except for two slits for its eyes.

"No more running, pet."

Nadya gritted her teeth. *No gods, no hope.*

The Vulture moved to strike and Nadya had nothing left to lose, nothing left that could save her. But she refused to die here.

It had been like a well the first time she used it, a well *Marzenya* had uncovered. Now it was a river, the dam burst. All of Nadya's frustration and fear channeled into power. Magic that was hers alone. The Vulture was knocked off its feet, crashing into a table and snapping it as if it were made of paper.

Nadya stared at her hand, horror churning her stomach. What was *that*? She scrambled for her prayer beads. *Maybe the veil parted, maybe that was Marzenya.*

But Marzenya was far away. That had been something else entirely.

Abruptly the prince skidded into the room, blood dripping down one hand.

What is he *doing here?* Nadya thought with a touch of despair. This couldn't get any worse.

"Józefina?" he said.

The Vulture staggered to its feet behind Serefin. Nadya

stood, flinging out a hand. Shards of ice shot off her palm and drove the Vulture back down into a pile of books.

Serefin turned. While his attention was diverted, Nadya sliced open the back of her hand. The prince stepped toward the Vulture.

"Leave," he said. A simple order that had enough command to it Nadya could easily see this boy as the king of Tranavia.

"This isn't your business, princeling," the Vulture hissed.

Serefin yanked a page out of his spell book and when he crumpled it in his fist the Vulture dropped, still as stone.

"Did you kill it?" Nadya whispered.

Serefin shook his head. "It takes more than that to kill their kind. I don't know if I could if I tried. They won't be down for long. Minutes, at most."

He offered his hand and helped her to her feet before he returned to the unconscious Vulture. He crouched down, taking a lock of its hair between his fingers. Nadya thought he was going to take off the mask, but he straightened.

"Return to your room," he said. "Lock the door, though I don't think they'll try again."

"What?"

"Go," he urged. His lieutenant, Kacper, jogged into the room.

"Blood and bone, Serefin," he said wearily when he saw the unconscious Vulture.

"I'm not leaving until you tell me what's going on," Nadya demanded. If there was a chance this hadn't been because of Malachiasz, Nadya needed to know.

Serefin glanced from her to Kacper. Kacper shrugged. Serefin raked a hand through his hair. When he looked to her again, his pale gaze was narrow.

"My lady, the participants of this grand game are in danger. *Please,* just return to your chambers."

She opened her mouth to protest but he held up a hand. His expression was beseeching and she sighed. Adrenaline was draining to exhaustion and going to bed sounded like a fabulous idea. She just . . . wanted to forget all of this. She darted back to the table to pick up the book she'd found and bade the prince a good night.

"Thanks for saving my life and all," she said.

"You seemed to have it rather in hand."

Nadya carefully opened the book as she walked back to her chambers. She didn't want to flip through the pages for fear of it falling apart in her hands. But the book landed on a page that had one line focused in the center.

Some gods require blood.

She stopped dead. All the creeping dread that had been building within her solidified into something she did not understand. A feeling that was far too certain she had found something that was truth. A truth she dare not confront.

She shut the book and ran for her chambers.

And straight into another Vulture. This one slammed its fist into Nadya's face and no amount of power could keep her from passing out.

Nadya woke up in a pool of blood. There were sharp points digging into the back of her body, fire burning through her veins. She could feel tears pouring from her eyes, coursing down her cheeks.

She reached out to her goddess.

And a door slammed closed before her.

Panic flared, white-hot in her chest. All her joints locked up and her limbs shook. No, this wasn't happening. No no no *no no no no.*

This isn't real.

Was this something the Vultures had done to her? Was she being punished for the power she used trying to escape? This was a different kind of quiet than before. This was worse than the veil. This was emptiness.

Calm down, she told herself. *Figure out where you are.* A stabbing pain went through her as the silence remained, the gods now more than just out of reach, but turned away completely.

Maybe she would never hear another quip after an errant prayer again. She shivered. It couldn't be that. The gods wouldn't have *abandoned* her. Not for a few doubts, not for kissing a heretic—not even that.

Brushing her fingers against the slab she was lying on, she winced as the delicate parts of her hands met nails and broken shards of glass in return. She attempted to sit up, the jagged edges digging even farther into the backs of her thighs. Her thin dress was in tattered shreds, fabric clinging painfully to her wounds.

A low, pained moan broke past her lips as she tried to shift off the slab. Her head spun; she had lost far too much blood.

She moved herself gingerly off the slab, wincing as her legs were sliced open at every movement. Her feet landed on cold stone, but her knees buckled the instant she tried to put weight on them. She bit back a cry, snapping her teeth down on a fist, instantly breaking the skin of her hand. Iron heat filled her mouth and she coughed, spitting blood.

She pushed herself up off the ground and felt in the dark for a way out, a door, anything. Even if it was locked, she would feel less like she had ceased to exist. She had become nothing but the blood slicking the floor and blinding pain.

She couldn't help the whimper of relief when her hand landed on a doorknob. She rattled it, though it was useless. It was fastened tight. Another surge of panic threatened to ruin her. She was starting to see things creeping out of the darkness. Things with nails for teeth and razor smiles.

She turned away from the dark and pressed her forehead against the door. The wood was cool and let her refocus before she tried to reach for the gods again.

The door to the heavens remained closed.

Anguish and a rage too fluid to fully define washed through her and she wanted to scream. She reached for the prayer beads she did not have and found nothing but Kostya's necklace. She yanked it over her head and threw it across the room. She heard it hit the wall with a feeble, metallic clang.

"This isn't *fair!*" she cried, to no one and to nothing because she was alone. Entirely alone in the kingdom of her enemies. Her best hadn't mattered.

"I have only ever done what was asked of me," she said, her voice feeble and broken. She leaned back against the door and slowly slid to the ground, ignoring the wrenching agony that followed, the blood that she could still feel dripping down the backs of her legs.

The veil had been uncomfortable, stifling, but she could always hear Marzenya's voice if she reached. This was different. This was purposeful and had nothing to do with Tranavia's machinations.

A line in a history book would half-heartedly mention the cleric who had tried to save Kalyazin but only managed to be forsaken by the gods. There would be no canonization after death for Nadya, just a quiet passing of the cleric who had *failed.*

She clenched a fist, ignoring the pain, only to cause more blood to slide down her wrist from her sliced-up palm.

Please don't let this end here. If she cried out with everything left within her would she get an answer? Or would she have nothing but the ashes of the only thing that had ever made her life worth living? *Zhalyusta, Marzenya, eya kalyecti, eya otrecyalli, holen milena.*

Her plea went unanswered. Nadya was dropping into despair when something flickered at the corner of her vision. Nothing more than her addled mind playing tricks on her.

But the light grew stronger. Nadya frowned and slowly crawled to the other side of the room, fingers reaching blindly until they closed over Kostya's necklace. The spiral at the center was giving off a low light.

Some gods require blood.

She swallowed hard. Taking the pendant in her fist, she let the blood soaking her hands drip into the ridges.

She held it closer to her face, peering at the soft, almost eerie light.

"You deserve to know the truth about the beings that chose you." Nadya startled at the unfamiliar voice chiming in her head. It was speaking in holy speech and usually she didn't understand the tongue without the gods' blessing.

Nadya inhaled sharply, hit with a sudden barrage of images. The wave of pain that slammed into her nearly knocked her out.

Creatures with knotted joints like the whorls of a tree, faces enshrouded in fog, four eyes, six, ten. Beings with eyes on their fingertips, mouths at their joints. Iron teeth, iron claws, iron eyes.

One after another after another. Sinuous wings, feathered

wings black as tar. Eyes of light, of darkness. And blood. So much blood.

Because that's just it. It was always, always blood.

Feeling sick, Nadya dropped the necklace. The images stopped. She was panting, fighting for air.

She tentatively reached out for the voice again, only to be met with silence. She wasn't used to silence in her own mind. When she picked up the necklace again, she was careful to not touch the spiral ridges but apparently any contact was enough. When the cool silver touched against her skin all her senses were flooded with white light. Purity with rivulets of blood staining it all. It fell in tiny droplets, from her fingertips, off her arms. There was nothing but the blinding white and the blood.

What is this? What are you?

"*Does that matter?*"

She was surprised when the voice—unusually high, like reed pipes—responded.

Are you . . . one of the gods? There were gods she had never spoken to, was this one?

There was a long silence, leaving Nadya suspended in the blood-soaked white space. She was vaguely aware her pain was only a dim buzz now. It surrounded her like a fog, barely noticeable.

Then: "*Once upon a time, yes.*"

And once upon a time that answer would have terrified Nadya. A few short weeks ago, the girl in a monastery who believed so wholly in her gods and her cause would have looked upon this with horror, disbelief. She would have written it off as hallucinatory heretical magic. But now . . .

Now she had allowed herself to doubt. Now she was tired. Now she had been forsaken and abandoned. She sat down, crossing her legs underneath her, conscious of the floor wet with blood beneath her. There was nothing left to do but hope for answers.

How does one become something that is no longer a god?

"How does a human girl become something divine and feared by the gods that gave her the power she wields?"

Nadya frowned, puzzled. *I think you're mistaken.*

"Mistakes are not things I generally make," the voice replied.

Where am I? What do you want? The being never answered her first question, but she held back asking again in hope she would receive *some* answers.

"Where you are is as irrelevant as it is immaterial. What I want is better answered by the question of what *you* want."

Can I see you?

"You do not want to."

Nadya flipped the pendant between her fingers. It had come with her. Had she been carrying this being around her neck all this time? Where had Kostya—of all people—found this? Why had he given it to *her*?

What . . . *did* she want?

"You have it already," the voice said from behind her. When she turned there was nothing but the white and the blood. "But you don't realize it. So long spent under the thumb of the pantheon has tainted your understanding."

Tainted? Nadya asked, feeling sick. Whatever this was, whatever this being wanted, would only lead to danger. But what option did she even have?

"You think they can take your power away from you?"

Nadya grew cold.

They can. They gave me this power; they can take it at their will.

"That *is* incorrect." The voice sounded amused.

Nadya trembled. Her vision blurred, shifting back to darkness before being flooded with white once more.

"Our time together grows short. You must make a choice, little bird. Do you continue on with your wings clipped or do you fly?"

Darkness plunged back around Nadya—abrupt and severe— as the necklace slipped out of her hands and pain crashed back down onto her.

26

NADEZHDA

LAPTEVA

Velyos is a god but not a god. He is a was and an is and never again, never again.

—Codex of the Divine, 50:118

When Nadya came to there was an itching in her veins unlike anything she had felt before. She shoved the necklace down into her pocket, careful to keep it off her skin, though it no longer glowed. If blood sparked the connection, she would have to be especially careful not to touch the pendant again, as blood was slick around her still.

The itching in her veins grew stronger, and Nadya shut her eyes. Remembering the well of power during the attack on the church when Marzenya had given her free rein of her magic, she groped in her own mind, trying to find that place once more. If what the voice said was true, it was hers to use, and she needed to find it.

Fog clung to her. It was as if she was lifting a heavy

curtain. What she found on the other side was white and shining and *powerful*. Refrains of holy speech unlike anything she had ever heard. Pure raw magic. She opened her eyes and stood, ignoring her body's protestations as her cuts reopened, blood dripping down. White points of light emanated from her fingertips and she touched the door, drawing symbols with the practiced ease of someone who had cast magic this way all her life. She knew—intrinsically—how she was to use this power, how she was to twist the words of an immortal tongue into raw magic.

The door shattered before her hands. She jumped back, wincing as shards pierced her already broken body. She wasn't going to stay conscious for much longer.

There was no one outside and Nadya wilted with relief against the doorframe, giving herself a moment to breathe through the pain and flashes of wooziness, before she put one foot in front of the other and slowly stumbled forward.

She turned the corner and ran directly into someone coming down the hall. The well of magic flooded down into her hands and she reacted without thinking, shoving out with the power. She saw the figure's arm lift, blood on their palm. Her magic crashed off them harmlessly, deflected by their own power.

"Nadya?"

She froze, taking a step back. Fear and relief tangled in her chest and she wanted to bolt. If the Vultures had Malachiasz again they could use him against her and she couldn't fight him. Not in the state she was in now. So she ran.

Nadya was tired and battered and it took him no effort to catch her. He grabbed her arm and yanked her to a stop. Dimly, she realized she was shaking. She heard him hiss out a low breath as he took in her mess of wounds.

"It's just me," he said, gently turning her to face him. "I went to your rooms. Parijahan was gone and the place was ransacked."

No mask; it was tied to his belt. It was just him. Hair tangled and dark smudges of exhaustion under his pale eyes. He was here looking for her, not because he had been brainwashed to kill her. She let out a long, shuddered breath.

He glanced over his shoulder. She lifted her hands, staring at them. What had she *done*? What was this power she was using? It was blasphemous; the door would never reopen to her if she kept this up. When she lifted her gaze, Malachiasz was watching her with a tentative expression on his face.

"My magic . . ." she started.

But then he tensed, head whipping around, and suddenly her feet were off the ground and he had swept her down the nearest hallway and into what appeared to be a closet.

It was dark. She was immediately hyperaware of just how close she was to him, face against his chest. His breath ruffled the soft hairs at the base of her neck, sending shivering jolts down her spine. She could feel his hands hovering inches above her waist, clearly afraid to settle on the chance he would place them directly over an open wound.

Footsteps clattered through the hallway. Loud and fast moving. Someone had discovered that Nadya was not where she was supposed to be. Once things grew quiet again, he shifted, taking her hands in his, her palms up.

"Show me," he said softly.

She swallowed hard. Grasped at the well of magic that flowed too deeply for her to understand. White light like cold flame sparked at her palms.

An odd little half smile flickered at his lips, lit by the glowing magic at her hands. Magic that was . . . hers? She didn't know. She opened her mouth to ask him, because he would know, but something stopped her. She didn't understand how he knew these things about magic; didn't want to be swayed to his heretical point of view. But . . .

What if he's right? He always seemed to be right about her, about magic. She didn't understand.

"The things you could do," he whispered. He touched his fingertips against hers and she had to swallow down her heart from where it lodged in her throat. A faraway look appeared in his eyes, but he blinked and it was gone. "We need to get out of here."

She nodded. There was a second, a tremor, where she wanted to break into pieces and cry. She wouldn't—she refused to crack so easily. But she threw her arms around him, fingers digging into his back, indulging in the comfort of his warmth.

He let out a startled breath and his hand weaved through her hair to cradle the back of her head. "I'm glad you're safe," he whispered, lips soft against her temple. "Let's get you to someone who can see to the worst of your wounds."

Nadya reluctantly pulled away. She reached out to the gods again as she reached for Malachiasz's hand. He twined their fingers together without a word.

And, again, from the gods, she was met with silence.

Nadya looked up at the winding staircase with trepidation. The glass tower was beautiful, light glittering through the panes. It had more stairs than Nadya would be able to climb in her current state.

"I could—" Malachiasz started, but quickly fell silent when Nadya held up a hand.

"I will not be carried," she said.

"It would be no trou—"

"Do not offer again." But the reality of the situation hit her and she leaned her head against his shoulder. She felt dizzy, each wave of pain threatening to knock her flat.

The witch lived at the top of the spiral staircase. Apparently she was their best bet to getting Nadya any help at all. Malachiasz softly kissed the top of Nadya's head.

"Are you certain?"

"Not at all," she mumbled. She was in pain and tired and didn't want to walk up however many thousands of stairs were in front of her.

She straightened, pulling away from Malachiasz and gripping the railing as she started up. He let out a frustrated breath behind her.

"I lived at the top of seven thousand stairs," she said. "What's a few more?"

Her head spun and she swayed backwards. She gripped the handrail enough to twist herself around so she was sitting instead of toppling down the stairs.

Malachiasz leaned against the railing. "Written in the history books will be the story of a Kalyazi cleric, killed before her time not by her Tranavian enemies, but because of a flight of stairs."

Nadya let out a pained whimper. Cuts reopened and started to drip blood down her back. "I hate you."

"*I* offered to help."

She looked up at him. "Written in the history books will be the story of a deranged former Vulture, murdered—quite terribly—after making one too many awful quips."

"Deranged?"

"*Abomination* is too biased a word. You have to stay objective in history."

"That's not even remotely true. Are you going to sit here all night? Someone is going to wonder where I am."

She was fairly certain the world had begun to spin around her in addition to her already dizzy head. She held a hand out in front of her face and squinted at it. She was seeing far too many hands.

"Are you in shock, Nadya?"

She squinted up at him. "Is that what this is? You lose a lot of blood and you're perfectly fine. *I* lose a lot of blood and I go into shock? How is that at all fair?"

He laughed. She grinned through her pain-filled haze. She liked the sound of his laugh. She held her hands out to him. He could at least help her stand.

As she rose, everything spun so hard around her she only had enough time to shift her footing so Malachiasz could catch her when she fainted.

Nadya woke for the third time that day, but this time it was on a chaise that smelled of mildew. There were bandages wrapped tightly around her torso and limbs. Her tattered dress had been replaced with a simple one of gray wool. She sat up slowly, every inch of her protesting.

"Ah, she awakens," a voice said from across the room. "Good, it was growing awkward with this Vulture here. Never did like his kind."

Malachiasz made an affronted sound.

Nadya rubbed at her eyes. "How long was I out?"

"Not long, not long at all."

The witch looked to be in her seventies. Her eyes sparked onyx bright in the dim light of the room. Her face was lined, her curls white but threaded with black.

Nadya met Malachiasz's eyes from where he was sitting across the room. He smiled faintly, but seemed preoccupied.

"Do you know my name, child?" the witch said. "Because I know yours and that doesn't seem fair."

Nadya stiffened. "H-how do you know my name?"

She waved a hand. "My name is Pelageya, in case you weren't aware. I know his name, too," she said, hooking a thumb in Malachiasz's direction. "Which is the true feat."

Malachiasz tensed, but he didn't move from his seemingly relaxed posture. His gaze grew wary as he eyed the witch.

Nadya frowned, puzzled.

"It's been a long time since I was in Kalyazin, but I recognize a girl of snow and forest well enough even with dark magic's touch upon her. And this palace has been without any blessing of the divine for so long that you were practically shining when you stepped inside. But . . ." she trailed off, peering closely at Nadya. "Not enough light to guide you now."

Pelageya grinned. "What if I provide some illumination for this dark path? You came to the right place, though I'm surprised your Vulture brought you here. I'll tell you a story." The witch promptly sat down on the floor. "A story about our king and a young prodigy Vulture."

Nadya looked up in time to see Malachiasz's fingers curl into a fist.

"Though," she considered, tugging at a spiral curl, "he's not your king. Not mine, either. He's not even *sterevyani bolen's* king, now, is he? Is it treason if we all here swear to different crowns? Except . . ." Her gaze narrowed on Malachiasz. "You can't really swear to your own crown, now can you?"

"Careful . . ." he murmured. He flexed his hand over the arm of his chair, nails flashing iron in the dim candlelight.

Pelageya smiled.

"You see, our Tranavian king has become a paranoid man, certain that because his son is a more powerful mage, it will spell his doom. So he needs more power, always more power.

"And amidst the Vultures was one who rose through the ranks at such a very young age. More clever than most and more dangerous by far, he spent his time with ancient books and old tomes and discovered the very secret the king was looking for."

Nadya felt a chill of dread settle in the pit of her stomach. Malachiasz leaned his chin on his hand, listening intently.

"So, he offered it to the king. It was theoretical, of course, nothing that could ever actually be *done*. But the idea was there and this talented Vulture wanted his cult to be on better terms with the Tranavian king. The Vulture queen who ruled before him did a poor job, you see. She ground the order down to near insignificance and *this* talented Vulture wanted his order to have power again. He wanted a partnership of equals between the crowns. Perhaps he even wanted something in return for this gift, but who could say? But then the king asked him to perform this theoretical ceremony. Surely, he could do it. He was the ultimate success of his cult, the one whose power had been tortured into him to a higher point than even the oldest Vultures ever reached. If anyone could do this, he could."

Pelageya giggled. "Can one have a crisis of conscience if one has no conscience to begin with?"

Malachiasz leaned back in his chair, gaze flicking to Nadya and away again.

"The Vulture disappeared. Poof! There one night, gone the next, leaving his cult to scramble in his absence. Because the Vultures need direction, they need their Black Vulture to lead them, and he had vanished."

Nadya was listening at a distance, refusing to let the witch's words catch up to her, to connect all that she was hearing, but she knew, she *knew*. Would that it had been so simple, that Malachiasz were just a Vulture recruit who got scared and fled. The world was falling out from underneath her and she had no anchor, she had nothing, because nothing was even real.

It was Malachiasz. It had always been Malachiasz. The leader of the cult, the one who had spun all of this into motion, the one who had smiled and charmed his way into Nadya's trust because he could do terrible things with her power if he had access to it. She wouldn't be sitting here with bandages covering her body if not for Malachiasz.

"But he fled?" Nadya asked. If she pretended the one they were speaking of wasn't sitting in front of them, listening in calm contemplation, maybe that would make this easier.

"He did," Pelageya said. "But he came back. Do you think that is coincidence? That this clever boy and his clever magic have returned now?"

"Malachiasz?" Nadya said, her voice smaller than she would have liked, weaker. She willed him to look at her.

He looked different, sitting in the witch's chair in a way that made it seem almost a throne. His black hair parted far on the right side, falling over his shoulder in inky waves, his pale eyes cold and blank. Less a boy, more a monster. Was that all he was? The silly boy who smiled too much and felt too deeply just a mask for the monster underneath?

Had she fallen for his lies exactly as he wanted her to?

He finally met her gaze, eyes softening, growing familiar. "It's all right, *towy dżimyka*," he said, voice soft.

It wasn't. Not at all.

Pelageya laughed. "Is that supposed to make her feel better?" She stood up, walking around Malachiasz's chair. "Is that supposed to earn her trust again?" She hooked a finger underneath his chin, forcing his gaze up to hers. She looked young. Nadya didn't know when the shift had happened but knew the witch was a force of nature. A magic just as old and dangerous as either of them possessed, made worse by the wisdom of her years. "What have you done, *Chelvyanik Sterevyani?*" she whispered. "What will you still do? I don't think love is such a force that it will stop you. I'm not sure you're even capable of it."

Nadya closed her eyes. Her breath hitched. She wasn't going to cry, she was too scared for that, too deeply shattered. She wanted to, though. Cry like a village maid who'd had her heart broken, not a girl touched by the gods who fell for a monster and was devoured. This was her fault. She'd ignored the signs, ignored her goddess even. Now it was too late. Now they were here and her heart had been compromised and maybe this was a mistake, maybe he wasn't lying at all, maybe he had changed, he would help them, and this was all just the witch trying to tear a rift between them that would ruin everything and hand the war to Tranavia.

"I just want to end what I started," Malachiasz finally said.

Nadya felt her heart lift with hope but she quashed it. She wanted to trust him, desperately, but how could she?

Pelageya's eyes narrowed. "How careful you are with words, *Veshyen Yaliknevo.*" *Your Excellency.*

"Don't," he said, pulling away from her touch.

"What?" she asked innocently. "I'm just giving you the respect you're due. Would you prefer if I used your name?"

His jaw clenched.

"I thought so. Malachiasz Czechowicz. Such power in that name. It was wise of you to hide it from Tranavia, but then you gave it away in Kalyazin. I'm still puzzling over that, surely you knew what you were doing by that act. You *have* proven to be exceedingly clever." She paused in thought, pulling a face of almost deranged glee. It was unsettling. "But, this isn't just about you, *Veshyen Yaliknevo*. *Chelvyanik Sterevyani*. *Sterevyani bolen*." She sat down on the arm of his chair and he shifted to the opposite side, as far from her as he could possibly get. "This is about the little scrap of divinity you've drawn to the depths of Tranavia."

Nadya lifted her chin. She wasn't going to let them see she was falling apart.

"She followed you a long, long way from home. What did you tell her to make her come so far without putting a blade in your back?"

Malachiasz mumbled something Nadya didn't hear. Pelageya laughed.

"Of course, of course. Without cutting your throat, I should have said. Now that you point it out she does have the look of a girl who goes for—" She leaned over and tipped Malachiasz's head back again, baring his throat. His fist clenched over the arm of the chair, nails now just long enough to be visible claws. "—sensitive flesh."

Malachiasz inhaled sharply.

"I never told her anything that wasn't true," he said, voice carefully restrained.

Pelageya looked to Nadya. For what, confirmation? She shrugged.

"Apparently it was all in what he never bothered saying, or how he chose to say it," she said. *It's all still lies.*

Pelageya slid her hand down Malachiasz's neck. "I don't think you realize just what you've done, *Veshyen Yaliknevo*."

He frowned, looking over at Pelageya for the first time.

"Oh, you think you do, for you are so clever, and all the pieces have fallen into place remarkably for you." She brushed a fingertip against a trio of gold beads that were threaded through his hair. Nadya narrowed her eyes; she didn't remember ever seeing those before. "How much will you come to regret this?"

"We're going to stop this war," Malachiasz said evenly. "There is nothing to regret."

Pelageya smirked. *"Dasz polakienscki ja mawelczenko."*

Nadya frowned. The words were Tranavian, but she had no idea what any of them meant. Clearly, Malachiasz understood, his face paled.

"Nie."

"I suppose you'll find out."

"I think someone should explain to me what's going on," Nadya said slowly, finally working up the courage to speak. She felt like a *child.* Far too young to understand what was going on. Their words were spinning just out of reach over her head. Right now it was hard to believe Malachiasz was only one winter older than her; there was a darkness around him that made him seem so much older and more terrible. She hated it and she wasn't going to let them do this to her. She wouldn't be used, not by Malachiasz, not by this witch.

Pelageya glanced at Malachiasz. Reluctantly he returned the look and waved a hand; suddenly this action that had seemed so benign before appeared uncomfortably imperious.

"By all means," he said. "She'll be killing me soon enough and I'm fascinated by what you have to say."

The condescension, however, made more sense now.

"No, actually, I'm more interested in your excuse," Nadya said. She wished her voice wouldn't shake. She wished she could face this without feeling like something was being ripped away from her.

The witch grinned and his expression wearied. He glanced at Pelageya again, clearly hesitant to speak in front of her.

"Why are you here, Malachiasz?"

"I have told you. My reasoning hasn't changed just because you know what I am now. I want to save my country. I'm one of the few people who can; surely you understand that."

He was giving her nothing, less than nothing.

"I don't believe you," she said softly.

Pelageya ran a hand through Malachiasz's hair. He looked like he was an inch away from tearing her arm off.

"You're young, *sterevyani bolen*," she said. "How were you to know that your heart still beat in your chest after what's been done to you?"

He snarled, knocking her hand away and standing in one fast, dangerous movement. "Don't mock me, witch."

Pelageya lifted an eyebrow, lips twisting into a slow smile. Then her attention was back on Nadya.

Nadya, who didn't know how to hold herself together after this. Nadya, who couldn't pull her gaze away from Malachiasz, unable to reconcile that the boy she had traded jokes with, that she had kissed, was a symbol of Tranavian heresy. A monster greater than all others.

She feared the Vultures more than she did the Tranavian nobles. She feared the Black Vulture more than she feared the Tranavian king. It didn't make sense. That the silly, anxious boy sat on a throne built on the bones of thousands of people. Idly, she realized her hands were shaking. The room was too cold. Everything was wrong, the world shifted too far to one angle, unfamiliar and treacherous.

She thought she knew what she was doing, coming here, but now she was in a foreign country, surrounded by her enemies, and the one she had anchored her safety to had been lying to her from the start.

Nadya pulled Kostya's necklace out from her pocket, holding it up to Pelageya.

"What is this?"

"A vessel, a chamber, *a trap*," she said. "Velyos is within. Did he give you his name? No, he likes to be mysterious. Mystery is something more appealing to someone divine."

Nadya shut her eyes. She didn't understand what was happening.

"Have you heard of him? I suppose not. The veil went up, Velyos broke away. Your gods were probably relieved, but now here he is once more. You cannot feel the touch of your gods because the king is sending blood magic out in waves around Tranavia. Why do you think he's kidnapped lovely young blood mages to siphon out their power? He's cut off any access to the divine in preparation for his end goal. It's been building for years in Tranavia, this veil, this darkness."

A chill cut through Nadya hard enough to frost her skin. A shard of ice digging into her stomach. His end goal, some theory Malachiasz had provided to him. *Power.*

"The veil isn't the problem," Malachiasz muttered.

Pelageya ignored him. "But, you see, your world has taught you there are only two things," Pelageya said. She slid off the armrest until she was lounging sideways in the chair Malachiasz had previously been sitting in.

He leaned against the fireplace, arms crossed over his chest.

"There is your magic, which is good, of course. And then *their* magic. Blood magic. Heresy."

"It's just magic," Malachiasz said.

"I don't think she wants to hear this from you," Pelageya sang.

Nadya glanced at him. Hadn't that been what he had tried to show her from the day they met? Hadn't that been his entire point when they were at the wayside shrine? He had been

trying to give her some form of freedom—his form of freedom—
and until this point she had been considering it, wavering.

"But then there is my magic, except a witch is just a girl who
has realized her power is her own. Then, perhaps, there is
something else yet."

Nadya forced her hands still before they reached for the prayer
beads she did not have. "What are you saying?" she whispered.
But she didn't want to know. She wasn't ready to indulge, she
wasn't ready to step away from her gods. She didn't *want* this.

She held her hand out in front of herself and small flames
lit around her fingertips. "That's wrong."

"That's magic."

Nadya shook her head.

"You're here to kill a king and change the world," Pelageya
said. "One will, of course, follow the other. How did you think
you were going to do that? How were you going to get around
the fact that your *Chelvyanik Sterevyani* doesn't have the control over his cult that he used to?"

Malachiasz's jaw tightened. Nadya felt almost relieved. The
witch had said it to sow more discord, but if he didn't have full
control of the Vultures, maybe that meant he actually *was* helping them? She shouldn't give in to hope. She hated that she
was so damn hopeful.

"Did you drag this out just to taunt us that our goal is impossible?" Malachiasz asked.

Us. Our. She looked at him just as he glanced down at her.
She was in a thousand broken pieces and she didn't know what
to do.

No, she did. His was a game she could play perfectly. She
would keep her distance, let him think he had gotten away with
it, and then she would get her answers.

"Of course. A bit. But also to help, because you *do* need help."

A sudden insistent knock on the door made all three of them pause. Then a voice, terrifyingly familiar, came from outside.

"Pelageya? I need to speak with you."

Of course it would be the prince.

27

SEREFIN
MELESKI

Svoyatovi Klavdiy Gusin: *A cleric of Bozetjeh, Svoyatovi Klavdiy Gusin was a master of time, bending it to his will. Until, one day he disappeared and was never heard from again, his body never found.*

—Vasiliev's Book of Saints

There was a rattling from inside the room as Serefin waited with Ostyia and Kacper. He could hear hushed voices snapping at each other before the door opened.

"If this is a bad time I can—" He cut himself off. Firstly, because he realized even if it *was* a bad time, he would not wait or come back. There was no time. Secondly, because when the door was opened it was by someone he thought he would never see again.

"Malachiasz?"

The boy on the other side of the door blinked in surprise, something undefinable flickering over his features.

Serefin realized immediately that Malachiasz didn't recognize him the same way.

His cousin had disappeared when they were children. He never thought he would see him again; his aunt acted like he was dead, so Serefin assumed some accident had befallen him that the family didn't speak of. But the lanky boy leaning in the doorway to the witch's chambers was the eighteen-year-old version of the wild boy Serefin had played with as a child.

"Your . . . Excellency?" Ostyia said, obviously trying to fill in the awkward space that had arisen between the boys.

Malachiasz lifted his eyebrows. "Yes?"

"This is unexpected."

Serefin felt his stomach drop as Malachiasz responded to the Black Vulture's honorific with a sharp-toothed smile. *How can it be him?*

Malachiasz pushed away from the doorframe and winked at Serefin. "My second informed me you were asking after my health. Truly, I'm touched."

"What a plot this is turning out to be!" Serefin recognized Pelageya's voice. "Get out of the way, *sterevyani bolen,* let your prince inside."

"Can he be *my* prince if his father isn't my king?" Malachiasz asked. "Since that was so important to you a moment ago."

But he opened the door wider, cutting Serefin another odd look as he took a step back. Józefina was sitting on a chaise by the fire. Blood stained her hands and face.

A sick feeling settled in Serefin's stomach. He should have walked her to her chambers; he shouldn't have left her alone. The Vultures must have taken her the minute he had his back turned.

Malachiasz stepped toward her, but received an icy glare that made him veer off, and he ended up leaning against the fireplace. She drew her knees up to her chin, finally meeting Serefin's gaze. She shot him a tentative smile.

"Józefina, I thought . . ." Serefin trailed off. "I'm glad to see you well."

"She was in a sorry state when I found her, do you know something about that?" Malachiasz asked. He tilted his head, waiting for Serefin's answer.

Is he goading me? Serefin thought, confused. *He doesn't know me.* Something knotted in his chest. It bothered him, that this boy—his cousin—didn't know him, that he only knew him as the petulant High Prince.

Serefin could feel a headache starting to form behind his eyes. He was so *tired.* He collapsed in an empty chair, indifferent to the broken image of himself he was showing to the Vulture. He could pick a fight at a later date if he survived this.

"Your Highness looks unwell," Pelageya noted.

"His Highness has been in a perpetual state of 'unwell' since he returned to Tranavia," Serefin muttered. "What is he doing here?" He pointed to Malachiasz.

"You know I was wondering that myself. Unfortunately, for all of us, he's as woven into this mess as the rest of you," Pelageya said. "I think you're all even working for the same goal, which would be novel, now, wouldn't it?"

Pelageya stood in the center of the room, hands on her hips, as she slowly scanned the group. She frowned at Ostyia and Kacper.

"Stumbling in a dark so thick you cannot see your hand in front of your face. I know, I know. I've been watching you all as you stagger toward a similar end, but none of you seem to know where you're going. You're close, you've planned well, but the king has eyes, the king has ears, the king *knows.*"

Serefin straightened. Józefina appeared troubled.

"What are you talking about, witch?" Ostyia asked.

"You. Want. To. Kill. The. King." Each word was emphasized by Pelageya flinging out one of her bony fingers from her fists. She held up her hands, showing six fingers, and grinned. "All of you do! Oh, how our Tranavian king is hated. I wonder, though, truly, will you all turn your attention on the Kalyazi *tsar* next? Or is this a one-ruler assassination plan?"

No one spoke. Tension fell heavily over the room.

"The girl, the monster, and the prince," Pelageya said with a sly giggle. "And here you all are."

Serefin lifted his head. There was more to that prophecy. He didn't miss the Vulture's frown, or Józefina's look of puzzlement.

"We are missing a few," Pelageya mused, rocking back on her heels. "But . . ." She shrugged. "Their part will come later, or never, for if you all fail none of you will survive! I wonder, truly, if you have a plan for this coup? How will you keep the nobles from revolt? How will you keep the Kalyazi from swarming Grazyk? Or, gods forbid, the Salt Mines?"

"The throne is mine," Serefin said.

The Vulture's frown deepened at the mention of the Salt Mines. Serefin kept a careful eye on him as Pelageya spoke. He didn't like that he was here, it didn't make any sense.

"If the throne still exists after all of this," Malachiasz murmured.

"Your throne likely won't," Serefin said.

"I don't *need* my throne. It's a bit of an empty symbol. Power is power."

Józefina grew very still, her face paling. She cast a horrified look Malachiasz's way before her eyes fluttered shut and she pressed her forehead against her knees.

"I want you all on the same page, my little revolutionaries, for I think you will all leave this room acting upon a singular plan."

"And it will be a mad witch who sets us upon it?" Serefin asked.

"Ah, but you came here for advice, prince, because you are desperate with a plan that you know will fail."

Serefin glowered and leaned back in his chair, sighing. He didn't know why the Black Vulture and Józefina were here. He didn't know what they knew or why they were—apparently—acting with the same goal as him. He didn't know and he didn't care. If this took him to the end, then he would work with anyone. "What will you have us do?"

Pelageya laughed, clasping her hands together. "Ah, this is a dream come true. What *will* I have you all do?"

"Within reason, witch," Malachiasz said wearily.

Józefina still had not opened her eyes or lifted her head.

Pelageya sat down on the floor in the center of the room, her skirts sweeping out in a wide arc around her. She ran through—tapping out on her fingers—all the details that had come to light during the past few weeks. Most of it Serefin knew, some of it he did not. But those were things he barely believed: intervention of the divine, blood magic being used to block off the heavens, that it had been the Black Vulture who had defected. The latter explained a few things, but not enough.

"So what do we do?" Ostyia finally snapped.

Pelageya looked to her before looking away dismissively. Ostyia wasn't a part of the witch's mad prophecy so she wasn't worth her time. However Serefin wanted to know the answer. What were they to do? If his plan was doomed to failure and seemingly he was to work with the Black Vulture? The Black Vulture who had returned to his cult. His cult that had been whispering in his father's ear.

"What do you have to gain from my father's death?" Serefin asked Józefina.

Her dark eyes were impassive. "I want to end a war."

"And killing my father would do that? Why not kill the Kalyazi *tsar*? Tranavia is winning, why not let the war end organically?"

Her eyebrows furrowed and she chewed at her lip. "And why would you want to kill your father, Serefin? He's your *father*, and you don't seem particularly hungry for the throne."

She's deflecting, Serefin thought.

"Oh, but the king needs one last element for this grand spell of his!" Pelageya said before Serefin could answer. "The blood of his firstborn son will take him from our mortal realm to one significantly higher."

Józefina blanched. It took her a second to recover. "So, how do we kill him? *When* do we kill him?"

"When he thinks he's won," Serefin murmured.

Malachiasz smiled. "Well, that's where you'll need me."

Serefin's eyes narrowed.

"The king doesn't know I'm in Grazyk," Malachiasz said.

"Yes, but we all know your Vultures have fallen to pieces in your absence," Kacper said.

Malachiasz stiffened. Józefina shot him a curious look.

"There are some who want me off the throne," he said. "How is that unusual?"

"Because the Vultures can't act against their leader?"

"Magic is imperfect, lieutenant," Malachiasz said. "How do you think I became king? Łucja had the throne for nearly forty years before I challenged her."

Even so, Serefin hadn't known the Vultures were truly split. It made sense now that the Crimson Vulture had come to him even while others were acting as his father's personal guards. He couldn't concern himself with uniting the cult, though.

"The Vultures are the ones who planted this seed in my father, who gave him this idea. Was it you? It makes perfect sense for you to be the puppet master here."

Józefina looked ill.

"This is entirely my fault," Malachiasz said.

Serefin flinched back as if Malachiasz had struck him. *This has become quite the family mess,* he thought.

Józefina stood, wincing as she did so. She slowly paced the room, walking with a bare limp. *What happened to her?*

She idly flipped a silver pendant between her fingers. "The king won't want to . . . proceed without you present, will he?" she asked Malachiasz.

"If he thinks he can do this himself, he is grossly overconfident in his mediocre abilities," Malachiasz said.

Serefin snorted softly. "That's what this all is at the core of it, isn't it? It's just power."

"Isn't it always?" Malachiasz asked.

Józefina cast a glance between them, eyes narrowing. "All right," she said softly. "It's safe to assume that the *Rawalyk* has been ignored in favor of harvesting participants for their blood." She grimaced, rubbing her forearm, and Serefin realized what had happened to her.

Blood and bone.

"I would say he's going to make his move soon," Serefin said. "I would like to avoid him reaching the part where he kills me. If that's possible?"

A weary half smile flickered at Józefina's lips. "Tell him you can do this without Serefin," she said to Malachiasz.

He lifted an eyebrow. "You want me to go to the king?"

She held his gaze for a long time, something dangerous sparking through the air between them.

"If not, then we need to reevaluate our understanding," she said. There was steel in her voice.

He looked as if she'd slapped him. "Understood," he said, voice strained.

She turned to Pelageya, who grinned. "Tension in the ranks, how exciting. You're on the right track, now it just needs some dramatics."

28

NADEZHDA

LAPTEVA

Svoyatova Alevtina Polacheva: *A cleric of Marzenya, she was an assassin who seemed to be more skilled at the art of death than the art of magic. She lost her life on a mission to Tranavia, killed by heretic blood mages.*

—Vasiliev's Book of Saints

"I need to speak with *on yaliknevi* for just a bit," Nadya told the others, ignoring the brief flicker of agony that crossed Malachiasz's face as she used his damn honorific.

What Nadya always had to her advantage was the element of surprise. When she slammed Malachiasz into the railing of the stairs to the tower, he seemed genuinely shocked.

"Nadya, please," he said through gritted teeth as she hooked her leg around his to make it easier to topple him over the side if she felt like it.

"Have you *ever* told me the truth?" She could feel her power swirling in her veins and it was a terrifying thought that she could so easily use it on him now. "How did the prince recognize you?"

"How he knew my name, I have no idea," Malachiasz said. He strained against her, but after realizing it was fruitless he relaxed into it, letting his head fall back. He hung, bent backwards over the railing, one foot and Nadya's hand gripping his shirt all that kept him from toppling over the side. "It was your spell that left the loophole that those who were not our enemies would be able to see me."

"So the prince has become our ally?" Nadya asked incredulously.

"Apparently. But this isn't why you're angry with me."

She pushed him back a little farther. His grounded foot slipped and he jerked, his hands scrambling to grasp at the railings.

"You lied to me," she said through clenched teeth. "You made me believe you were nothing but a boy, scared and in over his head, when you were the worst of them the whole time."

He sighed heavily. "Yes."

"Why?" Her voice cracked. She hated that he could affect her like this.

"Because I'm scared and in over my head," he murmured. "I also happen to be the worst of them. Nadya, please let me stand." His tone was weary. "I appreciate the threat, but I would survive this fall. You did better last time."

She took a step back, allowing him to straighten, before punching him in the face.

He staggered back against the railing again, laughing as he wiped blood from his bleeding nose. "I deserved that."

"You deserve more than that," Nadya said. "I should have dropped you."

He looked down, considering the fall. She shook her head, glanced at the door, then started down the steps. She needed to talk to him where there was less of a chance of the prince hearing. He was silent, trailing behind her until they reached the bottom of the stairs. Nadya grabbed the doorknob and that was when he finally spoke.

"Nadya, there was no other way."

It was her turn to be silent. She moved to open the door, but his hand landed over hers. She was very aware of his body close to hers, the heat of him at her back.

"Monsters are real, and I am their king." His voice was low, a whisper, his lips brushing the shell of her ear. "We both know lying was the only way to earn your trust."

She wanted to shove him away; she wanted him closer. That always seemed to be the crux of it. She didn't know what she wanted. Why hadn't the revelation cut whatever was tying her to this boy? Why did she feel herself leaning back against him?

"Was my trust really that essential?"

"Nadezhda Lapteva . . ." His hand slipped up her arm. She felt his other hand against her waist. Hearing her full name spoken with his Tranavian accent made her shiver. "More than you even realize, *towy dżimyka*."

She let out a shaky breath. His hand slid up her neck, tilting her head back. His lips pressed against her throat, sparks igniting underneath his touch.

Her resolve was fighting a losing battle. It surrendered when he lifted his head and kissed the corner of her mouth.

"This isn't fair," she murmured as he turned her around and pressed her against the door. "This is playing dirty."

"I'll not lie to you, Nadya," he said, a smile quirking his lips at the irony. "I play dirty."

Then her traitorous, heretical hands betrayed her as she reached up and wove them into his hair, pulling his face down to hers and kissing him. Because she was angry with him, furious with his lies, but not even her anger was enough to cool the burning she felt when he was near; the heat that spread through her nerves when he touched her.

He made a small surprised sound against her mouth, his hands pulling her closer. His hips pressed into her, hand tugging at her hair to draw her face up to his. She arched her back off the wall, letting her body form against his until there was no space left and it was just them, only them, and the heat of his body and the pressure of his mouth.

For all his lies and plots and the danger he brought into the shoddy plan they had, she held *this* over him, she realized. This monstrous king could be undone by the touch of her lips.

She only had enough sense to tuck that piece of information away before he kissed her harder, deeper, sliding his knee in between her legs, and every sensible thought she had fled her mind.

When they finally broke apart, Nadya let out a breathless laugh as she gazed up at the glittering rainbows cast by the tower.

"You're going to go find Parijahan and Rashid. I don't know what happened to them after I was taken and I'm worried," she said.

He nodded.

She took his chin in her hand, directing his gaze down to hers. "Prove to me with something other than words that I shouldn't kill you for what you are," she whispered.

But even now, she didn't know if she could ever do what needed to be done.

"Go to the cathedral when you're finished here," he said. "None of the Vultures will give you any trouble."

She felt a chill of dread, but she nodded. "Do the others know about you?"

"Yes."

They've all been keeping this from me. Every single one of them.

"Nadya . . ." he began, but she waved him off, stepping away toward the stairs.

"Go," she said. "I'll speak with you later." An undercurrent of a threat, a promise, a statement that this wasn't over and she wasn't going to let him sway her with charm.

He hesitated, and his hesitation did nothing but break Nadya down further. She didn't know what to do and she didn't have her gods for guidance. She hated feeling lost, betrayed, and broken.

Ultimately, it didn't matter. She had come here to stop a war, to bring about justice for her gods, to bring them back. Her heart wasn't a factor, no matter how much it was twisted and torn in the process.

She returned to Pelageya's rooms, bracing herself for the questions Serefin would surely have for her that she wasn't entirely certain she could answer. He still thought she was a Tranavian noble. It didn't make sense that he recognized Malachiasz, but there was something else, something there. They both had the same icy pale eyes, and it was probably nothing, a quirk of coincidence, yet . . .

Likely it was something that didn't matter. Nadya pushed open the door to find Serefin whispering fiercely with Ostyia. They both stopped when she entered.

"Where did Malachiasz go?" Serefin asked.

"We came here with companions who haven't been seen since I was kidnapped."

Serefin flinched. Nadya let some of her ice cool. He was fighting for the same thing they were, albeit in a roundabout way. She didn't know how he felt about the war, but the way he had spoken of it at dinner the night before had been weary.

"I'm sorry," he said softly. "I didn't know you all would be in danger from him as well."

"But you knew there was something going on?"

"I thought his focus was entirely on me."

She nodded. "Is that why you're willing to kill him? Because it's you or him?"

"That and you've seen Tranavia, you see what his obsession with power and this war have done to the country."

She had. She'd seen poverty and suffering, just as there was in Kalyazin. This couldn't continue, they couldn't sustain it for much longer.

"Do you trust him?" Serefin asked. "The Black Vulture?"

I didn't know that was who he was, she thought, *so the answer is too complicated for words.*

"I think it's safe to keep him at arm's length," Nadya said—a thing she clearly wasn't doing; her lips still felt bruised from his kisses. "But I also believe he will help us."

"It doesn't make sense to me," Ostyia muttered.

Nadya shrugged. "This is his fault—" Just saying that ached. "—it would stand to reason he would want to atone for it."

"Will it be enough, though?" Kacper mused.

Serefin frowned. He looked dreadful, dark circles bruising underneath pale eyes, his brown hair looking unwashed.

"What if we bring in a different variable?" Nadya said softly, a plan formulating. "What if we make your father come to us?"

Serefin lifted his head, meeting her gaze. So desperate, so utterly without hope. He didn't truly think his father could be stopped, that much was clear. A pang struck her like a knife to the side. She was lying to him, too. She had learned that the prince wasn't a monster as she had always believed him to be and the boy she was falling for was worse than she could have possibly imagined. And she was lying to them both to see her own goals to fruition.

But she couldn't tell Serefin the truth. She couldn't risk him turning on her before this was finished.

"Draw him into the cathedral—he'll think it's because Malachiasz is ready for this ceremony or whatever it is—get him to a position where he thinks he's going to be given everything—"

"And then take it away," Serefin murmured.

She nodded.

Hope flickered in his eyes and he smiled.

He sent Kacper and Ostyia off to prepare and offered to see Nadya back to her chambers. She was supposed to go to the cathedral, but she suspected Serefin would be less willing to go there, so she accepted. If only to get a little more from this prince before she made her decision on what to do about him.

Marzenya would tell her to kill him, to hell with the whole royal family, and to start Tranavia over with a new line of blood. Marzenya would also tell Nadya to slaughter Malachiasz *immediately*. Neither of those were things she particularly wanted to do. She didn't know what that meant about what she was. She had never wavered in her faith like this, going so willingly against what her gods decreed.

Malachiasz had hidden what he was from her, but she would be dead if not for him and she couldn't deny any longer that her fascination had turned to a fondness that even the lies hadn't managed to soil.

Serefin was clever and surprisingly caring. She had listened to the conversation of the *slavhki* at court; none of them thought of the war as anything more than an inconvenience. They didn't care about what it was doing to their people, they only cared if it got in the way of their dramatics. She wondered if the Kalyazi Silver Court was the same, if maybe they weren't so different after all.

"You'll have the crown if we succeed," she said. "What will you do?"

He was so blithely unaware that his answer would determine whether she spared him or killed him. He looked thoughtful, but she noticed how he tensed whenever they passed servants with their flat, gray masks as they walked through the palace halls. Spies of his father?

"It's never seemed real to me," he said, his voice soft. "I've been at war for . . ." He trailed into silence and there was more in that silence than words could fill. He was broken, she realized, a boy who had seen horrors too young. "I just want to be better than my father."

"Admirable, as your father is currently involved in planning filicide."

He laughed. It was strained.

"What about the war?"

He cast her a sidelong glance that made a jolt of fear run through her. She wondered if he suspected, though she didn't know how he possibly could.

"We don't know anything else," he said. "And that needs to change. And we're out of time. The Kalyazi are moving on Tranavia and I don't know if we're in a position to properly defend ourselves."

Nadya's breath caught. "Anna," she whispered.

"What?"

She shook her head, hoping he didn't press further. "And Tranavia's irreconcilable differences with Kalyazin?"

"What about them?"

"Would you let priests back into Tranavia? Rebuild the churches?"

His jaw tensed. Alarms rang in her head; she had stepped too far, but it was too late to backtrack.

"I'm not sure Kalyazin's gods have any place in Tranavia," he said.

She nodded as if it was a perfectly reasonable answer. Inside she was left fumbling. Serefin *would* be better than his father and the war did need to end. Was she willing to compromise? She was here to give Tranavia back to the gods, but she was here to stop the war as well. Was one more important than the other? She was only one girl; she didn't want the fate of nations resting on her decisions.

They were nearing Nadya's chambers. She wasn't entirely certain how to reach the cathedral from here and she asked Serefin for directions.

He frowned.

"Be . . . careful, Józefina," he said. "He is not one to trifle with."

Nadya almost laughed. It was touching that he seemed so concerned with her welfare. "Could you do me another favor, Serefin?"

"You're aiding me in patricide, I figure I owe you a lifetime of favors."

"Oh, I'll remember that."

He grinned. She couldn't help but smile back.

"Someone has surely noticed that I'm not languishing in a

dungeon by now. I would like to be confident in my knowledge that no one is going to come looking for me because I'm not where I'm supposed to be."

Especially as I'll be with the Vultures.

Serefin nodded. "I can do that."

"Thank you."

"I still don't understand why you're doing this."

Nadya didn't know how to answer that. Divine command was too much truth, anything else felt trite.

"The war took someone important to me," she said, fingering Kostya's necklace unconsciously. She couldn't think about how it had been *Serefin* who had led that attack. "I won't tolerate it any longer."

He leaned against the wall beside the door to her chambers. "And who are you that you can do what countless others have failed at over a century?"

No one. Just a girl. Some small scrap of divinity.

She shrugged. "I'm the first person who refuses to fail."

The Vultures kept residence in what once was the grand cathedral of Grazyk. Now that the gods were no longer worshipped, it was where the Carrion Throne resided. Malachiasz's throne.

The cathedral was an imposing structure. Massive and bleak, with grand spires and huge stained glass windows.

Nadya stopped before the entrance, staring up. She couldn't force her feet closer and after a few minutes she was dimly aware of Malachiasz's presence beside her, looking up at the cathedral as well.

Silence filled the space between them before he spoke: "War has made us all used to living in desecrated spaces once considered holy."

It had been painted black. Nadya knew there was no way it had looked like this when it was an actual church. There were ironwork vines and shattered statues worked into the bricks. All the statues had lost their heads but one.

"*Cholyok dagol,*" she swore under her breath.

Malachiasz followed her gaze. He paled. "You know, I'm honestly not sure how that one in particular has survived."

"I can't tell if you're lying to me or not," Nadya said wearily.

Svoyatova Madgalina. A saint who was supposedly the first of the clerics. Nadya didn't like the irony.

It started to rain. A freezing rain that fell in heavy, painful droplets. Malachiasz squinted up at the sky. He reached down and took her hand, twining their fingers together.

"You're not forgiven," she whispered.

"I know."

She bit her lip, blinking back tears. He tugged at her hand.

"Parijahan and Rashid are fine, come on, let's get out of the rain."

She followed him into the cathedral and tried to not feel as though it was swallowing her alive.

The foyer was tiled with cool, black marble. The door to the sanctuary black with gilded edges. Malachiasz pushed the door open. It was like he was leading her farther down into hell, a new level with every door he opened.

Yet still she followed him.

Her breath caught in her throat when she stepped into the sanctuary. Malachiasz glanced back at her, a half smile at his lips. He was wearing different clothes, a long tunic over breeches, all in black with a rich golden brocade belt tied around his waist. He looked more like nobility now, like he could reasonably be a young king.

The sanctuary was vast, with high, vaulted ceilings and pillars carved with figures that betrayed the room's religious origins. The Carrion Throne rested atop gilded skulls. Bones lined the long, open hall, inlaid into the black marble floor. There was a brutal, primal beauty to it, this combination of the profane and the divine.

Light filtered down through the high windows, flooding the room, softening its harsh lines. She was aware of Malachiasz watching her as she took in the sanctuary. She walked around the bones inlaid in the floor, while Malachiasz stepped from one to the next, like a young boy playing a game.

"Tell me what you wouldn't say in front of the witch," she said.

"The king is trying to become a god," Malachiasz said, without looking up, as he hopped from one bone to another.

Nadya drew in a sharp breath at the frank way he said it. As if it was nothing.

"My concept of a god, not yours, I think," he said. His shoulders lifted in a shrug. "But who knows? And, yes, the theory was one I discovered." He sighed, rubbing his forehead with his elegant, tattooed fingers. She wondered—not for the first time—what the tattoos meant; she wondered if it was too late to find out. "It was just a theory; the sheer amount of magic involved to make anything like it remotely a reality was so astronomical that I thought it was impossible. I shouldn't have told anyone, I know, but I did and here we are."

"Why were you researching it to begin with?"

"Curiosity, for one." He waved a hand at the sanctuary. "Because I saw the fault line in Tranavia and thought maybe— maybe I could fix it. Maybe I could be the one to save this crumbling kingdom. What's the point of all this power if I don't do anything with it . . ."

He'd never struck her as the power-hungry type. She wondered if that was just another facet of him he was hiding, if he had so perfected the image he wanted her to see that she didn't actually know him at all. Or if the idealism—the desire to save a dying kingdom—if that was the truth of him.

Except . . . He was picking at his cuticles, the rim around the nail on his index finger filling with blood as he tore too far. He winced and stuck his finger in his mouth to stop the bleeding. She didn't think a power-hungry monster king would have anxiety and play childhood games on the floor of his own grim palace.

"So, you abdicated? Fled the Vultures?"

"I fled *Tranavia*," he clarified. "Abdication is impossible. I have the throne until I die, until I'm killed for it, most likely."

Her eyes narrowed. "When the Vultures attacked . . ."

"I thought they were there for me, yes. Rozá is one of the ones who want me off the throne."

"But *you* sent them away?"

"It was a gamble. Like I said, the magic is imperfect, obviously, as they attempted to kill me there. They could have kept after us; they could have killed the others. We got lucky. I shook the order when I fled; I have created more chaos by returning. I . . . I don't know if I can command them like I did. No one has ever done what I did."

She frowned.

"You are searching for an apology for what I am; I will not provide one. I thought I had found something to end this war and save Tranavia. Instead I gave the idea of unlimited power to the one person who should never have considered it. I ran because refusing would have meant my execution. I can admit to being a coward in that respect."

Something cracked in her chest and she jolted. "All of it has been a lie? Everything?"

He closed his eyes, knuckled the bridge of his nose. "No. Nadya, that's not what I meant. I have grown so used to lies that I don't know what's true anymore." His voice trembled. "What you've given me is a truth I don't know what to do with because I've never had anything like it before. I can't bear to think I've ruined it."

They stood in silence, the light shifting outside, fading within the sanctuary, and lengthening the shadows around them. Here in this profaned place, Nadya found herself reaching for a monster.

She cradled his hand, lightly pressing her fingertips against his. She let the silence drag out, stretch between them, become something almost tangible. When she was certain he felt it, she reached up and took his face between her hands. His eyes closed, long eyelashes splayed like shadows against his pale skin. He rested his hands on her wrists, thumbs pressed lightly against her palms in a way that made her heart pound traitorously.

"Tell me the *truth*, Malachiasz, why are you here?"

He exhaled deeply, his breath feathering her face. "I'm tired, Nadya. I want to put an end to what I've started. I want this war to end without leaving Tranavia in ashes."

"I want to believe you," she whispered. "But . . ."

He opened his mouth, at a loss for words. Finally, he asked, "Will it always be like this?"

Would it? She couldn't say. Would she ever be comfortable with what he was? Or would it always be this constant hot and cold, friends one second and enemies the next?

"I don't know."

He nodded and there was such a deep well of sadness in his

pale eyes that Nadya felt her heart splinter to a shattering point.
It wasn't something she had ever felt before, this crack in her
chest, this void splitting her ribs open. His sleeve fell back, revealing the ridged mess of scars covering his forearm.

Frowning, she trailed her hand over the scars. "You said
the razors to cast magic don't scar." She had cut open her
arms in the arena and the wounds were already healing—not
as quickly as if she were a blood mage herself, but they were
healing clean.

"They don't," he said. "It was a reminder." Like the remind-
ers he whispered to himself of his name, always his name.

"Do you still?"

He shook his head. "Not for a long time."

She let her thumb brush over his, fingers toying with his,
before she dropped his hand, taking a step back. She turned
away, taking in the sanctuary again. Would he lose all of this
if he helped them? Did he even want it in the first place?

"How long have you been . . . this?"

"Two years," he said. "I was sixteen when I took the throne."

"You killed the last Black Vulture?"

She turned in time to see him nod.

"Why?"

"I wanted to know if I could," he said softly. "If anything
would become better if I succeeded."

"Did it?"

"No."

They were quiet again. Nadya wandered through the sanctuary and the voice in the back of her head that was still loudly
struggling against Malachiasz began to fall silent.

Eventually, Nadya heard his footsteps behind her. Felt his
lips press against her neck in a way that made her knees weak.

"I want to talk to the others," she said, flushing at the way her voice hitched. Her face flushed even hotter when she heard his soft laugh.

When he stepped past her, a smile flickered at the edges of his lips. There was darkness at the corners, something evil just underneath the surface, sinister. He turned and grinned at her, monstrous but beatific, holding out his hand, darkness gone. Maybe she'd just imagined it. She took his hand.

Malachiasz led her out of the sanctuary, up a flight of stairs and down a long hallway. They were stopped midway down the hall by a Vulture clearing her throat.

"I honestly didn't think you were ever going to come back."

Malachiasz tensed. He hastily dropped Nadya's hand and she ducked her head. She had to fight the instinct to flee.

"Rozá," Malachiasz said flatly. "I would apologize for leaving you in the dark, but it occurs to me that I don't care and you are not required to know my business. Żywia knew I was back and last I checked she was my second, *not you*."

Rozá wasn't wearing a mask and her bare face was softer than Nadya expected. She was pretty in a luxurious sort of way.

"Any longer and *I* would have been named Black Vulture," she sneered.

Malachiasz's smile had a knife's blade edge. "We both know that is impossible."

Her claws snapped out of her hands, but Malachiasz already had one long iron claw tipped underneath her chin.

"Don't, Rozá," he said softly.

"I should tell the king what you're doing," she said, but she swallowed hard and her voice trembled.

"Well, then, it's good for all of us that you cannot." Malachiasz's voice struck chords of fear in some primal depth of Nadya.

Rozá's eyes flashed but she nodded. Malachiasz retracted his claw, letting her take a step back.

"But you *can* tell him that I've been watching and I have thoughts about how he has chosen to handle matters," Malachiasz said. He glanced back at Nadya. "My chambers are at the end of the hall. I'll be with you soon."

Nadya frowned. She didn't want to leave him alone with this Vulture where she couldn't keep on eye on him. She shot him a warning look as she passed. He smiled faintly at her. It did nothing to make her feel better as she hurried down the hall, overly aware she could be stopped by a Vulture and no longer have Malachiasz's protection shielding her.

Not that she couldn't protect herself, but she was in a precarious position as it was. Stirring up suspicion was the last thing she needed.

Rashid was on edge when she entered Malachiasz's chambers. He jumped to his feet, wincing at the motion, but he relaxed when he saw it was her. She walked in slowly, taking in the lavish quarters. They didn't appear like they had been lived in for some time.

Paintings covered every open wall space and were stacked in the corners of the room. Mostly landscapes, strangely dark, as if the artist was rendering a grim future. A few portraits that didn't appear to be of anyone in particular that Nadya could tell. There was a bookcase that was overfull, books beginning to gather in piles around it.

"Oh," she said. She shot Parijahan and Rashid a reluctant smile before stepping toward a door and opening it. She wanted to know everything about this strange, secretive boy. He was a liar and she wanted his truths.

Inside the room was a study befitting someone with Malachiasz's title. More books were stacked in the corners. The desk was a mess of papers and razors and sharp tools that Nadya didn't even want to consider. The room felt wrong, off, and Nadya shut the door quickly, feeling ill. The corridor off to the back led to his bedroom. Nadya hadn't expected the rooms to all be so cluttered and messy. She moved back into the main sitting room.

"You lied to me," she said flatly.

Parijahan pursed her lips. Rashid, at least, looked ashamed.

"What did you expect? It was enough that you knew he was one of them—"

"You don't get to make that decision for me," Nadya snapped.

Rashid touched Parijahan's arm. "She's allowed to be upset," he said, voice soft.

"How did you find out?" Nadya asked.

"It's Malachiasz. He hedges. He hedged too far one day and I put the pieces together," Parijahan said.

"You trust him?"

"I trust him. He has questionable methods, he's desperate, but he's trying and that's more than can be said for most people."

It didn't feel like *enough* to Nadya, but she didn't know what would ever make it enough. But it didn't seem to matter. She could wander in mental circles about how she shouldn't trust him because he lied to her, but she would still follow him.

This was a battle she had lost. No amount of flipping back and forth was going to change how she needed him for this plan to work, that she cared about the anxious boy trying to correct a mistake, the boy she believed was not a lie. Even if he happened to be a monster.

"Where were you two?"

"Languishing in dungeons, trying to convince a rather keen

guard that 'No, Parijahan doesn't look familiar, you just think all Akolans look the same.'"

Nadya's eyes widened. "What?"

Parijahan waved a dismissive hand. "Could you see to his broken ribs?"

"Your *what?*"

Rashid smiled sheepishly, stretching out on the chaise with a pained groan.

"I think I'm dying."

"He's not dying," Parijahan said.

Nadya drew her magic forth, hating every second she used it without contact from the gods. She whispered holy speech she didn't understand under her breath as her fingertips heated. She carefully worked out which of Rashid's ribs were broken and set to mending them.

Rashid squirmed underneath her hands like a child who refused to sit for the healer. Nadya had to restrain from smacking him. "Sit still."

"Your hands are *freezing.*"

The door opened and closed with a slam. Malachiasz flopped face-first onto the remaining chaise. He let out a long, dramatic sigh and sat up.

"Rashid got his chest knocked in for trying to charm the guards?" he asked.

"You know me so *well*, Malachiasz," Rashid said, his face wrenching as Nadya worked.

It took her an hour to heal him. When she finished she leaned back on her heels, staring at her hands. She was dimly aware of the others talking, finalizing plans, but all she could think about was how she had healed Rashid *herself.* It hadn't been Zbyhneuska's power, it had been her own.

Maybe Malachiasz had been right all along.

What did that mean for her? When all this ended—if she even survived—would the gods turn away because she had discovered her power wasn't dependent on their whims? Was this true of every cleric in history or was this a flaw within herself?

She was jarred by Malachiasz moving to kneel on the floor beside her. He gently took her wrists and folded her hands between his. Tears burned at her eyes.

"We can't always understand how magic chooses to flow," he said softly. He tucked a lock of her hair behind her ear. "This is freedom, Nadya, you don't have to shy away from it."

She didn't have the words to explain that he could never understand, even if he was right. The gods were the reason she lived, the air in her lungs. If they were stifling, it was because it was necessary.

Except now she was living without the fear of them hovering, digging in her thoughts. Whatever she would have to do to see this plan to its end would be entirely on herself; there would be no danger of a god denying a spell or ignoring her prayers.

She made a final, tentative reach for the gods and when she was met with a stone wall of silence, she made up her mind.

This was about survival, about something bigger than Nadya's magic. She wasn't going to let herself be riddled with doubt and guilt. This wasn't something she should run from; it was something she should embrace.

"Thank you, Malachiasz," she whispered.

He smiled. "Are you all right?" He reached out a hesitant hand, brushing his thumb over a long cut that ran down her neck. "I wish I could help, but . . ." he trailed off. Blood mages couldn't heal.

"I like to know you have a weakness," she replied. She tugged on a lock of his hair. She wondered if that was what she had become, the thing that would cause this monster king to stumble away from his throne. Another weakness. "Explain to me what's going on—without lying, which I think is a perfectly novel idea—and I might consider forgiving you."

Parijahan snorted. Malachiasz's smile fell.

"You owe me forty *kopecks*," Parijahan said to Rashid.

He sighed. "In my defense the odds were against it from the beginning."

Nadya and Malachiasz exchanged a glance. She could feel the tops of her ears burning. They both pretended they had no idea what the Akolans were talking about.

Nadya climbed into the empty chair. Malachiasz shoved Rashid's legs off the chaise and sat down. Rashid protested and kicked Malachiasz in the head as retaliation.

Malachiasz liked the plan Nadya had formed with Serefin, though he worried it would cause the king to act against the prince early.

"You want to bring him here?"

She nodded.

He looked thoughtful. "It would be less public than acting in front of the entire court. And I do know which of the Vultures are acting as the king's guards now."

"Can you do this? With your order split the way it is?" Parijahan asked.

"I don't have a choice," he said.

Nadya's eyelids were heavy and she curled up in the chair, yawning. "Wouldn't your fleeing Tranavia be seen as treason?"

"It was directly in retaliation for something the king asked me to do, so, yes. But for the ritual to work, he can't do this without me. If what Serefin said about his father is true, then he's so desperate he'll look past my transgression."

Nadya pressed her face against the chair cushion. She could

dimly hear them discussing whether they should wait any longer—no—and when they should act—tomorrow.

Nadya was next aware of being lifted out of the chair, of smelling a pleasant mix of earth and iron and feeling the gentle brush of Malachiasz's hair against her cheek.

"I'm going to go speak with the king. I'll be back. You and Nadya can use my bedroom," she heard him say to Parijahan, his voice a low rumble in his chest. She shifted into the warmth of his arms.

"Is she asleep?"

"No."

She shook her head, but buried her face into his chest.

"She has had her worldview rocked far too many times for any one person in the past twelve hours, on top of being tortured and siphoned. All things considered, she's doing remarkably well," Malachiasz continued. "Especially as we expect her to assassinate a man tomorrow."

"All part of the job," Nadya mumbled. "We shouldn't kill Serefin."

"What?"

"Serefin. He's good." She nuzzled his chest. "I like him. He should live." She forced her eyes open. "Be careful, Malachiasz."

His eyes flashed sadness at her, but he blinked and it was gone. He smiled.

"What have you been told about worrying about me?"

"It's useless." She yawned. "Too late for that."

29

SEREFIN

MELESKI

Svoyatovi Milan Khalturin: *Svoyatovi Milan Khalturin was a holy man, blessed by no god yet a worshiper of them all, who wandered across Kalyazin. There are miracles attributed not to his life, but to his death, as his bones have been said to have healing properties.*

—Vasiliev's Book of Saints

Serefin was too anxious to sleep. He was mostly finished with the necessary preparations for tomorrow, but his mind wouldn't let him rest.

As he sat down at his desk with spells sprawled out in front of him, blood still drying on the pages, he couldn't shake the feeling there was something he still wasn't understanding.

What would they do to the kingdom when they started this coup? Tranavia was *his* kingdom. His land of swamps and lakes and mountains and marshlands. Of blood magic

and monsters. A kingdom with two kings. He didn't want to see it swallowed in the fires of war, and he didn't want to see it starve to death, either. Both were dangerously close on the horizon. But he also didn't want to *die*.

His father had come to dinner, seeming almost giddy about something. Serefin tried not to have misgivings—this was all part of the plan—but he was worried. If his father was to be believed, Malachiasz was the one pulling the strings. Even if the Black Vulture had admitted his fault, did that mean he wasn't going to hand the king exactly what he was looking for?

But it didn't matter. They were out of time. At dinner the king had mentioned that the Kalyazi forces had moved, that an attack was imminent. He'd seemed . . . overjoyed at the prospect, and that terrified Serefin the most. All he could cling to was the desperate hope he could save himself in the end.

A knock at the door startled him. Likely Ostyia or Kacper— he hadn't seen either that evening.

Żaneta looked washed out when he opened the door. She shot him a weak smile. Before he had a chance to greet her she reached out, grabbed the lapels of his jacket, and kissed him.

He stiffened in surprise, but soon relaxed into the kiss. His hands clasped Żaneta's waist and her fingers slid into his hair.

"What is this?" he asked, breathless when she broke away. He kissed the corner of her mouth, her jaw. She didn't answer. He lifted his head, searching her face. He felt a chill cut through him as he took in her bleak expression.

"Żaneta?"

She shook her head, forcing a smile. There were tears in her dark eyes. He gently cupped her face in his hand.

"Can you come with me?" she asked. She blinked hard and

the tears were gone, the discomfort gone with them. She looked as poised as ever. "Sorry, I'm fine. I shouldn't have—"

"Żaneta . . ."

She shot him a bright smile, no longer strained. "I'm fine, Serefin."

He hesitated before gently kissing her again. When he broke away, she reached up, combing his hair with her fingers.

"It will only take a minute," she said. She held her hand out. He took it.

"Have you seen Kacper or Ostyia?" he asked.

"I'm surprised neither of them were with you. I haven't seen them today."

He frowned. It wasn't like them to disappear. A heavy feeling began coiling inside him that felt suspiciously like dread. He had dismissed it before—Żaneta was the only person at court he trusted—but as he followed her down the dark halls of the palace he couldn't deny this was going to end badly.

He tried to think, to pull his hand from Żaneta's grip, but found his head suddenly fuzzy and his fingers slack. Żaneta went from leading him to dragging him down the hall.

Foreboding crept up his spine like cold fingers as they walked. Past the dungeons, in the back wing of the palace, far below ground, where any magic research the king was doing took place. Research not ordained by the Vultures.

There was blood trailing out from underneath Żaneta's sleeve and sliding over her fingers. She glanced back at him, wiping the blood off on her dark skirts, and cleaned off her mouth with the back of her hand, a smear of blood coming away on her fingers.

His brow furrowed; he hadn't tasted blood when he'd kissed her. The realization came slowly, his thoughts searching through a murky fog.

It was a spell. She put magic on her lips and now he was trailing helplessly behind her even though he knew he should flee. The only one he thought was on his side, and she had sold him away like all the rest.

They reached the entrance to the catacombs. The doors intricately locked and guarded on both sides. Serefin felt the jaws of his fate close in around him as he stepped into the dark.

Żaneta stopped. She turned back. The dark was choking and thick. Panic constricted his chest, making it feel as if no air was reaching his lungs. He felt her hand on his face, her touch light.

"I'm sorry, Serefin," she whispered. She kissed his cheek.

"What could he give you that I couldn't?" Serefin asked. It was hard to speak, his words came out thick and muffled.

He couldn't make out her features in the darkness. "I want to be the queen. It's that simple."

Queen alone.

"He's down here, isn't he?" Serefin hated that his voice broke. He hated that he was scared.

"He needs you," Żaneta replied.

She nudged him forward. Toward the darkness. Into the depths. He had no choice but to throw himself headfirst down into it.

30

NADEZHDA

LAPTEVA

Svoyatovi Konstantin Nemtsev: *A cleric of Veceslav during a rare time of peace between Kalyazin and its neighbors. That did not protect Konstantin from meeting an unfortunate end. He was captured by Tranavian blood mages and drawn and quartered. The peace did not last long.*

—Vasiliev's Book of Saints

Nadya dreamed of many-jointed monsters and creatures with thousands of teeth. Of gaping mouths and claws of bone. These monsters, they *knew* her. They reached for her, hissing her name, and even as she ran she could feel claws catching on her clothes. The thousands of eyes peeled away the flesh on her back. She dreamed of fields of blood, of blood raining from the sky, of a world already ravaged by war with rivers that ran red.

She woke up screaming. Horrible, throat-searing screams that shook her whole body. Her hair dripped with sweat.

She was only vaguely aware of Parijahan's cool hands brushing her hair from her face, of the whisper of Akolan words, rapid and fluid.

Of the door flying open, a pair of warm hands folding over hers, the bed sinking down slightly on one side as Malachiasz sat, pulling her against his chest.

"Nadya, it was just a dream," he whispered in her ear in Kalyazi. Her screams gave way to gasping sobs. "You're safe here, *towy dżimyka.*"

She curled against him, his heart beating fast against her ear. There was rustling on the other side of the room and she heard Parijahan and Rashid talking softly to each other. Little things to center herself in reality.

"What time is it?" she asked, her voice raw. It hurt to speak.

"Sometime in the middle of the night," he replied.

It felt like it should be nearly morning. She heard the door close as Parijahan and Rashid slipped out.

If she hadn't felt so awful, she probably would have blushed at the realization she was alone with Malachiasz on his bed. At this point she was too tired to care.

"I haven't heard the gods since I woke up in a pool of my own blood," she whispered. "What scares me is maybe it's a good thing. I don't know what's real anymore."

Malachiasz nodded slowly. He looked like he'd been torn from sleep; his long hair was tangled, his shirt hastily thrown on. It was open wide, half hanging off one shoulder.

"It's perfectly human to doubt, Nadya," he murmured.

"Not when you're divine," she said. She sniffed pathetically.

"No, I suppose not," he agreed.

"How do you do it? Live without faith?"

He was quiet against her except for the rhythm of his breathing. "Nadya, do you *really* want to know where my ethics come from? Me?"

Him, the king of monsters. The liar. The heretic.

No . . . she supposed she didn't.

She murmured her answer. He nodded, unsurprised, and gently kissed her forehead.

"I feel like I shouldn't ask what had you screaming bloody murder in your sleep but I admit I'm curious."

"Monsters."

He flinched. He thought she was talking about him. She almost wished she was, at least that would be easily explained. She considered letting him believe he gave her nightmares. But she wasn't that cruel.

"No, not like that," she said, when she meant *not like you*. He visibly relaxed and that made her curious. "Would that bother you?"

"Of course it would."

"But you like being what you are."

His expression shifted, became troubled. He didn't correct her. "I would not want to be the cause of your pain, even if it may be inevitable." After a long silence, he spoke again. "Perhaps you should try to sleep again? I'll let Parijahan know she can—"

"Stay," Nadya said, cutting him off.

He frowned, already shaking his head. He started to stand but she caught his wrist.

"I care about you, Malachiasz," she said, the words rapid as they rushed out of her. "I don't know when it started, but it's real and it *terrifies* me. You're the single most frustrating person I have ever met and I'm still a little convinced we're enemies and caring for you is literal heresy, but I do. You've been lying to me from the beginning and I can't make myself stop caring for you."

His expression was completely indecipherable and he wouldn't meet her eyes. Had she been reading him totally wrong? Had she said the wrong thing? She'd never done this before; she wasn't really sure how it worked. She didn't—

He kissed her. It was hungry and purposeful and spoke clearly of wanting. It surprised her, how desperate he felt. It frightened her—just a bit—as well.

It didn't stop her from shifting up on her knees, leveling herself to him, and knotting her hands into his hair. Her heart was pounding and every inch of her felt shaky because this was wrong. If she didn't die tomorrow she would certainly be punished.

But she didn't care. *She didn't care.* His hands gripped her waist as he pulled her closer. He broke away, his breath ragged and hot. His pale eyes were dark and dangerous as they searched her face.

"This is a terrible idea." He spoke in Kalyazi. She was tired of hearing Tranavian.

"I know."

"I wish you did," he said, his voice hoarse. He lifted a hand, gently tracing her features with his fingertips. She shivered. When he reached her mouth she tilted her face up to kiss his palm.

He let out a long, tattered breath. She pulled his face back to hers, kissing him hard, feeling his body notch against her. She drew one hand out from his hair and let it slide down his neck, glancing fingers brushing against his collarbone. His skin was hot and she felt his hand trail up the ridges of her spine. He pressed forward, lowering her back onto the bed.

For a split second, she froze, suddenly realizing just how dangerous this was, how much further down she could throw herself if she allowed it.

He felt her instant of indecision and pulled back. A similar misgiving flickered on his face.

"Just stay," she whispered.

He nodded. "Nadya, I . . ." he trailed off. Kissed her throat. Her jaw. The corner of her lips.

She was having trouble thinking clearly. Her mind focused solely on the feeling of his mouth against her skin. But she understood he wanted to say something serious to her so she opened her eyes.

"If something happens tomorrow . . ." He shifted so he was lying next to her. She turned on her side and moved closer so their foreheads were touching. "I want you to know you are the only good thing that has ever happened to me."

Was her heart supposed to be in her throat like this? Was she supposed to feel so alive and so much like crying right now? She had no idea. All she knew was she had gone against everything she ever thought *right* and had fallen completely, irreversibly for this terrible, monstrous boy.

She curled her fingers against his face, the scratch of stubble beginning to dust his jaw and cheeks rough against them. His voice scared her, and not in the way it scared her when he was speaking as the Black Vulture. This was different. This was sadness. Desolation.

How could *she* be the only good thing to happen to him? She had almost slit his throat, had hung him off a railing. She didn't even trust him, not really.

Maybe that wasn't true. He had lied, he was a monster, but still she cared. A part of her had come to trust him. And that was the most terrifying thing of all.

"We'll just have to make sure nothing happens, then," she said.

That earned her a strained half smile from the Vulture boy. She kissed him, once more, a soft and slow and equally purposeful kiss, before she tucked her head down and settled herself against him.

Nadya woke with her head pillowed on Malachiasz's chest, one hand pressed against his ribs. Soft, early morning light was slipping through the cracks in the curtains.

She sat up, trying not to think about what she would have to do by the day's end. Malachiasz stirred beside her. He didn't wake, just folded his body around her. She smiled and softly rested her fingers in his hair.

Lying on a nearby table was the iron mask he wore over his face as a Vulture. It was similar to the one she had seen him wearing when they first reached Grazyk, but this one had a vicious edge to it, designed to cover even more of his face.

Malachiasz stirred again, waking.

"How many more lies are you going to tell me before I finally hear the truth?" Nadya asked. She turned his mask around in her hands, the iron cold. She didn't mean it in an accusatory way, she was merely curious.

Malachiasz frowned; the expression tugged at the tattoos on his forehead. He took his time answering. "When we met I gave you my name," he said, his quiet voice scratchy with sleep. "It's the only truth I have left."

"It's a truth you've given others as well."

He turned, groaning, and pressed his face against her hip. "What do you want from me, Nadya?" His voice was teasing.

"I'm just pointing out: I am not the only person to know your name."

"You're just being difficult."

She laughed and looked down at him. His black hair spilled onto the white pillows like ink. She drew her knees up to her chest and wrapped her arms around them; thought about how when they were sitting in front of Alena's altar he had practically admitted to her he was evil. He closed his eyes and his face was pleasant, peaceful. A monster king, feral and beautiful.

Her chest ached in the oddest of ways as it struck her again just how much she cared for this broken boy and how it terrified her. It would never stop terrifying her.

She laid back next to him. "Is it part of you? I mean, has it always been with you?" She didn't need to clarify.

He was silent—she was getting used to his long silences—she hoped he said *yes*. That he had been born with iron in his body instead of bone. It would mean a curse of blood instead of something done to him by man. If he hadn't been born with it, then it had been tortured into him. Experiments more gruesome than Nadya was willing to contemplate.

"I was born with the potential for monstrosity, as all people are," he said finally. "The Salt Mines made it a reality. All I have is what they made me."

Nadya pressed her mouth to his bare shoulder, another fracture making its way down her heart. She didn't know what would happen to them at the end of this. She couldn't even think that far. Her future was bleak and she knew it.

What would he say, if he knew her end goal remained the same? That she was willing to bring the gods' judgment down on Tranavia. That when this veil parted she would still be theirs.

At least, she thought she would.

As Malachiasz turned his head to look at her, lifting a hand and brushing the backs of his fingers against her cheek, her heart squeezed painfully. He wasn't the only one lying. She was doing a perfectly good job lying to herself.

31

SEREFIN
MELESKI

Svoyatovi Dobromir Pirozhkov: *When Svoyatovi Dobromir Pirozhkov was a child, his sister fell into a frozen river and he miraculously returned her to life. Hers was an odd life, full of strange mishaps until finally she was killed in a bizarre accident, trampled by her own horse. Dobromir, who was not a cleric, was also chased by terrible luck throughout his life until ultimately he drowned in the same frozen river he saved his sister from years prior.*

—Vasiliev's Book of Saints

Serefin was used to the concept of pain. It was a familiar friend. When he was forced into the dark, what waited for him was something that could not be described in such easy, small words. This was not his friend. It was more; it was bigger than anything human vocabulary could name. It obliterated him—pulled him out of conscious existence

and threw him into a world where monsters walked and blood fell from the sky like rainwater.

He was losing his grasp of his own awareness, of the very essence that made him *Serefin*, the moody High Prince with far more blood magic talent than would ever do him good as a king. The High Prince who never thought he would be king because he would die first. It was slipping away from him. No, not slipping, being pulled. It was being taken. He was losing all that made him who he was and he would be left in this wasteland world of blood and monsters and magic.

This world, this world, this world.

This world that would become reality. That he knew, intrinsically, whoever *he* even was. It was an overwhelming sense of knowing, of horror, of the kind of foreboding that drove a man insane.

Something he was, once. Before. Before what? Was there a line, a point, a moment that divided him into the Before and the After? Or was there nothing but this blood raining from the sky and soaking him to his skin—skin?—and draining into rivers.

He was aware of the bitter punch of copper; that he had put his blood-soaked fingers into his mouth and tasted the crimson stain on his skin. But *why*?

Soft feather glances brushed across his face. Razor teeth nipped at his ear and he heard singing. No, no, that was wrong. He didn't hear it because hearing was a separate experience. It was something he did not have. He felt it, he *became* it. The song and the music and the whispery reed of a voice was what he was now—he was ever changing, ever shifting, and still blood rained down.

This song was not one he knew. He did not know the tongue, it felt wrong, it felt perfect but in a wrongness that made him shudder.

It was sudden, the shift from incomprehension to enlight-
enment. The moment when the words he was hearing made
sense to him in their perfection and their abhorrence.

It was someone else and this voice was angry, it was frustrated, it was sad. It had lost so much and gained so little and
it was tired of fighting and tired of war and—

War?

War and blood and magic staining the land and staining the
people. Heresy and—

No.

No, this was all wrong, this was wrong. Something still lu-
cid, still *Serefin,* was screaming because this was wrong.

The war meant freedom. The war was necessary.

The song changed. The song became an agreement. Cor-
recting itself midnote, apologizing for its mistake because of
course of course of course this land would never have peace
until one of its blasted kingdoms was eradicated.

That was wrong, too. Serefin—what was left of Serefin, if
anything was left of Serefin—scrambled for the word that
would describe this song. He had it, but it existed out of his
reach, just past the point where Serefin became something *not-*
Serefin.

It wasn't there, though, and so he felt himself fall, disinte-
grate, lose the last piece that made him Serefin until there was
nothing nothing nothing left.

And there was silence. And from that silence came a different song. Sly and sharp and slow. Needling through the silence
for something that had gone missing.

There were prophecies and there were visions of a world
where nothing was left. What was the point of a world of
nothing? But he needed four things: one that was lost, one
that was held in a different song's grasp, one that had stopped

listening to songs years ago, and one who was untouchable because they were too close to being a song themselves.

It made it difficult, especially with this world so focused on ripping itself apart. But a challenge was a riddle was a test.

Even if it meant putting back together what arrogance had torn apart. Even if it meant forcing one unwilling to listen. Even if it meant seeding doubt into a zealot's heart. Even if it meant bringing madness.

To fix the discordant notes ruining the music, it was willing to sacrifice most things, even those four essential pieces to its plans.

First, though, a stumbling prince.

Serefin saw an ocean of stars. A blackness stretching out into forever around him. It pressed upon him, washed over him, swallowed him alive. Surrounding him, guiding him, though he did not know where he was going. He just knew he had *been*; he once was. He was nothing—no one—and there was nothing but stars.

And moths.

Millions of dusty wings the color of starlight, dancing through moonbeams, flitting on him, around him. One moth, far larger than the others, soft and gray, landed right over his bad eye.

He took a step forward. His foot left a bloody print in the ash behind him. Blood dripped down his fingers, but he didn't think he was wounded.

But maybe he was. He existed. He was real.

He was dead.

He found he wasn't too bothered by that, if slightly irritated that his paranoia had turned into reality.

His hand crept to his face, nudging the moth onto his index finger. It complied, its slight legs barely heavy enough to register as a weight against his skin.

The moth and the stars swirled around him until they were one and the same; moths flying in constellations with points of light on their dusty wings.

Something was burning within him, hot in his veins. Something was changing and he didn't know what. Something within him—about him—had shifted amongst the stars and the dark and the glittering moths.

He thought, quite clearly, *This is not the fate my father intended for me.*

Blood and demons and monsters. A will to break. That was what he was supposed to see.

Not stars, not moths, not songs.

"Meddling with Izak Meleski's plans from beyond the grave," Serefin said aloud to the moth on his finger. At least, he thought he spoke aloud; he wasn't entirely sure in this place what that meant.

The moth fluttered its wings in acknowledgment.

His sight tunneled . . .

A world burning. Grazyk in rubble. The Tranavian lakelands filled with blood and death. Scorched Kalyazi mountains. Punched-in onion domes of the Silver Court, smoking. A world broken, a world starved. Blood falling from the sky like rain.

A future that could not—would not—be stopped. A future that had already been set into motion.

Serefin woke up.

32

NADEZHDA

LAPTEVA

Svoyatova Serafima Zyomina: *Little is known about Svoyatova Serafima Zyomina. Though a cleric, she was blessed with a strange magic that never seemed to work the same way twice. If one was an enemy, seeing her on a battlefield meant a slow and agonizing death, for she was a cleric of Marzenya and both were cruel.*

—Vasiliev's Book of Saints

The rain from the night before grew steadily worse, turning into a massive storm. Lightning flashed every few minutes, casting the sanctuary into stark black and white. It made the room feel violent, angry, a place of death—fitting for a king of monsters.

Malachiasz melded into his role seamlessly. He was wearing a hood in the shape of a vulture's head. It shadowed half his face with its vicious beak. A cloak of black feathers fell heavy over his shoulders. He was flanked on

either side by Vultures in banded iron masks that covered most of their faces. He sat on the throne in a way that was casual, comfortably arrogant. One leg was kicked over the armrest, his tattooed fingers steepled over his chest.

A boy made king of monsters for a kingdom of the damned.

Something itched in the back of Nadya's head. A shifting. It was uncomfortable. Something had changed. She couldn't put a name to it; she wrote it off as nerves.

When the king arrived he was flanked by only a few guards. Such blind trust in Malachiasz. Such desperation for a power so abominable.

Malachiasz pushed the hood back to hang over his shoulders. His nails were iron, held at a length just long enough to appear as visible claws. His eyes were rimmed with kohl and more gold beads were knotted into his long, black hair.

He looks like a king . . . Nadya realized, feeling her stomach drop. How had he fooled her into believing he was insignificant?

Feral and wild with his hair in braids and knots. A smile glinted at his mouth, his teeth iron, his incisors too sharp. A little further and those incisors would be fangs in his mouth.

Her heart pounded in her throat. She was wearing an intricate white mask of pearls and lace. Her hair woven into a complicated mess of braids. They had taken the glamour off her face and stripped her hair of the dye as well, and though she had long since stopped noticing Malachiasz's magic on her skin, she could feel its absence. Her old *voryens* were strapped to her forearms, their solid weight a comfort.

Izak Meleski, the king of Tranavia, paused in front of Malachiasz's Carrion Throne. He did not bow, but a smile stretched his lips.

"We heard rumors of the flight of one of your Vultures, Your

Excellency," the king said. "Imagine our surprise when the truth came to light!"

Nadya tensed at hearing an honorific from the king's lips.

"Mere exaggerations," Malachiasz said. "I did spend some time in Kalyazin for"—he paused, thinking—"academic purposes. I must offer my condolences, Your Majesty. His Highness was a testament to Tranavian magic; he will be missed." Chaos and madness were carefully cultivated threads in his voice.

"What?" Nadya whispered; her hand reached out and landed on Rashid's forearm.

He frowned, uncertainty apparent in his features.

Nadya felt as if she were scrambling for purchase amidst a landslide. *No,* they were supposed to save Serefin, not kill him. Malachiasz knew, he'd agreed. Letting Serefin fall to harm was putting the king one step closer to his goal.

What if that was his intention all along?

She watched Malachiasz, not the king as she should, searching for an indication that he hadn't meant for Serefin to die. There was only the cool expression of a monster.

The king carefully folded his hands behind his back. Nadya noticed Żaneta at his side, looking pale and withdrawn. She didn't see Ostyia or Kacper in the hall, either.

"Kalyazin will pay for the death of my son," the king said, his voice wavering slightly.

Nadya exchanged a look of alarm with Rashid. It wasn't possible.

"We will start with the Silver Court," he continued, fist clenched. "And we will bring them to their knees."

A sweeping sense of magic being used washed through the hall. Izak jerked his arm down. Lightning crashed outside, jolting the hall with erratic, frantic flashes. The magic was overwhelming, Nadya could taste it in the air, copper, blood. The thought of how much it would take to control the skies like that was . . . unimaginable.

Malachiasz looked up at the ceiling, his expression unconcerned. Then he smiled.

"So, it worked." His voice contemplative, but still audible. "I wasn't sure, you know. It had not been confirmed that using the blood of a powerful mage would heighten the process."

No. Nadya's blood froze in her veins. Parijahan's eyes closed and she leaned back against a pillar. Rashid's expression blackened.

"It feels little different to me," the king said, razor-sharp.

"How are you to know what the power of gods feels like?" Malachiasz asked. "You have nothing to compare it to."

"And you do?"

Malachiasz clasped his hands together. "Well, I was—how was it put?—the ultimate success of my cult before this. You got what I promised, did you not?"

A biting glint of iron teeth. A puppet master, pulling them all along with his honeyed words and panicked pleas for trust. Nadya watched from the shadows with narrowed eyes. They were supposed to let the king think he had won, but that had *not* meant giving him the power he so craved.

Nadya's will to fight leaked out of her. Had Malachiasz done it anyway? Orchestrated blasphemy in an attempt to destroy her kingdom?

She hoped she was wrong. She had to be wrong.

Except the king needed Malachiasz to complete the ceremony. Which meant Malachiasz had done it willingly. Had he betrayed them? For what?

But as she watched him sitting on his throne made of skulls and bones, she saw him for what he always was. Tranavian to his core: merciless and beautifully cruel. She had been a fool to believe him. There had been so many signs she had so willfully ignored, choosing instead to put her faith in a monster.

What could the king do to the heavens with the power he now bore? If man-made magic had created the veil keeping the gods out from Tranavia, what could *this* do?

Nadya thought fast. If it was down to her to stop this, then so be it. She looked at Rashid, who appeared as confused as she felt.

"I don't understand why," he said under his breath.

She tugged the silver pendant over her neck and eyed the spiral; she wrapped the cord around her hand as she would her prayer beads. If all she had was a bloodthirsty forgotten god-that-was-not-a-god, it would have to do.

The king took Żaneta's shoulder and pushed her closer to Malachiasz's throne. She stumbled, falling at the Black Vulture's feet.

Malachiasz leaned forward, tipping her face up with one iron claw. "You *did* wish to be queen," he hissed. "The price of power is blood; it always has been. The price of becoming like a god? Well, that's death." He crooked his head, the movement off-putting in its fluidity. "But such disloyalty. Such fickle whims belong to those who dream of rising above their station to places they do not belong." He trailed his iron claw down her cheek.

Her expression turned to horror.

His mouth tilted upward slightly at the corners. "Subtlety would have been better for a queen. Betrayal is a taint not so easily ignored. Can I tell you a secret?" His smile widened when she didn't respond. "My order was built on betrayal. You'll fit right in."

Nadya saw Żaneta's lips form the word *no,* her terror silent. Malachiasz straightened, towering over the girl as he waved a languid hand to the masked Vultures who grabbed her.

"We are *so selective* in those we welcome into the order," he said. "Congratulations. You've been selected. I do look forward to your next inevitable betrayal," he called as Żaneta was dragged screaming from the room.

Nadya shut her eyes.

"He wouldn't," she heard Rashid murmur.

But that was just the thing—he *would*. He had never been a tortured victim of his cult; any such implications had been a carefully painted falsehood to gain her trust. He was their ultimate success. There was nothing he wouldn't do to get what he wanted.

And that was what Nadya didn't understand. What did he *want*?

33

SEREFIN

MELESKI

Svoyatovi Nikita Lisov: *A cleric of the god Krsnik who chose to abandon the life of a holy man and instead use the god-given power bestowed upon him to entertain. While the Church fought against his canonization, the use of one of his finger bones turned the tide of a battle in 625 when it burst into flames and wiped out a full Tranavian company.*
— Vasiliev's Book of Saints

Serefin was trapped in darkness.

If I'm in a coffin, there's going to be hell to pay, he thought irritably.

He felt strange, oddly jittery and feverish. He pressed his hands up, prepared to feel the blank slab of a coffin lid.

His hands met nothing but air.

He let out a long sigh of relief. Now he had to get out

of here, wherever here was. He struggled to his feet, swaying as he stood. Blood and bone, he felt awful.

He considered casting a light and reached for his spell book. *Idiot, of course you don't have that.* But he paused. Stars and moths and music. He wondered . . .

He had nothing to use to draw blood. There were no razors in the hems of his clothes. He had no knife. All he had was himself and the dark around him.

He rubbed his index finger over his thumbnail. He kept his nails trimmed short, so that wouldn't work.

This is going to hurt, he thought with resignation as he pushed his sleeve off his forearm and bit down hard.

Blood flooded his mouth and with it came an intoxicating rush of power. He had no spell book, no conduit. It wasn't possible to cast blood magic without either, yet Serefin channeled the jittery trembling in his muscles, the heady rush of power from the blood.

He cast out a handful of stars. They glittered in the darkness, lighting enough for him to see he was still in the catacombs. At least he knew the way out.

He crashed his way out of the catacombs, disturbing the guards standing outside.

"Your Highness," one said, his tone oddly grave as he drew his sword on Serefin.

"Oh, is this how it goes? I'm murdered *and* everyone has orders to kill me on sight? Just to rub it in?"

He didn't know if he had actually died but damn if it didn't sound significantly more poetic.

He wondered if he could kill with the stars still floating lazily around his head. There was only one way to find out. The bite wound was still sluggishly bleeding, and he used it to coat his hands. Before he had a chance to use the magic, though, the point of a blade was sticking out of one guard's eye. The other fell beside him, revealing a one-eyed sorry sight.

"Serefin," Ostyia gasped. Her single eye was rimmed red, as if she had been crying. Serefin had *never* seen Ostyia cry. The closest she had ever been was the day her dog had been killed on a hunt when they were children. Even then, she took the news with a stony face.

She fumbled with the dead guards, and handed Serefin a dagger. She winced at the bite mark on his arm. "We have to go," she said. Pausing, she turned back and threw her arms around him. "You're not allowed to die," she said fiercely, her voice catching.

"Too late for that," Serefin said, a little shocked at her embrace. "I think. Perhaps not. What's happening?" He realized she was alone and felt a stab of panic. "Where's Kacper?"

A crash of lightning and thunder lit the hallway for an instant, before they were plunged back into the torchlit dim.

"We have to go," she repeated. "I don't know where Kacper is, I'm sorry, Serefin." She still hadn't let him go. If anything, she clutched him tighter. "Your father announced your death this morning. He's using it as leverage, saying it was assassins. He's at the chapel now . . . and Serefin?" She finally pulled back, her face pale. "Whatever he was trying to do, he succeeded. And you were supposed to stay dead."

"Well," Serefin said brightly, masking his horror as Ostyia stepped away. He strapped the dagger onto his belt. He didn't bother wrapping the bite wound. Let everyone see his desperation. "If my father wants to become a god, I'll have to show him what I saw on the other side."

Ostyia's one eye was wide. "What did you see?"

"Stars," Serefin said. He waved a hand at the stars still hanging in constellations around his head as he stepped over the corpses and started down the hall in the direction of the court-yard. "There was music. And . . ." he trailed off.

"Moths."

And thousands of glittering, dusty wings exploded around him.

34

NADEZHDA

LAPTEVA

Svoyatova Raya Astafyeva: *It was said that stars trailed Svoyatova Raya Astafyeva wherever she went. A path of flickering light amidst the darkness of war.*

—Vasiliev's Book of Saints

Nadya watched as the rain spattering the windows of the cathedral became thick and red. Blood. It was blood.

There was blood raining from the sky.

Parijahan followed Nadya's gaze and her lips tightened. This was all happening in the wrong order.

Nadya let her magic trickle out from where she stood, hidden in the shadows of a marble pillar. No one would notice her there. A pale slip of a girl wouldn't be seen while the king of Tranavia turned the skies to blood and toyed with more power than any mortal should ever possess.

All that power could bring Kalyazin to its knees in

moments. All they had by way of magic was one seventeen-year-old cleric. And while her power was significant, it was nothing compared to this. Not while the gods were out of her reach.

But not all of the gods, not quite. She rubbed her thumb over the pendant in her hand. *Some gods require blood.*

She was already so far past what she had thought was truth. There was nothing stopping her from going further, not if it was going to save them all. She might live to regret this but she also might not live at all and that was enough to make her decision for her. She had power now, power of her own, and while she couldn't press against that veil of magic before, perhaps that too had changed.

She let one of her blades fall into her hand. Praying under her breath, she tugged the mask off her face and dropped it. She cut a careful spiral into her palm, the same pattern that was on the pendant, then pressed the cold metal into her fist.

Blood it is, then, if that's what it takes.

She could feel the oppressive weight of the veil cast over Tranavia bearing down on her. She pushed her power against it, a single point of light against an expanse of darkness. There was the smallest splinter. The king's head snapped up as he felt it too. Malachiasz stiffened, fingers fluttering in an odd way as his hand moved to press over his heart. He looked up at the ceiling, a puzzled frown passing over his features.

Blood was dripping between her fingers and down her hand as she clenched her fist.

Malachiasz gave a lopsided grin and it was another spike through Nadya's heart. He stepped away from the king, folding his hands behind his back. The king's attention locked onto her.

There was no warning when the king's power moved against

her. A heartbeat and the stones of the floor were rippling like water, the floor soon gone from underneath Nadya's feet. A blink and she slammed to the ground in front of him, her *voryen* flying out of her hand and clattering across the floor.

"What is this?" The king of Tranavia grabbed a fistful of her hair and yanked her head up.

She bit back a cry of pain and shoved her magic harder up at the veil. If this was when she died, then fine. *Fine.* She would tear this veil down first and bring the gods back to Tranavia with her dying breath.

There was no chance to respond to the king's question, no time for even a clever quip; the king slammed his hand against the side of her face and this time she *screamed*.

Lances of white heat drove through her skull. Everything splintered—black and white and red and black again—and she nearly passed out. The king dropped her.

She caught herself on one hand. Her stomach churned, threatening to upheave its contents onto the grotesque floor of bleached bones.

"Well, child, you're in a rough spot now, aren't you?"

Hello, Velyos. It felt good to be able to commune with a god once more, even if Velyos was something else. Something not quite a god. But something with power Nadya could harness nonetheless. Her vision was blurry when she opened her eyes, and blood dripped from her nose. She felt a shift of power, saw the king's hand move down toward her. A killing blow.

She caught the power against her own. It rattled her to her bones, her elbow buckling underneath her. She couldn't stop it. It was too much, too strong, all she could do was hold it off for a few seconds before it consumed her.

"You don't want to break the veil, you know that, right?" Velyos said. *"Do you really want to destroy this country and all within it?"*

If I don't bring the gods back, the king will win. Tranavia will win. I can't do this on my own. I came here to bring the gods back.

"*I have shown you the truth, and still you want their aid?*"

Nadya faltered and her magic with it. The king's power flooded through the cracks in her shield and with it her dreams came back to her.

Too many people have thought me so naïve that they could control me. I won't allow you to do that as well.

But she still couldn't do this alone.

"*Perhaps you don't have to.*"

The cathedral doors came crashing open. The magic slamming her down ceased.

Serefin Meleski, covered in blood and surrounded by a constellation of glittering lights and fluttering moths, strolled into the room. Nadya's chest clenched as she touched the power roiling off him. It was unlike anything she had ever experienced before. Unlike the Vultures, unlike the horror his father had become. This was ethereal and darkly enchanting.

As she grasped what his power felt like, it was as if she had been doused in ice water.

It was like the power of the gods. Or, no, like the power she was glancing upon when talking to Velyos.

As Serefin scanned the room, his gaze caught hers. She tensed as recognition flickered in his pale blue eyes. But then his lips twitched just so into a smile.

Not alone, then?

"No," Velyos responded. "*Not quite.*"

SEREFIN

MELESKI

A day before and Serefin would have had the cleric arrested on sight. A week earlier and he would have immediately killed her for the power her blood harbored. But, now, seeing the girl crumpled on the floor with blood smeared across her face and murder in her eyes, Serefin had never been so happy to see anyone in his life.

Of course the girl from some backwater Tranavian city was the cleric hiding in plain sight. Serefin would have deemed himself foolish for missing all the signs, except he had the excuse of being worried about other, greater things. A pointless excuse, all things considered.

"Father," he called radiantly. "I don't know which I'm more offended by, that you *murdered* me, or that you used my death for your own gains—if I died. Did I die? It's all very unclear. But, I'm here now! While I applaud the imagination required to get so much from my death, really, I do—I had no idea I was so important and everyone likes to feel special—I'm hurt that I don't get to reap any of the rewards from it. Because, you know, I'm apparently dead."

The shock on Izak Meleski's face was the greatest gift Serefin's sad life had ever given him.

"Serefin," he said, his voice choked.

"Oh, don't sound so surprised," Serefin said. "As if you *care*."

The Black Vulture stepped down from his dais, hands folded behind his back, face carefully impassive. He approached Serefin slowly. The moths fluttered in nervousness around Serefin.

"Your Highness," Malachiasz said, bowing his head. "You do realize what this means, don't you?"

Serefin had no idea what the Vulture was talking about. He eyed the younger boy as he circled him, slowly.

"I can't say I do, Your Excellency," Serefin replied.

Malachiasz spun on his heels, facing the king again. "I believe this is a coup." His cheerful smile revealed iron teeth.

Izak's face darkened and power roiled in the black corners of the hall. Malachiasz turned to Serefin again.

Serefin drew the dagger from his belt and cut a thin line down his forearm. The stars around his head brightened. Malachiasz looked up at them, a hand lifting to nudge one of the moths in the air with an iron claw.

"Fascinating," he murmured.

Then he was gone and darkness was sweeping across the floor in an inky flood toward Serefin.

So, now I have to fight off my father's magic—the likes of which I do not understand—with my own which I also do not understand, Serefin thought grimly.

The Black Vulture swept back up to his throne. He idly spun a chalice on the armrest and Serefin watched as the cleric stood and darted for a dagger that rested a few steps away.

It was time to test just what he could do with this power.

NADEZHDA

LAPTEVA

Malachiasz's eyes closed. He tilted his head back, baring his throat to Nadya's blade.

"Did I make a mistake not killing you?" she whispered, her voice cracking. Tears burned her eyes.

"Almost definitely." His hand tightened over the arm of the throne. His eyes opened, flickering onyx.

Nadya lifted her gaze in time to watch as all the Vultures—the ones who had defected from Malachiasz—toppled. She hissed out a breath, pressed her forehead against the side of his head. "What have you done?"

"There was no way to stop this," he rasped. "It was set into motion a long time ago. It was always going to happen."

"And you returned to see your great victory through," she said through clenched teeth. "Bring the cleric—she'll be useful—she can watch her kingdom fall."

A flicker of pain crossed his face. "Are we so different, Nadya?" He lifted his hand, fingers tipped with long claws, and pressed his thumb against her lips. "We both long for freedom. For power. For a choice. We both want to see our kingdoms survive."

A few of the Vultures struggled to their feet. Parijahan slid out of the shadows to deal with them herself. Serefin couldn't hold off his father much longer.

"We both know we're the only ones who can save our kingdoms," he continued, voice soft.

Her blade slipped in her shaking hand, cutting a shallow line on his throat. Crimson trickled down the pale of his skin. He stilled, icy eyes never breaking from hers.

Nadya had been so terribly naïve. She had listened to her heart as it whispered that the boy with the charming smile and gentle hands didn't mean any harm; he was dangerous, he was thrilling, but he meant well. Lies, lies, lies.

They had all had their eyes on the king of Tranavia; she wondered if they should have been watching Malachiasz the whole time.

"You'll help me stop this," she said.

He was silent a beat too long.

"I *will* destroy your carefully laid plans to accomplish my own."

"No," he finally said. "They align, you see."

It didn't make sense and she didn't understand. Her heart but shredded bits of flesh, pounding between her ribs. He but a monster, darkness in the shape of a boy. She was numb.

She lifted her blade from his throat, reaching down and sliding her hand over his wrist. She pulled his hand up, dragging her blade into the same spiral she had cut into her own. He hissed as she pressed the pendant over the cut, closing his hand around it, interlacing her fingers with his.

"I could do a lot with blood like yours," she whispered, her mouth at the shell of his ear. "And I want you to know that some gods require blood."

His eyes flickered from onyx to pale, his chin tilting down as a smile pulled at his lips. "Complicit in heresy, indeed."

She felt his power collide with hers, nightmarish and black. Aching and roiling like a poison and seeping inside her. She let it in, let it mix with her own well of light and divinity.

"Now you've tasted real power, *towy dżimyka,*" Malachiasz murmured, "what will you do with it?" He laughed softly and slipped the pendant back over her head, trailing his bloody fingertips down her cheek. "What will you do with freedom?"

She stared at him, at this broken boy who was a horror and a liar and had started this disaster. His power was intoxicating. She moved her face closer, her lips achingly near his. Her numb naïve heart screamed at her to forgive him again, one more chance, but he didn't deserve more chances.

"I'm going to save this world from monsters like you."

"Then here's your chance."

She pressed her lips to his temple and pulled away. Serefin was on his knees, hunched over in pain, blood oozing from his head, one hand white-knuckled on the ground holding him up. Dead moths littered the floor around him. The stars around his head began to flicker out.

Nadya punched another hole in the veil. She didn't break it completely, not yet, just enough to feel Marzenya's presence. Her rage, her ice, her anger. It was enough for Nadya to take the two halves of power she had within her—her own and that of a monster—and form them into something she could use. For a blinding, terrible moment holy speech flooded Nadya's senses. She saw only light; she heard only the chimes of divinity; copper filled her mouth.

Izak Meleski turned toward her and Nadya was hit by a crushing, agonizing weight. The man's power could send horrors into Nadya's mind, but she had seen horrors. There was little left to frighten her.

She pulled her *voryen* up to use as a channel for her power, pushing flames down onto the floor and toward the king. They were tinged with darkness. The flames touched the king, but he backed away, forcing a new horror into Nadya's mind.

She shook it off. Light tipped her fingers and she called a pillar of blinding power down from the sky—from the hole in the veil—to slam down upon the king.

For a heartbeat, she thought she had him. But a constricting power beat down upon her, forcing her still.

Blood vessels burst in her eyes from the strain weighing down heavy upon her. Blood dripped down from her nose, leaked from her eyes, she could feel it pooling in her ears.

She was dying.

SEREFIN

MELESKI

When his father turned away, it felt like Serefin was coming up for air after being drowned. He gasped, choking on blood, and forced himself to his feet.

The cleric stood, frozen. White light surrounded her head—almost a halo—but something about it was tainted and it shivered in erratic tremors. Blood drained out of her like water. Serefin took a step closer but his knees gave out. He had nothing left; a few moths that fluttered weakly around him, not enough blood left to cast. He was drained dry.

Like a shadow, the Akolan girl whom Serefin had seen trailing the cleric slipped into the center of the room. She snapped out with her wrist in a violent blur. It was a whip, Serefin realized dimly. The blunted leather struck Izak Meleski directly in the temple and he stumbled.

"*Nadya!*" the Akolan girl screamed as the king's attention turned on her. Her limbs seized.

Serefin glanced at Malachiasz, who watched impassively from his throne, chin in his hand. All that power and yet he did nothing. Hatred burned in Serefin's veins. He had known the Black Vulture was a danger, yet he had let himself believe with foolish hope that perhaps he had an ally, when he was just another monster.

35

NADEZHDA LAPTEVA

Svoyatova Valentina Benediktova: *A cleric of Marzenya whose path became clouded when it crossed that of the Tranavian blood mage, Urszula Klimkowska. All records of Valentina end there. No one knows whether Valentina killed Urszula, or vice versa. Her canonization was due to the miracle she performed when she was twelve of defending the city of Tolbirnya. There is no record of her death; her body was never found.*

—Vasiliev's Book of Saints

Nadya pushed her hands out and shattered the king's hold. He stood with his attention on Parijahan, torturing her. Nadya gripped her blade in her bloody hand and tugged at her power, putting herself across the room in the space of a heartbeat. She slammed her blade into the king's back.

Divine magic and blood magic and something else,

something *different*. Power that should not be combined; power strong enough to take apart the one who wielded it. Magic that was so in opposition that in another circumstance, held by another person, it would destroy itself before being bound into a formidable spell.

But Nadya knew divine power, and she had touched Malachiasz's power, knew the shape of it, dark as it was, and she knew her own well of magic.

She forced the torrent of magic through the blade and into the king. This would kill even a god.

He jerked, his body shuddering. Nadya pulled the blade out, staring at it in abject horror before she plunged it back in his body a second time. She stumbled to her knees. Parijahan crumpled, blood welling at the corners of her mouth.

There was silence.

Then the single, ringing sound of footsteps on the marble floor. Nadya lifted her head with some difficulty to watch as Malachiasz stepped down from his dais, the chalice he had been toying with back in his hand.

The expression on his face was strange. Eyes glassy, sweat beading at his temples. He swallowed hard, gaze flicking to Nadya in a glimmer so fast she wondered if she imagined it.

"Thank you," he said, his voice soft. "I didn't think it would work, you see, there were so many variables along the way, so many things that could go wrong, but you have done exactly as I hoped."

Nadya stiffened. She watched, mutely, as Malachiasz kicked at the body of the king, adjusting it so the fast flowing blood drained into the chalice.

"No . . ." she whimpered. She tried to get up, to knock over the chalice and stop whatever Malachiasz was about to set into motion, but she couldn't. Her limbs refused to move and she remained frozen in horror as Malachiasz lifted the chalice, swirling the blood inside slowly.

"Malachiasz, please." Nadya had to force the words past her lips.

She felt Rashid's hand on her shoulder. He approached Malachiasz.

Malachiasz lifted a hand and rested his iron claws on Rashid's chest, his eyes still on the chalice of blood. "Do not try to stop me," he said softly. He slowly met Rashid's pleading gaze. *"Please."*

"This isn't going to fix anything, Malachiasz," Rashid said.

"You don't understand," Malachiasz snapped. "This"—he waved to the body of the king—"won't be enough to stop this war. Those Kalyazi gods will grind Tranavia to ash like they've ground out their own country. I cannot let it happen. I won't."

"This won't help."

Nadya struggled to her feet. She took a shaky step toward him, curled her fingers over his on the cup. He was trembling.

"Is this what you wanted?" she asked faintly. "All the lies, all the planning, for this?" A flash of clarity, the understanding that he had wanted Serefin's death, to take the secular throne out of the equation entirely and claim it all. "You think you're going to save these countries," she whispered, horrified. "This will just cause more destruction, Malachiasz, please, the gods aren't *like this.*"

"Nadya, I showed you freedom. You know what will happen now." His voice shifted, tone accusatory. "You knew it the whole time."

She did. And she had been willing to sacrifice Tranavia to save Kalyazin. Her quest was divine and the Tranavians were heretics. But he was wrong; it wasn't going to end that way.

"I'll become more," he said, sounding frantic. "Can't you see? I *told you*."

She blinked, startled. He had. He had told her the Meleskis needed to be deposed. That the *gods* needed to be deposed.

She'd been too wrapped up in him to put the pieces together.

She reached up, winding her hands through his hair, clasping them on either side of his head. "Are we so different, Malachiasz? It's over. Let it go. This will destroy you."

The Black Vulture shook his head. "I've waited for this too long." He lolled his head, gaze unfocused. "Why go back when you can go further? Why let Tranavia burn when I can save it?"

His knuckles whitened as his grip tightened further. He pushed away from her and tipped the chalice back, draining it in one long draught.

No.

Nadya's heart sped in a fluttery, sick way. She felt Malachiasz's power still within her burning against her hold. *What has he done?* She stepped back.

Malachiasz shuddered, and the chalice fell from limp fingers. His head tilted back, Adam's apple bobbing, as he swallowed hard. His face wrenched. Blood dripped from the corners of his eyes.

Iron claws, iron teeth, blackened horns that twisted back into his long hair. Vast, feathered wings drenched with blood sprouted from his shoulder blades. His pale eyes flickered onyx.

Physical changes that had been burned into his body by those of his kind. *Why go back when you can go further?*

What was further? Further was a power so corrosive that Nadya—through her terrible connection to Malachiasz—could already feel it eating away at him. Further was the veins underneath his pale skin turning black with poison.

Further was the power of a god—not even a god, this was

worse than any divine power Nadya had ever touched. This was something horrible and eldritch, twisting his body and choking his soul. Draining the dregs of his humanity to be replaced with something vicious and mad.

Nadya let out a scream of pain. It felt as if every manifestation was happening on her. The cut on her hand heated, burning up her arm, filling her veins with fire.

Iron spikes jutted from his body, dripping with blood. As he stood, chest heaving, Nadya gasped. He fit the image of the monsters that terrorized her nightmares.

"Fascinating," Malachiasz murmured. He pressed his clawed hand over his heart and frowned, as if he was feeling something only mildly unusual. His head twitched, wrenching painfully. Lightning and thunder and a groaning in the earth crashed around them.

She stepped closer. Rested one hand over her racing heart. Tears spilled over as she reached out and brushed her fingers against his cheek.

"What have you done, Malachiasz?" Everything she had felt for him was nothing more than ashes at her feet, but still her broken heart lurched at the thought of losing him.

There was madness in his black eyes—madness and something terribly close to divinity.

Which was, in essence, the same as madness.

He didn't speak, just shook his head. He took a step away from her. Desperate and heartbroken, she pulled him closer and ignored his iron teeth, his madness, and kissed him.

He tasted like blood; he tasted like betrayal.

"I can feel it," she whispered, her hands smearing blood on his neck. "What have you done? I can *feel it.*"

His eyes flickered back to their icy pale, agony stark within them. *"Myja towy dżimyka. Myja towy szanka . . ."* He tilted her face up. Kissed her again, careful with his razor claws, his touch achingly gentle. When he pulled away his eyes went onyx once more, the ice bleeding away into darkness. "It's not enough."

"Malachiasz?" Her voice broke and she clutched at him even as she felt him moving farther and farther away.

One of his hands lifted; the backs of his fingers brushed against her cheek.

He thought this would heal the gaping wound of his tattered soul, *save his kingdom.* She was watching him destroy himself. Spiraling into pieces as he was twisted into something far past a monster.

But he still has his name, she thought, a desperate, fleeting, irrelevant thing.

Tears dripped down Nadya's face and she caught his hand, pressing it against her cheek. She kissed the back. His hand slipped from hers.

His vast, black wings snapped open and he rose, crashing through the high window in the chapel and sending fragments of broken glass raining down upon them. Nadya stood, blood staining her skin, fingers to her lips.

The veil over Tranavia was ebbing away, the gods' touch returning. Now their presence felt wrong. Nadya braced herself for Marzenya's anger, but nothing came.

She could feel the gods, but they did not speak to her.

36

SEREFIN

MELESKI

Svoyatova Evgenia Dyrbova: *The last known cleric, Svoyatova Evgenia Dyrbova, a cleric of Marzenya, fell on the
battlefield. Her last words were considered a prophecy of
doom—the gods would recede, their touch would lessen,
clerics would be even more of a rarity. Kalyazin would be
doomed, if nothing changed, if the war continued.*
                               —Vasiliev's Book of Saints

Serefin woke on the sanctuary floor surrounded by dead
moths and shards of glass. He opened his eyes just in time
to see the cleric faint, her Akolan friend not quite reaching her in time to keep her from crashing to the floor.

Light still haloed her head.

"Nadya," the boy whispered, picking her up. He glanced
at Serefin, going rigid when he noticed he was awake.
He gently set the cleric down and picked up a discarded
dagger.

"You know, if we killed you as well we could end this war even faster," he said. He crouched next to Serefin, the dagger held lazily between his long, brown fingers.

"Go ahead," Serefin mumbled. Where was Ostyia? He'd lost track of her in the madness.

The boy studied him. He looked out towards the entrance to the sanctuary. He shook his head. "No. I don't think you're anything like your father."

Those words flooded Serefin with relief. "Is she going to be all right?" He worked himself up to a sitting position. He shouldn't be moving at all; he had lost *far* too much blood.

The Akolan boy looked at Nadya. His features softened. "I don't know. But your asking makes me even less inclined to kill you." He stuck out a hand. "Name's Rashid."

Serefin stared at him, amused by the absurd normalcy in the gesture. He shook the boy's hand. "Serefin."

Rashid stood and walked over to the Akolan girl, unconscious a few steps away. As he was checking on her, one large, gray moth fluttered down to the ground in front of Serefin.

"Are you the only one left?" he whispered, nudging the moth onto his index finger. The moth's wings fluttered. *No.* The moths would return; the stars would return. He had been altered and now he had to figure out what that meant.

"Get off me, I'm fine, I'm fine." The Akolan girl's voice rang out. She sat up, holding her head. Her eyes narrowed as she scanned the room. "Where's . . ." but she trailed off, her question going unfinished.

She moved, kneeling next to Nadya. Lightning jolted the room, too near for comfort, but the rain outside was now only rain. Serefin scrambled to his feet, searching the hall for some sign of Ostyia.

He found her lying underneath a pillar like a discarded rag

doll. Panic gripped his chest. It didn't look like she was breathing. *No, not Ostyia.* He knelt beside her, hesitant to look any closer. He didn't want confirmation of a tragedy. He didn't want to know.

"You're not allowed to die," he rasped. When he touched her, a constellation of stars formed around his hand. "If I'm not allowed to die, you're not either."

Ostyia took a gasping breath. She began to cough, shoulders shaking. "Serefin?" Her voice was scratchy.

"Didn't we have this conversation already?" He tried to joke but it came out flat. He'd almost lost her. He had so little; he was unable to even consider what might have happened to Kacper. He couldn't lose them.

"We have to find Kacper," she said, straightening. Her eye grew wide as she reached up to touch the skin underneath his left eye. "Can you still see out of this?"

When he closed his good eye, his bad eye was still a blurry mess. "It's the same, why?"

"It's full of stars, Serefin." Her voice was hushed, awed. "You're surrounded by stars."

He leaned back on his heels, unsure what to say. *Yes, this is what happens now* just didn't seem to do it justice. He didn't know what it meant.

Behind them, the cleric stirred.

NADEZHDA
LAPTEVA

Nadya's head pounded. She stared up at the beautiful ceiling of the cathedral and contemplated giving up.

Maybe what they had done would change things. Maybe things would be better now. Or, maybe, they had just set into motion something far worse. Her hand ached with a dull, throbbing pain. The spiral would scar into her palm, a reminder.

Nadya sat up slowly, looking up to the window where Malachiasz had disappeared. He had lied to her, betrayed her, and now he was gone.

She felt hollow, utterly used up. The prince knelt down in front of her, obviously in pain.

Nadya smiled faintly. She stuck out a hand.

"I don't think we've ever been introduced," she said softly. The tight hold she had been keeping over the way she spoke Tranavian loosened, and her Kalyazi accent melted into her words. "My name is Nadezhda Lapteva, but you can call me Nadya."

His scarred eye looked different. It was a deeper blue than his other pale eye, and stars glittered in constellations in its depths. He took her hand. His was warm as his fingers wrapped around hers.

"Serefin Meleski, and *please,* just call me Serefin," he replied. A huge gray moth fluttered down from the ceiling and landed in his brown hair. "Did you know you have a halo?" he asked. The awkward, strangely charming boy was still there, underneath the exhaustion and the stars. Underneath the power that felt divine.

She raised an eyebrow. "Did you know you have a moth in your hair?"

He smiled and nodded.

A crash of lightning struck right outside the chapel doors, making them all jump.

The dead body of the Tranavian king was across the room. A chalice lay on the ground beside him. His blood had dried on Nadya's hands, leaving them stiff.

Her gaze passed over the body, locking onto the chalice. She felt like she'd been punched in the chest as she looked at it.

So she had done what she set out to do; so she had killed the king, she had broken the veil. At what cost? A higher price than she had been prepared to pay and more questions than she had been willing to answer.

She cast a prayer up to Marzenya. She had no prayer beads, she had nothing.

Her prayer was met with cold, deliberate silence and it needled at Nadya's heart, but she knew the goddess heard her. The veil was finally, truly, gone.

Nadya looked up at the shattered cathedral window once more, glass fragments dusting the ground around her. Malachiasz's black power itched underneath her skin as it fought against her own divine magic.

She would release it if she thought she could; if it would do any good at all she would purge it, break off the last piece tying her to the Black Vulture.

Her palm ached and she shifted the fingers of her left hand, feeling the skin stretch and tighten around the spiral wound. She rose to her feet, movements slow. Lying on the ground some space away from the body of the dead king was an iron crown. She picked it up, returning to where Serefin sat looking vaguely confused.

"The king is dead, long live the king," she said, handing it to him.

He looked up at her. His eyes were otherworldly now, ghostly and divine in the way stars swirled in the darkness of his left eye, a contrast to the icy pale of his right. Serefin laughed wearily. "Words I never thought I would hear."

"Where are all the Vultures?" Ostyia asked.

"Most probably fled with their king," Serefin said.

"I guess the next question would be, where are your nobility?" Parijahan asked.

Serefin shook his head. "Waiting to see who leaves this cathedral alive, most likely. Whatever requires the least amount of dirtied hands."

He was clutching the iron crown tight in his hands.

He doesn't think he's ready for this, Nadya realized. *He's scared.*

It was strange to see Serefin as a boy and not as the terrifying blood mage who had been whispered about throughout the monastery where she'd grown up. The monastery he had burned to the ground.

Ostyia touched his hand. "I'll go," she said, voice quiet.

Serefin nodded. She slipped out of the cathedral.

Parijahan picked up the chalice lying near the king. Nadya cringed away from it when she brought it near.

"I trusted him," Parijahan whispered, her gray eyes misty. She met Nadya's gaze, sympathy evident.

Me too. Worse, I think I loved him.

Without thinking, Nadya's fingers closed over the stem, taking it from her. It was made of silver and glass. There was still blood pooling at the bottom. Her fingers absently glanced across the rim.

Everything felt murky and fog-like. As if they were all waking from a dream. It was clear Serefin felt the same.

Serefin still gripped the crown in his hands, fumbling with it, face puzzled and torn. He stood and took a step toward his father's body, a flicker of pain passing over his features. Parijahan moved to stop him, a hand on his arm.

"Let me," she said gently.

"The ring," he said, relief cracking his voice.

Parijahan nodded and she moved to slide a heavy signet ring off the king's hand. She handed it to him. He thanked her quietly, the ring in one hand, the crown in the other. He hesitated before slowly sliding the ring over the littlest finger of his right hand. The crown remained clutched in his hand.

Nadya nearly tried to contact the gods again, but something held her back. She'd never been afraid of the gods before. But after nearly losing everything, and after realizing her magic was something *she* possessed, not a thing given or taken away at the gods' whim, she worried they wouldn't treat her the same. She had doubted too much, gone against their will too many times. She had loved the wrong person.

But she still believed in them; her version of gods, not Malachiasz's, and she dearly hoped that meant something. It didn't mean she didn't have questions—she had a thousand—but she was willing to ask them. But . . . maybe not yet.

Nadya sighed heavily. Serefin glanced over at her. He lifted a hand and the moth shifted over to land on the signet ring.

A boy who is mortal and maybe a little divine, Nadya thought. He held no belief in the gods, he was still a heretic, whatever had been done to him she doubted it had changed what he believed. He was still a blood mage.

He smiled at her, though, and she wondered if maybe that was all right.

"Will this be enough?" she asked him. "To stop the war?" Malachiasz was wrong, he had to be wrong.

Serefin twitched his hand and the moth flew away. "It will."

epilogue

THE BLACK
VULTURE

He didn't know what it wanted.

The hunger. The raw, scraping need that had hollowed him out, clawed out the core of him and left him with nothing but *wanting*. There was no name for it, for what the hunger wanted. For the dissonance that rattled apart and reformed and created a cacophony of words and voices and *too much too loud*.

He knew where to go from here. A place to hide, to recoup, to plan. Pieces to be moved and taken away and brought forth. He needed to . . . he needed . . .

(He'd never expected to make it this far.)

(He'd never expected *survival*.)

What he needed didn't matter; the darkness was clawing through him. He had so little time left. More time than expected.

(Being unmade was such unpleasant business.)

A point of clarity, insistent in its rhythmic return, battered against the corners of his awareness, a single note: regret.

Regret.

Regret washed away by the intoxicating thrill of power that was *greater,* that was *more.* Swept away with the last dregs of paltry weakness that tried to force him to look back, *look back.*

(There was no turning back.)

It grew greater, a vastness in the switch from *human, barely,* to *something not.*

Stone doors flew open before him, leading into a darkness so complete that walking down the steps toward it would be like ceasing to exist.

(How fitting.)

Lightly he touched a symbol, roughly hewn into the stone wall, that his hands had glanced upon so many times before.

Dimly, he considered how his enemies called this place hell on earth. This place where blood flowed too freely—unwillingly given.

His hand pressed into the stone, finding it sticky with fresh blood. He hesitated; a pressing thought needled at his heart, a reminder, a mantra.

He whispered to the darkness: "My name is . . ." He shook his head.

It was gone.

Once there was a boy who was shattered into pieces and put back together in the shape of a monster. Once there was a boy who clutched at the remnants of what he had left as it fell through his fingers. Once there was a boy who destroyed what little there was remaining because it *wasn't enough.*

The boy was gone. The monster had swallowed the heart that beat in his chest.

He let the darkness take him.

ACKNOWLEDGMENTS

First and foremost, all gratitude to my lovely agent, Thao Le, plot wizard extraordinaire. Thank you so much for seeing the spark of something good in my mess of an early manuscript, giving me a chance, and pushing me to be better. And also thanks for using Kylo Ren to get me to figure out Malachiasz. I can't believe that worked. Here's to working together on many more books.

To my editor, Vicki Lame, for getting this weird little book and my ridiculous Monster Children so totally and *completely*. And also for all the Kylo Ren gifs. There's a bit of a theme here.

Thank you, thank you, thank you to the Wednesday Books team for welcoming my book and me with such incredible enthusiasm. To DJ, Jennie, Olga, Melanie, Anna, and Meghan.

Thanks to Rhys Davies for bringing this strange world to life.

Thank you to Mark McCoy for the most black metal illustration a book cover has ever had.

Many thanks to Allison Hammerle, who survived living with me while I was writing this book. Thanks for all the nights of talking out my plot issues and dealing with me lying on the floor and agonizing relentlessly. You're the real MVP.

To my amazing early readers: the evil queen of consistency, Phoebe Browning (yes, there's *finally* a wall around Grazyk), Basia P, Revelle G, Jennifer A, Angela H, and Vytaute M. You're all so wonderful and I don't know if this book would exist without your feedback and encouragement.

To my Tumblr crowd: Diana H, Hannah M, Marina L, Chelsea G, Dana C, Lane H, Jo R, Sarah M, Ashely A, and Larissa T. I can't believe you watched me publicly draft this book. We have all been on that blue hell-site for far too long.

To the fantastic writers I've met along the way: Lindsay Smith, R. J. Anderson, Rosamund Hodge, Melissa Bashardoust, Alexa Donne, June Tan, Kevin van Whye, Margaret Rogerson, Rosiee Thor, Emma Theriault, Deeba Zargarpur, and Caitlin Starling.

To Leigh Bardugo, publishing coven leader and all-around wonder. Thanks for supporting an earnest young writer on Tumblr and for all the timely, sage advice. But really for being the person I can shout at about that ridiculous Dragonlance musical.

To Christine Lynn Herman, my witch queen, thanks for crashing my DMs and proclaiming us friends. Rory Power, I probably won't fight you in a parking lot. And Claire Wenzel, I aspire to be half as bitingly witty as you; also, finish writing your book.

Thanks to the phenomenal artists who have already shown my book so much love: Nicole Deal, Therese A, and Jaria R, especially. To the booksellers who gave this book a chance and so many kind early words.

ACKNOWLEDGMENTS

And, ultimately, thank you to my family for their lifelong support of my weird interests and hermit ways. Thank you for letting me be secretive about my writing until I was ready to show it to the world.

bonus scenes

MALACHIASZ

CZECHOWICZ

The last thing Malachiasz expected was for his plan to work. For Izak Meleski to show up in a fevered state in the middle of the night, claiming he had figured out the solution to their little problem. He very much doubted it—the king wasn't a particularly skilled blood mage.

Malachiasz was still half asleep when he opened the door to his chambers. He felt a flash of panic when the king's eyes narrowed on his face, some strange vague recognition flashing over his features before it was gone.

"Your Majesty," Malachiasz said, swallowing hard and trying to remember where he'd left his mask. If he could get it inconspicuously. "Please, if you could, my study might be more comfortable?"

He kicked open the door to his study and tried not to think about the mess. He needed his mask.

The king was speaking—saying something about the

answer to Tranavia's troubles—but Malachiasz walked as swiftly as he could back to his bedroom and scooped his iron mask up from the bedside table, fitting it over his face.

He felt more like himself when it was on now. It didn't stifle anymore. He was also grateful that he could leave the king alone and not find himself in unimaginable trouble for it. The king looked to Malachiasz for everything, it seemed. So much so, it was exhausting and a bit troubling. Malachiasz had his own matters to attend to; he couldn't handhold the king's obsession with the blood magic the man could barely comprehend.

He raked his hands through his hair as he returned to his study, finally opting to tie it back to hide how much of a mess it was.

When he resembled something close to the Black Vulture and not a bleary-eyed teenage boy rudely woken from a dead sleep, he entered his study.

The king was pacing.

"You can do it," the king said, more a demand than anything else. He waved a stack of paper at Malachiasz, who took it carefully.

Malachiasz slowly sat down at his desk. "I'm sorry, Your Majesty, I need you to explain," he said, scanning the spell.

He went cold, dimly aware of the king speaking. There was a rushing in his ears as panic chewed its way into his throat and clawed down his chest. He flipped through the paper. Blackmail and the promise of disaster. That was what the king had handed him.

"What is this?"

"A way for you to give me what I want," the king said smugly.

Malachiasz felt all control ripped from his hands. He had been so close; the pieces had nearly lined up perfectly. But he had underestimated the king. He had underestimated Meleski's greed for power and his comprehension of the magic Malachiasz had always only half explained.

Malachiasz spread out the pages, forming a single spell, in front of him. He read without speaking. Let the silence spread out until it was thick and cloying and the tension so pressing that the king was overwhelmed by it.

He needed the king to feel it.

What he was reading would destroy Tranavia.

"Could you explain this to me?" he asked. *Prove to me you understand what chaos this will cause.*

"What do you wish to know?"

"The logistics of this spell, mostly," Malachiasz replied, keeping his voice pleasant. "Did you write this?"

The king didn't respond to his jab. Probably for the best.

"The theory you proposed was sound; it just needed refining," Meleski said.

Malachiasz fought the urge to roll his eyes. He didn't know who had done the refining, but it hadn't been the king.

The spell before him would require a large number of blood mages to be siphoned for their power. *Murdered,* he couldn't help thinking. The chosen subject would be infused with their power, and it would—theoretically—be enough to give a single mage sufficient magic to finally stop this infernal war.

Except the spell had taken a darker turn. For all Malachiasz had nudged the king in this direction, he had not expected *this*.

Meleski was willing to sacrifice his own son.

Malachiasz didn't know the prince. Serefin Meleski had barely stepped foot in Grazyk in years—he was a prodigy tactician, essential for the war effort, and thus he was always at the front.

But Serefin was a powerful mage. Tranavia would need him. "This is untested, Your Majesty, there's no guarantee—"

"Careful, Vulture, this sounds like a refusal."

Malachiasz froze. He had to refuse. Giving Meleski this level of power wasn't going to fix anything because Meleski couldn't even comprehend what the problem was. He would be the final nail in Tranavia's coffin.

But if he refused, Meleski would do everything in his power to destroy him. The Vultures would be safe—Meleski was obsessed with them and their power—but Malachiasz wouldn't be spared.

"Not a refusal, Your Majesty, not at all. May I hold on to these? You are correct in your assumptions: you have discovered something that could make this possible." *If totally destructive.*

The king nodded, waving him off. "You will do this, Vulture. You *will* give me this power."

Malachiasz smiled thinly, but internally he was screaming. "Of course, Your Majesty. Absolutely."

He fled in the night. He couldn't decide if it was a crisis of conscience or something deeper, a pin in the map. He would return—surely—but this was not the way things were supposed to work. He needed to get away; he needed to regroup, rethink, reconsider just how he could fit the pieces of his plan together in a way that would put him back in control.

Meleski had wrested it from him and that would not do.

Żywia found him before he fled. Somehow she always knew. Of everyone, she would be the person to sense that Malachiasz was frantic, that he was falling apart, that losing control was not what he wanted and it was breaking him into pieces.

She blocked the doorway. Her dark hair was wild and tangled, her dark blue eyes hurt but mostly angry. She was as tall as him; it would take effort to get past her.

"I'm not letting you leave until you tell me exactly what you're doing."

He dragged his hands through his hair. She wouldn't understand. She would try, and it would make everything worse, and he needed to leave.

He took her by the shoulders. "There will be a time when I explain everything. But right now, I need to leave."

She blinked at him, something fracturing in her face. "I'll be ripped apart if you're not here," she whispered.

He let out a breath. It . . . didn't change anything. He wished it did; he wished knowing that she was right, that she would have difficulty controlling the Vultures without him there to lead, was enough, but in his efforts to fix things, he had only succeeded in making everything worse.

He needed to leave.

"Where are you going? At least tell me that," she said.

He took a step back, swallowing hard. Then he did what he did best.

He lied.

"Kyętri. I'll be back. I need to . . . reevaluate what the king asked of me."

Her eyes narrowed. She knew what he thought of the Salt Mines. They terrified him. He would never go back, under any circumstance, because it was easier to ignore the agony of what had been done to him if he didn't return to the place where it had happened. He would never descend into that hell ever again.

He was leaving Tranavia. He was going somewhere no one would ever look for him.

Malachiasz was going to Kalyazin. If he was the only person

who could stop their gods from shattering his kingdom, he would go to the source.

It was always cold. It wasn't even the kind of cold that chewed at Tranavia in the winter; this was something else. It was almost a living thing, nestling down in Malachiasz's bones and making them ache every morning.

There was a part of him that liked it, how it chipped away at him, bit by bit.

He reached the refugee camp of Tvir in the early morning, as light was just beginning to glitter against the snow. He stopped at the edge of the trees and wondered if this was worth it. His clothes were ragged, but Kalyazi made. The markings he had taken when he joined the ranks of his order would be unusual here, but he had seen a few Kalyazi with odd tattoos, so they wouldn't be totally out of place. He hoped.

He had stuffed his spell book and military uniform so deeply into his pack that it would take upending the entire thing for anyone to find them. It was unwise of him to have both, but it was far more dangerous to be without his spell book, and the uniform . . . well, it was sentiment.

No one knows I'm here, he reminded himself, anxiety beginning to sink its claws into his throat. *I've made it this far without a second glance. I can keep going.*

He wouldn't think of the upheaval he had left behind; the problems he had left for Żywia to handle because he was weak and cowardly and something during his indoctrination must have gone horribly awry for his conscience to still cut at him so badly.

He scrubbed at his face with his hands. It would be better

if he didn't think about what he had thrown away so soon after fighting tooth and claw for it.

Malachiasz hitched his pack over his shoulder and stepped into the camp. The soldier he met at the edge looked as tired and worn out as he felt. He gave Malachiasz only a short glance.

"What village are you from, boy?"

"Kievya," Malachiasz said.

The soldier's eyes narrowed, and it was like he was finally really looking at Malachiasz.

"Did it finally fall to the heretics?"

Malachiasz nodded, internally bristling at the branding. He'd found it best to speak as little as possible. His Kalyazi was flawless, but he hadn't managed to completely eradicate his Tranavian accent. Saying he was from Kievya was explanation enough for most people: the village was very close to the Tranavian border. It had held on admirably but recently fallen to Malachiasz's people.

A reasonable explanation that would mask just about anything from tired people not looking for trouble.

The soldier leaned against a Kalyazi weapon Malachiasz didn't know the name for. For a tense second, he thought the man was going to turn him away. It would be fine, he could figure out a different plan, but he was nearly out of food and they were deep in the Kalyazi mountains. Malachiasz could usually manage for himself well enough, but it was so cold.

After a long silence, the guard jerked his head toward the camp. "Go ahead, boy."

Malachiasz couldn't help the weary smile. The guard's eyes softened as he waved him away. Malachiasz had found Kalyazin to be an exhausted kingdom full of tired people just trying to scrape by as war tore them apart.

He thought he would hate them, but instead he could too easily empathize.

It left him confused and bewildered and continually putting on hold his plan for figuring out just how to twist his former plans back into his control. The idea was draining, and he liked not having the fact that he was a monster coloring every person's interactions with him. No one knew what he was. He was simply a weary boy fleeing the war like everyone else.

It was . . . nice, to be unimportant. To be able to crack jokes with Kalyazi he came across in desolate inns and receive a surprised laugh in return.

He had never had a chance to be no one; he found he was fond of it.

Malachiasz passed through various Kalyazi villages and encampments, never staying in one place for long lest someone look too close or listen too hard to the way he formed Kalyazi words.

The months passed quietly. He grew used to it, comfortable— until he crashed into two Akolans and they spun his world back out of his control.

He was passing through a minor Kalyazi city when something slammed into him. He almost reacted instinctively, claws nearly sliding out of his nail beds. Instead he drew a dagger from a sheath at the small of his back. He hadn't used magic in months, and the ache of its absence was starting to get to him.

"Move! Move!" The blur of motion and dark hair pushed past him, catching his wrist and dragging him along behind her.

He was too bewildered to pull away, and so he found himself tripping over his own feet as he was yanked into a nearby alleyway.

Shouts erupted from farther down the road and a boy spilled into the alley, bleeding from an ugly wound on his side. He fainted immediately at Malachiasz's feet.

Malachiasz chewed on his thumbnail and regarded the Akolan boy bleeding out. "Hello," he said.

The girl who had grabbed him turned, looked down, and groaned. "The soldiers will be here in minutes." She darted to the boy's side, checking his pulse. "If you would like to keep your pretty head on your shoulders, Tranavian, you should probably help us."

Malachiasz beat down a flash of panic. "I'm sorry?" he asked pleasantly.

She glared up at him. Her gray eyes were steely and fierce. Her thick hair was bound up in a single loose braid. Blood dripped from a cut on her cheek.

For some reason, that was enough.

He sighed.

The Akolan boy was shorter than Malachiasz, so he managed to lever him onto his shoulders without difficulty.

"My name is Parijahan," the girl said, voice soft as she nudged Malachiasz toward where the alley spilled out near the wall. She nodded to the Akolan boy. "Rashid."

A distant part of him knew he was supposed to feel the impulse to give her his name in return. After a few seconds ticked away, she glanced at him.

"Fair enough," she muttered.

His spell book was buried so far down in his pack that there was no way he would reach it in time. He watched as Parijahan moved to check if the coast was clear.

I guess I'll have to kill them after this, he thought with a vague pang that he was fairly certain was supposed to be regret. But he couldn't exactly have people wandering around who knew he was Tranavian when he had slipped past so many. He followed her as she rushed out of the alley. She had a heavy-looking bag slung over one shoulder.

The last thing he needed was to be wrangled into something that would draw attention from Kalyazi soldiers.

"This way," she said, and tore out into the streets.

Malachiasz groaned, shifting the way the boy was draped over his shoulders, and followed after her. Shouts were still following them, but Malachiasz couldn't tell if they were getting closer.

He followed Parijahan into a decrepit building, and she slammed the door behind him.

"Who are you running from?" he asked.

She shushed him. He frowned, still unused to being treated so casually. As much as he liked being a nobody, sometimes he missed the automatic respect his title gave him.

She moved to a crack in the boarded-up windows, peering out. After a few moments of tense silence, she let out a long breath.

"They moved past," she said softly.

"Who are 'they'?" Malachiasz asked.

She turned and looked to where Malachiasz had set Rashid on the ground, then knelt next to the unconscious boy.

"City guards. Nothing too scary, eh?" She looked back at Malachiasz. "What are you doing in Kalyazin, Tranavian?"

Malachiasz leaned back against the door. He folded his arms over his chest. "How are you so certain I'm Tranavian?"

"Accent. Also—" She waved to him. "—you look like one. It's in the face."

His frown deepened. That couldn't *possibly* be true.

"Thanks for getting Rashid out of there," she said. "We probably don't have much time before the guards start poking inside these buildings." Malachiasz eyed the Akolan girl as she dug through a bag and took out a handful of bandages. She busied herself with wrapping the boy's wounds. After a few minutes of silence during which he contemplated leaving, he eventually sighed and slid down the door until he was sitting on the ground.

Her gaze flicked over to him.

"What did you do to get the guards' attention?"

"Stole supplies," she said quickly.

He lifted an eyebrow. She met his gaze defiantly.

"Why were you stealing supplies?" he asked innocently.

She cast him a long look, and then smiled, a thought seeming to occur to her. "Are you a blood mage?"

He did not answer. She was probably only asking because of her unconscious friend, which he couldn't do anything about. "Blood magic can't heal."

"Shame."

"You never answered my question."

"Should I? You never told me what you were doing far past enemy lines."

He frowned. She had a point.

"Defecting?"

He blinked as she handed him the excuse he needed, then nodded curtly.

"I thought so," she murmured. "Well, c'mon, blood mage, you help me get Rashid out of here in one piece and I know a place where no Kalyazi is ever going to find you."

Well, now he felt bad about planning to kill them both.

That was new.

"You can't make that kind of promise," he said.

"You think the Kalyazi aren't going to know what you are?" she shot back.

He let out a hard breath through his nose. "I've been doing quite fine for myself." Something slammed into the door, and Malachiasz shot to his feet. He was going to get himself caught and hanged at this rate. "Should've left you both in those gutters."

"Well, you didn't!"

He was terrified to discover that he might actually like this girl.

"So, Akolan, we have two options here," he said.

The door made a cracking sound as another slam found it. "Do tell."

"We go through that window and run for it."

She looked at the window in question. It wasn't big enough for either of them to make it through, and they had an unconscious Rashid to consider.

"Tell me option two is better."

"Option two does mean I'll have to kill a lot of people."

"I don't think you know what *better* means," Parijahan said. "Any options with a little less death?"

"I'm sorry," Malachiasz said. "I don't know what 'less death' means, either."

She laughed, which was unexpected. "Minimal death. Run like hell. If we get separated, meet me south of the city walls. Can you carry Rashid?"

Malachiasz met her eyes and considered that he might be getting into something he wanted absolutely no part of. He nodded.

She grinned. The door slammed open.

They had found a pair of Kalyazi in the mountains. Malachiasz held one of the Tranavian soldiers in a spell, watching as

Parijahan and Rashid . . . negotiated, which apparently meant pointing a crossbow at one and holding a dagger to other's throat, as if they hadn't all seen one of the two girls take every star out of the sky.

He couldn't take his eyes away from the shorter of the two girls. There was blood on her hands and flecked in dark spatters across her face. Her hair caught the moonlight, pale strands captured by the cold wind as her braid unraveled. Malachiasz tugged at his magic, killing the Tranavian in one quick act, but he barely felt the use of his own power, too thrown by the dark eyes of the Kalyazi. Eyes that widened with fear before her expression hardened to a steely determination that piqued his curiosity. He could feel her terror, drawn to it by the monstrous part of himself that had been sleeping for some time. It was the way her terror seemed to shift to something else, something vicious and sharp, that made him step closer.

"We could have gotten information out of him," Parijahan said, a disapproving frown tugging at her lips.

Malachiasz barely registered that she was talking about the dead soldier. He had forgotten about him. He felt a *little* bad about killing him, but it was all part of a greater game. If that was what he kept telling himself, it would remain true, right? He had spent months with the two Akolans and he had little desire to return to the chaos he had left behind.

He knew he should pull his gaze away from the girl, but the monster had stirred and it dragged him closer still, like a moth to a flame.

He glanced at the other Kalyazi girl, wondering if she would have the same effect, but he dismissed the passionate hatred in her eyes immediately. It wasn't the same.

"Names?" he asked hopefully. He needed her name, needed to have something from this girl.

Parijahan shook her head.

"We very politely gave them our names, but I suppose Kalyazi don't appreciate manners," Rashid said.

Malachiasz couldn't help smiling. She knew how this game was played.

"Wise of them," he said.

He took another step closer until he was standing right before her. There was a string of beads around her neck, shimmering with some kind of magic that Malachiasz had never seen before. Before he could stop himself, he reached out and took them in his hand. He heard her breath catch, saw her hand clench into a fist.

"You both came from the monastery, yes?" he asked. It was obvious they had, but he wanted to hear her speak. He wanted her to admit that the breathtaking power he had felt was hers.

She didn't respond, only watched him with wariness, looking like she would bolt at any second.

"So which of you is the one with magic?"

"Kalyazi don't have magic," the other girl snapped.

Malachiasz spared her a passing glance before returning his gaze to the girl with hair like snow. Her dark eyes were a warm, deep brown.

"It was you, wasn't it?" he asked.

"Don't be ridiculous," she said, her voice soft.

There was a quiet edge to her words, a dangerous thread that nearly made him step back. This was a Kalyazi that Malachiasz might fear.

He took her hand, pressing his lips to it as he gave her something he had never thought he would willingly give someone who was, technically, the enemy.

"My name is Malachiasz Czechowicz," he said.

She stared, fingers tensing against his for a split second.

She peered up into his face, her expression revealing nothing but curiosity. The seconds that passed with her hand still in his stretched on.

She did not give him her name. He dropped her hand.

It didn't matter. He would get it.

He knew what she was. As much as she was trying to hide it, there was no way for her to hide the fire of magic that burned under her skin.

"We need to get out of here," the second girl murmured, stepping protectively closer.

She merely nodded, leaning down to pick up a fallen blade from the snow. Malachiasz stiffened, unable to shake the feeling that she was seconds away from stabbing him with it. *He* should want to turn his magic on her, because if she had done what he suspected, she was the one person who might turn the war in favor of the Kalyazi.

"The danger has passed, and we haven't yet finished our introductions," Rashid said. He glanced at Malachiasz, who returned his look with a slight smile.

She scowled, her nose scrunching as she considered the three of them. Her pale skin was dusted with freckles. "There's a prince on our trail and the longer we spend out here, the closer he gets. We thought the group you had your sights on was part of his company, but it looks like they were merely stragglers. We'll be on our way now, before he has the chance to catch up to us."

A beat of alarm. Malachiasz knew there were Tranavian companies that had made it this far past the border but . . . Serefin? Why?

"Prince? The Tranavians have as many princes as you Kalyazi do. You'll have to be more specific," Rashid said.

Malachiasz had to keep from rolling his eyes. The Kalyazi wouldn't know a low prince from a general.

"The High Prince," the second girl snapped.

Both the Akolans looked at Malachiasz. He stifled a sigh.

"The High Prince is this far into Kalyazin?" Parijahan asked, something in her tone directed at Malachiasz. As if he should know. He didn't want anything to do with the High Prince. That would only lead to the king.

"The monastery burned yesterday," the girl said, her voice trembling.

Malachiasz took a step back as Parijahan nudged him so she could move closer.

"So you need somewhere safe to wait him out?"

She blinked. "What?"

"Parj . . ." Malachiasz said, but he wanted the girl to agree. He wanted to know what her magic was. He wondered if, maybe, she could fix his mistakes. There had to be a way to stop Meleski from becoming unstoppable, but Malachiasz couldn't return to Tranavia without being blackmailed into helping him. Maybe there was another way.

But this girl was almost certainly more trouble than she would be worth. They should keep moving, leave the girls here—but he couldn't help drawing closer and hoping Parijahan had her way.

Parijahan ignored him. "Come with us," she said earnestly. "We can keep you safe from the prince."

The girl's gaze found Malachiasz again. Her eyebrows tugged down, just slightly. Her grip on her blade tightened.

"He won't harm you," Parijahan said.

"I make no promises," he murmured. Because, truly, if she was a cleric, there was a lot he could discover from some blood, and it didn't have to be freely given.

"I won't have anything to do with any Tranavian," she said. "Except to kill them."

"Yes, I can see that," Malachiasz said. He nudged one of the dead soldiers with the toe of his boot. There were a lot of them. That was not good, all things considered. He had become a little too complacent in his time away from Tranavia; he shouldn't be comfortable with the deaths of Tranavian soldiers, even if he was set apart from them as a Vulture. "An admirable skill set. She's not going to take you up on your offer, Parijahan. We should go."

"The *actual* High Prince is near?" Rashid asked.

"Blood and bone, I should have left you both in those gutters," Malachiasz muttered. He wandered over to one of the dead soldiers and picked up his spell book, flipping through it. The spells were almost childishly simple, but there were a lot of empty pages that Malachiasz could use for his own. He took the book, glanced at Rashid, inclining his head slightly, and started off back into the woods.

But not without one more look at the girl. She was talking to Parijahan, her voice too low for him to hear. He watched her tuck a lock of white hair behind her ear, and something in his chest shifted dangerously.

Rashid caught up to him quickly. "Well?" he asked.

"Well what?"

"You were staring."

"I absolutely was not. If she comes with us, we're asking for the Kalyazi army to fall on our heads."

Rashid made a noise of disbelief. "Parijahan is talking to her. She's coming with us."

Malachiasz let out an exhausted sigh. Rashid was right. Parijahan always had her way. He glanced over his shoulder again, but they had moved out of sight.

"You were perfectly civil to the other Kalyazi Parj picked up, what's the difference with this one?"

"Magic," Malachiasz replied tersely. She wasn't just another Kalyazi orphan Parijahan was keeping out of the snow. She was something more.

She had ripped the stars out of the sky, and Malachiasz had a bad feeling he had met his match, if not his doom.

ABOUT THE AUTHOR

EMILY A. DUNCAN is the *New York Times* best-selling author of *Wicked Saints*. She works as a youth services librarian and received a master's degree in library science from Kent State University, which mostly taught her how to find obscure Slavic folk-lore texts through interlibrary loan systems. When not reading or writing, she enjoys playing copious amounts of video games and Dungeons & Dragons. She lives in Ohio.